"HOW MANY AFFAIRS DO YOU THINK I'VE HAD?"

Sara spoke without looking up, her tone curious.

"With all the men drifting around your bohemian tenement, how would I know? It doesn't matter!" Luke lied, aware now of fumbling badly. "I'm sorry."

"I can't fault your assumptions," she replied evenly. "I am an artist. The place where I live isn't much to look at. And I am not logical—simply a bundle of emotions unsuitable for your scientific life. For the Other Luke it would add up to a love affair to drool over in his old age...."

"Stop it, Sara!" he ground out. "I am not your Other Luke."

"And I am not your next affair, either. I have never had an affair—I cannot handle it—never with you! Oh, God," she cried, "why didn't you just make it clear in the beginning that I was to be only an interlude...?"

AND NOW...

SUPERROMANCES

As the world's No. 1 publisher of best-selling romance fiction, we are proud to present a sensational new series of modern love stories—SUPERROMANCES.

Written by masters of the genre, these longer, sensual and dramatic novels are truly in keeping with today's changing life-styles. Full of intriguing conflicts, the heartaches and delights of true love, SUPERROMANCES are absorbing stories—satisfying and sophisticated reading that lovers of romance fiction have long been waiting for.

SUPERROMANCES
Contemporary love stories for the woman of today!

THE HEART REMEMBERS

EMMA CHURCH

Harlequin Books

TORONTO • LONDON • LOS ANGELES • AMSTERDAM
SYDNEY • HAMBURG • PARIS • STOCKHOLM • ATHENS • TOKYO

For Karen Schattner:
A promise kept.

Harlequin first edition, September 1981

ISBN 0-373-70007-5

Copyright © 1981 by Emma Church. All rights reserved.
Philippine copyright 1981. Australian copyright 1981.
Except for use in any review, the reproduction or utilization of
this work in whole or in part in any form by any electronic,
mechanical or other means, now known or hereafter invented,
including xerography, photocopying and recording, or in any
information storage or retrieval system, is forbidden without
the permission of the publisher, Harlequin Enterprises Limited,
225 Duncan Mill Road, Don Mills, Ontario, Canada M3B 3K9.

All the characters in this book have no existence outside the
imagination of the author and have no relation whatsoever to
anyone bearing the same name or names. They are not even
distantly inspired by any individual known or unknown to the
author, and all the incidents are pure invention.

The Harlequin trademark, consisting of the words
SUPERROMANCE, HARLEQUIN SUPERROMANCE and the
portrayal of a Harlequin, is registered in the United States
Patent Office and in the Canada Trade Marks Office.

Printed in U.S.A.

CHAPTER ONE

LUKE DRISCOLL, a lean dark man in an impeccably tailored suit, left his car and strode through the night toward the flagstone steps of Spars' Nest. He moved with an easy masculine grace that echoed the silent prowl of the tall mountain men who had once slipped through the forests cloaking the Colorado mountains above them.

Reaching the steps, he paused, his cool eyes scanning the house rooted in the foothills above Denver. It was a solid house of stone and oak, with a small tower in the angle of its two wings.

Outside of the entrance lights, the only lights on were those of his grandfather's sitting room on the ground floor of the right wing. The remaining windows reflected only the gleam of a full moon.

As he drew in a tired breath, his dark eyes lifted to the peaks of the Rocky Mountains thrusting into the still night, and for a moment he let his mind relax and float in the peace of the midsummer's night, inhaling the garden scents and drawing strength from the mountains as he had since his childhood.

His lack of expression as he stared upward contrasted oddly with the male power of his tanned face.

A dark face scored by a thin scar running from a primitive cheekbone to a hard jaw.

But as his gaze dropped to the windows of his grandfather's room, he frowned, and with his hand tightening on the handle of his briefcase, he continued toward the broad, carved oaken door.

It opened before he reached it to reveal a gaunt elderly woman bundled in a faded robe, who greeted him with an air of disapproval that seemed natural to her humorless face. "It's very late!"

Luke eyed her with amusement, and ignoring her forbidding image, as he had learned to do as a boy, he said dryly, "You make me feel like a schoolboy sneaking in after hours, Grey."

A corner of her mouth creaked into a smile. "Mr. Elijah wants to see you."

"At this hour?" He crossed to the small fruitwood table where his mail waited. Riffling through it without interest, he added absently, "Did Jess drop off that report?"

"It's in your den."

"Good."

"She's a sensible woman, that one. *She* knows her responsibilities."

He stilled at the unexpected implications of her remark, but all he said was a quiet, "Go on to bed, Grey. You shouldn't be up this late."

"There are sandwiches and hot coffee in the den." With her lips compressing, she turned and left.

Staring after the woman who had looked after him since he was seven, he wondered bleakly, why now? Why bring up the past now?

He scowled, dropped the mail back on the tray, extracted a magazine from his briefcase and slowly walked down the hall toward his grandfather's rooms.

"...a sensible woman...." The words echoed in his mind. "...knows her responsibilities...."

Not like Sara.

Sara, who would appear in paint-stained jeans or in an artistic gown, reeking of turpentine, and proving that once again she had forgotten their guests.

Completely unlike Jessica, who always appeared perfectly attired, her black hair in madonnalike simplicity and her poise as firm as the rocks on which Spars' Nest rested.

"You should have married Jessica!" Sara had once told him angrily. "She is what you need! An impeccably elegant addition to your robot world. Something that I'll never let you make of me!"

He stopped outside the sitting-room door and drew in a deep breath. What was he doing with his life, he found himself suddenly asking. Perhaps Grey was right. It had been nearly five years now. Years of silence. If he freed himself legally and married Jessica, it would be a sensible conclusion to a long friendship and to shared interests, as well as a step he knew everyone except Elijah, and perhaps Paul, would agree was long past due.

Sensible. His mind frowned, and the unbidden thought came that however sensible marriage to Jessica might be, it would never approach the ecstasy of having loved Sara.

"Or the misery," he muttered with grimness, and

half hoping Elijah had retired so that he might get on with the latest project report left by Jessica, he pushed the door open.

The soft glow of a single lamp barely reached the shadowed corners of the room. Pausing, Luke surveyed with quiet affection the white head resting against the back of the winged chair , and when a distinct whuffle escaped his grandfather's lips, a half smile softened the grimness of Luke's mouth.

He was still smiling when a glimpse of color caught the corner of his eye. His head turned toward the fireplace.

In an instant his carefully organized world dropped from beneath his feet.

Blood drained from his face as he stared at the portrait propped on the mantel. The portrait of a girl with haunting gray eyes, and hair the color of autumn wheat that framed high cheekbones whose hollows were brushed with shadows that touched the vulnerable line of her lips.

He tried to turn away from her eyes. Eyes that could still spin their ethereal soul-binding web, in a face that hovered in the swirling mists of a twilight world. Eyes that pleaded for something indefinable and still made him ache to provide whatever it was, at whatever cost.

Inexorably he found himself drawn back in time to where he had first seen the portrait.

Drawn back in time to Toronto, the Canadian city that had shivered in the November winds sweeping the shoreline of Lake Ontario.

There he had stared at the portrait on the wall of a

cold, bare attic room that smelled of age and turpentine, not yet realizing that his orderly life was about to disintegrate under overwhelming emotions that would leave him scarred more deeply than any physical injury.

He was still spellbound when a husky voice with its Canadian inflections had spoken dryly from behind him.

"It would never, Mr. Driscoll, qualify as an investment."

Startled, he had turned to find Sara.

She was taller than he had expected from her portrait, and gracefully slender as she smiled politely up at him with gray eyes that held a hint of disdain and were very different from the lost pleading in the portrait.

"I'll buy it anyway," he surprised himself.

"It's not for sale," she replied flatly, and turning from him with a gesture that held an irritating hint of dismissal, she crossed the room to stare into the rain as if he were longer there.

His eyes narrowed on her until he was only vaguely aware of the old Victorian tenement creaking in the wind and of the strains of Tchaikovsky's violin concerto flowing from somewhere through thin walls in mounting crescendos of emotion.

"I can meet any price," he said finally.

"It is not for sale."

He studied her with rising annoyance. She was dressed in black, a high-necked sweater and trousers, with the curve of her breasts half-covered by an open paint-stained smock. Her hair seemed antique gold in the gray November light. "I think that's a matter for the artist to decide, not the model."

Her head lifted, and even as she replied, he was aware of an irrational desire to feel the coolness of her lips against his.

"I am the artist." When his dark eyebrows hooked upward, she added wryly, "Is that so surprising?"

"It is surprising for a self-portrait to have such character." He examined the chilly room. "Yet the evidence is before me. An easel, a palette with colors that match many of those on your smock, plus Jeffrey's high recommendation of you to assist me in selecting a painting for my grandfather. But most of all the painting on the easel. It has the same touch of fantasy mixed with reality."

He paused, studying the portrait on the easel, and then, half smiling at the dowager who regarded him smugly, he remarked, "She reminds me of an overfed Pekingese who has never known anything but silken boudoirs and is quite pleased about it, too."

His eyes shifted to find her regarding him oddly, and he asked, "Do you prefer oils?"

"Yes."

"I imagine they allow a longer creative dialogue as well as time to develop feelings."

Surprise flickered across her face, and almost reluctantly she nodded.

"The expression in your own portrait is...." He looked again and felt its magic drawing him. "It's...haunting."

"It was my last painting for my teacher. He died shortly after."

His eyes found hers, asking questions he was as yet unaware of, and she looked away. After a silence he said quietly, "You're a very talented painter."

Her long lashes lifted. "I am an artist."

"My apologies." He smiled slightly. "As a scientist and mathematician, I should detest being called a mechanic who is good at figures."

A suggestion of a smile hovered in her gray eyes, and feeling that they had been talking on two levels from the first, he asked softly, "Must it be a matter of, I do not...like thee, Dr. Fell, the reason why I cannot tell?"

She did not move. He had an impression of her as a wraith in the deepening shadows of the room before she smiled and with an easy grace dropped onto a workbench. One slim leg bent beneath her as she settled herself. "You yourself are a man of conflicting evidence, Mr. Driscoll."

"Oh?"

"When I look at you," she said, as if speaking her thoughts aloud, "I feel rich dark velvet. But when you move I think of a panther's lean and merciless power. The angles of your face are so strong that they cry for a palette knife, and yet...." She paused, her eyes cooling. "Your impeccably tailored clothes, your expensive tan, and your need to hire an artist to help you buy 'an investment' as a gift all seem evidence of a rigid, insensitive sort who has to buy his taste in elegance."

He said nothing as she finished with an air of challenge. He was torn by conflicting reactions—anger, amusement, responses to a bewitching young woman perched on her bench as if she were a princess, and half-formed thoughts of culminating too many years of study and work with an interlude that he was half-afraid to begin. "As I mentioned earlier, I'm a scientist. A successful one, I might add."

"What sort of scientist?"

"Physics...electronics."

"Should I be addressing you as Dr. Driscoll, then?"

"My colleagues do," he said in an uncaring tone.

She shrugged, stared down at her slim hands a moment and then looked back at him without comment.

As the silence grew, his dark eyes searched the silver of hers, and all his thoughts blurred.

He wanted only to tear aside the veils in her eyes and to walk into their clouds of infinite grayness, and once there, to somehow satisfy an inexplicable yearning growing within him.

The soft pelting rain on the windows almost drowned his words as he whispered, "Who are you? Where are you from?"

For yet another moment he held her eyes, aware that her assurance was faltering and her confusion increasing.

With a visible effort Sara pulled their gazes apart and resumed staring at her hands. Finally she drew in a breath and then recited evenly, "I am your guide to good taste, Sara Marshall Hayes. Born in Toronto, and at the age of five, when my parents died in a boating accident, I was taken to Muskoka, the land of blue skies, to live with my great-aunt."

"Were the skies blue?" he asked softly.

She glanced up and then quickly down, and after a pause continued, "Sometimes. I was usually at boarding school here in Toronto. After school was over I kept house for my great-aunt, taught riding at a girls' camp, and was a part-time housekeeper for Christopher Avery, the artist. My great-aunt died when I was eighteen and Christopher a year later."

"Did your great-aunt approve of your painting?" he prodded.

"No." She hesitated, then added almost dutifully, "Aunt Ruth meant well."

As Grey had meant well, he thought, after he had lost his parents and grandmother, when Elijah had become a bleak grief-stricken figure with no time for anything but consuming work. "Did Avery teach you?"

She nodded. "Almost everything I know."

"And what have you been doing since then?"

"Barely eating," she acknowledged dryly. "And studying. I'm beginning to gain recognition, though not enough yet to refuse guiding an American through galleries for a commission."

"Someone has to buy or artists would starve," he replied with an odd gentleness that he did not yet understand. "I can pay well."

"It is not for sale!"

"Why not?"

"Because...." She hesitated, then whispered, "It would be like selling myself."

A week later, instead of attending the Boston conference on energy as reason dictated, he stood beside Sara on the edge of the windswept half-frozen Lake of Bays near where Sara had spent her childhood.

"Now," Sara asked briskly, "what do you see and feel?" She smiled mischievously. "No numbers or centigrade or molecular structures are permitted."

"Snow and ice, so cold beneath my feet that it's almost hot," he obliged, ignoring other feelings for the moment. "And the keen cold edge of the wind barely softened by the first sun in four—"

"Disqualified!" she pounced with glee. "You have a long way to go, my poor scientific Luke."

Irritated, he demanded another try, opting for smells. "There's the clean soul-scouring smell of a winter's day. The scent of your hair blow—" Her clear giggle interrupted him, and he hooked an arm around her and glared into her eyes. "What is so damned funny!"

"My hair probably smells of oils."

He grinned reluctantly, his irritation fading, only to be replaced by his awareness of her glowing skin, the curve of her mouth, and the flush slowly spreading up her cheeks as he continued to stare at her lips.

"I never could remember poetry precisely," he murmured, his body tensing against the softness of her, "but isn't there something that goes somewhat like, 'the sunlight clasps the earth and the moonbeams kiss the sea...what is all this sweet work worth, if thou kiss not me?'"

Very slowly he lowered his head. She did not move away as she had before, but waited. As his lips touched hers she quivered, and when his mouth parted hers he felt her slender body stiffen against him, then relax as his kiss lengthened and slowly deepened until he was shaking. He broke free to hold her against him as he drew in deep controlling breaths.

He knew then that he wanted her more than any woman he had ever known. So much so that she made him feel as unsure as an adolescent in the throes of his first infatuation.

Until he met her, he had not realized how vulnerable he was, how much he had missed the barely remembered warmth and laughter of his childhood before his world became bleak. Half resenting and half fearing his own emotions, he released her.

She instantly withdrew to stand half-turned from him staring out toward the frozen wastes of the lake. She did not look at him as she said rather quickly, "I used to wander along the lake here thinking and dreaming all the profundities of growing up. Christopher found me scribbling here, as he called it, and ended up teaching me in the summers—and later on, after I finished school, there were lessons almost every day. We made our bargain here."

"Bargain?" he managed, gradually regaining control of himself.

"He would teach me if I would pose for him." She smiled slightly. "At twelve I thought it was a reasonable bargain, not knowing there were people who would have paid a packet for an hour of his tutoring."

"Did he ever paint you?"

"Several times." She turned and pointed to a nearby hill. "The one I liked most was of me sitting up there. I was staring toward the horizon at all my life that was yet to be." Her eyes met his and skidded away. "Aunt Ruth always thought that he hired me to clean house. Instead, we created."

"Did he become your lover?" The question broke harshly through his control, a sudden unbidden jealousy streaking through him.

Her breath caught audibly. "He was in his seventies, Luke. He was my father, my grandfather, my teacher, my mentor—and above all, my only true friend."

"Sara... I'm sorry."

She would not look at him, only at the horizon as if she were still trying to see what was yet to be. He watched, afraid to speak, afraid of her spell, of appearing a fool, and of what he wanted to say to her.

But despite himself his attraction to her conquered his fears, and as the days passed he ignored most of the conferences he was scheduled to attend. Instead he found himself using his influence to gain access to the private collections Sara yearned to see, found himself entering a world he had thought lost, and found himself watching silently when she resisted his lures to paint with the touch of fantasy that was Sara. And gradually he was caught up, and his own world seemed millennia away.

"I should have been in Washington today," he remarked one night as they walked slowly through the snow-covered streets, their steps matching in the quiet hours.

"The Other Luke should have been."

"Other Luke?" He halted, and she looked up uncertainly. "Tell me," he said. "Tell me about this Other Luke."

She started walking again, and as he joined her she said quietly, "The sober little boy who forgot how to feel and dream, who stopped lying in mountain meadows watching a bird on the wing, a star in the sky, when he found that he could gain his grandfather's notice only by learning facts and numbers and by studying with admirable discipline."

His throat tightened, and it was some moments before he could ask, "And this Luke?"

"He...he can be sensitive and tender and passionate. He can give laughter and strength and dreams. I...." She stopped.

"I love you, Sara." His voice was hoarse with tension.

Her steps faltered until she stood searching his eyes in the dim light of a streetlamp, fine snowflakes falling on her hair like jewels. "We're worlds apart, Luke," she told him softly. "And we're lonely. The Other Luke knows that...and even I do."

"I *love* you!"

"Don't!" Unshed tears suddenly glistened in her eyes. "Only our inner selves match, Luke. We don't have tomorrows. They are not for us."

His hands cupped her face, feeling its cold wetness; and half-afraid of losing her, half-afraid of the Other Luke, he kissed her with a fierce longing that she matched unequivocally, even desperately, until they stood in the gathering snowstorm shaking and holding each other.

"Let me stay with you tonight," he whispered huskily.

She stilled on a caught breath. "Stay?"

He loosened his hold enough to look down on her bowed head. "Let me take you home and dry you and warm you with our loving." He waited tautly in the eerie snow silence. "Sara?"

Slowly her head lifted, and in the faint light, so briefly that he was unsure if he had imagined it, there was the same indefinable plea in her gray eyes that was in her portrait, and then her lashes dropped. She pulled free and whispered, "I...I don't know, Luke. I need—to think."

"Think! Oh, Sara, you of all people! Here we are, standing here cold and shivering. What is there to think about? Or do you usually have to think out your love affairs in advance?"

In a curious tone, still not looking up, she asked, "How many do you think I've had?"

"With all the men who drift about in your bohemian tenement, how would I know? It doesn't matter!" he lied, fighting the knowledge that he had fumbled badly. "I'll take another month off. I'll take you to the Caribbean islands...to the sun and sea. This is our...*our* affair. This is what matters! This moment in time."

"Luke?"

She said his name softly, as if she were calling to him, and brushing the impression aside, he said tensely, "Sara, you want me as much as I want you. And that is as much a fact as feeling."

"The answer is no."

He regarded her with disbelief and a sense of dread. "Why?"

" 'I am—yet what I am who cares, or knows?' " she quoted tiredly, and turning, walked away in quick long steps.

"Sara!" She did not even pause. With growing anger at himself, at her, at everything that had gone wrong, he followed. When he caught up and fell in step with her, his voice was stiff. "All right! There's no need to behave as Victorian as that place you live in! If I've offended you I'm sorry. I didn't mean to be so damned clumsy."

"Don't worry," she replied evenly. "I can't fault your assumptions. After all, the facts are all there. I am an artist. My friends obviously have casual affairs. The place where I live is not much to look at. And I am not logical—simply a bundle of emotions unsuited to your scientific life."

"Sara...."

"For the Other Luke, it adds up to a love affair to drool over in his old age, and—"

"Stop it!" he said through his teeth. "I am not the Other Luke!"

"And I am not your next affair, either. Facts or not, I have never had an affair—not what you mean. I don't know the rules. I cannot handle it...never with you. Never for a brief while and then polite farewells! Oh, God!" she cried. "Why did you not just make it clear in the beginning, before—"

"Sara, listen to me!"

"No! You're the Other Luke...in the end."

In silence he walked next to her, fighting the Other

Luke who knew Sara would never be more than an interlude, who knew she would not fit in Spars' Nest, or with his friends. He had to be sensible. He had to be.

They entered her building and in the hallway he stopped, his hands gripping her shoulders and forcing her to face him. The snow melted on her face like small tears waiting to fall privately.

"Oh, God, Sara!" he groaned.

"Luke...." Her voice wobbled. "Poor Luke."

He stared at her as the strains of a sonata permeated the rickety building, mixing with the quarreling of a couple somewhere, and the moldy odor of age and dampness assaulted his nostrils.

She was right, he told himself with a sudden yearning to be back in his orderly, predictable world.

As if she read his thoughts, she whispered, "Goodbye, Luke."

He did not move or call out as she left him.

Two weeks later, haggard and beaten after days of missing her, of wanting to turn and share a moment with her, he stood outside her door staring numbly at the sign tacked on it: Gone.

He knocked on doors until someone told him she had gone north, and then he knew where to find her.

She was walking along the shoreline bundled against the cold, her footprints following her in the clear snow. And standing on the hill above, he was aware of a raw relief so profound that he could not move or speak.

In that instant she slowed and stopped. Hesitantly, a fey creature sensing a presence, she half turned and her eyes lifted to where he stood against the backdrop of dark snow clouds.

It seemed the very world held its breath as their eyes met, and throwing aside logic, order and safety, he called, "Sara...we need you! Both Lukes! Marry me, Sara! Love me, and give me peace."

She stood unmoving, her eyes still reaching out to him, and in that moment he had been more afraid of her refusal than he would, or could, ever admit. Only later did he ask himself if she had paused to weigh his assets before replying, "Yes, my Luke! Oh, yes! For all the days of my life."

All the days of her life had, in the end, meant a year, Luke thought with cold bitterness, and his hand clenched the magazine he still held as he closed his eyes against the power of her portrait, against the mind-blurring mists surrounding her, and above all, against the memories.

"When she did your portrait," Elijah said suddenly, "she painted you in sunlight. I told her that she should have painted gears and dials and wiring. But she said that for her you were like sunlight—at least in the beginning. She was going to give you your portrait on your birthday that year."

Luke pivoted sharply, turning his back on Sara's portrait to ask harshly, "How did it get here?"

"I've had the galleries in Canada and the States watching for it since she left. Someone who had seen the photograph that I mailed out ran across it a few weeks ago."

"Up for sale?"

"On condition that it would not be publicly shown."

"Her priceless painting!" Luke crossed to the sideboard, and discarding the magazine with its feature article on Jessica, he poured himself a drink with shaking hands. A long swallow of the heating liquid, however, did nothing at all to disperse the cold emptiness within him.

"You're being a fool, boy."

He faced his grandfather, his hard features expressionless. "Did you expect me to rejoice?"

"She's in trouble," Elijah said tiredly. "You know that she would not sell her portrait unless she were."

"Hypothesis or fact?"

"Facts!" The old man moved angrily. "You as a scientist should know that facts can lie. They can fit the wrong theory. You need feelings, too!"

"You helped make me what I am." Luke moved to the mantel, his back to Sara's portrait, his eyes cold. "My feelings meant little enough to you until you noticed my brain." Even as he saw the parchment skin gray, swift regret made him add, "I'm sorry." His hand raked through his dark hair. "I was wrong to say that."

"I was wrong!" Elijah replied brusquely. "I was a damned fool! But with Hannah...and your parents, too, gone in one blow, I felt dead myself. My work saved me." His white head lifted and his dark eyes met Luke's. "Could you honestly say that if Sara had died and left a child, you would not have buried yourself in your experiments?"

"If she needs help, she knows where I am."

"And if your situations were reversed and you needed her? Of course you would call her."

The scar on Luke's cheek paled. Without replying,

he drained his drink and walked to the window to stare sightlessly into the darkness.

"She's as proud as you are," Elijah said, and after a pause added gruffly, "I want to see her. I want her back at Spars' Nest."

Luke stiffened. "She has no right to be here."

"You didn't lease her, boy, you married her. For better or worse."

Quelling memories, Luke asked with an effort, "Where is she?"

"In Key West, Florida."

He started inwardly, unwilling to admit to his grandfather that he had, in fact, swallowed his pride long ago. Enough to search secretly throughout Canada and the States. But he had never, he realized, even recalled the place he had casually mentioned to her on their honeymoon.

"Where were you planning on going before I interrupted your schedules?" Sara had asked idly one night as she lay in his arms before the fire in their snowbound cabin.

"After Washington, to Key West. A little island in a cradle of islands at the southern tip of Florida. A magic place."

"Magic?" She had lifted herself on an elbow to smile down at him with curiosity.

"Only a small part has the magic," he had explained. "The old town. It's another world. There's a dab of Britain inherited from the Tories who fled there, loyal to England to the end, and a dash of the Bahamas. It's a peaceful spot. A place where your soul can pause to catch its breath."

Pulling himself out of his memories, Luke stared blindly into the moonlit night. "Is she...ill?"

"She needs our help."

His face tightened and his insides went taut as he asked, "Conjecture?"

"A report by a local man whom I hired."

There was a long silence before Luke turned and said coldly, "Then I'll send a check."

"I want you to go there, boy! Find her! Bring her back before I die."

"We're close to a breakthrough in the lab on the stability problem," Luke countered instantly. "And—"

"Forget the damn project!"

"That from *you*!" Luke gibed. "If I leave now, it could delay testing at a crucial stage. We've too many rivals, as you well know, who are anxious to beat us to the finishing line."

"A few days won't be critical."

Luke hesitated, then, "John Gordon informed me an hour ago that one of his security friends tipped them off that the next issue of *Electronic Newsletter* will have a comment that Driscoll Electronics is onto something big."

Elijah started visibly and said sharply, "A leak!"

"Apparently," Luke replied shortly, containing a renewed spurt of anger.

"How bad?"

"We won't know until it's out."

There was a grim silence. Luke knew that Elijah was shaken by the implications. For years nearly all their profits along with a good part of their own money had been poured into their project. Everything was being gambled on their ability to produce a system of cheap and practical solar energy.

"Who?" Elijah demanded roughly. "Who talked?"

"John's working on it. But we may never know."

"Damn!" Elijah's hands clenched.

"With this latest development, I have to be here."

"Or you can let Ralph Beaumont, your general manager, manage. Jessica can stand in for you on the project. If they can't, you need a new team."

"We'll also have to accelerate the project now or see everything go down the drain."

With barely repressed anger and frustration, Elijah shook his head. "I want Sara here."

"And the project?"

"I'm not too old or feebleminded to hold the fort and make any decisions they can't handle."

"No deal."

Their eyes locked, both gazes dark and willful. With an indrawn breath Elijah rose, and across the chasm between them he said firmly, "Then I'll go. There should be some honor in this family."

"You'll kill yourself!" Rising anger darkened Luke's features. "She left without honor! We owe her nothing."

"For better or worse," Elijah said without room for compromise, and reaching for his cane, he started from the room without a backward glance.

Swearing under his breath, Luke watched until Elijah reached his bedroom door. Only then did he grind out, "I'll go."

Elijah paused, looked back, and again their dark gazes locked. With a slow nod, Elijah walked on.

Luke stood alone in the still room, the grandfather clock ticking away time. When he slowly turned to stare up toward the mountain peaks again, he felt oddly old and exhausted.

"You see only granite and karst and geological formations," Sara had once accused as they stood together looking at the mountains. "Can you not see the harebell and mauve mists? The golden roses of the high peaks? Can you really not feel the beauty, the cruelty and the dreams of the high country?"

"No more," he replied to his memories. A pulse throbbed at his temple. When he found her, he would not become emotionally involved again. This time he would be cool...and logical...and implacable. Above all, he would be in control.

CHAPTER TWO

DARK BILLOWING CLOUDS that were like sails hovered on the horizon of the Gulf of Mexico, creeping inexorably toward the island.

From where Sara sat on the sunlit beach regarding them bleakly, they seemed like the ghosts of the treasure galleons that had once plied their way past Key West.

Her gaze dropped from the threatening darkness that would soon swallow the blue sky to the small waves curling across the wet sand toward her toes with a relentless persistence that seemed to match the forces in her life that were pushing her into a corner.

"It's going to thunder, mummy. Tricia doesn't like that."

Starting slightly, Sara smiled at the small boy who had quietly joined her, and her hand automatically reached out to smooth back his sun-whitened hair. "You don't like it, either, do you? But it probably won't reach us for hours yet, Toby. By then it may be only a few grumbles and mumbles."

"Can we go see the turtles?" His blue eyes were hopeful.

"And come back here, too," Tricia added, trudging up to her twin's side, her brown eyes sharing his hopes as one small hand tugged on a dark braid. "We could picnic!"

"I have to work tonight. We'll only have time for supper together."

"Again!" they chorused with clear disappointment.

"I have to," she affirmed gently, wincing inwardly as their faces lost their sparkle.

"I don't like you to work all the time!" Toby protested.

"It's only for a little while," Sara answered, only too aware that "a little while" could be very long for four-year-olds.

"It's so mummy can get money to fix your leg," Tricia said in a lofty manner that failed to conceal the uncertainty creeping into her dark eyes.

"I don't care 'bout my old leg!" With the angry words, a shimmer of tears touched Toby's blue eyes and he turned to limp rapidly away, his sturdy body stiff with feelings he could not yet control.

"Toby!" Tricia trailed after him, and after a pause she suggested hopefully, "Let's make a sand castle!"

Toby stopped, expressions shifting across his small face as he fought between his hurt and Tricia's proposal. He stood still, sunlight bathing his head, a small boy uncertain of what to do, which way to go.

Feeling much the same, Sara let her breath out with a soft sigh as Toby gave in and limped toward his sister, who was already scooping wet sand into a pile. "Wait for me!" he shouted as he hurried to join her. "Wait for me!"

Sara watched them for several moments before her eyes slowly returned to the distant clouds.

The sense of hopelessness came without warning, threatening to overflow in a torrent of tears. Choking on a sob, she forced herself to take deep breaths until gradually she regained control.

She would not cry, she told herself fiercely, a sense of shock rippling through her. It was only the strain of the past months. The strain of working not only days, but also nights, of rising early to have these moments with the children, and of trying to gather enough money to support the three of them through the months of Toby's convalescence after his operation.

She was tired. That was what made everything seem an effort—to the point where even small decisions, much less large ones, loomed over her like the dark clouds on the horizon.

Drawing in another deep breath, she tilted her face to the warm wind and morning sun, and watching the nearing shadows, she wondered if she was forever destined to be a shadow among shadows because she had loved unwisely.

Luke.

A surge of confused emotions accompanied the surfacing of his name and propelled her to her feet. She shivered as if to shake off physically the knowledge that she might yet be forced to seek his help. He would never forgive.... She dammed the flooding fears and turned quickly to call the children. "Tricia! Toby! Time to go!"

"Now?"

"Now!" she echoed firmly, and ten minutes later at the nursery school she said just as firmly, "I promise."

"Cross your heart?"

"Cross my heart," she repeated softly. "I don't work tomorrow, so if it's not raining we will go on a picnic and see the turtles." Bending, she dropped a kiss on Tricia's dark head and Toby's fair head. "Now go! And have a nice, nice day."

They left her reluctantly, rather like puppies dismissed in disgrace with their constant backward glances. Glances she met with a smile. A smile that died when she turned and walked away, haunted by their newly faltering faith in their small world.

It was time, she knew, to decide. To decide whether to keep on trying to go it alone or to surrender and contact Luke.

Luke... With a half-angry movement of her head she paused by a stone bench below the tall palms fringing the beach, and then sat down.

For a long moment she stared out at the turquoise waters trailing into indigo depths before the advancing storm.

Dear God, she had loved him! So much that she still felt as if the death of her loving had amputated some part of her until nothing—not even the children—seemed able to replace her irretrievable loss.

Yet, she thought, she should have known from the first moment she saw him that only grief would come. Had Aunt Ruth been alive, she would certainly have warned her.

He had seemed so arrogant that day when she

found him in her studio—until she had looked into his dark eyes and thought she saw someone else behind the armor. Someone as lonely as she. Someone with a nameless yearning in his soul that matched hers.

"Your romantic notions will lead you to disaster, just like your mother," Aunt Ruth had often lectured with dreary relish. "Look what your mother got, running off with a musician! An early grave, that's what!"

And she had me, Sara would silently add to herself as she retreated inwardly from the recriminations.

"Find yourself an ordinary man who's solid. A man who wants a family. Do your duty by him and forget that nonsense you read and moon over!"

Duty.... It had been Aunt Ruth's substitute for the three-letter word *sex*, Sara reflected wryly. How wrong she had been there, but how terribly right in all else.

Staring at the bleached sand of the beach, she saw instead the white snow surrounding the small cabin where she and Luke had spent their honeymoon. A small three-room log cabin hanging on the side of a mountain, one of a circle of mountain peaks ringing a high Colorado valley. A world of soft white velvet that had shimmered in the eye-aching sunlight.

"It's beautiful," she had breathed that first morning as they looked down upon the snow-covered ranch where his mother had been born and raised. "What a beautiful world you come from."

"Our world," Luke had whispered huskily, his arms bringing her against the hard muscles of his body.

Her own body had stirred instantly with newly discovered desires and knowledge, and a small pleasurable gasp had escaped her lips as his hands slipped inside her jacket to caress her with arousing expertise.

Mindlessly her hands had moved beneath his sweater, digging into the male sinews of his back and feeling the power of her effect on him as his body responded to her. Inevitably they had returned to the cabin to continue her initiation into uninhibited passion.

That had been their time of loving, belonging and joy. Days when he had been Her Luke. Days whose passing she had resented, as if somehow some part of her had sensed that they were days that were numbered.

And numbered they had been. For Her Luke had gradually disappeared from the moment when she had confronted the reality of him on his home ground. The reality of a home run by another woman, Luke's housekeeper and surrogate mother, who had thoroughly disapproved of Luke's bohemian bride.

The reality, too, of the woman whom everyone had expected Luke to marry, the cool Jessica Pettiway. Jessica, his beautiful, scientific associate, who had shown her clear contempt of Sara whenever Luke was absent.

She had needed help. Instead, Luke had been too busy with his work and projects. Not too busy, however, to lecture her and judge her wanting, and behind his criticisms, Sara had heard, "I don't love you. I wish I had never married you."

She had been too different. Unable to instantly become the poised wife that he evidently wanted, especially in a hostile world, she had hidden her growing loss of self-confidence behind defiance—even as within herself she had cried out to him to love her for herself.

It was her mindless defiance that had driven her to ignore Luke's cold warnings against friendship with Rufus Petrofsky, a fellow artist and a man of intense blue eyes and silver hair.

She had been a fool, Sara reflected for the thousandth time, for she had insisted that Luke trust her. It had all seemed so clear at twenty. If he loved her, he would trust her.

In the end it had been brutally swift. Luke, returning early from a conference in New York, had found her breakfasting at dawn with Rufus in his studio home. Luke had refused to believe that she had spent the night nursing the other man through a high fever; and Rufus, with a wicked amusement and for reasons she still could not understand, had not denied Luke's accusations. He had simply watched with mocking silence as Luke dragged her away.

On the way home to Spars' Nest, driving the winding mountain road with reckless anger, Luke had lost control of the car. Sara had been concussed and bruised. Luke had broken a leg and had slashed his face.

The first day she had managed to walk, they had had their final bitter quarrel in the cold sterility of his hospital room.

"Get out," he had said icily. "Get out of my life...."

As Sara stared now into the restless sea, her throat ached with remembered pain. She had believed that she could open his world. Instead she had been imprisoned in his. She had given everything, and it had been too little.

Never again, she promised herself. She was finished with loving. She had the children now. If it was not enough, there was still purpose and a contentment of sorts, and she had kept Luke from the children while they were still young enough to become warped and twisted to the ways of his world.

With a sigh she pulled herself out of her pit of memories and rose. The dark clouds were closer, though sunlight still showered the island. The sun in the east and the clouds in the west...where Luke was.

She shook off the thought and hurried away from her memories toward the art gallery where she was employed.

For several hours there was no time to think. In the noon lull, however, present realities dominated as Sara sat at the small Regency desk in the showroom staring down at the figures she had added and subtracted and adjusted dozens of times.

"That storm isn't far off," her employer, Madge Wintertree, murmured from the door of the gallery.

"I'll keep an eye on it and bring in the outdoor displays before it starts," Sara assured her, and raised her head to stare through the bow window fronting the gallery.

"Before I forget," Madge continued, "don't accept another order from Mrs. Ridley unless she pays half down."

"She didn't refuse another special order!"

"Yes, and short of finding a drunken tourist, we are stuck with her appalling taste."

Sara smiled slightly, and then her smile faded as she returned to computing possible budgets. Selling her painting and her engagement ring had helped—but not enough. Yet.... Soberly her eyes scanned the figures, totaling her estimates. She might be able to do it. Just.

Rising, she pushed aside the worn and fingered sheets of facts and walked to the screened door of the small gallery to stare out at the quiet street.

"I wish the storm would veer off," Madge grumbled behind her. "Summers are slow enough without rain to keep stray tourists indoors."

"It may miss us." Sara peered doubtfully at the sky. The clouds were definitely nearer. Clouds whose rains would pelt the mosquitoes down for a short while and briefly cool the island. "Every cloud has its silver lining," she added wryly.

"Are you working tonight?"

"Yes." Sara walked to a table where decorated driftwood plaques and a small watercolor waited to be hung. Aware of her employer's eyes following her, she gathered them up quickly.

"Sara, must you work in that nightclub?"

"It pays well and the office is quite separate from the club," Sara replied evenly, avoiding the concern in Madge's eyes. "A few months more and...." Biting her lip, she hugged the plaques to her breast. Her gray eyes were defiant as they lifted.

"You'll be ill yourself and it won't be enough in the end," Madge snapped, her graying red hair seeming to stand on end. "Look at you! You're losing weight, your face is drawn and you're exhausted! What good will it do Toby and Tricia if you collapse?"

"I won't."

"Sara—"

"I am not writing to him!" It helped to say it aloud.

"He is the one person who could help without—"

"I will not!" Sara drew in a controlling breath. "He would take the children. He'd never forgive my keeping their existence a secret from him."

Madge regarded her with a clear mixture of compassion and irritation.

"I can manage alone. Really I can, Madge."

"How? I've watched you add and subtract numbers for weeks."

"If...if I'm wrong, I would rather beg as a last resort than beg at the start and risk everything that means anything to me."

With a scowl the plump woman in vivid clothes that were a gallery advertisement in themselves turned away heavily to stare down at the scraps of paper filled with Sara's jottings.

Eyeing Madge with affection, Sara wondered, not for the first time, where she would be now if it had not been for Madge's kindness. When she had found herself in a daze in northern Florida, after days of buying bus tickets anywhere east, Luke's words, "A place where your soul can pause to catch its breath," had sent her to Key West instead of back to Canada.

She had fainted walking past the gallery, and with the shock of learning that she was pregnant there had also been the gaining of a new, if gruff, stranger as a friend and employer.

"I've been thinking," Madge offered brusquely. "I could get a second mortgage on the gallery."

"No," Sara refused gently. "You can't afford it, Madge. I keep your books, and you are barely in the black. It's too much after all the hard work you've done to make this gallery pay. Not when I can go elsewhere, if I must."

"You should have made some rich friends."

"I've known rich people, and you can keep them."

"Send the letter, Sara!" Madge raised her head. "Don't break yourself carrying the load alone."

"I don't need him—or his charity."

Madge sighed. "It's your life, child. But sometimes pride only ends up hurting us."

"Sometimes," Sara returned bleakly, "it is all that one has left."

"They certainly breed you stubborn in Canada, if you're an example." Madge shook her head and added, "Go along and hang those. I'll cover the shop in case a tourist dares to brave the coming storm."

With a nod of relief that Madge had dropped the subject, Sara walked through the gallery toward the garden. The polished floors and white walls of the renovated Bahamian house made a narrow but simple and airy backdrop for the many sculptures and paintings. Paintings ranging from original oils by promising Key West artists to watercolors and sculptures of driftwood, shells and minerals. It was a combination that attracted tourists fleeing northern winds in flocks.

In the garden where weather-hardy sculptures edged the paths that were trimmed by flower beds of sweet william, cathedral bells and azaleas, Sara slowly climbed the old wooden steps to a small tree house of sun-bleached cypress.

Inside it was cooler, with the wind strained by shade and drifting lazily through what had once been a child's hideaway. Placing the plaques on the window shelf, she stared down at the watercolor of a couple walking on the beach in sunlight—not in the mists of childhood dreams as in her portrait.

"Well, it's gone!" she said aloud. "Gone and sold."

Would Luke care that a prosperous tourist had fancied it and bought it? Would he care that the Sara in the portrait was gone, too?

What did it matter, she asked herself tiredly. The portrait had brought a check for Toby. It had been no more than a relic of a foolish child so starved for loving, despite a childhood filled with Aunt Ruth's warnings against love, that she had been ridiculously vulnerable when Luke strode into her life.

As she hung the watercolor, her fingers tightened on the frame. Why, she cried silently, had she had only a few brief moments of loving and being loved? Why for her only a brief span of rapture before the terrible time of emptiness?

Biting down on her lip, she placed the remaining plaques on the walls, reminding herself that she had too many responsibilities to indulge in self-pity. The past was dead.

She had learned her lessons—most of all to be realistic. Luke had worshipped facts, and now the irony was that she, too, did. And a current fact was that she needed money desperately for Toby.

As she left the tree house, the first cool thrusting fingers of wind portending the storm plucked at her skirt. A glance toward the sky pushed aside her brooding thoughts and she started moving the perishable displays indoors.

Madge greeted her return with a harassed expression. "I can't find them!"

"What's lost now?" Sara asked with a faint smile over a typical Madge predicament.

"I detest superior sorts who never misplace a thing!" Madge muttered even as she pounced upon a pile of papers. "Aha! Found them!"

Recognizing the bank receipts, Sara shook her head. "If you had asked me, I could have told you that they were there."

"You know, it's a marvel I ever hired you," Madge reflected audibly. "Can you take over while I go to the bank?" The creak of the front gate made her glance outside. "Here comes Mr. Godfrey, one of your fellow Canadians. He must have decided on the von Marbod that his wife admired."

"I'll take care of him. You go on." Smoothing her hair, Sara walked forward with a smile.

Twenty minutes later, oddly comforted by the soft

sounds of his Canadian inflection, she waved goodbye to George Godfrey and entered the gallery as the first flashes of lightning streaked through the still air.

She was standing uncertainly in the center of the front display room, her tired mind fumbling for what needed to be done next, when above the rumble of thunder the creak of the gate caused her to lift her head. With a sigh she looked through the square panes of the bow window.

Even as her eyes reached the man walking through the gate, they widened with shock. Stunned, she watched the man pause, his features grim as he slowly scrutinized the gallery, apparently oblivious to the gathering wind and flying leaves—a nemesis materializing out of the storm.

In split fear-frozen seconds she was aware of the changes in him that set her heart jerking with anxiety. There was no response in the face of the half stranger. A dark, powerfully male face slashed by the scar etching its way from his left cheekbone to the corner of his hard lips. A face that was harsher than in any of her memories. A face that had tempered into that of a man of relentless, ungiving pride.

When Luke moved forward suddenly, Sara moved backward involuntarily. Numbly she heard a pottery bowl crash to the floor behind her as panic scrabbled through her brain. Thunder growled again and black clouds shadowed the island as she lost sight of him between the steps and door.

Did he know? The question shrieked through her mind. In its echo came the frantic realization that if by some miracle he did not know of the children, this would be her only chance to drive him away. Drive him away before he could think, probe or question.

The door opened and her mind blanked. Somehow she found herself crouching on the floor, picking up the pieces of pottery with trembling fingers and half cowering as she groped for control, half wanting to crawl beneath the pieces and hide.

So it was that Luke found her. Crouching, the neat line of her cotton dress belling, as she scraped up the shards. He had thought merely to probe a bit himself before seeking Elijah's representative; to see the gallery, to get the lay of the land.

Now she was before him, and his first jarring shock was followed by the greater shock of the changes in her.

She was far too thin, though still graceful as she rose to face him with her hands cupping the broken pottery. Pieces of their life, he thought with a part of his mind, as he absorbed the finely drawn skin across her cheekbones and the shadows below the remembered clouds of her eyes. Held by them, he found himself irrationally wanting to step forward to comfort the wary, controlled Sara facing him.

"Luke," she whispered, still in shock, and knew instantly that she could never ask him for help. The implacable, unfeeling grimness confronting her denied any remnant of the Luke she had loved, of the man who just might have helped without questions.

This man would destroy the life she had rebuilt if he learned of their children, and she marshaled her defenses to drive him back to his mountain lair without pausing to question or wanting to return. Or did she have to fight? Did he know?

"I see you remember me." His muscles tightened before her seeming indifference. She had said his name as if labeling an artifact.

"Of course." Her dryness matched his. She forced herself to walk to her desk and sit where her trembling legs would not betray her. With an effort she held her silence, waiting to learn how much he knew.

For a long moment, only the streaking fire of lightning and the growling of thunder sounded. Outside the trees bent before the hurtling storm and the narrow house shivered.

"The real Sara?" Luke finally said. "Or is it the Other Sara? Cold, unfeeling, controlled—"

"You taught me, Luke!" she attacked instantly. "You taught me how unreliable feelings are, and I learned well from you."

"Learned!" he mocked, rejecting the unbidden image of Sara giving freely and loving warmly.

"Why are you here, Luke?" Her heart seemed to halt as she waited for his reply.

"Elijah thought you were in trouble when your painting showed up on the market. He sent out photos of it and a high bid after you disappeared, hoping to locate you."

"Elijah." A terrible relief surged through her as she understood that it was Elijah who had sought her. Luke did not know about the children, then. Not anything.

"Certainly *I* wouldn't search for you," Luke drawled the lie, her lack of reaction piquing him.

"Elijah's old now, Sara. He had a stroke after you left, and moved back to Spars' Nest from the ranch."

"Is Grey still there?"

"Yes." His fist clenched. "Elijah wants to help you, if you're in need."

"I am not in need. I need nothing." Her chin rose fractionally, and with a half-forgotten knowledge of her, he knew that she was lying.

"Nothing?" His eyes narrowed, darkly alert eyes.

"Nothing."

"Then you would be free to visit Elijah?"

She looked away, fixing on a small sculpture of a battered lighthouse, vaguely aware of the driving rain outside, and frighteningly aware of a chaos within her. "No."

"He's ill. He wants to see you." His tone implied that he could not comprehend Elijah's wishes.

In a sense, she also was surprised, for though Elijah had in some ways seemed an ally once, he had also been brusque and somewhat intimidating. "I've wondered if he was still alive," she said neutrally.

"I've wondered if you were."

Her startled gaze met his cold eyes and instantly returned to the sculpture. She shrugged. "Why should I not be?"

"You were battered, bruised and in shock when you left."

Her head lifted, the dull light of the storm shading her hair into pewter, and her eyes were hard. "Don't tell me that my state of mind and body then has belatedly disturbed you?"

His neck reddened, but the hardness of his eyes matched hers as he replied, "Not enough to forget your extramarital activities."

"I was innocent."

"And I was not born yesterday, Sara."

Reason versus emotions, she thought, unable to deny it still hurt. It was the sum of their marriage and the cause of its failure. He had no reason for having so little faith. Even though he, too, had lost his parents as a child, he had not had to live with lectures on his mother's foolishness and his father's infidelity.

With a tired sigh she said, "It no longer matters to me, Luke, whether or not you believe me."

"You left me. You were the one who walked out."

"How marvelously you've twisted it!" she mocked. Then she smothered the shaft of anger spiking through her to say calmly, "It was your home, your life and your work. I never belonged. And you told me...to get out."

"You never wanted to belong."

"Luke's mistake—that's all I ever was." She said it carelessly, as if it did not matter, yet inside she cried despite herself, *why didn't you help me? Help me when I was so afraid and uncertain....* Drawing in a quick breath to regain control, she said abruptly, "I can't go to Denver. That is final."

"You won't, you mean."

The rain thrummed evenly against the windows. "No."

"He is in his eighties!" He felt shocked despite himself at the change in her.

"Perhaps later... next year," she replied, knowing that she could never go back safely.

"He may be dead by then."

His bluntness made her wince inwardly. "I can't go."

"He was always your supporter."

But not Luke, she thought dully. "No."

"Why the hell not?"

"I don't want to."

"You don't want to," he repeated flatly.

"No."

"Just like that."

"Yes."

"An old man who never hurt you."

She stared fixedly at the jagged base of pale stone supporting the loneliness of the sculpted lighthouse. She, too, had to stand alone to protect the children. Yet she was unable to look up into the certain contempt she knew would confront her, and she let the silence grow.

Luke eyed her and even in anger noted the fatigue in her bearing. "You sold your painting. Why?"

The non sequitur made her look up, then quickly down at her hands resting on the scraps of paper filled with her calculations and budgets. She nodded.

"Elijah seems to believe that you would sell it only under duress."

"There comes a time," she returned evenly, "when childhood things are put to rest."

Silence closed in again, and the desultory pattern of the abating rain was a deadening background. "Then you're not in any trouble—financially."

"No."

He felt locked out, blocked, as if he were staring at a lost object and not seeing it. His eyes rested idly on her hands, and then narrowed on the pale band of skin next to the slim gold wedding band. "You sold your engagement ring, also—and recently."

With alarm she jerked and rose to cover her reaction as she realized from his gaze how he knew.

"Why?" he pursued. "Why both your portrait and your ring—at this particular time?"

"For a new car," she offered quickly. "I need a new car."

His one dark eyebrow hooked upward with open disbelief, but before he could speak, Madge rushed in shaking off the rain like a shaggy dog. "Whew! What a day!" She stopped abruptly, her eyes widening as she saw Luke.

"M—Madge, this is my...." Sara stopped, aware that she did not even know if she was still married to this Other Luke, this unloving stranger.

"Husband," Luke tacked on shortly, realizing as Madge Wintertree was introduced that she knew exactly who he was.

The awkward introductions were barely over when, with a look at Sara's pale controlled features, Madge said, "I'll be in the back office if anyone comes."

The difficult silence Madge left behind was broken by Sara with a low, "So, we are still married, then."

"Yes."

"Despite my scarlet history."

The scar along his cheek twitched. "It was for life."

"Not for you."

"Surely your marital status doesn't affect your love affairs?"

"Naturally not," she replied, knowing he would distort her meaning, and stiff with anger.

"I will never... forgive you, Sara."

Her eyes lifted to find such a hard coldness that her hands shook as she turned away and rested them on the windowsill. Bleakly looking into the weeping world outside, she realized that with Luke still legally her husband, he was more a danger than ever to her and the children. "It doesn't matter if you do forgive now, just as it doesn't matter if you believe me."

Regarding the rigid line of her slim back, the distant coolness of her in the rain light, an anger unequal to any he had felt in years threatened his control.

With a cool, "It doesn't matter," she dismissed her betrayal and all the pain of their marriage as if it were an old story. He was still fighting for control, determined not to allow his emotions to become involved, when she turned to meet his gaze with cool gray eyes.

"Luke, there is nothing left for us to say to each other. Go back. Back to Jessica, Grey and Elijah. Forget the past. Get a divorce and forget me. We were totally incompatible—art against science, logic against faith. All we ever had was a sexual attraction that died."

He sucked in a breath. "I came because Elijah wanted to see you."

"We all fail sometimes—even you."

His lean body tensed. "Your expenses and a generous fee will be paid."

"I am not for sale, Luke."

"Everyone is... as you proved when you sold your portrait."

Her eyes flicked away; she was startled that he recalled how she'd felt about the painting. "The Other Luke," she whispered.

Pivoting to hide a resurgence of anger, he glared into the renewed fury of the storm. "Sold to buy a new car!"

"Yes."

Emotions as erratic as the gusting wind shaking the walls of the gallery made him say curtly, "You are still my wife, Sara. If you need money it won't dent my funds to help—provided they don't line the pockets of a lover."

"How can you—"

"How much, Sara?" he asked without turning. "Everyone does have a price. Let's just say I'll rent you for Elijah. To make an old man happy. With a bonus for a good performance."

She was briefly tempted. To have enough money, to stop worrying; she could fly to Denver for a few days and with the money disappear.... No, it was far too dangerous, she told herself. "I want nothing from you, Luke. Not hypocritical concern nor a salary."

As he repudiated her reply with a shake of his dark head, her image flashed back at him from a mirror angled on the wall. An image showing her hands clenching and unclenching. "I always do it when I'm scared," his memory echoed.

He prodded instantly, "So you don't need money desperately, after all."

"No." Again her chin lifted betrayingly. "The fact is, Luke, I have enough for the car now and I simply don't care to trek across the continent to satisfy an old man's whim."

He paled. "Damn! I think if I could find a way to hurt you, to crack that icy thing you call a heart, I would! You put me through hell and now you dare to—"

"Considering any inconvenience to you or disruption of your obsessive research was what you called hell, I—"

"Don't push too far, Sara!"

"And don't threaten me, Luke—just because you've failed. I tried. It was more than you ever did. You might have been a lover, but you were never a friend or husband!"

"I don't think Elijah would care to see you as you are, and I'll be damned if I'll suffer you even for his sake."

She didn't move and his eyes drilled into her with pure contempt until a completely unexpected awareness of her, the scent of her, the remembered passion of her, seemed to explode inside him, and he looked away.

As if he had laid out his thoughts for her inspection, Sara somehow knew the direction his mind had shifted, and instantly rejected her echoing awareness of the pure maleness of him with something closely akin to fear. Her insides shaking, she managed, "There's nothing else to say, then."

"Except that I curse the day I first laid eyes on you," he ground out.

With icy pain she quoted the words he had said to her nearly five years before. "I don't need you! I don't want you. I don't love you. Just get out of my life! The very sight of you—" She was unable to finish as buried anguish threatened to surface, and her words fell into a near silence as the storm suddenly abated.

Luke was still. It was as if he had turned into the granite of his home mountains. Only the need to protect Tricia and Toby by driving him away enabled her to meet the flint of his eyes without visibly flinching and to say coldly, "Goodbye, Luke."

Vividly he saw her again at the foot of his hospital bed in the same frozen, determined stance, and for a moment he could not speak.

When he did speak, his words reached Sara as if he were speaking from the end of a long tunnel. "I won't intrude again."

For yet another taut moment he stared into her shuttered eyes, his face expressionless but his eyes narrowed, hidden from her. It was almost as if he were passing his final, irrevocable judgment upon her before he wheeled and left her staring numbly after him.

CHAPTER THREE

THEY WERE SAFE, Sara told herself that evening despite an inexplicable uneasiness that refused to be alleviated even after the hotel clerk had confirmed Luke's departure.

They *had* to be safe. Yet the pods of the woman's-tongue tree clicking and clacking in the night winds outside her window seemed to mock her.

She stared into the tangled shadows on her bedroom wall, trying to think of some way to be certain, knowing that she could not use the money set aside for Toby's convalescence to flee. They just had to be safe, she reiterated desperately while the cicadas burred holes into the night.

Uninvited, the image of Luke as he had confronted her suddenly intruded. Too vividly she saw the tempered leanness that he had acquired in the past years, which only emphasized the hard taut power of his male body.

Flushing and appalled by the route her wayward mind was taking, she rolled over in bed with a groan and forced her thoughts back on track.

If only, she thought tiredly, she had not sold her portrait. If only.... A sudden soft moan made her still.

By the time a small cry followed, she was already on her feet and crossing the narrow hall to the children's room.

It was instinctive reaction, for she had become accustomed to the nights when Toby was awakened by the gnawing ache of his leg. Nights that were spaced apart and yet were still too frequent.

Sitting on the side of his bed, she smoothed his rumpled hair back, murmuring, "Mummy's here."

"I hurt," he whimpered.

"I'll get your medicine," she told him softly, and within a moment was back at his side watching him swallow the pill while her hands rubbed his aching leg.

"I don't like hurting," he mumbled as he returned the glass.

"I know," she soothed, "I know. Soon it will be gone."

"Will the op'ration make it go away?"

"It has for all the other boys and girls."

"And I won't hurt ever again?" he said hopefully.

She hesitated, wanting to tell him what he begged to hear. But knowing that he trusted her implicitly, she followed the doctor's advice and said truthfully, "It will hurt more at first. And then it will all go away."

"I don't want to hurt anymore!" His chin wobbled.

"It will only be for a little while," she promised.

"No!" he quavered, and his small jaw jutted forward.

"Shhh!" She glanced quickly toward Tricia, who was curled up in sleep in the next bed.

"I won't!" he insisted belligerently in a loud whisper.

Sara sighed, her fingers still kneading his leg as she tried to find the words that might help him understand. "Do you remember when you were sick last time? Your head hurt, and your chest and throat ached, too, whenever you coughed?"

A slow nod replied.

"And then the doctor gave you medicine with a needle. Remember?"

"I don't like needles."

"They hurt a bit, don't they?"

"A lot!"

"But then the hurting in your head and throat...it all went away." She paused. "Didn't it?"

"Yes," he agreed with patent reluctance.

"After the operation it will hurt, too, but that hurt will be the kind to make you all better."

"Why does it hurt?"

"Because," she said, groping for patience, "your leg will be sore after the doctors fix it."

"Why?"

"Because they have to fix it inside."

"Why?" he persisted.

"It's the only way to fix it."

"Why?"

"Because!" she ground out with mild exasperation, knowing he would recognize the word and tone as her final say.

"Oh."

Smiling slightly, she smoothed back his hair again, and doubting that he really understood her point, she bent and kissed him, saying, "We'll think about it tomorrow. Okay?"

"Okay." He sighed, his eyelids drooping.

Gently she tucked the sheet over his shoulders, and remained yet awhile to rub his back lightly until the medication allowed sleep to claim him again.

Back in her own bed, she found sleep evading her and tossed restlessly. She tried to convince herself that everything would work out in the end, but the memory of how tenacious Luke could be nibbled at her self-assurances.

Dawn found her still awake with a day of promises to picnic and visit the turtles ahead of her, and her mind and body heavy with fatigue.

A fatigue that by late afternoon, after hours on the beach picnicking and harvesting the early sea grapes for jelly, made her long to crawl home and sleep for a year.

Instead she waited in the shade of a banyan tree with its dark glossy leaves and aerial roots half caging her while she watched Toby and Tricia leaning enthusiastically over the rails of the turtle pens with their old friend Eduardo.

"How old is that one?" Toby asked Eduardo, pointing down at a huge turtle with fascination.

Eduardo tilted his graying head and narrowed his eyes on the turtles destined to become soup, oil and leather bits. "Two...maybe three hundred years old."

"That's awful old," Tricia decided.

"That turtle was probably flapping her flippers when the wreckers were salvaging doomed ships off our reefs and rumrunners were sneaking across the seas. If she had kept away from the shrimp and sponge boats, she'd still be free."

"I want to ride one," Toby announced, patently unimpressed.

Watching silently, Sara found herself regressing to a childhood habit. She had been five when Aunt Ruth had taken her in. From then on, nothing Sara had done had been right. Soon, no matter what she was doing, she had learned to keep one eye constantly alert for Aunt Ruth bearing down upon her with a frown and a ready lecture.

Now she found herself once again keeping one eye constantly scanning the tourists exploring the nearby galleon, which had been restored to smart paint and trim and seemed much too small ever to have sailed an ocean. From there her eyes moved to search the straggling crowd exploring the wares on sale—natural sponges, shell jewelry, conch horns and other island specialties.

But she found no tall, dark and bleak figure watching from the shadows or bearing down on her.

They *were* safe, she assured herself as she and the children left the square to walk slowly across the small island. Yet despite herself she felt an odd sense of leave-taking, as if her small world on the island, her place of respite, had somehow been permanently violated by Luke's intrusion.

"Mummy?" Tricia tugged on Sara's hand. "Didn't a man steal a lady from there?" Tricia pointed to the old graveyard across the way with its white vaults raised above sea level and guarded by stone angels.

"Yes," Sara replied shortly.

"Why?" Toby pursued promptly.

Sara frowned down at them. "He was ill. He didn't know what he was doing."

"Oh."

Where, she wondered, had they heard of the demented lover who had stolen his beloved's body and taken it to live with him, playing hymns to her in her mildewed bridal gown for eight years before he was discovered?

She shivered. It seemed impossible that this quiet island lazing in the late-afternoon sunlight had seen centuries of violence. Its name seemed so innocuous—unless one knew that Key West came from the sinister name Cayo Hueso, or Island of Bones, as the first Spanish explorers had named it upon finding only sun-bleached skeletons to greet them.

But now it was tranquil, she reminded herself, as if its history were only fragments of the old people's imaginations. Now artists and writers who followed Hemingway's pathway shared the peace of the old town and left the modern side of the island to the tourists and the naval base.

As they turned onto the street where the house she rented rested tiredly in the neutral winds and evening sun, she scanned the street warily. But no one waited.

By the time they reached their gate she found herself relaxing, and feeling somewhat foolish, she paused to let the children race on. Looking at the house, she could not help but wonder what Luke's reaction would have been had he seen it.

Contempt, she decided without hesitation. The

same contempt he had felt for her studio loft in Toronto. She eyed the weathered cypress of the house, which leaned slightly, and the veranda steps that sagged sadly as if the probable hundred summers they had seen were far too many. It had been neglected, but it was cheap and clean. In all, with the yard of sparse grass and sand and the twins' red wagon, long since bleached into pink, it looked like a faded photograph in a family album—except for the flowers.

Flowers so alive with color they had often nearly tempted her to paint again. It was not only the vivid lavenders and roses of the bougainvillea, or the mauve and cream of continually blooming hibiscus, but also the brilliant greens of the palms, orange trees and the noisy woman's-tongue tree someone had once planted with care.

Yet not all the flowers, or even the soft golden rose of sunset, she was forced to admit, could hide the shabbiness of the old Bahamian house.

For an instant she could see Spars' Nest—cared for, solid, commanding. An intriguingly eccentric house with its two stone wings at right angles and the small cozy tower that joined them.

"Boo!"

Sara jumped, her heart thudding, and then smiled as the giggles rippled through the quiet evening from the vicinity of her knees. Spinning around on the culprits, she crouched. "You frightened me! Look!" She pointed to her hair. "I have white streaks now."

"The sun did that!" Toby shouted, reaching out a small hand to touch the pale streaks in Sara's hair, which matched his own.

"No," Sara solemnly insisted. "You did it."

"We did not!" Tricia giggled.

"Sure?"

"Sure!" they both chorused, enjoying the ritual.

"Ah, well if you are sure." Sara grinned and stood. "Now, how about playing ball together for a while. With Aunt Madge coming to supper, I have to get busy."

"Can't," Tricia said.

Sara's eyebrows lifted. "And why not, young lady?"

"Toby threw the ball and it's stuck on the roof."

"All stuck," Toby agreed. "But I didn't mean it."

With a sigh Sara peered up at the roof and spotted the ball in the rain gutter above the veranda.

"You can get it," Toby observed confidently.

"Thanks," Sara returned dryly.

She was panting by the time she had climbed to a precarious balance on the veranda rail. Pushing away fatigue, she stretched up and out toward the vagrant ball. She was fully extended, her fingertips almost touching it, when Tricia spoke from somewhere below her.

"Who's that man, mummy?"

Sara's head jerked around.

There was a brief glimpse of Luke stalking through the gate, and a glimpse of grim cold fury that fulfilled every fear in her heart, before she lost her balance. She clutched wildly at the drain guttering, felt it rip loose from rotten moorings, and then the ground rushed up toward her.

Her breath exploded from her lungs as the ground

slammed into her and a streak of pain sent her spinning into darkness.

A darkness barely broken by distant voices, someone holding her, and pain. A long wavering darkness.

Finally she was able to hold on to a distant fuzzy light without it being swallowed by more darkness, and as her eyes focused, she found Madge's face hanging over her.

"You fell, Sara. You're bruised and you have a mild concussion. You'll be fine soon." Madge bent nearer, her hand lifting Sara's head. When Sara moaned at the searing pain slashing through her head, Madge murmured, "Try to relax. I know it hurts. Just take these and sleep."

After that the world blurred and darkened again into deep black velvet.

When she wakened uneasily, it was nighttime. The small lamp on her dresser cast a soft light that barely held back the shadows. Outside she could hear the clicking of the tree pods and the drone of crickets.

With an effort she turned her head. The sight of Luke jolted her heart against her rib cage and swept her vague uneasiness into focused memory.

He was asleep. His big lean frame was bent into an upholstered chair that he had apparently commandeered from the front room. His dark hair was disordered, his suit rumpled, and in sleep there was none of the terrible fury of her last memory.

As she watched him an inner shivering spread through her until she was shaking despite her efforts to stop. She struggled to sit, and the pain in her head increased so swiftly that a croak of agony escaped her.

Luke roused instantly to find her trembling uncontrollably. Her gray eyes were dark with pain or fear or hatred—he did not know which.

Quickly rising, he moved to her. When she shrank from him, his mouth compressed, and picking up the medication and a glass of water, he said without expression, "This will help the pain."

"I don't want it."

"Drink!"

It was a command bordering on a threat, she thought dazedly, yet when his hand slipped beneath her head, there was only an odd gentleness. Too weak to argue, she swallowed the medication and her head barely touched the pillow before darkness possessed her again.

When she wakened next it was daylight, and Luke was still in his chair. This time staring levelly back at her. Dully her eyes met his in a long look that was surrounded by the ghosts of a thousand unspoken words.

"The...children," she whispered, her fears coiling again like roused snakes.

"They are asleep. Madge is looking after them."

"Luke, I...." Her voice cracked.

"Why!" he asked harshly. "Why didn't you tell me?"

He looked barely able to resist striking her, and unable to prevaricate or dress up her words, she said tiredly, "I didn't want them to grow up at Spars' Nest. To see only contempt for me in your eyes. Or to watch you drying their souls until they became... machines, unable to feel or trust. It destroyed me, and I couldn't let it happen to them."

Turning her face away from him, she battled tears that threatened to escape. She had not wept since Toby and Tricia were born. All the doubts and uncertain guilts she had locked away suddenly were clamoring for release. Unaware that the color had left Luke's face at her words, she added in a whisper, "I wanted them to know faith...and loving."

There was a long silence between them before Luke finally said, "You left me when I was tied to my bed with a broken leg. There would be a rough justice if I took the children right now. Before you could get out of that bed and stop me."

Her head pivoted sharply. His face was half in shadow, the stubble of his beard accenting the scar on his cheek almost satanically. "No!" She shook her head, fighting the suffocating pain. "No! *No!*"

When she attempted to sit, he was next to her in a swift moment, and although she tried to resist the hard hands pressing her back, she was snatched into the possessive darkness and went limp.

His mouth grim, Luke settled her back on the pillows, and as he pulled the covers around her, he was aware of a feeling of disgust with himself for taunting her when she could not fight back.

He was still staring down at her bleakly when a small noise in the hall caught his attention, and a moment later he was in the hall, startled to find Toby and Tricia crouched together in a huddle against the wall outside the room.

"What are you doing here?" he asked them softly.

"Is mummy dead?" Toby quavered.

Appalled, Luke dropped to one knee to meet the pairs of eyes, one blue and one brown, that were glued with open anxiety to his face. He shook his head. "She's asleep. She's very tired and the bump on her head hurts."

"You promise?" Tricia whispered.

"I promise."

In a simultaneous move they rushed to him, and he found himself kneeling awkwardly with a small face buried in each side of his neck. Without time to think he put his arms around them, and holding them, smelling the sleepy scent of them and feeling the warmth of their small bodies, he was startled by a wave of emotion that made him hug them even more tightly to him.

He was still groping with new feelings when the sound of the front door opening intruded, and by the time Madge Wintertree appeared, he was on his feet watching Toby and Tricia running to greet her.

Within moments she shooed them off to dress, before following she eyed his drawn face. "Bad night?"

"Fairly quiet."

"You look as though you need a good cup of coffee and breakfast. Why don't you freshen up while I get things started."

With a nod he briefed her on the night and Sara's condition, and an hour later, breakfast over and his third cup of coffee before him, he leaned back in his chair and eyed Madge thoughtfully. "As Sara's closest friend, why aren't you treating me like a pariah?"

She glanced out the window to where the children were playing, and then back at him. "Perhaps because I've had more time to study human nature than either of you," she told him somewhat wryly. "Both of you are babes in the woods when it comes to understanding relationships."

Even as he frowned over her reply, the phone rang. Setting down his cup, he murmured that it was probably for him, and a moment later Jessica's cool voice was greeting him with a casual, "Hi! Grey gave me your number. How are things going?"

"Well enough," he said neutrally.

"It's raining here. I'll bet you are enjoying sunshine, though."

"And mosquitoes."

"I called because you left so quickly that I didn't have a chance to ask you if you would bring back a couple of those natural sponges they have there, and a conch shell for my nephew."

Scowling, he said abruptly, "Will do."

"Thanks."

"Anything else?"

"When will you be back?" she asked.

"I'm not sure. A week, perhaps."

"You found Sara, then."

"Yes."

"Grey told me that you were searching for her." She hesitated. "Luke, don't let her destroy you again."

His hand tightened on the phone as he said in a grim tone, "Whatever I do will be my decision."

"I'm sorry. I'm concerned. As a friend, allow me that much. I remember what she did to you last time...and to your work."

He drew in a breath, but before he could reply Tricia poked her head around the door to ask, "Can we go to the beach today?"

"This afternoon," Luke told her. "Now scoot! I'm on the phone."

"Who was that?" Jessica asked sharply. "Was that a child?"

"It was," he returned dryly. "As a matter of fact, it was one of my children."

When a stunned silence followed, he added, "Say hello to everyone, will you, Jessica? I'll see you whenever I get back."

Hanging up, he walked slowly out to the veranda to stand with his long fingers gripping the post as he absorbed the true message underlying Jessica's call.

A call that he and his security officer hoped would appear innocuous to any eavesdroppers, but which had actually briefed him on what the rumor, published only hours ago, contained.

With the request for sponges indicating that Driscoll Electronics had been specifically named, and the request for a conch shell indicating that solar energy had been identified as the general nature of the project, he knew the key information. Jessica's failure to use other code words told him that was the total scope of the printed rumor.

Still, it was enough, he thought tiredly. It would attract trouble faster than carrion attracted vultures. It would place in jeopardy the livelihood of every employee as well as the company's existence.

All it would take now was one vulnerable employee in a key position or a successful industrial spy operation, and years of work and effort would go down the drain—just when they were so near to success that they could almost touch it.

Reason told him he should return to Denver quickly and take charge himself. But if he left, part of him countered, there was no one he would trust to ensure that Sara did not disappear again with the children.

His hand tightened on the rail post and his jaw tightened to the point where pulses throbbed along its hard line.

"Do you hurt, too?"

Luke looked down to find his newfound son regarding him with clear concern. "Hurt?"

"You look like you hurt. Your face was funny."

"I was thinking about something." Luke dropped to a crouch so that he was on eye level. "Sometimes when I think, I make faces."

"My leg hurts sometimes. Then mummy gives me medicine." He grimaced. "And she rubs my leg." He cocked his head. "Did you ever have an op'ration?"

"Yes...." Luke's dark eyes were pinpoints as he pushed aside memories. "On my leg."

"Did you really?" Toby asked, entranced.

"I did really."

"Did it hurt?"

Luke hesitated, noting the anxiety confronting him, and in the pause Madge Wintertree appeared in the doorway.

"I imagine it did," she said casually. "For a while."

"Oh!" Toby looked somewhat rattled.

"But the hurting stopped," Luke assured him, picking up on Madge's approach. "And then my leg was fine."

"The hurting stopped?" Toby asked. "It all stopped?"

"It all stopped."

"Oh." He seemed to mull this over, then looked up. "Are we going to the beach?"

"This afternoon," Luke promised, blinking at the sudden change in subject.

"He's still uncertain about the whole idea of an operation," Madge said quietly as Toby trotted across the yard with his uneven gait. "The doctor advised that we tell the truth without making a fuss."

"He seems too small to be facing surgery," Luke replied as he tensed inwardly with a wave of protectiveness that shook him with its force.

"They make fun of him sometimes. They call him 'gimpy,' and other names. When that happens he's ready to face any 'op'ration.' But being made fun of is also a great deal for a small boy to handle." She paused, then added evenly, "And being torn apart between his parents might be more than he can handle at this time. He'll need Sara desperately."

"Which means?" Luke prodded, his mouth tightening.

Her eyes met his without flinching. "It could mean that you face the choice between revenge and your son's future."

He regarded her narrowly with a grudging respect

before replying grimly, "Toby won't face that dilemma before surgery. Sara will be there—I assure you."

Two mornings later Sara wakened with her mind clear and her memory unsure. Faint throbbings reminded her of her fall, but for the first time in months her body felt completely rested. The sense of peace lasted until the last clouds of sleep left her and the memories rushed in. Instantly her body stiffened and her eyes opened.

"Hi, mummy!" Toby and Tricia chorused in greeting, their faces level with hers as they leaned on the edge of her bed. "You're awake!"

"Wide awake," Sara agreed, and pushing aside everything for the moment but the relief of knowing Luke had not taken them away, she held out her arms.

"We missed you," Tricia confided after the first excitement passed.

"I missed you, too."

"Uncle Luke let us kiss you when you were asleep," Toby revealed. "Could you tell?"

"I had a lovely dream," Sara assured them, her voice shaking, "so I must have."

"Uncle Luke's nice," Toby offered.

"And he's fun, too," Tricia added.

Fun. It was so far from her own feelings that Sara turned her face away to hide her reactions, and found Luke watching them from the doorway. Involuntarily her arms tightened around the children, and meeting his dark, unrevealing regard, her eyes were suddenly hard and defiant.

Without expression he asked, "Coffee?"

Nodding, she held on to her control, aware of the presence of the children, who instantly popped up with, "Me, too!"

"They usually have it with milk and—"

"A dash of coffee and sugar," Luke finished and left.

Within a short time they were sharing coffee in her bedroom, and Toby's and Tricia's delight in their newfound uncle was clear. Despite herself, Sara felt betrayed.

Yet, she reminded herself, as far as they knew, he had helped her, and they were seeing only the charm he was exerting to win their approval. Her effort to rationalize, however, did not help, and by the time they cheerfully obeyed his order to play outside for a while, she found herself feeling hurt and somehow more alone than ever.

How long would it be, she could not help wondering as she watched Luke stacking the cups on the tray, before he tired of playing the benevolent uncle, before he found them nuisances and started regimenting and disapproving and—

"Madge went to the gallery," he said suddenly, without looking toward her. "Do you feel up to dressing and sitting on the veranda?"

He could have been a valet for all the interest he showed, and part of her wanted to explode, to break through the cold judgments behind his mask. Another part of her, however, wanted only to hide, aware that the reckoning was coming and that she was unarmed and wounded and unable to stop it.

"Sara!"

"Yes—I feel well enough." With her reply she stood on legs whose weakness startled her.

He closed the distance between them in a long stride. "You'll probably need help to the bathroom."

"No!" To her horror, she flushed. "I can m-manage."

"Whether you remember or not," he said dryly, "I have been carrying you there for three days—not to mention other occasions of intimacy in the past."

Trembling with weakness and resenting his strength, she said nothing as his arm circled her.

By the time she was settled in the wicker rocking chair on the veranda, she was taut with apprehension, and in her effort to maintain a calm facade her eyes sought the peace of the blue sky. Suddenly she wished desperately that she could escape into the past. The past before Luke.

Escape back to the cool blue lakes of Muskoka, to the early mornings when she would slip from the house before Aunt Ruth wakened and race off to the riding school. To the blissful freedom of riding across the fields, leaving all her cares far, far behind. In Denver, too, she'd had the outlet of riding at Paul Girard's ranch until Luke's suspicions had extended even to his best friend.

The giggles of the children playing nearby drew her back to the present, to the acceptance that there was no going back. Even as Key West was changing under the flood of tourists—many from her own Canada— so, too, had Muskoka probably changed. There would be nothing to go back to anywhere, she reminded herself.

"They are fine children, Sara."

With a start she looked up to find Luke in the doorway watching her. The trembling started again as he approached. He settled so purposefully in the creaking chair opposite her that the inner tremors spread until she had to clasp her hands in her lap to still them.

"You're too weak to fight," Luke observed as he subjected her to a detached scrutiny. "Perhaps it will save a great deal of argument."

"Luke...."

"I've been thinking it out these past days. You know that you almost succeeded in driving me away without stopping to check into your life or ever wanting to return. I presume that was your goal."

She nodded tiredly.

"Unfortunately for you, Elijah hired a local man some weeks ago to discreetly investigate you. I was to stop and see him first. Instead I went to the gallery first." He drew in a breath. "On the way to the airport I finally stopped in to see him. Between him and your friend Madge, the picture is fairly complete."

"I'm doing all right! I don't need—"

"You just slept for more than three days, and not only from your fall, but also because you've been working two jobs, caring for the children and, I suspect, shorting yourself on food, as well, to save money. That is not handling everything all right by anyone's standards."

"In a few months—"

"No."

"I won't—"

"Now, you listen to me, Sara!" He leaned forward, his muscles rippling and the scar on his cheek whitening with cold anger. "When I arrived the other night, I did not even know if I could keep my hands off you! You had one hell of a nerve keeping my children from me! And I don't give a damn what you thought or why you thought you had to. They are my children, also."

"You didn't want children!"

"That is a lie!"

"And you have a convenient memory," she retorted bitterly.

Luke drew in a harsh breath. "We are not going to beat the past to death. The situation—now—is this. Toby needs care. Elijah wants to see you. I intend to know my children. So next week you are returning to Spars' Nest with me."

"No."

"Oh, yes, you are, Sara! I can walk out now with the children and leave you here. With my legal staff, I'll keep the case in court for years. We will drag your history through court. Rufus, the nightclub work, your inability to care properly for Toby...everything and anything."

"Luke—"

He overrode her. "As far as anyone in Denver is concerned, during the time here we will have agreed to a trial period together for the children's sake. You were an amnesia victim and your memory is still returning, our future uncertain."

"No one will believe it!"

He shrugged. "That's our story." Her eyes told him that he had won, and the victory felt oddly flat. Yet he drove in his last points relentlessly. "You will pretend to be recovering. You will appear to be trying to make our marriage work as far as onlookers go—even Elijah. And you will be kind to him. In return Toby will have the best possible care...every chance available."

"And if I refuse?" she asked without spirit.

"You will never see Toby or Tricia again."

CHAPTER FOUR

A WEEK LATER, with Toby asleep in her arms after their long flight, Sara looked up at Spars' Nest.

It was as she remembered. The small tower and two wings of stone and dark wood, solidly built on the mountainside. The lawns, embroidered with flower beds, spread their trim skirts through the moon-dappled shadows below the dark firs, broad oaks and ghostly aspens. Above, the moonlit mountains soared to an indigo sky, while below, the lights of Denver were scattered like carelessly tossed jewels.

She had been enchanted when Luke first brought her to Spars' Nest. Now her apprehensions over what awaited her within its stone walls blurred all other feelings.

"You *are* coming in?" Luke asked dryly as the airport limousine purred away.

Not replying, she stared up at Luke as he stood on the steps with Tricia asleep in his arms. The gaslight of the lanterns by the oaken doors flickered across his scarred cheek and threw his long shadow toward her. He could have been some dark duelist out of a bygone era but for the small child in his arms.

She had tried to purge him from her mind and had fought against seeking his help for so many years.

Now he was back in her life, and regardless of her feelings, he had once again taken it over.

As Aunt Ruth had. As he had after their honeymoon, when he no longer wanted a wife quite so emotional and artistically involved, but rather wanted someone quite, quite conventional...like the cool and brilliant Jessica. The unimpeachable Jessica Pettiway.

Her eyes lingered on his face, the male line of his lips, and she tried to deny that, even as she wanted to run, somewhere within herself there was a yearning to do the impossible. To walk back into the past where for a brief time she had loved and been loved passionately by this dark, lean, waiting man. *Don't,* she warned herself instantly. *Don't even think of caring again.*

"Sara!"

"Yes...I'm coming." Drawing in a breath and shifting Toby's weight in her arms, she stepped forward.

"It's good to see you home again, Mr. Luke. I...." The dry, dusty voice halted as Sara entered. There was a brief hesitation before the housekeeper granted Sara a short nod as if she were no more than an upper servant following the master in.

It was uncanny, Sara thought wildly. Grey might well have planned it all. Once before Grey had said much the same and had committed the same omission in her greeting. And once before Grey had stood there in her black dress, her veined hand almost possessively gripping the newel post, and her gaunt body stiff with disapproval as her colorless eyes pinned the intruder.

There had been no welcome then. There was none now.

"Mrs. Grey." Sara did not nod or smile. She was no longer the young bride who had wanted to be liked, who had foolishly cared whether this woman accepted her.

Grey stiffened, the pupils of her eyes pinpoints of affront.

"Let Grey help you with the boy," Luke ordered.

"I can manage."

With a shrug he turned to Grey. "Is everything ready?" When he was assured that his instructions had been followed, he added, "Then, let's get the children to bed." He eyed Sara neutrally. "Do you need anything?"

"Two small glasses of milk." She met the housekeeper's pale gaze again. Grey's glance instantly shifted, and without even an indication that she had heard Sara, she turned and disappeared into the shadows in the direction of the kitchen.

"You could have greeted her civilly," Luke said tersely, and started up the stairs.

"She could have greeted me civilly," Sara threw after him.

"Bravo!" a cool mocking voice cheered from the shadows, and Luke halted, his dark brows lifting as Jessica Pettiway strolled out of the den where she had evidently been standing watching everything.

"What are you doing lurking about?" Luke asked irritably.

She yawned, her slender fingertips covering her mouth, and contradictory dark blue eyes quite alert.

"I dozed off waiting and wakened upon your arrival—not precisely lurking, dear Luke." She drifted over to Sara. "Are these the newfound children?" She peered at Toby. "Ah, quite blond." Her eyes lifted to meet Sara's. "Are his eyes brown or... gray?"

"Blue," Sara replied evenly.

Jessica's groomed brows lifted and she turned to eye Tricia. "Now this one, Luke, could have your mark on her. At least she is dark."

"You'll excuse us," he said abruptly, "but they need to be in bed." Looking past Jessica to where Sara stood, pale and strained, he turned and continued up the stairs.

"I'll wait!" Jessica called lightly after them.

By the time Sara reached the landing, Denver's high altitude forced her to pause for breath, and she half turned to look down into the hall. Jessica was gone and the lights were on in the den. She had forgotten, Sara realized, how immaculately beautiful Jessica was—and how incredibly insensitive.

Her eyes moved over the entrance foyer with curiosity. It was as it had been the first time she arrived—white walls and dark beams. Monastic. The paintings, the plants, the curtains she had added to lighten its austerity were gone. Her brief year at Spars' Nest erased.

The bedroom she had shared once with Luke, however, was the same as the day she had left in tears. Unnervingly so. The pale blue walls, cream carpet and even the cushions of the small upholstered chairs by the window, with their blue, cream and lemon print she had searched months to find, were the same. Above the fireplace the Danish figurines still peered indifferently down upon her return.

"I moved downstairs shortly after you left," Luke offered abruptly, as if to forestall questions. "The rooms have been closed."

"Where are the children sleeping?"

He crossed to the short hall connecting with what had been their dressing room. There he paused, and for an instant seemed uncertain, a dark figure hovering over the small room with two beds. "It's a bit crowded, but near you," he finally said, and bent to lay Tricia on one of the beds.

Not replying, Sara applied herself to rousing the children, who were irritable despite their nap. Luke assisted, patient with Tricia's grumpiness, and a smile twitched at the corner of his mouth when, as he tucked her in, she lifted her arms and ordered, "Hug me!"

He obliged with his easy grace and then turned to include Toby.

Watching him thoughtfully, Sara found herself unable to reconcile his gentle humor and firmness with the children with the cruelty she had seen in him. Her sober gaze was still on him, and on the contrast of his dark hair with Toby's fairness, when Luke looked up.

His smile faded instantly, and by the time he straightened, his face had closed. There was a curt nod and he was gone, leaving Sara pushing back an irrational anger.

"Mummy?" Toby said sleepily.

"What is it?" she whispered, clamping down on her emotions.

"Where will you sleep?"

"Right in the next room. Through there."

He nodded, and she settled both children down and then slowly walked back through the short closet-lined hall paralleling the bathroom between the two rooms. The sight of Luke dropping her luggage in the center of the room halted her in the doorway. She eyed him warily.

"Your luggage," he announced shortly. "Do you want a tray of sandwiches and coffee sent up—or tea?"

She said nothing. Jessica was waiting downstairs and there was not even a token invitation from him. Appearances evidently did not extend to Jessica Pettiway. But, she reminded herself sharply, what else had she expected?

"Sara?" She seemed wraithlike to him as she hovered in the shadow of the doorway.

"I'm not hungry. Just tired." Not moving, she stared back at him. It was oddly disconcerting to see him against the background of their room. The room in which once they had loved and raged and laughed together. Now he looked at her as though he had never known her or cared for her. Perhaps, she thought, he never really had.

"It seems," he said dryly, "that you intend to spend the next months eyeing me reproachfully and playing out a classical tragedy."

"No," she denied without spirit. "Not at all."

A sudden impatience with her apathy prodded him

to say deliberately, "It would be more sensible, Sara, if you would pull yourself out of this Victorian decline. Start eating normally and rest. You might find that you'll enjoy these months without cares."

"Without cares!" The first sparks of anger in days propelled her chin upward. "You call being here under threat without cares?"

"Without cares," he agreed blandly. "We have our bargain. I see to it that you and the children are secure, and you keep up appearances."

"However, appearances don't apply to Jessica!" she snapped, and instantly was furious with herself for saying it.

"Jessica has nothing to do with you, Sara," Luke returned grimly. "You forfeited editorial rights on my life the day you first went to Rufus. Remember that in the future."

"Yes, sir!" she choked out.

"Don't try me too far," he warned, and suddenly he was closing the distance between them with long male strides.

"No!" It was a gasp as awareness of him flared searingly through her, shocking every cell in her body. "No!"

He stopped abruptly, his eyes dilated into complete blackness, and then, without another word, he pivoted and strode out of the room.

Behind him Sara sagged against the door frame, her forehead pressing against the cool smooth wood.

"You're strong," Madge had told her early that morning at the airport. "Whatever happens, Sara, you are strong enough to cope."

But she wasn't, Sara cried silently to herself as her head slowly lifted. She had coped alone because there had been no choice. And as much as she resented Luke's taking command of her life again, there was also something about his ungiving strength that was frighteningly seductive. Victorian decline.... Her mouth tightened, and lost in her thoughts she stared into the fireplace. Its hearth was clean. Not even the ashes were left.

At the head of the stairs Luke paused, his fists clenching against the knowledge that he had wanted to shake Sara with an unreasoning fury and instead the impulse had in a split instant shifted in nature to a raw desire.

Sucking in a hard breath, he told himself savagely that he would not allow that to happen again, he would not let himself become involved. But for her own good, he promised himself without examining his motives, he would force her out of her apathy. He would make that temper of hers flare. He would— Abruptly he became aware of Grey at the foot of the stairs eyeing him curiously.

"What is it, Grey?" He descended the stairs.

"Was there anything else tonight?"

"A tray for Mrs. Driscoll. Coffee...." He hesitated, recalling that Sara preferred tea when she was tired. "Make that tea and a sandwich." One hand raked through his thick black hair tiredly. "Is my grandfather asleep?"

She nodded. "He said that he would see you and— her, in the morning."

"Her?" he repeated dryly.

Two spots reddened on Grey's sharp cheekbones. "Mrs. Driscoll."

"You didn't greet her. Why?"

"If she's complaining—"

"She is not, but you seem ready to."

He watched Grey stiffen, and the memory of Sara half shouting, "She does not like me, Luke!" surfaced. He shrugged it away mentally. Grey was a creature of habit who disliked change, nothing more. Sara had been young and far too defensive with her lack of sophistication.

"...she still have amnesia?"

He jerked his focus back to the conversation and, catching the drift of it, nodded. "She recalls more every day."

"I've always done my best by you. You know that I would never—"

"Not you, too! First a Greek tragedy, and now the noble retainer of an Edwardian play. Dammit, I've had enough!" Grey's clear shock forced him to add wearily, "Look, we are all tired. Let's call it a night."

He saw her swallow visibly before saying, "Very well, but there's still that girl your secretary hired for the children."

He sighed. "Jeannie Schneider?"

"Does she work for me or for—" Grey stopped.

"Her?" he supplied dryly. "She works for my wife. You have enough to do without extra burdens."

He watched her as she finally left, and not moving, he stared into space. Instead of the stark white walls of the entrance hall, he saw Sara.

Sara in the past week in Florida; gentle with the children, lifeless near him. Sara as he had first seen her years before, with her gray eyes hostile as she faced him in that dreary Victorian attic she had called her studio. Sara, her face filled with guilt as he walked into Rufus's studio that dawn.

Swearing softly, Luke turned and walked toward his den where Jessica waited.

"Ralph thought you might like to read this tonight," Jessica said a moment later as she handed him a clipping.

Forcing aside his thoughts of Sara, he read, "Rumor is that David—Driscoll Electronics—is taking on the Goliaths of industry in the solar-energy arena. Is history about to repeat itself?"

"It's really rather general," Jessica commented.

"It's enough."

"But—"

"And if I find out who couldn't keep his mouth shut, being blacklisted in industry will be mild compared to what I'd like to do." At Jessica's expression, his mouth relaxed. "No need to shiver. I've been moderately civilized by now."

"You looked so...fierce," she said with a shaky laugh.

"Perhaps a good meal will calm the beast."

"Then let's hurry."

"If there aren't any other messages, fine."

"No. Ralph and John said what they have can wait until the meeting tomorrow morning. There is something, though, that we ran into. One of the tests came up with an unexpected side effect that—"

"Let it wait until tomorrow," he interrupted. "I need to relax."

She gave him a narrow look, her lips tightening briefly, and then without commenting preceded him from the room. As they left the house he found himself wondering if Sara was watching, and had to make a conscious effort to restrain himself from looking back.

An hour later, after toying with his food, he pushed aside his plate and signaled to the waiter to clear the table before focusing his attention more sharply on what Jessica was telling him. "In other words, you're saying everyone is panicking."

"They are splitting into factions," she modified. "Ben is promoting the idea of a deal with an industry leader. Specifically ETI. His brother-in-law is a vice-president there."

He was thoughtful for a moment, his mind computing Ben Hadley. In his thirties, a bachelor, Ben was sharp and hungry for power, specifically for the general manager's position. He was quite capable of bailing out if he thought the company was sinking, or if the price was right. Unfortunately, conditions were approaching both requirements. "If he's contacted ETI...." His mouth compressed.

"I shouldn't think he would without your approval."

"I only hope you're right. What else?"

"A few think we should make a deal with a power company, and others favor a federal grant or going it on our own."

"They seem to be covering most of the bets," he

drawled. "And you? Where do you stand amid all the factions?"

"With you." She leaned forward tensely. "We can't let anyone else in, Luke. This is our project. Our ideas. Our years of work! Any agreement with another company or corporation will mean that they'll put in their own high-powered team and they will walk off with all the honors!"

"So you favor going for an energy grant?"

"Only if we have to."

"Oh, we'll have to—unless you can find us fifteen or twenty million lying about to transform our brassboard model into a practical product that can be mass-produced."

"At least with a grant it stays our idea," she replied earnestly.

"We hope," he murmured, and as the waiter appeared with their after-dinner drinks, he eyed Jessica assessingly. Instead of the tailored business suits and blouses and neat chignon of her work attire, she wore a casual dress of deep blue with her hair a black silky curtain around her face.

Broodingly he wondered why he had never really been attracted to her except with respect to her intelligence. She was a valuable addition to his staff. Given an idea, she could produce a workable design if anyone could. She was also beautiful and had more than once hinted his interest would be welcome, yet....

"Worrying over work—or Sara?" Jessica asked when the waiter had gone.

He shrugged and sipped his drink before saying

mockingly, "Between what's happening with our project and finding myself a father, I believe I have something to worry about. With a son and daughter to pass on the company to, it makes this current threat take on new dimensions."

Jessica started to speak, then stopped.

Luke's eyebrows rose inquiringly. "Go ahead," he prodded.

With a sigh she leaned forward again, her hand moving to cover his on the table as she said jerkily, "Luke, they are... *your* children?"

Shock jolted through him, and drawing in a quick breath, he managed, "Of course they are!"

"But the boy looks— Oh, never mind!"

"They're twins!" he measured out, his eyes hard now.

"And one looks exactly like Rufus!" Jessica retorted with a rush. "Whom we all know was her lover then."

"He looks like Sara. The other—"

"The girl may be dark like you, but it's a common coloring, and Sara's father was dark, if you recall the picture she had of her parents. Luke, a brown-haired, dark-eyed girl is about as average as one can get, and the boy obviously looks like—"

"Jessica!" His hands clenched into fists.

"Why did she never tell you?" Jessica insisted. "Most women would—unless they had something to hide. I just hate the thought of you acknowledging another man's children! No, wait! Use your head, Luke, not mindless emotions as you did last time. We have too much at stake now."

Rising, he threw down his napkin and with an effort controlled himself enough to say curtly, "I appreciate your evident concern, but understand this, Jessica. If you ever...ever repeat or even hint at what you have just said to me, to anyone at all, our friendship is finished."

The dark fan of her eyelashes dropped to conceal her eyes. "I'm very sorry, Luke. As a—friend, I had to say it."

"It's said. Don't repeat it."

Her head shook and the cream of her skin flushed.

For yet another moment he stared down at her, then he turned and signaled the waiter for the check.

It was nearly an hour later when he arrived home, and leaving his car, he stood looking up at the silent, unrevealing face of Spars' Nest.

Grey would be retired in her small apartment above the garage, still in a huff, he suspected. Sara's windows were dark.

An odd reluctance to enter the house held him motionless. Behind him the metal of the car's engine crackled as it cooled, and the wooing cry of crickets blended with the night wind sighing down the mountainside.

He felt alone. Uncomfortably alone in an infinite universe.

Shaking off his mood, he entered the house, locked up and flicked off the lamp in the entrance hall. It was not, however, as simple to flick off Jessica's words concerning the children, and after a moment's hesitation he slowly mounted the stairs instead of going to his room.

Outside the children's room he paused, and even as he did, there was a small choked sound within the room. Quietly he pushed the door open and found Toby sitting up in his bed with tears rolling down his face.

"What's wrong?" Luke whispered, aware of the open passage through to where Sara slept.

"Uncle Luke?"

"Yes, it's...Uncle Luke." He eased himself onto the bed and in seconds a warm boy crawled into his arms.

"It's...funny here," Toby whispered.

"It's a nice room. You'll like it. It even has two teddy bears over there just waiting for you and Tricia to be their friends."

The tousled blond head lifted to look into the shadows. "Where?"

Lifting Toby, Luke crossed to the bears, and at Toby's insistence he laid one beside a sleeping Tricia.

Hugging his bear, Toby asked, "Where's mummy?"

"Shhh! I'll show you." Carefully he walked through the short inner hall to pause in her doorway.

She lay with her head beneath her pillow, something she had always done when she had trouble sleeping. Scanning her sprawled form, he thought she had no right to look so innocent and vulnerable. Not when she had deliberately hidden from him. Not when, despite himself, for years he had looked up from the middle of conversations whenever he even glimpsed a woman with fair hair. And not when for years he had lived with the fear that she had lost her memory and was wandering about somewhere in shock...or was dead. His mouth tightening, he pivoted and returned Toby to bed.

"I like you," Toby offered tentatively.

Luke looked down at the small face, into intense blue eyes—not gray like Sara's or brown like his, but very, very blue.

"Don't you like me?" Toby asked uneasily even as he moved closer until Luke felt his heartbeat and the warmth of the small hand clutching him.

"Yes...of course I like you," Luke assured him gently, and yet as he hugged Toby to him, he found himself looking over at Tricia searchingly.

CHAPTER FIVE

SARA STOOD in the small tower at the junction of the two wings of Spars' Nest, looking down on the shaded lawns below with a feeling of apartness.

"Good morning."

She tensed inwardly as Luke suddenly spoke behind her, her gaze remaining fixed on Tricia and Toby, laughing and playing below with Jeannie Schneider. The girl had appeared only an hour before, ready to work and unaware that Luke had not said a word about her to Sara.

"You were up early this morning," Luke commented, eyeing her stillness with irritation.

Hardly hearing him, she lifted her gaze above the tops of the blue spruce, pin oak and aspens to where she could see the golf-leafed dome of the neoclassical capitol building of Denver gleaming in the morning sunlight. The thirteenth step, she recalled absently, was a mile high, and from it the high plains upon which Denver was built rolled slowly downward for more than two hundred miles into the prairies. What a long, long upward trek it must have been, she thought, feeling as if she, too, were struggling up an endless hill.

"Sara, I'm speaking to you!" He paused, eyeing

her slim back narrowly. "Is this a fit of pique, or have you decided to simply sulk?"

She shook her head slightly and for yet another fraction of time clung to her little world, reluctant to turn and face him and his ungiving condemnation. Her eyes strayed south of the city to where she had once ridden Paul's horses across the open fields, and somehow the memory calmed her.

"Dammit, Sara! Do I have to fire a twenty-one gun salute to get your attention?"

Drawing in a sharp breath, she broke free of her trance and turned jerkily to face him across the small square room to which she had retreated to think.

The room was barely four strides across a soft lemon-colored carpet between the cushioned window seats. Her drawing table, installed by Luke as a gift during their months together, still remained beneath the northern windows. And on one side a small wooden rail guarded the stairs dropping through an opening in the floor. It was a cool bright room with sunlight pouring through the Colonial-paned windows.

"Good morning," she said cautiously, doubting that it would be. The thoughts and memories that had added to her restless night in the room they had once shared seemed foolish when facing the reality of him.

"About time," he half grunted as he stared down at her. His wheat-colored summer suit, accented by a crisp white shirt, set off the darkness of his skin, hair and eyes.

The man whose hard black eyes moved over her

without politeness did not seem even related to the man she had once thought she loved, and her apprehensions shrouded her again, her pulse shivering, her hands beginning to tremble.

"I might have expected to find you hiding here," he murmured, his gaze lingering on the shadows below her eyes. "From the look of you, it is not at all a good morning. You look worn out."

Confused by a sudden gentleness in his voice, Sara blurted, "I think we're past conversational minuets, Luke. I assume you've come with my orders for the day?"

His eyes hardened. "It's a shame," he drawled, "that I can't lock you in this tower as men once did their wives—especially those whose glances strayed. It might have prevented so much."

She turned her back on him, her fingers gripping the edge of her drawing table as she stared blindly out the window, and fought back the hurt his words inflicted with anger.

"No comment?" he prodded.

She shook her head; her throat had gone rigid. What right had he to be bitter, she protested silently; and having assured herself that she no longer cared what he believed or said, she was deeply shaken to realize that she did care. Yet he had been the one who lacked faith, not she. He had made his miserable bed, she told herself angrily, so let him lie in it. Muscle by muscle, she fought back her rage.

"Sara?"

"Yes."

"Elijah would like to see you this morning. He's in

the sitting room at the end of the wing downstairs."

"Very well." She did not turn.

"I'll remind you of our bargain. Be kind to him. He's under the impression that your memory is foggy yet."

"You don't really think he believes that," she said tiredly.

"I told him that we are trying to see if there is a future for us. That with the children we are—"

"Stop it!" She wheeled. "Stop it, Luke!"

His dark eyebrows shot up, and he observed mockingly, "The Victorian decline has just ended!"

"Luke, I ca—won't take this for months! Please!"

Resenting her appeal, her very defenselessness, he replied coldly, "Perhaps I failed to make myself clear when we last discussed the terms of your stay. If you dislike it here, you are free to leave."

"Is that what you want? Is that what you hope to do—drive me out?"

He shrugged. "Go or stay—it's the children I care about."

"Not even the kind of man you are now could drive me from them!"

"I am what you made me."

"No one makes you anything, Luke! You do it to yourself."

A peculiar expression entered his eyes, and for a moment her gaze was trapped by his before he asked soberly, "And what have you done to yourself, Sara?"

Her emotions trembled at his unexpected shift in mood, and once more she turned away to stare down upon the lawns below. The children were no longer in sight, and her eyes moved to the drawing table, fixing on a small Indian jug of earthen pottery that she had once used for her drawing pencils. Picking it up, she cradled it in her palm.

"Sara, this...." He stopped when she looked up at him, her gaze level.

"Luke, the past is gone. Whatever we thought we once felt for each other is also gone. It doesn't matter now whether I'm guilty or you lacked faith. I'm not a child anymore. I've supported our children alone for more than four years. And if we are to bear these next months, we have to either meet as adults or not meet at all."

"Why? Why, after all these years, do you still deny your guilt?"

"Perhaps because I am not guilty!"

"The facts were indisputable!"

"The facts," she repeated bitterly.

"Without facts, Sara, nothing is reliable. There would be nothing you could depend upon."

"There is trust. And faith. I would have had faith in you no matter what the facts."

"Talk!" he dismissed with a contempt that shocked her.

"Then, as a scientist," she managed, "you should certainly know how misleading facts can be out of context!"

"If you think you can make me believe that Rufus was not your lover—"

"I don't think I could," she cut him off, her voice shaking. "And I don't even want to anymore!" She looked down at the jug she was holding, her teeth biting into her lower lip as the words with which she had perjured some part of herself echoed in the silence.

Staring down at her bowed head, Luke found himself caught between an angry frustration with her stubborn refusal to admit guilt and an entirely irrational desire to believe her. His eyes rested on her hair glinting in the sunlight, and moved on to the golden tan of her skin, its glow drained by an underlying pallor. Briefly his dark gaze lowered to linger on the curves of her breasts, and then abruptly he looked away and asked curtly, "How does the girl, Jeannie, seem to you?"

Sara looked up, her eyes expressionless. "The children like her."

"She's the eldest in her family, so she is accustomed to young ones."

"And Toby and Tricia are accustomed to strangers looking after them." She paused. "Why didn't you tell me that you had hired someone?"

"It was an unintentional oversight."

"I'd rather look after them myself."

"You'll need Jeannie with Tricia when you're with Toby at the hospital."

"Yes...of course," she agreed, quelling her anger at what seemed like high-handedness to her.

"She works for you, not Grey."

Sara simply nodded, fighting small tremors of anger that were not soothed by the caressing breeze drifting in the windows.

"I'll be busy at the office and lab for the next few days," Luke continued.

"Naturally," she murmured tightly.

He eyed her sharply. "What does that mean?"

"It means," she answered stiffly as she met his hard gaze levelly, "that work has always been your first priority—more important than our marriage years ago, and now more important than the children!"

"The week after our honeymoon," he informed her coldly, "I hired Ralph Beaumont to take over the general operation of the company so that I would have more time with you."

"With me? Or with your research projects?" she taunted.

"With you... *and* my research," he ground out.

"Of course," she said flatly, her eyes dropping to her hand as it clenched the small jug.

His jaw tightened. "Don't try acting the neglected wife on me! You had more than enough interests with a home and charge accounts most women would envy, not to mention your obsession with painting to the point where you resented my interruptions—except," he said deliberately, "when you wanted sex."

Her head snapped up, and for an instant there was a naked pain in her gray eyes that startled him. It was gone so quickly, to be replaced by a cool gray curtain, that he half believed it had been his imagination as she said evenly, "It seems that we have our marriage properly labeled now, Luke. None of the responsibilities or sharing of a wife, just the duties of a highly paid call girl!"

He paled and with a harsh laugh threw back, "Well, you certainly acted like one in the end!"

Her face was completely without expression as she absorbed the wounds he had inflicted. Inwardly she cringed, her own hastily spoken words hurting as much as his. Yet, she reminded herself savagely, there was a raw truth in the angry words they had flung at each other. For he had never shared with her why he had worked such long hours that year, his time spent more with Jessica and in the office and lab than with her; his house belonging to Grey, not her; and her painting relegated to a hobby that she was expected to drop the instant he deigned to appear.

"I'll call the children's clinic today," Luke finally said bleakly. "They have one of the finest staff of surgeons in the country for youngsters like Toby."

"Bargain made...bargain kept," Sara murmured, her eyes on the jug in her hand.

With a muffled expletive he started to leave, then halted on the steps, his gaze sweeping her. "One other item. See that you do some shopping. Those rags won't do here. In a month you and the children will need something warmer as well as more presentable. I'll see that accounts are opened immediately."

"I'll pay for whatever we need myself." Her head lifted defiantly.

"Considering that it is my requirement—for appearances—I'll pay. You'll also need evening wear along the casual line. I'll expect quality."

"I—"

"On second thought," he added, starting down the steps, "perhaps Jessica had better go along to advise you."

He had barely taken another step when something

sailed over his head, narrowly missing it. Recoiling instinctively, he sucked in his breath and, spinning, stared up to find Sara looking as stunned as he felt.

Her heart thudding wildly, she stared back at him, appalled at the suddenly surfacing fury that had impelled her to throw the small jug. Fear caught her breath as her eyes locked with his, and tension threatened to erupt within her into hysterical laughter.

She watched the scar on his cheek pale, the pulse at his temple throb, but all he said was a soft, "If you feel that strongly about it, I'm sure the salespeople can advise you." He continued down the steps then, and only his dark hair was visible when he tossed back, "Don't forget Elijah!"

Motionless, she barely heard him as she stared into space, distinctly rattled by the violence that had erupted within her. She could not even clearly remember why. She never lost her temper anymore. Yet she just had.

Mechanically she walked down the steps and picked up the broken pieces, and her mind slipped back to the scene in the gallery. There, too, there had been broken pieces. Was that what was happening to her, she wondered numbly as, lost in her thoughts, she returned to the tower room to sit at her drawing table holding the shards cupped in her hand.

She would put them back together, she decided. Somehow it was important that she should. Opening the drawer to put away the remains, she stilled at the sight of all her paintbrushes, pens, charcoal just as she had left them more than four years before.

Perplexed, she carefully set down the fragments of

the jug, pushing aside scraps of paper to make room. The sight of a small sketch made her catch her breath. It was a work sketch for the first painting that she had sold through Rufus Petrofsky's gallery. Brimming with her exciting news, she had raced home to Luke, who had remarked irritably, "Why all the hurrah? You don't need money now."

His failure to understand, and his assumption that it was the money, not the affirmation of her talent, that had been so exciting, had produced the first tiny gulf between them.

Abruptly she pushed the drawer shut, wondering why all her lovely hanging plants were gone, all external signs, yet not her brushes, paints and pens. What did it matter, she asked herself, and rising, she descended the tower steps, pushing away Luke and all the disturbances associated with him.

Elijah Driscoll turned from a table as she entered his sitting room. His tall spare figure, capped by hair as white as the snow already crowning the distant mountains in August, was still straight. He had been bending to sniff the fragrance of a rose in a crystal vase. Now he subjected her to a piercing silent study with dark eyes; Luke's eyes and Tricia's eyes, and eyes that were quite alert beneath the thick white brows.

"So you're back," he greeted her brusquely.

"For a while."

"You were a fool, girl!"

"So was Luke."

"Hmmph!" His look was so nearly baleful that suddenly she wanted to smile. "Learned to stand on your own feet, eh?"

"I had to."

"Ah, well, you'll find when you look back in life that the growing happened in the hardest times. My grandson's become a man these past years."

"I rather doubt that applies to me," Sara said, and did smile. "It would be most uncomfortable."

Amusement sparked his eyes. "Sit down! Stay awhile."

She chose a chair across from where he settled by the dark fireplace. Her eyes scanned the room to find it much the same as she recalled. It had been a sitting room for guests, though Elijah had added personal touches.

"Well?" he said gruffly.

She regarded him silently, noting the fine shivering of his hands that had not been there before. "I should be saying that after the way you've been studying me since I walked in."

"What happened to you?"

"I'm sure Luke told you everything," she evaded.

"Amnesia?" He snorted and reached for his pipe. "Cock-and-bull story if I ever heard one!"

"Did he—"

"He told me a story," Elijah muttered, tamping down the tobacco. "I'm too old and frail for the truth, you know. Got to be sheltered. As if I hadn't lived through my shares of shocks—four wars, inflations, depressions, my Hannah and our children dying. Pah! What did you do? Run off with another man and then lose him?"

"I had motive enough to leave without needing an incentive, as well."

"Did you?" He shot a narrow look at her over his pipe. "Still think so?"

"It was Luke's decision."

He scowled. "Wouldn't believe you ran off with someone. Whatever your faults, you were besotted with the boy."

"Luke prefers his version."

"You were both too impatient. You were too young and dreamy to understand, and Luke married a girl and expected a matron overnight."

"Perhaps... but it's all over now."

"Is it?" He puffed on his pipe. "Well, I've too little time in this world to be tactful. Not with eighty years behind me and a tired heart."

"Elijah—"

"Let me warn you now, and I've told Luke the same. There's no sense in looking back at what once was. That's looking backward instead of forward. It's trying to put the past into now and the future, and it's impossible."

"I am not trying to do anything but—"

"Let me finish, girl! You two are married in the eyes of the Lord. But for you to have any future, you have to build on what you both are right now—as the years have changed you both. Not on what he was and you were."

Her lips compressed.

"And don't tell an old man like me," he added, leaning back, his eyes seeking hers, "that you don't give a hoot about him anymore. Won't wash, girl. The heart always remembers."

His words provoked conflicting emotions and she

wanted to protest vehemently, but instead she returned his look and said in a company-polite tone, "Do you miss the ranch?"

"A safe subject, eh?" He nodded, apparently accepting her change of subject. "Some ways I do, but this will do for whatever time is left."

"You'll live another twenty years!"

"If I don't, girl, I don't mind." He drew on his pipe. "It's been more than twenty years without my Hannah. It will be good to be with her again."

His eyes shifted to a faded photograph on the table next to him of a young girl in an old-fashioned lace dress. Sara watched the expressions crossing his face and found herself moved by the longing, the smile that crept into his eyes followed by a sadness, and she held her silence.

It was not until he started and seemed to return to the present that she said, "I never really knew you."

"You were young then. Scared of men, I often suspected—probably that aunt of yours. Scared of Luke in some ways, too, though you sure could let fly when you were riled. Reminded me a bit of my Hannah. You always did remind me of her at times. Did you know that?"

She shook her head.

"On some of my visits back then, I'd hear you two at night—and then the sweet silences." He chuckled as Sara's color rose slightly. "It was the same with my Hannah." He shook his head. "I met her when I was eighteen. I worked in the old mines up there." He gestured south toward the mountains. "She was a schoolteacher's girl. Taught me to read and write and to do sums. But most of all, she taught me loving.''

"Elijah...."

His eyes returned to the framed photograph. "Never understood, girl, why she picked me. But, Lord, was I glad that she did! I worshipped her that first year! In time, of course, I saw her faults, too. Then I simply loved her."

He broke a thick silence with, "You have loving in you. It showed in your paintings. It shows with the children. I watched from my window this morning, and even Luke spoke of it."

She refused to ask precisely what Luke had said, and only commented, "Children are easy to love."

"And safe—at least while they are young."

Her startled gaze met his, then shied away quickly. "I used to believe that you disapproved of me. As much as Grey did. I was the upstart. Too lower-class for Luke."

"Hannah and I between us built a fortune. I began making radios in cardboard cigar boxes to sell to miners. From there I went on to making a few fancy ones, then started a factory when the war came. Luke's father, our Simon, moved on into electronics after his military service. But we never had pretensions, girl! I admit that I didn't really try to know you, and I should have. Grey's a different story, though."

"She resented me in every way, and still does."

"Well, after Hannah, Simon and Elizabeth were lost in that air crash, Grey ruled our male household. You were a threat. She's afraid of you as much as anything."

He puffed on his pipe, and Sara recalled the hostility of Grey's pale eyes the night before as he added, "Doesn't make her harmless, though."

"What does that mean?" she asked, thinking instantly of the children.

"Not arsenic," he assured her with a faint smile. "More like molasses with a heap of hot spices. Loyal but dour, she is."

"I was here only a week when I heard her agreeing with Jessica that I was trash. Luke would get rid of me soon enough, she prophesied. You'll see, she told Jessica. And she was right, too. He did."

"Did he?"

Sara rose abruptly and walked to the window, her slender back tense. "Whatever he believes," she whispered nakedly, "I was innocent." She pivoted to meet Elijah's eyes. "I loved him! There was no one in my world important to me except Luke. And he turned on me. He refused to help me. He could only criticize me and accuse me, and finally tell me to get out of his life."

"And so you did," Elijah said softly.

"Yes! Yes, I did! What else could I have done?"

"You could have stayed and fought it out, instead of running," he suggested gently.

Sara paled. "I tried! I tried to reach him at the hospital. He... he refused to see me or to listen."

"He may have refused at first, but in the end he would have listened. Underneath he is as sensitive and vulnerable as his mother, Elizabeth, was."

"Sensitive!" She rejected it harshly.

"He was very close to his mother. She was an artist, too—but with words. She often read her poems to him, teaching him to see the world through her eyes. Had she lived, she might well have become a poet of some standing. She was already gaining a reputation in the West when she died."

"His mother was...a poet?"

Elijah frowned. "Didn't you know?"

"He never told me. He never wanted to talk of his parents. I thought that perhaps he didn't remember them well, or that their death hurt too deeply."

Elijah seemed nonplussed, and it was a moment before he gestured toward the bookshelves flanking the fireplace. "There, to the right—chin high. See the narrow books bound in red leather?"

Slowly Sara walked over and extracted a slim volume. As she opened it, she groped to understand why Luke had never once mentioned these volumes written by his mother.

"To my own Robert," she read aloud softly. "Let me count the ways...."

"They had a fine marriage. For Elizabeth, our Simon was her Robert."

"Why?" she whispered. "Why did Luke never tell me?"

"I don't know. I just...don't know."

Holding the slim volume to her, she returned to the chair across from Elijah and proceeded to tell him about the children, of her hopes for Toby after his surgery. When she caught Elijah nodding, however, she rose. "I had better check on the children."

"Looks like I need a nap," he admitted. "I get more tired lately."

"So do I, at times."

His dark eyes searched hers. "Was it hard, girl?"

She stared back at him. "Yes."

"It was hard for Luke, too. Don't forget that. Something I regret is going back into my work when Hannah died. But, girl, I would have gone mad if I had not! Trouble was...it hurt the boy. The core of him was warm and solid, but I didn't give it a chance to develop. So we are both guilty in our way."

"Whatever Luke was," Sara told him tiredly, "he's hard now. And now, as you told me earlier, is what I am living with."

"But underneath there is the foundation of his early years."

"Perhaps," she said doubtfully, and moved toward the door.

"Girl!"

"Sara," she corrected softly without turning.

"Eh?"

She waited, a half smile forming.

"Sara, then. Come back and see me."

"I will."

"And bring those great-grandchildren of mine if you don't think I'll frighten them into the shivers."

"I raised them to resist tyranny!"

His chuckle followed her from the room. But as she walked through the house, her smile faded as she mentally fingered the bits of their conversation. Luke's mother had written poetry, and he had never—

"Mrs. Driscoll."

She looked up as Grey materialized from the hall's cool shadows. "Yes?"

"Miss Jessica is calling." Grey paused. "She would like to speak to Mr. Luke."

Her eyes cooling, Sara said, "You know that he's left for the office. I'm sure she can contact him there."

"Of course... Mrs. Driscoll." Grey started away.

"One minute!" The woman stopped but did not turn. "In the future please see that all calls reach my husband... without delays."

Grey was motionless, and then, without looking back at Sara, she nodded and disappeared down the hall to leave Sara aware that, however clumsily, Grey had wanted her to know Jessica was calling Luke; that Jessica was part of his life.

As she left the house, Sara crossed the lawn slowly toward the children. Nearing them, she paused to stare up at the house with an inner sigh, fighting the knowledge that already the tensions of Spars' Nest were once more weaving their web around her despite her efforts to stay aloof.

Some miles away, Luke also paused to look up at a building as he fought to put aside his own tensions and regain his customary detachment.

Before him sprawled a long, single story, H-shaped building of brick. Green lawns, trim flower beds and tall shady trees softened the lines of the factory and its headquarters offices, giving it the air of a university campus rather than that of a production center for light industry.

Driscoll Electronics designed electronic equipment to do specific tasks according to the needs of the buyer. Twenty radars, each priced into seven figures, were now being designed to meet the special needs of the air force, and provided for full employment for the next years. Another contract for airport radar equipment was already on the drawing boards.

The responsibility for those contracts, for the nearly two hundred employees, damn well had to have a high priority, he told himself with a growing inner anger. In addition there was the responsibility of carrying on what Elijah, and then his father, had built. Something Sara had never tried to understand, nor asked to see or learn about.

His hand tightened on the handle of his leather briefcase, and with a grim expression he strode into the reception lobby, past the security guards and along the carpeted halls to his suite of offices.

His secretary, Ellen Ross, met him and, well aware of his impatience with the mundane, briefed him professionally and concisely, informing him that his general manager and security officer had requested to see him at the earliest possible moment.

Waiting until she had notified them that he was in, he impassively told her of Sara's arrival and gave her the explanation he had developed for the curious, finishing with, "Contact the children's clinic immediately, find out who's who on the staff and get back to me right away."

"Dr. Minelli," Ralph Beaumont said, entering the office as Luke finished. "That's who you'll want. She's the best they have."

"Then look into getting an appointment with her,

Ellen," Luke ordered, nodding to his general manager.

"I have a cousin on the staff," Ralph added. "Let me see what I can do. I've heard she carries a very selective case load."

"If she's the best," Luke replied, thinking of Toby looking up at him as he asked about hurting, "then I'll get her."

His general manager, a spare, ascetic-looking man with a passion for football that seemed to contradict his image completely, nodded and waited until Ellen Ross had left before saying, "I have bad news for you."

Luke's eyes narrowed. "Let's have it."

"Hadley has definitely been negotiating on the sly with ETI."

"Proof?" Luke asked quietly, his mind rapidly calculating the degree of knowledge Hadley would have in his possession as a staff member outside of research.

"One of John's men...." He paused, looking up as the security officer entered. "Let John tell you now that he's here."

John Gordon, a former air-force security officer, strolled into the room in his habitually rangy manner. There was always a loose, almost sleepy look to him, belied by alert eyes that missed nothing.

Accepting Luke's offer for coffee, he poured himself a mug, then settled his lanky frame into a chair. "One of my men followed Hadley—"

"Followed?" Luke questioned sharply.

"Only because some remarks Hadley's been making to several people here indicated he was recruiting support for an ETI merger. I put a man on him to see if he was meeting with anyone, and he was."

"Go on." Luke swore silently.

"He had lunch yesterday with his brother-in-law and the head of research at ETI. My man clearly overheard Hadley being cautioned to bide his time on passing the offer on to you."

"Did you take any action?" Luke asked.

"None. Reported to Ralph and, with you due back today, decided to wait."

"Ralph?"

"My recommendation is to request his resignation, remind him that his security contract prohibits working on any projects related to our work, and provide a restricted professional recommendation. There is no way he could have negotiated this far without violating security."

Leaning over, Luke pressed the intercom lever. "Ellen, contact Ben Hadley. Have him report to me immediately!"

"We've tightened security in general," John drawled, filling the silence as they waited. "There's a virtual freeze on new hiring, new area badges have been issued—more selectively—and supervisors are on alert. You'll find a new security checkpoint outside your lab."

Luke nodded, and as his eyes lighted on a gray file folder he found himself thinking of gray eyes that could be as soft as a mist, or hold the flash lightning of a storm, or look back at him filled with silent pain.

Scowling, he looked up as Ellen announced Ben Hadley.

With a sense of distaste, Luke watched Hadley cross the room, a dapperly dressed man whose eyes held a decidedly cautious look as he seated himself.

"John's come up with something I thought you might like to comment on," Luke said dispassionately, his eyes watching Hadley's face closely.

"Oh?" There was the barest flicker of unease, and before Hadley could say more, John handed him a copy of his security report.

There was total silence in the office as Hadley read it, his face losing its color and his body tensing. When he looked up, however, he said almost glibly, "This is a misinterpretation."

"How?" Luke asked softly.

"I did have lunch with my brother-in-law and Dave Webster. We discussed a piece of property I'm considering buying. That was the offer referred to—nothing else. As for the other, yes, I'd favor approaching ETI over most other corporations if we consider that option, but surely I'm allowed my own opinions."

There was the barest silent exchange between the three men listening, before Luke pressed the intercom. "Ellen? Get me David Webster, research director at ETI, on the phone." Leaning back, Luke raised his eyelids and fixed a cold intent gaze on Hadley. "We can spend a great deal of time arguing, accusing and defending. When I pick up that phone, I'm going to say that after talking to you I'm interested in his deal. His answer will decide the issue, I suspect."

"Now, just a minute!" Hadley protested, rising to his feet. "He could assume that I discussed something on my own!"

"Let me put it this way," Luke replied grimly. "If he confirms that you've been negotiating with him, you'll be fired. Until the moment he does, you have the choice of a resignation."

The phone line buzzed at that instant, and not taking his eyes from Hadley's he picked up his phone.

"I...." Hadley looked at Ralph Beaumont, at John Gordon, then back at Luke, and with a cold fury said, "You have my resignation."

"Sorry, wrong number," Luke said coolly into the phone and hung up. Regarding Hadley wearily, he said quietly, "I'll expect it on my desk by four."

"I don't give a damn anyway!" Hadley snapped. "There are better places to go, higher places with ETI than here."

"If they'll take on a Judas goat," Luke replied evenly, adding softly, "and an unsuccessful one at that."

John Gordon rose and drawled, "I'll walk with you, Hadley."

Well aware that he was under escort until he left the building, Hadley turned on his heels and walked out.

"He didn't care for that last remark," Ralph remarked.

"John won't let him out of his sight. I doubt that he has much to offer ETI at this moment."

"I'd like to move Fred Berry into Hadley's position, if you have no objections."

"That's fine with me," Luke agreed. "I'd like you to take over in the next months and free me for the project. We'll have to accelerate."

"Right. I'll...oh, hullo, Jess."

Jessica nodded at Ralph with marked coolness, not bothering to reply as she crossed to Luke.

"See you later," Ralph said, his eyes amused, as if Jessica were a gnat that had tried to bite him.

"I can't stand him!" Jessica snapped as she helped herself to coffee. "He thinks he's running the place."

"For all intents and purposes, he is and will be," Luke replied with irritation at her refusal to conceal her dislike of his key man. She had been informed more than once of the rules of business that dictated a surface harmony conducive to teamwork was more important than individual likes and dislikes. She had countered that she was being honest, and had bridled when he informed her that, from the management point of view, her lack of control was a disrupting weakness.

"What happened with Hadley?" she asked, settling into a chair. "He looked as if he could kill."

"He's resigned."

"Oh? Did he leak the project?"

"Perhaps."

"Perhaps!"

"Leave it to security. John will track it down sooner or later."

She shrugged. "As long as we can get on with the project. That's one thing that no one is going to prevent...and we'll pull it off with flying colors."

"I wish I had your faith," he rejoined, and unbidden heard the echo of Sara's accusations, and saw the pain in her eyes when his own anger had led him to retaliate. Feeling suddenly tired, he collected himself with an effort to ask, "Where are those test results?"

She passed him a folder. "Look at the skew!"

With a sense of relief he immersed himself in the precision of statistics, and after several moments looked up. "Curve B is anomalous?"

"Yes. I've spent every day and half the nights for the past weeks trying to account for it."

"You've discounted water vapor?"

"Naturally."

He rose abruptly, everything else momentarily forgotten as his mind applied itself to the data—sifting, correlating and analyzing. "Let's get down to the lab."

Once there, time slipped away. Jessica and his staff became extensions of himself as he lost himself in the need for precision, for seeking exact balances and the mixture of forces and elements that would eventually solve the mystery of the skew, and perhaps reveal yet another small secret of nature.

When Ellen Ross entered the laboratory, he glanced up from the computer console with a frown. "Can't it wait?"

"You asked for the report on the clinic staff as soon as possible," she reminded him, unperturbed by his impatience as she placed her report on the worktable of the computer console.

Reluctantly relinquishing his absorption, he eyed

his watch to find it was already late afternoon. "What did you find out?"

"Mr. Beaumont has arranged for you to meet with his cousin at the clinic, tomorrow morning at ten—with the boy's records."

"That will mean half the morning, if not half the day gone!" Jessica interjected irritably. "Why not have our courier run the records over?"

"Confirm the appointment," Luke told his secretary as if Jessica had not spoken, and after reviewing his messages, he waited until Ellen had left before addressing Jessica. "I'm leaving nothing to chance with Toby. Let's get on with it now; I'll be leaving for home in an hour."

"Luke, the whole project is stalled until we break this! How much time are we going to lose from now on because of Sara?"

"Whatever is necessary," he returned curtly, and back at the computer he immersed himself in the trial equations only to find himself once again struggling with the tension between the new demands on his time and those of the project and firm. Yet Jess was right, he conceded. He would lose valuable time in the next days and weeks, and the project was stalled.

With a muffled expletive he pivoted from the computer console and reached for the phone. Seconds later Sara replied, and after a polite query about the children he said brusquely, "I won't be able to make it home tonight. It will probably be late before I'm in."

There was a barely discernible pause, then a cool, "I'll let Grey know."

"And Elijah. Tell him we've run into a few problems."

"I'll inform him of your priorities."

"Do that!" he snapped and hung up the phone.

With a feeling of near-savage anger, he stood unmoving, staring down at the phone. For an instant he wrestled with the impulse to call back, to explain that he would be compensating for the time he would lose in the morning; and then, telling himself that he didn't give a damn what Sara thought, he returned to work, ignoring Jessica's curious look.

As the hours passed, however, his vagrant thoughts persisted in wandering back to Sara's description of herself as a call girl, to the stricken look in her eyes as he had agreed.

With unaccustomed discomfort he knew that he regretted those words, as he had often regretted words flung in the first year of their marriage. It had been a cheap shot.

Yet she could also inflict verbal wounds, he defended himself, and provoke him to such fury that he lost control.

"Luke!"

The exasperation in Jessica's tone jerked his thoughts back on track, and feeling that somehow he was once again losing control, he forced his thoughts back into disciplined channels where facts and not fancies reigned.

CHAPTER SIX

THE FIRST DAYS after her return to Spars' Nest passed quietly for Sara. Apart from the scene in the tower, which she carefully avoided thinking about, she did not see Luke at all.

She knew that in the mornings the children saw him for a bare half hour, while she straightened their rooms and dressed before descending to breakfast. Invariably he was gone by then, almost as if he were deliberately avoiding her.

And each night he would return in the early morning hours, and she would lie in her bed listening tensely to his footsteps as he climbed the stairs, looked into the children's room and quietly left.

She preferred it that way, she told herself firmly. It allowed her to settle the children into a routine and to regain her equilibrium. She was determined above all never to allow herself such a foolish display of temperament again.

As the end of the week approached, however, she felt a rising resentment, not only because Luke's absorption in his work proved her accusation that it took priority over anything and anyone, but also because after long years of busy days, the slow pace since her arrival made her feel restless and frustrated.

Jeannie Schneider, a cheerful copper-haired girl whose personality combined the best of her Irish-German ancestry—cheerfulness and common sense—could only chatter on endlessly about her fascination with an apparent retinue of young admirers. Elijah talked to Sara of the old days, of his Hannah, and traded books with her as she caught up on reading. While Grey simply behaved as if Sara were a necessary evil to be tolerated and granted the minimum of courtesies.

In all, she felt very alone, and beneath the unperturbed facade she kept firmly in place, she felt uncertain and apprehensive.

Her hopes that at least Paul, Luke's closest friend and once her friend, would call never materialized, and as she walked along the winding road outside the gates one afternoon, she stared down to the plains below, half-tempted to call him herself.

"Mummy, it's going to rain!" Toby announced, pointing to the side of the road. "See!"

"It will!" Tricia seconded. "Like Uncle Luke said."

Puzzled, Sara followed their gazes and could see only dusty grass and dry earth over which ants were scurrying.

"See!" Toby said triumphantly.

"No," Sara admitted.

"The ants are walking in a line!"

"So?"

"So it's going to rain," they chorused, with Tricia adding, "Uncle Luke said so."

"They always do that before it rains," Toby elaborated, and then added sorrowfully, "I wish I had chalk."

"Why?" Sara asked.

" 'Cause Uncle Luke said, if you draw a line, they won't cross it."

"Uncle Luke said," Sara murmured under her breath, and as they walked through the open gates toward the house, a nameless apprehension stirred within her. She felt caught in time, in neither the past nor the present, as the iron will of Luke seemed to control her whether or not he was actually there.

In an attempt to break her mood, she abruptly suggested with forced gaiety, "Let's play hop-tag!"

"You're it!" Toby shouted gleefully as he and Tricia tagged Sara and then hopped rapidly away.

"Unfair!" Sara cried after them as she chased them hopping on one foot.

From the French windows of Elijah's sitting room, both Elijah and Luke stood watching Sara and the children playing tag.

"She invented hop-tag," Elijah said to Luke, "so that Toby could play on an even level."

Leaning against the door frame, Luke did not reply. He had solved the skew with the help of Mike Maguire, a bright and imaginative young engineer who had come up with an idea that had triggered the solution in Luke's mind. Now he was simply bone-weary.

He let his mind drift, and his eyes idly followed Sara as, laughing and flushed, she moved with agility. Almost absently his gaze lingered on the graceful lines of her slender body, the curve of her waist, the shifting of her breasts....

"Makes me want to join in the game," Elijah murmured as Sara and the children paused for breath in the high altitude. "Only wish I were a mite younger."

Drawing in a breath, Luke removed his gaze from Sara, and quelling a rising heat stirring within himself, he turned away. His hand cupped the back of his neck, and rubbing taut muscles he said, "I'd better be getting back to the office."

"I thought you finished the job."

"There's still a backlog of paperwork. With the weekend coming up, it has to be done tomorrow and in the mail."

"And your family?" Elijah asked mildly.

"Dammit!" Luke snapped, as inner tensions exploded. "Why the hell do you think I've been working day and night since I came back? I lost a whole day between two visits to the clinic, and Monday will be another half day. Tomorrow evening is the best I can do!"

"Priorities sometimes have to be shi—"

"To hell with priorities!" Luke said savagely, and ignoring his grandfather's startled reaction he took his leave abruptly. Pausing only to extract the sheet of scrawled equations he had returned home for from the safe in his den, a moment later he left the house.

Sara, leaning against the low stone wall separating the lawn from the wooded area surrounding the house, looked up as she heard the accelerating growl of the car. There was only a brief glimpse of the car through the shrubbery, and then it was gone.

Her mouth tightening, she pushed away from the wall, and slowly walking toward the children she said, "No more now. I'm worn out."

"Mummy's all worn out...worn out...worn out!" they chanted, trailing her back to the house.

She let the repetition wash over her, wondering if Luke was on his way to join Jessica for the evening, and then was angry with herself for even bothering to speculate about anything he did.

"LUKE WILL BE HOME for dinner tonight," Elijah told her the next morning as she stood with him on the lawn beneath the huge shade trees.

Her eyes on the children, who were playing with Jeannie, she replied in a dry tone, "How nice! Is he certain that the company can manage for an evening without him?"

"Sara!" It was a rebuke, though gentle.

"He has seen the children for half an hour each morning in the past four days. For all his claims of wanting to know them, he evidently does not want to enough to give up work."

"He would be here if there hadn't been trouble with the project and—"

"He has the brilliant Jessica. Let her do it."

"It's Luke's mind that has the ideas. Jessica can only execute them. Once he's caught up, he'll have more time for you and the children."

"Time to train the children to be cold and logical," she retorted, "and to kill their creativity and warmth."

"Bah!" Elijah snorted with clear disgust. "You're still as much a snob as ever."

She stiffened. "I am not a snob!"

"Why you ever married Luke," he went on as if she hadn't spoken, "is beyond me! Especially when you've always looked down your nose at his work."

She said nothing, staring down at her hands, remembering the sensitivity, the poetry and warmth of Luke when she had first known him.

"Luke is as creative as you ever were!" Elijah stated emphatically. "You use paints to create. He uses the elements of the universe. He takes from the earth we're standing upon, from the sun above us, and uses the forces of each to create. Have you ever credited him for that?"

"Electronic equipment is hardly aesthetic," she countered shortly.

"Then, the writer who transforms ideas into words everyone can understand, the realistic school of painting, and plays about real people—all of them can also be dismissed as uncreative."

"It's not the same," she said stubbornly.

"A man of science with a mind like Luke's is a creative being in his own right! It's a God-given talent, as surely as your own is. Only, Luke didn't quit when your marriage collapsed. No matter how he bled inside, he went on creating...as I suspect you didn't."

Stung, she answered angrily, "No, I haven't painted. I not only didn't have the time with two children to support, but I also didn't care to paint the true ugliness, the true—"

"He could have created something destructive!" Elijah interrupted firmly. "Instead he is creating a new system of solar energy that could change the lives of everyone. It will replace petroleum, just as petroleum replaced whale oil when that became too expensive. He's matching nature, Sara. Look at that tree!"

Involuntarily she looked, a memory stirring within her that she instantly rejected.

"That tree," Elijah said, "is nature's original solar system. It takes light from the sun—energy— and changes it into a fuel that we can use to get back the energy anytime we care to. Tell me, could you do that? Could you create a system of capturing the power of the sun in a way that will someday mean power for millions at the costs of pennies?"

"No..." she finally said when the silence stretched. "I couldn't begin to."

"And you think he's not creative! That boy will— But what do you care? What do you care about his responsibilities, his dreams and his challenges? He's just a cold, unfeeling scientist. Not a superior artist!"

"I never...." The denial died on her lips. She had called him far worse than that, she knew, both within herself and in angry confrontations. Her head lifted. "Whatever he can do, he worships facts. He always has."

Elijah sighed, nodding, then pursued, "No one is all one thing. We each have many parts to ourselves. Sometimes we get out of balance." He paused and asked quietly, "Did you ever go down to the company? Did you go through it and try to understand what he does? What he is responsible for?"

"He never...asked me," she defended.

"Perhaps because he was waiting for you to show an interest. Don't you think he could feel your disdain?"

"I don't know!" she half cried. "Please, Elijah, stop meddling!"

"Go with me to the company. See what he does, and that he is an artist in his field as well as an astute businessman—which is an art in itself."

"I...." Her head was shaking.

"Come! I'll set it up."

"Very well," she found herself agreeing, simply to stop his harassing words. "But not with Luke."

There was a glitter in Elijah's eyes as he acquiesced to her condition. "Just you and I, girl."

"It won't change anything," she warned him.

"At least you may understand what he does and come to respect his abilities more."

She didn't bother to argue, and apparently satisfied, Elijah took his leave and wandered back into the house.

Slowly Sara crossed the lawn to sink down on a redwood bench circling the trunk of a maple tree. If she had been totally honest, she knew, she could have told Elijah that Her Luke had always been creative. His creativity was for her the essence of Luke, that which drew her as much as the intense physical attraction he had always held for her. Her Luke.... Her throat tightened.

Tilting her head back to rest against the rough bark of the tree behind her, she looked up toward the crest of the foothills above the house, remembering despite herself the day soon after she had first arrived at

Spars' Nest, when she and Luke had climbed to the ruins of a mansion to picnic.

"It's not haunted," she had grumbled as, replete from their luncheon, she lay back in the grass to stare up at the sun sprinkling through the trees that formed a semigrove around them.

"Good!" Luke had murmured with a grin, his hand moving to the buttons of her blouse. "I'd rather not have witnesses—in or out of this world."

"Someone might come!" she'd protested feebly, her body already weakening with anticipation.

"We'll have enough warning," he whispered, his lips slowly traveling, nipping, tugging over the softness of her skin as he drew apart her blouse.

Sara moved uneasily, withdrawing from the memory of the lazy hours of lovemaking and shifting instead to afterward, when she had lain in his arms in the glade, drowsy and replete as the wind caressed their bodies.

His voice still husky, Luke had said almost the same words that Elijah had only a short while before. "Look, Sara! Look at the sunlight and the trees!"

"Mmm," she had replied sleepily.

He had rolled over and peered down at her, his skin golden in the sunlight, the hairs on his chest gilded. "Someday," he had told her roughly, "I'm going to capture the sun so that anyone can use it—rich or poor. I shall create, in my way, for you."

"For me?" she had replied huskily, melting inside, and loving him so.

"You have opened doors inside of me. I can feel, think, create—as never before. Sara, without you—"

"Don't!" she had said quickly, and drawing his face to hers, she had kissed him, arousing a sweet heated passion that swept them both away again.

Without her, she thought bitterly, as her mind left the past, he had evidently managed quite well, according to Elijah. Rising, she started toward the children to seek the distraction of their demands.

The sound of a vehicle turning into the drive made her stop and turn, her slim body tensing until she saw that it was a blue van with the Driscoll Electronics emblem on the front door panel, not Luke's sleek car.

Retracing her steps, she intercepted the two men at the front entrance. Each wore a blue jacket with an emblem on the pocket, and each carried a workmanlike satchel.

Addressing herself to the older man, she asked, "May I help you? I'm Mrs. Driscoll."

"We're with security," he replied with what might have been a flicker of surprise in cold blue eyes. "John Gordon's office."

"My husband isn't in at the moment."

"Your housekeeper is expecting us."

"Right this way," Grey said at that instant from the doorway, and as Sara turned, she added, "They're here to fix Mr. Luke's safe."

"If you'll excuse us, ma'am?" the older man murmured as he started past.

"You do have identification," Sara asked, as she always did.

The man paused, his eyes flat as he smiled. "Of course."

Accepting their identity cards, she was aware of Grey's silent disapproval, and of the younger man's apparent boredom, though his eyes swept the grounds restlessly. Checking the photos, she returned the cards. "Thank you."

"You're welcome, ma'am."

She watched Grey lead the way, the second man saying nothing but looking everywhere, and when Grey had ushered them into the den, Sara followed her into the kitchen to ask, "Aren't you going to stay with them?"

"No need for company men," Grey returned, clearly affronted. "Security called about them already."

"Still..." Sara said doubtfully.

"I do have dinner to prepare!"

"Very well," she sighed, and left feeling like an upstart who had just been reprimanded.

When she returned to the foyer, however, the movement of the den door, as if it had been hastily eased shut, caught the corner of her eye, and she stopped, regarding the door uneasily.

Telling herself that she was being foolish, she walked quietly past the den and on to Elijah's sitting room. He was watching television and looked up when she entered.

"That project of Luke's," she said without preamble. "Is it secret... valuable?"

"The company's future could depend on it. Why?"

She hesitated, then, "Two security men are here from the office to fix his safe. I can't explain why, but... but something's peculiar."

"What do they look like?" he asked sharply as he rose out of his chair.

She gave him a concise description, honed by her training as an artist. "Grey did expect them," she finished, uncertainty returning.

"There's one way to find out fast." He went to the phone and moments later his expression told her something was wrong.

Not waiting, she left the room, ignoring his call, and sped silently down the hall and across the entrance foyer to the den.

Even as she slowed, forcing an exterior calmness upon herself, she saw the den door once again in its last split second of movement. Biting down on her lip, she drew in a breath and reached out to open the door.

It was locked.

Instantly she rapped on it sharply. Her only answer was the sound of hurried movements, low swearing and then total silence.

"Are they still there?" Elijah asked quietly, joining her.

"I think they just went out the French windows into the garden," she said hurriedly, and started for the kitchen.

"Sara, don't!"

"The van's in front," she called back, and raced on past a startled Grey, through the kitchen garden and around to the den. The windows opening onto the lawn were wide open.

Staring across the garden, panting for breath, she saw that she would never catch them, and instead entered the den, hurrying toward the yawning opening behind a section of the bookcase.

The safe was still closed, but two neat holes marred its polished steel surface, and a betraying acrid smell lingered behind the intruders. She was tugging on the safe door to confirm that it was locked when she heard the roar of an engine and knew the men were gone.

Spinning, she ran back through the house, ignoring Grey's attempts to question her, and arrived on the front steps to find Elijah looking after the van as it careered through the gates.

"Did you get the number?" she asked breathlessly.

"No, dammit, it was covered with mud." He swore under his breath. "Luke and our security officer, John Gordon, are on their way."

"What were— The children!" Her heart jumping, she pivoted and then went limp with relief at the sight of them still playing across the lawn, completely unaware of the excitement. Crossing to the front steps, she sat down before her knees gave way. "We had better call the police."

"Luke may want it handled within the company."

Three hours later Sara had been thoroughly questioned. John Gordon had patiently and courteously reviewed everything that had happened, to the smallest detail, clearly pleased when she provided him with sketches of the two men. But he sidestepped all her questions and referred her to Luke, who, with Jessica at his side was concentrating on questioning a nearly hysterical Grey, and conferring with Elijah and John Gordon's assistant. Photographs were being taken, the safe was being checked and a series of phone calls were being made, all adding to the confusion.

Tired and irritated, and resenting the idiot treatment, Sara finally left to feed and bathe the children. She was in their room brushing Tricia's hair when Luke appeared.

His manner was relaxed, but she knew by the set of his shoulders that he was inwardly tense. Briefly a dark assessing gaze rested on her before he smiled down at Tricia. "I see you're being groomed like a proper filly," he teased. "Did your mummy ever tell you that she used to ride and brush horses every day?"

"I know. I want to ride horses, too."

"Me, too!" Toby shouted, bouncing on his bed, his picture book forgotten.

"Not you!" Tricia said loftily.

"Of course Toby will," Sara reprimanded. "Now stop bickering and settle down."

Tricia's answering mumble was lost as Toby, holding his arms out to Luke, asked, "You like me, don't you, Uncle Luke?"

Luke swooped down, and tossing Toby into the air, he caught him with a laugh. "Of course I like you!" he assured him.

"Mummy, hurry!" Tricia squirmed impatiently, and Sara returned to braiding her hair.

As she wove the long dark hair into a loose single braid for the night, she could not help watching Luke with Toby, nor avoid the knowledge that she was jealous. Jealous of how easily everything seemed to come to Luke and always had. Jealous of how, in a matter of weeks, the children adored him. Her hands stilled with dismay at the direction of her thoughts.

"Oh, mummy!" Tricia quavered, eyeing her imploringly over one shoulder.

"Sorry." Hastily Sara finished the braid and released the little girl.

For yet another few seconds she was motionless with a sense of surprise as she realized that she had always resented deeply the ease of Luke's life compared with her own. What he had considered trifles from the day they met were luxuries all her childhood. Strangers who were barriers to her presented no problems to him. He had been experienced, confident and poised, emphasizing the prison her life had been before her marriage.

Collecting herself with a start, she busied herself pulling back the bedcovers before telling the children, "Time to put your friends to bed."

"Oh, yes!" Tricia said eagerly. "Uncle Luke can help."

Sara's eyes lifted to meet Luke's, unaware that her resentment showed despite her effort to hide it. Looking away, she bent and kissed the children, finding comfort in their quick hugs and the clean warm scent of them. "I'll let your Uncle Luke put you to bed, too."

She left quickly, not seeing Luke's dark gaze following her thoughtfully before he turned to the task of laying some two dozen small toy animals on their sides on the bookshelves, and covering them each with a handkerchief in the nightly ritual.

When the children were settled, Luke entered her

room, closing the connecting door behind him. "They can wear you out in minutes," he said wryly, his eyes on her profile. "How about joining us for a drink before dinner as soon as I've changed. We can all use one tonight."

"We?" Her thoughts flew to Jessica.

"Elijah and myself."

"Oh." She picked up her hairbrush and began stroking her hair. "Elijah asked for a tray in his rooms. He said that he would prefer to relax and watch television tonight."

There was a grunt, then, "You've evidently made friends with him in the past few days." A faint mockery edged his words. "No more quaking at the sight of him?"

"I like him. Very much." She stared at him almost defiantly in the mirror.

"You didn't particularly like him before," he countered evenly.

"It wasn't that. I was unused to men then. He seemed terribly brusque."

"And now you're used to men?"

Her eyes lifted and met his in the mirror of her dressing table. She sensed the sudden anger in him and was too aware of his dark arrogance just behind her. "I'm not a naive twenty-year-old with a fourteen-year-old's experience anymore. Bearing and raising two children on one's own tends to force some degree of maturity."

"It was your choice."

"Was it?" Her expression was drawn and suddenly she rose, wheeling around to ask with intense anger, "Tell me, Luke! Would it have satisfied you if I had crawled back on my stomach to lick your boots and beg, instead of having to be blackmailed? Would you have cut our child in two if there hadn't been twins, or—"

"Shut up!" he growled, his hands moving to dig into her shoulders with a careless strength that made her wince.

"Why should I?"

"You walked out!"

"You told me to get out! At least I—" She caught herself with fright and looked away.

Luke, feeling her trembling beneath his hands, prodded, "At least you what?"

"Nothing. It doesn't matter." Her face smoothed. "Would you let me go, please?"

His face stiff, he released her. Stepping back from the scent of her perfume, which tantalized his nostrils, he said evenly, "I'll have Grey set table trays for us in the den."

Though she yearned to ask him dozens of questions about the events of the past hours, she said coldly, "I'd prefer a tray here—alone."

He regarded her with frustration before saying in a hard tone, "John told me that you had several questions. There are answers you should know, and we have to discuss Toby's surgery."

Defeated, she nodded tiredly. "All right—when?"

"Half an hour."

He left, his expression grim, and once in the hallway he drove his right fist into his left palm with sheer exasperation. He was furious without being quite clear as to why, and drawing in a long breath, he held it until the muscles of his stomach and chest were rigid. Slowly, letting the air slide from his lungs, he forced himself to relax.

As he descended the stairs, however, an inner tension returned, and despite his efforts to thrust it aside, the image of Sara's hair rippling about her shoulders as she brushed it stubbornly lingered in his mind.

An hour later, her hair bound back, Sara broke the silence that had reigned throughout the meal with a bland, "If it won't inconvenience you, I would like to use the tower as a sitting room."

"Go ahead."

"It will mean...I'd like to hang plants there again."

"So?" he returned with clear disinterest.

"It *is* your home, Luke."

Though something that she suspected was unpleasant flickered in his eyes at her emphasis, he only said carelessly, "Do as you please. I'll have Grey call the handyman to set in the ceiling hooks or whatever."

"Thank you." Returning her attention to her plate, she stayed by her resolve to not ask a single question about the two men, and finished her meal in silence.

Luke made no attempt to speak, either, and when he had finished he set aside his table tray and lounged back in his chair with his long legs stretched out comfortably.

As, apparently lost in thought, he drank his coffee, Sara found herself surreptitiously studying him.

The lamplight to his left highlighted his scarred cheek and the strong bone structure of his face, while the casual polo-necked knit shirt and tailored denims he wore defined the contours of the powerful muscles of his body.

As well as she had once known and explored that body and face with her fingertips and lips, she found herself wondering if she had ever really known him at all. Perhaps, she reflected sadly, there had never been someone who was Her Luke, or any Luke such as she had believed in, and her gaze lingered on his male lips, moving hastily away as he lifted his mug.

"About Toby," she said abruptly.

His eyes lifted to meet hers. "First, I would like to thank you for what you did this afternoon."

"It was...nothing." She looked down at her hands as an unexpected flow of pleasure moved through her.

"What made you suspicious?"

She shrugged. "Something about their eyes. The older man's were cold, even when he smiled." She looked up. "He also seemed surprised to find me here. They simply felt wrong." She smiled crookedly. "Nothing logical at all."

His head nodded slightly, acknowledging her point. "There were some working papers in the safe that could have caused some damage to the project."

"Why—" She stopped, annoyed with herself for forgetting that she was not going to ask any questions.

"Because about a month ago someone in the company spoke carelessly, and the remark was published in an industry magazine. As a result, the word is out that we are onto something big. Anyone who could steal it would make a fortune overnight."

Soberly she reflected on what he had said. "Are the...children in any danger?"

"No. Of course not! No one would go that far!" he rejected sharply. "After today's fiasco, they'll probably focus on the company. Most likely on bribery, or possibly blackmailing an employee."

"If anything...happened, Luke...." She stopped.

Leaning forward in his chair, he said tautly, "Look at me, Sara!"

Her eyes, filled with apprehension, met his.

"I've put five years of my life into this project. If it hadn't been for—" His eyes flickered and he shifted to, "Those years and the jobs of my people are at stake. If they steal our work and we can't recover what we've put into it, the company might not survive."

"I don't care about—"

"Listen!" His dark eyes held hers. "If I even *thought* that you, the children, or the safety of anyone at all was endangered, I would publish every bit of work I've done in the daily newspaper! I'd give it away—even if we went bankrupt. Believe me!"

She searched his eyes for a long minute and knew that he meant it. He would not count the cost.

"I promise," he told her quietly, still holding her gaze captive. "Whatever our differences, I promise that I will do just that."

"I know," she whispered with a tremulous sigh,

and looking back down at her hands, she repeated softly, "I know."

With an audible indrawn breath, Luke stood. "Drink?"

"Please."

"Bourbon?" he asked, remembering.

"On ice."

The ordinary exchange was calming, and for several moments neither spoke as they tasted their drinks. Finally she looked across at him. "What was it that you were going to tell me about Toby?"

"I've been over to the clinic twice this week with Toby's medical records. We now have an appointment on Monday morning at ten for a conference with the doctor and a decision on surgery."

"Decision?" Her heart seemed to stop. "What do you mean, decision? Who is the doctor?"

"A fellow Canadian of yours. She trained at Sick Children's Hospital in Toronto and she's one of the finest surgeons in her specialty on the continent."

"She?"

"Nancy Minelli. The children call her Dr. Nan." He paused. "They've asked that we both be present; and since Toby is a twin, that Tricia come along, too."

"What did you mean by *decision*?"

"Apparently Dr. Nan only takes on cases she believes her skills will help. If she believes another surgeon could do just as well, she won't accept Toby."

"But why? Why, if she could do it?"

"I don't know. All I know is that she limits her case load." He paused. "How is your driving?"

"Driving?" she repeated blankly.

"Would you be comfortable driving on mountain roads, with snow and ice?"

"I managed before, and I've managed since in Florida through storms and high winds."

"You'll need a decent car here, not a wreck like you had there. I'll arrange it next week. The clinic is about an hour's drive from here, and I may not always be going along, especially later when there are therapy visits." He set his glass on the tray. "Or would you prefer to have a company driver at your disposal?"

"I can manage myself."

"What color would you prefer?"

She stared at him in confusion.

"The car! If you would like it, I'll take you around next week to look at what is available."

"If I need a car," she said stiffly, though it would deplete her resources, "I will buy it myself."

"I am not having the children riding around these roads in the sort of rattletrap you could afford. When you leave, you can roll if off Lookout Mountain if it pleases you!" He shot to his feet and she recoiled slightly.

"Luke!"

"You never could accept a gift from me," he almost snarled, rounding on her. "Not without destroying any pleasure in my giving!"

"That is not true!" She rose to face him warily, if with an anger of her own.

"Isn't it? Your engagement ring was beautiful—so you said—but a terrible waste of money. You went on about it for days and then wore it only when I asked where it was!"

"Luke—" She stopped. For though she had in fact been afraid of losing the ring, she realized it could have looked that way to him.

"You also returned my wedding gift," he continued, his tone an indictment in itself. "Anything—*everything* that I tried to give you to make up for the years when you had nothing you somehow interpreted as either ostentation or conceit on my part!"

"I never meant it that way."

"Didn't you?" he asked tiredly.

Her head bowed, her voice shook when she finally whispered, "Perhaps I did. But...I don't think I knew why then."

"Why?" He found he wanted to know.

"I resented how...easy everything seemed for you." She looked up pleadingly. "You never had to muck out stables or skip a meal to buy a tube of paint. You never had to count pennies. Anything unpleasant, you ignored. Even your parents' death. I didn't know how to...to understand, and underneath I resented it."

"Oh, Sara," he sighed, and his hand moved to her cheek, touching its softness—everything else forgotten for a moment but the growing realization of how little he had known her.

Sara, finding herself unable to move under the mesmerizing touch of his hand against her face, slowly lifted her eyes to meet his, and the shadows of the room seemed to move intimately around them.

Luke stared back, conscious of the delicate lines of her face, of the uncertain quivering of her lips and the fragile scent of her. He felt the heat rising within him, his muscles tensing, and almost of its own volition his hand moved gently around the slender column of her neck.

"Luke...no..." she whispered hoarsely, her eyes darkening betrayingly and her slim body quivering as, before she could control it, a surge of almost painful desire rushed through her.

She tried to pull free, to escape before it was too late, but his hands cupped her shoulders and drew her almost roughly against the hardness of his body with a sure strength. When she twisted her face away, his mouth inexorably teased the soft silky places of her throat, nuzzling and nipping seductively.

She went limp, holding herself passive while her nerves screamed for release, and when his hold eased as his long fingers moved up to thread into her hair, she pushed away from him with desperate fear, and her fist drove into his midriff without compunction.

Luke's eyes widened and his grip loosened. In an instant she was across the room and through the door, running as if pursued by a demon.

He did not follow, but stood watching, and long after she was gone he still stared at the doorway. Then, turning away abruptly, he rubbed his neck with thoughtful fingers as the memory of the brief moments when she had trembled against him, when her slim body had adjusted to the length of him and the pulse in her neck had beat wildly against his lips, told him what he did not want to know.

At the small bar by the bookshelves he poured himself another drink with a hand that shook visibly. Emotions argued with reason, and standing there alone, the heat of the liquor joining the heat in his body, he told himself bleakly that he was a fool. A damned fool.

CHAPTER SEVEN

ON SATURDAY MORNING Sara descended to breakfast inwardly braced to face Luke with an impervious facade that would deny the events of the night before, only to learn from the children that he had gone to the office.

"He's bringing us a special surprise," Tricia whispered loudly.

"This afternoon," Toby added. "Something awfully special."

The surprise was a puppy, and Sara watched grimly as Luke presented a fawn boxer pup of about two months to the children, informing them that it was his puppy, but he needed their help to take care of it.

"Why did you get the pup?" she tackled Luke the instant the children and Elijah had wandered far enough away not to hear.

"Children should have a dog." His hands were thrust into his pockets as he leaned against a tree trunk, and his manner was so casual that the electric moments of the night before might never have happened.

"It is almost impossible to find a place to live where they will take a pet as well as children," she informed him angrily. "They will never give it up. It's thoughtless and cruel to allow—"

"You heard me tell them that it's mine."

"Marvelous!" she drawled with sarcasm. "Then there's no problem at all. You have spoken!"

"Sara...." It was a warning growl and it instantly ignited her still precarious emotions.

"Oh, go to hell!" she snapped, spoiling for a knock-down-drag-out fight.

When he merely regarded her expressionlessly, his dark eyes as cold as the mountain winds, she stalked away. All across the lawn she felt his eyes upon her, and fighting back tears, she summoned up her self-control and managed to smile cheerfully by the time she reached the children.

The weekend was dominated by the pup, and although Sara was not about to admit it, she found him an engaging, if clumsy, little creature. With a face that only a mother would love, the pup would have suited a name like Attila, but the twins fastened on Bumper because he constantly bumped into them.

"From the sound of him," Elijah remarked on Sunday morning when they returned from church to be greeted by happy barking, "we have a watchdog."

"Or a pest," Sara muttered, shooing the children up the steps. Pausing, she asked Elijah as the words triggered the subject, "Have they found out anything about those two men?"

"They have both been identified," Luke said, joining them. "There will be no more trouble."

"But what if...?" She stopped as Luke glanced at his watch, and said instead, "Don't let me keep you!"

His eyebrows lifted in a way that made her palm itch. "From what?"

"From your first priority!" Not waiting for his reaction, she climbed the steps. A short while later, as she was trying to unscramble the children and the pup, she heard the car growl down the drive, and her mouth tightened.

She did not see Luke again until the following morning when it was time to leave for the clinic. Caught between anticipation and dread, she was subdued and barely spoke to the distant Luke, who drove silently, his eyes on the road, his long fingers in grim command of the wheel.

When they arrived at the white stone buildings of the clinic, she paused on the front steps. Half-afraid that the doctors within the clinic might disagree with Toby's doctor in Florida, or refuse to help, she stood biting her lower lip, fine shivers coursing through her body.

"Sara?"

She raised her eyes, unaware of their silent plea, conscious only of the touch of Luke's hand as he took hers and hooked it through his arm.

"Chin up!" he said roughly, and guided her firmly into the building.

"Look at the fishes!" Toby shouted the moment they entered the reception room outside Dr. Minelli's office, and with Tricia hard on his heels, he rushed over to peer into the large tropical-fish tank set in the wall.

"I strongly suspect," Luke murmured as the elderly nurse at the desk looked up and greeted them, "that the aquarium has just performed its intended function by drawing off the children."

Sara hardly heard him. Her insides had become rubber knots, and after a night of tossing and turning as horror stories about operations that had gone wrong pulsed through her brain, she had the wild impulse to grab the children and run.

"Go right in," the nurse told them. "Leave the children here. I'll keep an eye on them."

"Keep that chin up!" Luke ordered softly in her ear as she preceded him into the inner office, and for a brief comforting instant his hand rested on her shoulder.

Crossing the room decorated in soft greens and cream, with a book-lined wall, she was further reassured by the sight of Dr. Nancy Minelli, a woman in her forties, slim and dark haired with warm blue eyes, who radiated serenity.

"I'm Dr. Nan," she introduced herself lightly. "The children call me that, and as their parents soon follow suit, we may as well start off with it." The soft Canadian inflection was a further balm, as she greeted Luke and then invited them both to have a seat.

"I believe," Dr. Nan said as she sat down behind her desk once more, "that I can reduce some of your tension by saying that I am accepting Toby as my patient. I know I can help him."

Sara glanced at Luke and saw his big body relax visibly as he replied, "Nothing could reassure us more than to know that. Your reputation is so impressive that had you refused, I was quite prepared to kidnap you."

She laughed with delight. "It would not have helped, I assure you. I am quite adamant about taking only those children who especially need my skills."

"So I was told," Luke conceded wryly.

"I was forced to establish limits," Dr. Nan said, "when some years ago I accepted every child I possibly could, even when other surgeons could help equally well. My average day was sixteen hours long, and a day off was rare. My husband, also a doctor, was a stranger, my young son was calling the maid and cook 'mother,' and I was normally incoherent with exhaustion."

She stopped as a young orderly arrived with a tray of coffee and Danish pastries, informing them that the children had been served milk and cookies.

When the coffee was poured, Dr. Nan gestured to the refreshments. "This is part of why I reduced my schedule. Sometime in life, I learned, one has to choose between a career and family. I settled for a less hectic schedule and time for my family." She sipped her coffee. "I suspect that most working people face that decision sometime in their lives when their needs pull them in two directions at once."

"Oh, yes!" Sara agreed with feeling, unaware of the sharp look Luke slanted at her.

"Now," Dr. Nan continued, "I do surgery three or four days a week. Mondays I reserve to meet the parents and my new patients." She eyed Sara perceptively. "You are somewhat apprehensive, I think."

"He's so...small," Sara admitted shakily. "Before...this was all in the future somewhere. If something went—"

"It's natural to worry," the doctor assured her. "By the time we operate, I think we can help you understand more of what will happen and ease those worries." Her attention moved to Luke. "How do you feel?"

"I have every confidence in your skill," he replied coolly.

Her mouth quirked. "How do you really feel?"

Luke regarded her almost haughtily, and then his face relaxed. "I've had my moments of doubt, too."

Sara looked at him with surprise, as much at his admission as at the idea that he actually had qualms. A mocking glint silently replied, and confused, she turned away to find Dr. Nan assessing them both.

"We have a program," the doctor said, "for the parents and children. While years ago hospitals assumed that parents only upset the children as well as the sanctity of the hospital routine, we've changed. It was not the parents who were upsetting the child by being there, but the departure of the parents—the apparent abandonment of the child to strangers."

"What sort of program?" Sara asked, intrigued.

"Today there will be a brief tour with Katy, my assistant. She greets all my youngsters the day they are admitted. Then, about a week before surgery I'd like you to spend a few hours with us, and finally, the day Toby is admitted we'll conduct a final review of procedures with him."

"He has a twin sister," Luke said. "Should she go along?"

"Are they supportive of each other or do they squabble a great deal?"

"Tricia is quite supportive," Sara assured her. "And they've never been separated before."

The doctor toyed with her pen as she thought a moment. "We'll try taking them both through the program and see how it goes. The second part, you know, involves having the children play hospital, handle the equipment and meet the people who will be on duty the day of surgery. We'll also provide you with reading materials today, and you'll find advice in them on answering the children's questions. Parents play a large part in how a child reacts to the whole experience."

"Toby and Tricia do not know that I'm their father," Luke said quietly. "My wife and I were separated until recently. I met the children only a few weeks ago."

"And their reaction?"

"They adore their Uncle Luke," Sara said firmly when Luke hesitated uncharacteristically, earning herself a peculiar look that made her add jerkily, "If you haven't the ti—"

"I'll be there!" he cut her off, his jaw shifting forward a fraction, not unlike Toby's expression when his back was up.

"You realize, of course," Dr. Nan said calmly, apparently unaware of, or ignoring, the byplay, "that Toby may reject you when he is hurting and still recovering from the anesthesia."

"Yes," Luke said shortly.

"I'll notify the staff, then, to refer to you as... Uncle Luke."

"When will you operate?" Luke asked.

"Toby has been in Denver for only about ten days," Dr. Nan replied. "Is that correct?"

"Yes," Sara confirmed, tensing.

"It takes a month for the blood to adjust to the oxygen level at this altitude. As there is no emergency, I would say...six weeks tomorrow—assuming his physical condition is normal."

"Six weeks!" echoed Sara.

"It will be a more simple process than the surgery your doctor in Florida recommended. It's a new procedure here with an excellent success record. He should be home, walking in a cast, a week after surgery. Five or six weeks later the cast will be removed and there will be exercises, some in the form of games, and some physical therapy. By the new year Toby should be walking normally."

Sara clung to the last words, her hands clenching. Suddenly Luke's hand, hard and strong, was covering hers, and she looked up at him startled. There was no mockery or anger in his dark eyes, only a warm gentle strength.

Throughout the remainder of their visit, everything blurred slightly. Toby and Tricia had their own separate interview with Dr. Nan and emerged full of information about their new friend who was going to fix Toby's leg.

Katy was almost a younger edition of Dr. Nan. Slightly plump and petite, with curly brown hair and laughing eyes, she was a woman who obviously knew children.

As she crouched at eye level to greet the twins, her infectious hilarity soon won them over, and when she took them on a tour of the playroom, including an inspection of the red wagon that would convey Toby to all his tests on the day he was admitted, she won them over completely.

"Be sure to answer any questions they ask," Katy told Sara and Luke as they parted. "Don't tell them anything is silly... talk it out seriously. The booklets you have will help guide you."

By the time they returned to Spars' Nest, Sara felt drained. The children were irritable with fatigue and overexcitement, and she turned them over to Jeannie gratefully.

"Brief Elijah, will you?" Luke directed, picking up the mail waiting on the foyer table.

"Are you leaving?" she asked with a feeling of dismay.

"I have work to catch up on." He dropped several letters back on the tray and handed her one. "From Madge. I'll probably stay and work tonight, as well."

"Luke?"

"Hmm?" His attention was obviously on the letter he was reading, and eyeing his broad shoulders and the muscles of his back visible under his summer jacket, she said nothing, waiting until finally the silence brought his head up. He frowned. "Well?"

"You will be there when Toby has his operation?" she asked, faltering slightly at the remoteness of his regard.

"I plan to be."

"What does that mean?"

"Precisely what I said."

"What's wrong?" she asked, a chill creeping into her. "At the clinic—"

"We were on public display," he finished brutally, and not even waiting for her reaction, he walked out of the door.

She felt sick. Unmoving, she stood alone, fighting waves of nausea. She had reacted to his spurious concern like a dumb animal receiving a pat on the head. She had actually believed.... Believed what, she derided herself savagely. That the man who had callously rejected her was not the Other Luke?

With an effort she fought back the pain and humiliation, and made herself walk calmly down to Elijah's room to tell him of their visit as if nothing else had happened. For nothing had.

THE FOLLOWING AFTERNOON a small blue station wagon was delivered by a smiling salesman.

"Dr. Driscoll asked us to bring it right out," the salesman said with a broad grin as he handed her the keys.

"Thank you."

His grin faltered in the face of her evident lack of delight, and sobering, he handed her the registration papers to sign. When she returned them, he quickly briefed her on the car and its features and then drove off hastily, his head shaking.

"Good-looking car," Elijah remarked, walking down the front steps to examine it. "Nice of Luke, wouldn't you say?"

"It will save him time if I drive," she said dully.

Elijah's eyebrows lowered. "Going to take it for a spin?"

"Only into the garage."

"Hmmph!"

For an instant she felt uncomfortable, remembering Luke's accusations. But it was not a gift, she reminded herself, and lifting her chin defiantly, she walked around the car and drove it directly into the garage.

"Ants have cows," Toby confided to Sara the following morning as she helped Jeannie ready the children for a picnic. "They milk the cows. They herd them, too. Just like cowboys."

"Don't tell me you want ant milk now!" Sara replied with mock horror.

"Their Uncle Luke told them about milking aphids this morning," Jeannie elaborated.

"And Grandpa Elijah said they have ant doctors, too. They operate!" Toby added.

"Maybe they can fix Toby's leg 'stead of Dr. Nan," Tricia said eagerly.

Sara laughed. "Would you both mind staying with a people doctor? Dr. Nan seems very nice." She tousled Toby's hair. "If you changed her for an ant, you might step on your doctor by mistake!"

As Toby and Tricia dissolved into giggles, Sara shook her head at the latter with mock despair. "Tricia, come here. Just look at your shoelaces!"

She plumped her on the kitchen chair, and while Jeannie combed Toby's hair, Sara loosened the tangled lacings.

"Bumper is coming with us," Tricia announced. "Jeannie said he could."

"I hope she knows what she's doing," Sara answered wryly, and then smiled as the pup stared up at her with interest and woofed. "He might be better staying here."

"He's our doggy! He can come!" Toby challenged.

"He is Uncle Luke's dog," Sara countered firmly, resolved to nip any such ideas in the bud.

Bumper immediately launched into a series of small yipping barks.

"See? He wants to go," Toby cried with delight. "He's good, mummy."

"He got Mrs. Grey mad!" Tricia said saucily.

"How?"

"He left his calling card," Jeannie supplied blandly, "in the kitchen."

Suppressing a smile, Sara said, "Then, we had better keep Bumper out of her way for a few days."

"Grey has good cookies," Tricia put in.

"That's nice, but Grey...." Sara paused, eyeing Toby, who was staring at his middle shirt button with interest, and decided to say only, "Grey is away today anyway, but do try to keep Bumper from pestering her. After all, she is older and tires more easily than we do."

"I'll keep an eye on them," Jeannie promised, gathering up the picnic basket.

With a quick smile Sara finished straightening Tricia's laces, and moments later she gave the twins a pat on their bottoms and shooed them toward Jeannie with, "Take these two ants out of the house!"

A house that seemed unnaturally quiet after they

had left, and with a rueful smile Sara filled a mug with coffee and slowly made her way to the tower room.

Although she had not touched anything in the remainder of the house, the tower room was already becoming hers again. She had solicited asparagus and rabbit's-foot ferns, baby's tears and kangaroo ivy from the groundsman, and hanging them in baskets, she used them to add warmth and life to the small sunny room.

For several moments she simply sat, letting the peace of the day seep into her and resisting the invitation of the thick branches stretching over the roof toward her to slip out and sit high in their shady boughs. That belonged to childhood, she reminded herself, and she was no longer a child, despite that very charge by Luke earlier in the morning.

She had seen him briefly after breakfast, when he asked neutrally if the car was satisfactory. She had replied with a curt affirmative.

"Have you driven it yet?"

"No," she returned shortly, despite sensing that he was angry—or more likely, she corrected herself mentally, piqued.

"Then do! Stop acting like a child. Use it! Go shopping. We could have a cold snap any day now with September here."

"Yes, sir!" Her eyes met his defiantly, if not without an inner qualm as she faced the hard power of him.

With a muffled oath he reached for his briefcase and in long male strides was gone.

She would use the car, she knew, so her small triumph was empty. And she would also shop rather than have him forcibly drag her through the stores or, worse yet, sic Jessica on her.

Her eyes followed the flight of a woodpecker, its brilliant red head feathers creating a dash of color amid the green leaves, and wished the children were there to see and feel the beauty of it. Or would they? All they seemed to want lately was facts.

Already they regarded Luke as a veritable fount of knowledge on everything, not just their latest interest in ants. His computerlike mind had not failed them yet, and she half feared that in some insidious way he was beginning to convert them to his world of facts and figures.

Restlessly she leaned back in the window seat, and passing by a book on solar energy that she was delving into to please Elijah, she selected the slim volume of poetry written by Luke's mother, Elizabeth.

Within moments she was lost in the sensitive music of Elizabeth's poetry, and somewhere in her reading the words became linked to Her Luke. To the sensitive man she had loved so futilely.

She raised her head and tilted it sideways to rest against the windowpane.

"Luke...." It was a whisper, a sad call, to a man who had probably never truly existed except in her foolish dreams.

Yet even now she shivered at the memory of his touch, of his lips against her skin, and her hand moved to touch the base of her throat, then sharply away.

"No!" she rejected out loud, and pushing aside the volume of poetry, she picked up the text on solar energy. Elijah would expect her to know something when they toured the production lines, she told herself.

She was dozing when the low burring growl of a car on its way up the drive roused her. Shifting, she leaned forward and peered down as a small yellow sports car buzzed up to the front door like an irritated bumblebee. With a grimace she rose, straightened her shirt and hair and descended into the cool shadows of the house, the door chimes urging her to hurry.

Fixing a polite smile on her face, she pushed back an errant lock of hair and opened the door.

The young woman facing her was a complete stranger.

Her chestnut hair fell to her shoulders and there was an eager expression in her warm hazel eyes that faded at the sight of Sara into uncertainty. "Is Luke in?"

"No, he's out," Sara informed her with matching uncertainty, not untinged with a sudden suspicion. "He's probably at the laboratory."

"You must be Sara, then." The woman smiled. "You say 'out' and 'laboratory' the Canadian way. I'm Beth Girard. I had hoped that Luke would introduce us. He asked me to stop by one morning, but didn't say when, so I thought I would wander over this morning."

"Girard?" Sara repeated, stepping back to let her in.

"Paul's wife," Beth Girard said, walking into the hall and giving Sara a sharp look. "Didn't Luke tell you? No, I can see he did not."

"He didn't tell me," Sara admitted, and aware that Luke had for some reason deliberately not told her, she had to quell a spurt of anger before adding, "But I'm delighted. Please come in, and we'll introduce ourselves."

"I'm Beth," Beth repeated promptly with a smile so warm that Sara felt a surge of instant liking for this woman whom Paul had married.

"And I am Sara."

"We are introduced!" Beth grinned, and paused in the double doorway opening into the living room, her eyes sweeping the fieldstone fireplace, the beamed ceiling and heavy furnishings. "You can certainly tell Luke's life these past years from this room. Technically perfect, but lacking in warmth. Paul tells me that you're an artist—quite talented, if the painting that he has of yours is typical. My only talents seem to be schooling horses and loving Paul." She laughed. "That is an odd combination, I admit, and not very special."

"Quite special, I would say," Sara managed, her lips curving over Beth's volubility. "Especially if they are related talents."

Another low laugh escaped Beth as she settled on one of the graceful chairs at the table by the bay window. "They just may be related. But, you know, it seems training is involved in loving. So many people don't know how. My mother always said that loving had to be learned in childhood, otherwise it could be difficult to know precisely how. Oh, anyway...before I become horridly philosophical and chat your ears off...Paul tells me that I am a typical Gemini—wall-to-wall mouth!"

"There's plenty of room here," Sara said, wondering if Beth always did chatter streams of words or if she was nervous. "The children are off with Jeannie on a picnic, and Elijah is out visiting, so don't feel inhibited."

With a mock-fearful look toward the hall, Beth whispered, "But where is the dragon?"

"Dragon?"

"Dragoness, actually," Beth amplified, her hazel eyes alight as she added irrepressibly, "Or should I say snapdragon? Whenever Paul and I are here, Grey seems to hover about like a mobile gargoyle."

Sara's startled eyes met Beth's, and for an instant she was unsure if the other woman was simply joking or asking something. But before she could probe, Beth was off on a new subject.

By the time they had shared tea, which Beth preferred, Sara had laughed more than she had in months. There did not seem to be a mean bone in Beth Girard for all her quick wit, and Sara found her friendly chatter filling a void she had felt since she had left behind Madge Wintertree's gruff companionship.

"I'm not holding you back from anything, am I?" Beth asked suddenly, with a quick shift of subject that Sara suspected was typical. "I mean right now? It's belatedly occurred to me that I could be keeping you from something. Peace and quiet, for instance."

"Nothing immediate," Sara assured her, laughing. "All I have planned for this afternoon is some shopping for winter clothes for the children and myself—per my orders for the day."

Beth's eyebrows lifted and her eyes danced. "Orders? Ah, Sir Luke!"

"His Lordship," Sara confirmed wryly, thinking of his arrogance.

"I'm just rattling about today by myself. Paul is off to Colorado Springs and won't be back until Friday night. I had to marry an architect who travels!" She shuddered. "Here he is, just back from Brazil, and off he went this morning. Honestly!"

"Then, he's been away!" Even as Sara exclaimed with involuntary relief upon learning that Paul had not been avoiding her, she saw Beth look quickly away. Not quickly enough, however, to prevent Sara from glimpsing something indefinable, and puzzled, she added lamely, "I wondered why he didn't call to say hello."

"I'm sure he will when he gets back," Beth answered in an oddly uncertain tone. "And we will be here for your dinner party, a week from Saturday."

"Oh...good!" Sara stammered, and afraid that Beth might realize this was the first she had heard of a dinner party, she rose, glancing at the grandmother clock in the corner. "It's almost noon already," she said awkwardly, managing a smile in Beth's direction. "I'd best be starting. I haven't driven the car yet, and I'll probably drive rather slowly."

"Could you use some witty conversation, a running dialogue and scintillating company?" Beth asked, her high spirits apparently back.

Confused, Sara met Beth's eyes and found only cheerfulness. The odd tension was gone. Or had it ever been there? "Yes," she agreed impulsively. "I'd like some company, if you're willing to risk my driving."

"I'm ready, willing and able!"

With a sudden access of high spirits, Sara ran up the stairs to change. Slipping on a simple dress, she paused by the window as it occurred to her that if she left, no one would be in the house.

Uneasy, she frowned, and then telling herself that there was nothing in the safe now, she finished dressing. Luke would have mentioned it if he didn't want the house empty, she reassured herself, and Elijah was due back shortly.

CHAPTER EIGHT

THE CAR DROVE BEAUTIFULLY, and had it not been for the circumstances, Sara knew she would be raving with delight. Within a short time she felt comfortable with it and by the time they reached the shopping mall she was able to zip it into a parking spot as if she had been driving it for years.

The urge to buy clothes only for the children was submerged not only by common sense, but also by the lure of being able to buy without worrying about her budget, and in a short time her scruples were tattered and her arms full.

"I think you caught the short end of the stick," Beth pronounced later that afternoon as they entered a shop rich with the scents of leather, rope and Indian blankets. "A coward could drive with you and never quiver."

"Does that mean I don't have to listen to your chatter now?" Sara asked with pretended hopefulness.

"No deal."

Smiling, Sara scanned the English and Western tack arrayed about them. "This is absolutely our last stop. I can use my old boots, but the children haven't any and they're eager to go riding."

"Don't you yearn to join our local hunt club? Tacky tack won't do, you know."

"Ugh!" Sara rejected. "Dressing in pinks and a bowler lid to chase some confused coyote across the plains? Not me!"

"Thinking of it, I can always see a vivid picture of some poor mangy coyote howling his way across the plains, desperately trying to explain that he is *not* a fox!"

They were still laughing when the sales clerk approached, and knowing Toby and Tricia would be fascinated by Western boots, she chose a pair for each. As they waited for them to be wrapped, Sara admitted candidly, "How I've missed riding!"

"Our stable is your stable, as they say to the south."

"You don't even know whether I can ride decently!"

Beth's fingers were still on the intricately carved silver-and-turquoise belt buckle she was examining as she murmured without looking up, "Paul said that you always rode at our place before, and I have several horses that do need exercise—and a few ponies for the children to ride."

"I...." Sara frowned, once again sensing Beth's sudden withdrawal despite her offer, and then a chill went through her. She had forgotten that she was a scarlet woman; someone Beth might be willing to get along with because Paul was Luke's close friend, but not someone she wanted too near. Swallowing, telling herself that she was innocent, so why should she care, yet caring, Sara managed to say lightly, "How nice of you, but really, there are several stables around."

"No...absolutely not!" Beth looked up smiling, as cheerful as ever, but for a flicker of alarm in her hazel eyes.

"But, Beth—" Sara started, confused.

"You'll ride at our place! And I shall love helping you teach the children."

The sales clerk's return cut off further discussion, and driving back to Spars' Nest with Beth chattering about her horses, Sara found herself wondering if she had not been oversensitive. Perhaps she had only imagined a wariness in her new friend.

Beth stayed on to meet Toby and Tricia and to chat with Elijah while Sara prepared coffee and cake.

By the time they had finished, and Elijah had left for a quick nap, the lawns were a deep emerald green and a heavy golden sun hovered just above the mountain peaks. Leaning back in her chair, Sara sighed, "I am tired! It's ridiculous. I have Jeannie helping me, no chores or job, and yet I'm worn out after a half day of shopping."

"Shopping is tiring. And not only have you been ill, but you also have those two imps." Beth regarded Toby and Tricia with amusement as they stomped across the room in their new boots, mimicking a cowhand's swagger, while Bumper raced around them in circles. "You know, I always thought twins would be a marvelous idea—two for one. Now I'm rapidly revising my opinion!"

Groaning, Sara admitted, "There have been times

when, as great as they are, I thought I would never survive."

"Luke mentioned that Toby would be having surgery soon."

"As soon as he's adjusted to the altitude. Meanwhile...." She stopped at the sight of Luke's silver sports car gliding up the drive. Rising, she stared out the window, the contentment of the day sliding away and tension returning as she said, "There's Luke now."

"Uncle Luke!" The twins looked up, shouted and ran for the front door calling out to him.

A moment later Luke appeared with Toby and Tricia and a wriggling Bumper in his arms.

"Beth! Glad to see you came over." His dark eyes shifted to Sara as he greeted her with synthetic warmth, and then he scanned the parcels piled on the sofa.

"They're mostly the children's," Sara said quickly.

"I hope you managed to find some things for yourself," he murmured. "Some suitable things?"

"If not, I'll return them. After all, it's your money."

For an instant his hard gaze froze on her, and then he turned to lower the children and pup to the floor.

When he straightened, it was to talk to Beth with a calm friendliness. And glaring at his back, Sara knew that he was as angry as she. Yet even as her eyes hostilely scanned his hard profile, she found herself jarred once more by the unbidden memory of his lips sensuously caressing her skin, of the hard lean strength of his body against hers, and of.... Flushing, she suppressed the images and sensations, and hurriedly busied herself with folding the new clothes.

By the time Beth had left, however, she had regained her composure. Sending the children off to Elijah, she turned to Luke to ask without preamble, "Why didn't you tell me that Paul had married?"

His dark eyebrows lifted, giving him the saturnine, mocking look she detested. "Does it matter why?"

"Yes," she replied heatedly, wanting to throw something at him again. "Yes, it does matter!"

"Then I'm—"

"He was the only real friend I had while I lived here! Yet you couldn't tell me that he had not called because he was away, or that he had married?"

"Married. Just as you are."

"He was my *friend*, Luke. Not my lover!"

"And I don't want Beth made miserable by you."

"The great Protector of Women," she jeered.

"Don't push me, Sara!"

"Don't push *you*! I am not a walking target, Luke. And I am damn tired of your potshots, and of having my nose rubbed in your imagined smut!"

"Sara—"

"I am not finished! All I've heard from you is, 'Don't upset Elijah! Don't upset Grey! Don't upset Jessica!' And now—'Don't upset Beth!' What about *me*? After what you—"

"That is enough!"

"You pompous...*ass*!"

His face darkened with a flush, the thin scar prominent on his cheek, and he stepped toward her, one hand rising to grip her shoulder.

Sara shied violently, only belatedly realizing that he was not going to strike her.

"My God!" Luke froze, clearly shocked. "You can't really believe that I would hit you!"

"Why not?" she countered, her voice wobbling. "You assault me with words every chance you get."

For a long moment her eyes, dark with emotions, met his. Abruptly she turned her back on him, fighting for control as tears threatened, and at the same time furious with herself for revealing even for an instant how vulnerable she still was.

There was a brief silence behind her, and then a muffled expletive as he forcibly spun her back to him and drew her roughly against the length of him.

"Let me go!" Her words were muffled as he pressed her face into his shoulder, his hand gently stroking her hair.

"Hush," he told her tiredly. "Don't cry."

"I'm...not."

"It's going to be all right."

"It can never be all right," she said dully, her defenses collapsing. "We're so far apart." Despite her words, however, she lingered within his arms. It was so seductively peaceful to lean, to be comforted, that she did not care if she was being rational or irrational.

As the seconds passed, gradually an insidious awareness grew that she could not deny. An awareness of the male scents of him, of the feeling of her breasts against his chest and of the dangerous weakness pervading her limbs. Appalled, realizing that it was insanity, still she lifted her head and her lips met his.

Instantly she recoiled with alarm, and pulling free, she avoided his eyes as she smoothed back her hair with shaking hands.

She could not trust him, she reminded herself savagely as she clamped down on her emotions. Not ever.

"Sara...." He paused, his gaze roaming over her hair with its pale sun streaks, the warm honey of her skin, and meeting the wariness in her eyes. He moved angrily. "Sara, listen to—"

The door chimes, vigorous barking and the sound of the front door being opened interrupted him, and swearing softly, he turned away, his hand raking through his hair distractedly. Confused by emotions he had promised himself would not occur, he stood tensely still.

Then Jessica Pettiway, immaculate in a tailored blue dress, her black hair in a perfect chignon and a slim briefcase in her hand, entered the room. The sight of her was like a dousing of icy water to Sara, and she stiffened.

"Hullo, Sara," Jessica tossed out, her cold eyes sliding past Sara, as they always had in the past, to Luke, and her greeting denying any importance to Sara's presence. "Luke, darling, what *was* that scene I glimpsed through the window? A grand reconciliation? Forgiveness of all sins?"

The grimness of Luke's expression upon hearing Jessica's words was more than enough to inform

Sara that the other woman had made her point. Tiredly she turned and started picking up the clothes from the sofa, barely hearing a thing as Jessica extracted some papers from her briefcase and began discussing them with Luke.

Then Luke was saying, "Give me time to change, and I'll follow you back. We can eat in town."

Lifting her head, Sara found his dark eyes resting on her indifferently as he added, "I'll be home late," before striding from the room.

He was no sooner gone when Jessica spoke. "Don't leave, Sara. I want to talk to you."

Tensing, Sara said, "This is not your home yet, Jessica."

Jessica shrugged, glided onto the sofa and crossed her slim legs. As she sat tapping a cigarette absently on her thin gold lighter, her eyes narrowed. "Touchy, aren't you?"

"What do you want, Jess?"

"Blunt. But then, you never were much on the social graces."

"Or on hypocrisy."

Jessica lighted her cigarette, drew on it and exhaled a thin stream of smoke. "As we are being so frank, I didn't particularly care for the touching scene between you and Luke."

"That's a personal problem," Sara returned evenly.

The chiseled features of Jessica's face hardened. "If you're deluding yourself that Luke will take you back, or feels anything but an obligation toward you, you're wrong. As soon as you and the children are disposed of, we plan to marry."

"And if I were you, considering the circumstances, I wouldn't hold my breath, Jess." Before Jessica could speak, she added in a tight voice, "Oh, don't mistake me! I don't want anything to do with a man who has a programmed computer for a brain and a digital heart!"

Jessica smiled slightly, a reptilian smile. "I'm glad you realize that he would not want you back with Rufus's fingerprints all over you. Not that he's immune to a bit of sex. After all, Luke is a passionate man, and you are known to be available."

"And married to him," Sara reminded her coldly, feeling sick inside that this woman should know anything of Luke's passion.

"Now, you sound," Jessica murmured silkily, "as if you do have hopes. How sad!"

"What *is* sad," Sara retaliated as silkily, "is your refusal to face failure. After...what is it—eight, nine years—you are still his...assistant."

"I am more than that!" Jessica assured her, stiffening visibly as she angrily stubbed out her cigarette. "Much more."

"I'm sure you think so, but—" Sara shrugged, taking a deep pleasure not only in standing up to Jessica, which she had not dared to do before, but also in baiting her "—the facts speak for themselves."

"You damn fool!" Jessica hissed, and was on her feet.

Recoiling despite herself, Sara could only stutter, "J—Jess, calm—"

"Can't you *understand*? You are destroying him! Our work will benefit millions of people. We'll make millions. And he cannot be distracted! He cannot waste time running after you and your children and petty problems! We are making history!"

Stunned by Jessica's vehemence, by the intensity of feeling from a woman she had always believed to be essentially cold, Sara fastened on one word. *"We?"*

"We! Together nothing can stop us! We'll win the Nobel Prize one day!"

"Ah! Madam Curie, I presume?" Sara managed.

Jessica flushed. "Why not?"

"Tell me," Sara asked evenly, recalling Elijah's remarks, "what did *you* contribute?"

"What?"

"What part of the breakthrough, of the basic ideas," Sara said with false patience, "is yours?"

"I have worked day and night, side by side with Luke every step of the way. My life has been dedicated to the project."

"Yes, but whose mind produced the key ideas?" Sara persisted.

"As an artist you couldn't possibly understand what I have contributed. Your mind is untrained, unscientific and unorganized."

Shades of Luke, Sara thought as she eyed Jessica with deliberate contempt, calculated to egg her on. "My being an artist has nothing to do with the fact that you cannot answer my question. You're nothing but a tagalong, Jess. You recognized years ago that Luke had what you lack—a creative mind. And any

Nobel committee would see in a flash that you're a second-class engineer riding his coattails."

Jessica went pale. "Whatever you think, you little slut, I'm the one he's with, the one whom he spends his days and nights with, and when you're gone—"

"Don't bet on it, Jess!" Sara cut her off, trembling with anger. "Don't bet on anything!"

Wheeling, Sara left the room so enraged that she collided with Luke in the hallway before she saw him. His strong fingers clamped on her shoulders, steadying her.

"What's wrong?" he asked harshly, and when she tried to break free, "What did Jess say to you?"

Her chin lifted betrayingly. "Nothing of importance."

"Don't lie."

"Nothing but the truth, then."

"Such as?"

"It doesn't matter."

"Then why are you shaking with anger?"

"Let me go, Luke!" With a twist she broke free and rushed past him.

A short while later, when the soft growl of Luke's car, then Jessica's car, started up and faded away, Sara did not lift her head as she knelt with the children and played with the pup in Elijah's room.

"Where is he off to now?" Elijah grumbled.

Sara shrugged, and picking up the puppy, she cuddled him for a moment, her nerves still jangling. "Off to dinner with Jess."

"Don't you mind, girl?"

"Not at all," she lied. Abruptly she placed Bumper on the floor and with inner confusion watched him trot to Tricia.

"Nice pup there," Elijah remarked in the silence. "Good blood."

"Toby's blood is bad," Tricia offered out of the blue, her attention on the tug-of-war she was having with Bumper.

"Stuff and nonsense!" Elijah spluttered, his eyes warning Sara to silence.

"But his leg is crooked."

"You know that Dr. Nan will fix it," Elijah replied.

"Oh, that's right! And I'm going to help her. She said so."

"It will be all fixed," Toby said. "Won't it?"

"All fixed," Elijah confirmed, and Sara held her silence although she was burning with the desire to question Tricia, well aware that with children, what went in one ear generally came out of their mouths, not the other ear.

Meanwhile Luke, speculating on what Jessica might have said to Sara, drove with a swift control, losing Jessica within a few miles, but unable to lose the image of Sara's expression as she had rushed into him.

His mouth compressed and his hands tightened on the wheel as an increasingly familiar conflict raged within him, part of him wanting to spin the damn car around and go back, and another part of him knowing that he had to iron out the wrinkles of the latest crisis immediately if they were going to meet the testing schedule.

The swing shift, operating from four in the afternoon until midnight, was moving at full pace as he strode past the assembly line and headed for the photo shop.

"Dr. Driscoll!"

Spotting the head of his machine shop approaching him, Luke halted and waited. "What is it, Mac?"

"This." He waved a drawing. "If you plan to have the hydrogen feed here—" he pointed "—I think the plate should be designed more as I've drawn it in."

Controlling his impatience, Luke assessed the suggestion, listening to Mac's arguments, and then nodded. "Go ahead. Let Ed know about it, too."

"Right, sir."

At the photo shop Luke requested that a copy of the schematic for the troublesome circuit be reproduced as an enlargement and sent to Jess's office immediately.

"The design engineer would have a copy," the technician replied.

"The offices are closed at this hour," Luke reminded him, and strode off toward Jessica's office.

"There you are!" Jessica greeted him. "I was just going to call the photo shop for a print."

"I've already done that." He closed the door and leaned back against it. "What did you say to Sara?"

"We were talking about the project," Jessica said. "She asked about it."

"And...?"

Her eyes flickered. "And I tried to tell her how significant the project is."

"What else?"

"That's about all."

"What else?" he ground out.

"I'd rather not— Oh, all right! She said that she couldn't care less what you did. She wants no part of a man with a programmed computer for a brain and a digital heart. Then—" she eyed him "—I'm afraid I lost my temper and told her that she was a fool. I'm sorry, Luke."

"Forget it!" he said grimly, and crossing to the drawing table, he looked down at the schematic unseeingly. "Let's get to work."

HER WORK DONE, Sara sat on the floor by Elijah's chair, silently watching the fire he had lighted to celebrate the first ghostly fingers of autumn brushing the trees with color.

The children were in bed, and with Grey off, she had served an omelet filled with ham and cheese, garnished with mushrooms and bean sprouts for dinner. Having cleared away the dishes, and with the empty evening stretching ahead, she let her mind drift.

Despite herself, her thoughts kept drifting back to the children, and looking up at Elijah she asked, "Do you think that Grey could be...." She hesitated, then, "Tricia has never talked like that before."

"I'll have a talk with Grey and see, but I doubt if she would say anything like that about Luke's children."

"I think I should talk to Tricia."

"Unless she brings it up again, I would let it slide. You make too much of a fuss over something and it will grow roots in a child's mind."

"Perhaps it's a stage." Sara propped an elbow on one knee and rested her chin in her palm, her eyes back on the flames in the fireplace. "But if I ever find that Grey is causing that kind of trouble—I'll leave. No matter what."

"Why not talk to Luke?"

Her mouth crooked cynically. "And have him accuse me of paranoia? I learned the last time that when it came to me against Grey, she wins and I'm being immature."

"She's been with him all her life, girl. When his parents died, it was Grey who stood by him. I was lost in grief. Try to understand that to him she was a mother of sorts for years, and she would never be cruel to his children whatever she thought of you."

"Elijah the peacemaker," Sara sighed. "I shall miss you."

"Not killing me off, are you, girl?" His hand moved to rest gently on her head.

"No." She looked up. "Of course not! I only meant that I shall be leaving eventually."

His dark eyes, disturbingly like Luke's, brooded down into hers, and whatever he saw made him shake his head slowly. "You're a fool, girl," he said softly. "A fool."

Resting her cheek against his knee, she sighed again. "Perhaps you're right." And after sharing a soft silence, she added, "In more ways than one. I had an absolutely horrid fight with Jessica this afternoon."

"Oh?" Elijah grinned. "Who won?"

"I'm not sure," she admitted ruefully, "but I suspect she did."

"Am I permitted to ask what the subject was?"

"She seems to think that I am an impediment to Luke's career, and that he is her vehicle for a ride to Oslo."

"Oslo!"

"The Nobel Prize, no less."

"What did you have to say about that?"

She grimaced. "I stole a leaf from your copybook and asked her what key ideas she had contributed."

"And?" he prodded with a chortle.

"She was... quite nasty." She paused, then added thoughtfully, "I don't think she even cares much about Luke himself. She's obsessed, and if she marries him, it will be to steal some of his glory."

"*You* are married to Luke."

"Not really... and I never was, really. Not the way you and Hannah were."

"That didn't happen overnight, child. Luke courted you for two weeks, went off and came back to marry you. I knew my Hannah for nearly two years before we married."

"You did so much together," she said wistfully, and leaning her head against his knee again, she stared into the fire a moment before saying, "I feel so useless here, Elijah! I can't interfere with the house or even help Grey. Jeannie is with the children several hours a day. And I haven't work anymore. It should be perfect, yet...."

"You could do something for me, if you would. Something very special."

The hesitation in his voice made her straighten and look up. He was staring at Hannah's photograph.

"Paint her for me, Sara! It's fading, and I want Toby and Tricia and their children to see my Hannah with all her warmth and spirit. The words I'm writing for the family history aren't enough!"

"I can't!" Sara retreated slightly. "I can't paint anymore!"

"Stuff and nonsense," he replied, as he had earlier to Tricia. "It's in your soul, and just as beautiful as words were with Elizabeth."

"But she shared loving—not hatred."

"Hatred?" He eyed her sharply and then asked gently, "You would paint Hannah with hatred?"

"N-no, of course not!"

"Then, you *will* do it."

"Elijah, please don't ask!"

"I am. You have a magic within you. You could make her alive, not stiff and unreal."

"I...just...can't."

"Still running, Sara?"

Her gray eyes flew to his and quickly away. "I did not run. He threw me out."

"He has never thrown you out, child."

She rose then, ignoring Bumper's startled protest at her feet. "I think I'll turn in."

At the door she heard him call after her, "You can't run forever, girl."

She wanted to turn and deny that she ever had. Instead she slowly climbed the stairs and sought the silence of the tower with Elijah's words echoing in her brain.

A moon so clear and full that the land was etched in stark shadows with only vagrant clouds sailing by to cast patches of darkness met her uncertain gaze as Beth's words joined with Elijah's.

She wondered suddenly if she did know how to love...or had she let her years with Aunt Ruth cripple her? Did it matter, she thought tiredly. Did it matter if she did run when Jessica was waiting like a harpy for the pickings?

The odd moments with Luke that afternoon returned with an unwanted vividness. His dark eyes looking down into hers almost as if.... She moved restlessly and rose from the window seat to leave, wanting not to remember but to forget and forget and forget.

It was nearly midnight when Luke returned to Spars' Nest, his eyes seeking Sara's window to find it dark. Leaving his car before the entrance, he started for the house, his head bent thoughtfully.

"Luke?"

He stopped, turning toward Elijah with a start. "What are you doing up?"

"Walking the pup."

"At this hour?"

"A good excuse for a late summer night's prowl after napping in my chair."

Bending to fondle the pup, Luke straightened and stood by Elijah staring down at the lights of the city below.

"Busy evening?" Elijah asked after a moment.

"We're stumped. Everything was set for the test and at the last moment.... I'll have to get back on it tomorrow."

"Enjoyed your dinner with Jess?"

Luke glanced sharply at his grandfather. "We were working and had food sent in."

"Only asked idly," Elijah replied blandly. "No need to get het up."

Luke stared into the night, aware that he had let Sara believe otherwise and that he did not want to examine why. Drawing in a long breath, he let it go on a soft sigh.

"Well?" Elijah grunted.

"Well, what?" Luke grunted back.

"Know what you're doing?"

"No."

"That's a start, boy. A start."

"Is it?" Luke said dryly. "Every time I think I can break free, something comes up. The safest thing we can do on the project is to finish the component testing and get the model functioning. Then we can sweat out the patent process."

"And then?"

"Then? You know as well as I that even if it comes through with flying colors, it's still another five years before it could be ready for production."

"Working day and night, of course," Elijah said casually. "Not much time for anything else."

Luke thrust his fists into his pockets. "What other choice is there? I can't drop the project; the company would be financially crippled with no return on the money we've poured into it. And if we go for an energy grant, or let another company in, I'll still have to be on it full time and overtime."

"Maybe...maybe not."

"What does that mean?" Luke asked cautiously.

"There might be a way to let someone else take it over with you keeping an eye on it."

"Hand it over!" Luke gestured angrily. "There's more than five years of my life tied up in it, and it's *good*, Elijah. It *will* work! I've more ideas, too, on how the fuel produced could be used by householders for their cars, as well! Think of it! Dammit, man, I can't give it all up!"

"Not saying you should," Elijah returned calmly.

"Then, what are you saying?"

"I have a friend. Known him more than fifty years now. He just might be the man to talk to. Interested?"

It was a long moment before Luke finally said, "Yes."

"I'll give him a call, then."

They walked along in silence, the pup chasing scents, the air crisp, and then Elijah said, "By the way, I promised to take Sara on a tour of the Driscoll empire, so to speak. Any particular day better with those radar contracts on board?"

"Sara wants to see it?" Luke asked with disbelief as Jessica's comments still rang jarringly in his ears.

"Seems as if she does. Promised her a while back I'd take her on a tour."

"A while back," Luke repeated.

"I thought she would like to see it. Production lines and all."

"I'll see if I can break free and join you," Luke said thoughtfully.

"No need, boy. Rather show it to her myself. You have your project."

"Dammit, don't you start on me!" Luke snapped, not pausing to think. Then, realizing Elijah had no idea that he had touched on an increasingly raw spot, he added roughly, "Sorry...I'm beat."

Elijah nodded and after a short while said, "Guess I'll go on in. No sense looking at the moon at my age."

"I'll bring the pup in." Luke watched him walk away, and slowly his eyes were pulled upward to Sara's windows.

With an effort he looked away and almost angrily strode off into the cooling night, feeling as if he were caught in a minor war. He had to stay neutral, he told himself, absolutely neutral.

Yet when he turned back his eyes sought her windows again with a yearning that he tried in vain to stifle. There was no way back to the beginning, he reminded himself tiredly, and tried not to wish he could be free again to walk inside to the warm welcome of her embrace, to lie with her, to laugh, talk and love in her arms.

CHAPTER NINE

Two DAYS PASSED before Sara saw Luke again, and then it was only because she deliberately waylaid him outside on his way to the car one morning.

"Why," she challenged, "didn't you tell me that we are having dinner guests next week?"

He was looking disturbingly tall, clean-shaven and well-groomed. His mouth crooked ruefully and amusement glinted in his dark eyes. "I clean forgot!"

Thrown off stroke, as if she had swung hard and connected with a pile of feathers, she regarded him suspiciously. "Really?"

"Really," he returned with light mockery. "I'm not perfect, you know."

"Oh, I know!"

"You needn't say it in such a heartfelt manner." He paused. "And you can bail me out by telling Grey."

She grimaced.

"Are you going to let a little old lady back you down?" he asked silkily. "Especially after the way you take me on?"

"How many?" she sighed, absently noting the sunlight tipping his heavy fringe of eyelashes with gold.

"Probably four guests, if Jessica brings someone. She'll let you know. Just ask Grey to prepare generous portions and we'll make do."

Her eyes fell, the news that Jessica had been invited leaving her feeling oddly deflated. "I'll tell Grey."

"Thanks." His eyes narrowed slightly, sweeping over her slim figure clad in jeans and a pullover, and pausing on her boots. "Going riding?"

"Yes."

"Alone?" he asked sharply.

"At Beth's. I'm starting the children off today. Why?"

His shoulders relaxed. "I'd like to be there to see it."

Her eyes met his. "You could be."

"It's not that simple, Sara," he said, holding her gaze, and as her gray eyes darkened involuntarily—revealingly—his insides went taut.

She did not reply, only looked into the dark spinning depths of his eyes, inhaling the masculine scents of him and feeling the heat moving thickly through her body until she was trembling.

Almost in slow motion his head lowered, inching down, closer and closer....

With a choked cry Sara stepped back and, pivoting, ran into the house. Slamming the door behind her, she stood in the entrance foyer, her fists clenching as she tried to drown out Elijah's taunting charges and his challenge to stop running. Yet if she had stayed, if she had felt the touch of his lips, she knew that she would have lost control, and it would have ended in her own humiliation.

Even now her insides were in knots and she still shook. Feeling almost ill with reaction, she fumbled for her defenses, propped up a tottering wall and went to speak to Grey.

Grey, it transpired, already knew of the dinner. "Miss Jess dropped by for coffee the other day. She often does. She told me, and I have it all planned already."

"But I...." Sara stopped, and unable to muster the will to challenge Grey at the moment over planning, she said tonelessly, "I'm sure it will be superb."

For an instant it seemed that Grey was about to make some comment, then thought better of it before finally saying, "I'll do my best."

"She probably will do great," Beth remarked several hours later as they watched the children playing on the back terrace of the ranch house. Beth's eyes touched them with a wistfulness as she added, "They did so well today. I wish...." She sighed, and let her wish remain unspoken.

About to make a quip about Beth's day coming, Sara suddenly bit back the words as a terrible suspicion entered her mind. Looking away, she took a deep swallow of her drink to wash away the dust that was still stuck in her throat, and let the silence rest between them.

"They certainly take to riding," Beth said suddenly with the air of someone consciously pushing aside other thoughts.

"We'll know better next time, when they are up on a pony alone," Sara qualified, knowing from experience that while their half hour each in the saddle in front of her as she rode around the pasture had at least acquainted the children with the reality of a horse, the test would be when they were on their own.

"If you'd like," Beth offered, "take the mare and go off for a ride by yourself. I'll look after the kids for you."

Sara hesitated, and then, seeing that Beth sincerely meant it, she accepted the offer. Moments later she rode off along the trail, waving to the children and then urging her mount into a smooth rocking canter.

In seconds the exhilarating sense of freedom she had always felt swept everything away, and for a short while she was a child again, escaping from all restrictions.

When she turned back, however, it was almost like turning to face the increasing tangle of her life as the tense moment of the morning returned.

From the very first time she had seen Luke, some primitive part of her had soared to life—the female recognizing the male, an instinctual mating response so strong that the thought of its return petrified her.

He was like an addiction, she thought. For five years she had not tasted the delights of him, and had believed herself cured.

Now, like an alcoholic who had tasted the dangerous forbidden drink, she knew she was gradually beginning to crave what could only bring disaster upon her head.

She would not let it happen, she resolved, and closing her eyes to the strength of her growing addiction compared to her crumbling defenses, she rode back.

"Oh, Sara!" Beth greeted her, disheveled and flushed from her games with the children. "You don't know how lucky you are! They are darlings."

"Not always," Sara warned, smiling at Beth despite a growing inner conviction that for some reason Beth couldn't have children. "They do have their days. That's when I find myself wishing that they were back living inside of me again, where I didn't have to put up with tantrums or rebellions."

Only a few days later, Sara recalled her words to Beth and wondered if she had tempted fate with them. Regarding Toby with clear exasperation, she was quite aware that he was in one of his most muleheaded moods.

Tricia wasted no time allying herself with her brother, declaring, "I want to go, too!"

"No."

"Why don't I take them down to the plant this afternoon?" Luke interceded.

"A no is a *no*!" Sara repeated, flashing Luke a warning look that sizzled. "I'm going tomorrow, and these two will stay with Jeannie—and behave, too!"

"Won't!" Toby said, his lower lip jutting.

"Won't!" echoed Tricia, promptly pushing out her lower lip.

"I know you're both upset," Sara said firmly, "but you're not going."

"Sara...."

"Luke, I said *no*!" She rounded on him, glaring fiercely.

"I wish Uncle Luke was my daddy," Tricia said truculently. "He wouldn't be mean."

"I wish, too!" Toby seconded sulkily.

Sara stilled, feeling as if she had been knifed in the back even as her mind told her that it was a typical remark for thwarted children. Another part of her, however, was suddenly frightened. She was still fumbling for words when Luke spoke.

"If I were your daddy," he said harshly, "I would be ashamed of you both! Don't you ever talk to your mother like that again!"

Tricia and Toby stared up at him, lower lips quivering, and when he ordered them off in disgrace, they shuffled across the lawn and sat down staring at the grass.

"I'm sorry, Sara. I should have known better than to undermine you, especially in front of them."

She raised her eyes to his, then dropped them, unable to speak.

Hard fingers hooked under her chin, forcing her head back up. "Look at me!" he commanded softly, and when she reluctantly did, he searched her gray eyes a moment before adding, "You know the children were just piqued—nothing more."

"Why shouldn't they prefer you?" she burst out, her whole body trembling.

"Nonsense!" His mouth tightening, he pulled her against him and his hand pressed her head against his shoulder. "Utter nonsense, and you know it."

"Do I?" she asked, her voice uneven. "All they know is that whenever they see you, however short the time, you give them all of your attention, plus presents of fascinating scientific tidbits—"

"I am not trying to win them away from you! You know that, Sara."

"But they don't! And you don't know what being a father is, either!"

"Oh?" His face became expressionless. "And what is your definition of a father?"

"It includes listening to the children even when you're tired or busy and don't want to." She drew away from him, continuing angrily. "And it's spending time with them when it's damned inconvenient! It's denying or disciplining them when you'd rather spoil them. It is *not* just playing charming, attentive daddy when your schedule and mood permit!"

"Thank you!" he said stiffly, a peculiar expression flitting through his dark eyes. "I'll see that it's programmed into my computer brain immediately."

He walked off, leaving her appalled by the realization that Jessica must have quoted her angry words to him.

"Luke!" she called after him, her hand going out, only to drop when he continued. Without quite knowing why, she knew that of the many things she had thrown at him, this had hurt him deeply.

The knowledge gnawed at her through the night, and the following morning she resolved that she would find some way to apologize to him while she and Elijah were touring the complex. Surely, she thought, as she drove toward the sprawling building, they would see Luke at some time or the other during the tour.

Frowning at the sight of a chain-link fence topped

by barbed-wire strands, Sara said, "I don't remember the fence... or the guardhouse, either."

"They just installed it," Elijah replied as she rolled to a stop by the guard. After signing a card, she parked inside the fence and proceeded with Elijah through the lobby, where once again they signed their names at a second checkpoint.

"I feel as if I'm entering a prison," Sara murmured nervously.

"Any company with classified military contracts must match military security requirements," Elijah explained. "And with Luke's research, as well, we can use it all."

She nodded, eyeing the carpeted halls lined with offices and photographs of the Rocky Mountains, and felt the tension increasing in her as she realized they were approaching Luke's offices, the only part of the complex that she had ever visited.

They were met by the news that Luke was in his lab, and after refusing his secretary's offer of coffee, Sara followed Elijah down the hall again with a sense of reprieve.

"First," Elijah announced, "we'll look at the meat-and-potatoes part of our operation." He paused to say hello to an engineer and introduce Sara, and then proceeded down the hall. "We start with a contract to build a piece of equipment that will do a certain job for someone."

"Like the radars."

"Right. Radars for the air force. These offices here—" he gestured to the small offices flanking them, each with a desk, chalkboard and shelves of reference books "—are where our design engineers design the electronic circuits to do the job."

"It looks rather ordinary," she murmured.

"It's all brainwork for the first year or so, Sara. Scribbles on scraps of paper. Then the mechanical engineers take over and design the container that will hold all the electronic circuits, the control panels, antennas and so on."

She peered into another office, eyeing a drafting table with the rough sketch of what looked like some sort of lever lying on it, and then was led by Elijah into a huge high-ceilinged room filled with equipment and people working in different areas.

Trying to look everywhere at once, she tripped over a cable and staggered after Elijah into a partitioned-off area where she found herself surrounded by heavy machinery.

"This is the machine shop. The mechanical engineer brings Mac rough drawings of what he wants and the specifications, and Mac makes the part."

Backing off slightly from the sparks flying from a welding torch, Sara found herself beginning to realize the immensity of the task of designing something from start to finish.

In the photo shop, the technician showed her the equipment used to shrink circuit drawings to one-fourth of their size, and the positive print that resulted.

"Over there—" the technician, a young black woman, pointed "—are vats full of chemicals. Using the positive, we make a print—just as if we were printing a photograph—except that instead of printing on photographic paper, we print on a sheet of photo- or light-sensitive copper that is joined to a backing of fiberglass board."

"And those chemical baths?" Sara asked, a bit confused.

"When I dip the copper sheet in, the chemicals etch off all the copper touched by the light. You end up with copper wherever there was a line drawn in the circuit drawing. You do understand what the drawing represents?"

"Not really," Sara admitted, ignoring Elijah's muffled snort.

"Before these came, they had wires leading every which way inside radios or televisions. Tangles of wires."

"Oh, I see! The lines on the board are just like wires."

"But much neater," Elijah put in, and after thanking the technician, he led Sara to a small assembly line where men and women were working, handling circuit plates and minute parts with miniature tools.

"Here they drill holes into the circuit plates and fasten the parts in place. Those tiny plastic-looking rectangles and sausagelike parts replace the glass tubes you once found in anything electrical. When they are connected they are tested and go into the casing. In the end we will have twenty custom-made, radars for the air force."

"There's so much to it," she said, and looking at the myriad parts, added, "I don't think I'd like working on the assembly line at all!"

"One day we hope to replace our assembly-line workers with robots."

"But they'll be out of jobs then!"

"They won't," Elijah said as they left the production area and started toward the other wing of the building. "They'll get better jobs."

"Will they?" she asked doubtfully.

"When computers came in, everyone said it would put millions of clerks out of jobs. Instead there are more and better jobs for them and many others. So it will be for assembly-line workers. Japan has already proved that."

Sara only mumbled some reply, her pulse jerking as she glimpsed Luke striding ahead of them. Then he turned the corner and was gone. Realizing that Elijah had noted her straying attention, she said with embarrassment, "Sorry."

"Quite all right," he returned blandly.

There was another security guard waiting when they turned into the research wing, and after they'd signed in again, the guard tapped a series of numbers on a dial that looked like a push-button telephone set in the wall, and the door opened into another corridor lined with offices.

"Here is where the basic research is done," Elijah told her. "Here is where we start with a concept and make it into a workable product that people can use. It means Luke has to dream up many of the parts, experiment and innovate."

"Doesn't he use any parts already made?"

"Some. In all, however, it takes years—even decades—to take a totally new breakthrough from someone's brain to the store counter. All that time, we have to carry the load of salaries, parts, designing, of equipment running six or seven figures; and if someone else beats us to the punch before we patent, we lose all the money we put in, plus all the time."

"And if you win?" she asked.

"The profits for years can go to paying back what we put into the research, and when that's paid off, paying for new research so our competitors don't make us obsolete."

"Aren't you going to show her our model?" Luke asked directly behind them, and Sara felt her whole body become vibrantly alive as her breath caught.

Elijah scowled, though his eyes were amused as he grumbled, "Stealing my thunder, eh?"

"Precisely," Luke returned. "This way, Sara."

Slightly breathless, yet wary that Luke might once again be wearing a mask of friendliness to disguise his feelings in public, Sara entered a sprawling room to stare at what looked to her like a giant hodgepodge of circuit boards, panels with a peculiar-looking gray pebbly panel, pipes and other paraphernalia.

Luke, distractingly close to her, gestured at it with pride. "That, Sara, is tomorrow's power plant for the home. Every home will use the sun, be independent of petroleum. It won't need batteries that run down, but will create a fuel."

"It's huge!" she exclaimed, somewhat disappointed by its looks. "The roof would fall in!"

"It's only the first working model. Once we prove the concept, we go to work on, er, making it look attractive—packaging. Some models start the size of a room and end up the size of a teacup."

"When pocket calculators were first designed," Elijah said, "they were so large and bulky they could hardly be moved."

"We also have to be sure it can be made on a production line. Mass production will be a key factor in its future. We have to—and I think we can—produce it as cheaply and reliably as a pocket calculator is today."

"Explain the differences between your system and most other systems," Elijah prompted.

When Sara nodded, Luke spoke eagerly. "So far, all the solar systems using 'light' cells—photovoltaic cells—convert the sun's energy and store it as electricity in batteries."

"Which can store only a limited amount. A week or so of rain and you're out of electricity," Elijah offered, ignoring Luke's frown.

"Two basic solutions are," Luke went on, "to make better batteries or to convert the sun's energy into a fuel that you can use whenever you need it. That is what I think we've done here."

"But how?" she asked. "How can sunlight be changed into fuel?"

"Look!" He guided her to his bench model. "Instead of using flat wafers of silicon the size of tea saucers, I've attached thousands of tiny spheres of the light cells that convert sunlight into electricity to a base. It's like attaching sand to sandpaper."

"It sounds more complex."

"No, it's more simple. We cut production and testing costs tremendously this way, and if a few cells are defective, the system is barely affected. Not like what they use now. See?"

"Yes," she assured him, aware that he was simplifying for her.

"For the next step, instead of collecting the electricity in batteries, I take hydrogen iodide and wash it over the light collectors."

"Oh," she murmured somewhat blankly.

He grinned slightly. "The electric current that the light cells produce splits up the liquid into its components, and we draw off the hydrogen to charge a fuel cell whenever we want electricity—day or night."

"It's a self-contained unit," Elijah added.

"What's important," Luke broke in, "is that it means rich and poor will be able to have it, and petroleum could become obsolete." He drew in a breath, adding wryly, "All I have to worry about is, will it prove out, and has someone else come up with the same system or a better one already."

"Luke?" Jessica was suddenly there, nodding at Sara, greeting Elijah with far less coolness, and saying, "Would you come take a look at this computer analysis?"

"Later."

"But—"

"Later," he said curtly.

Her lips compressing, Jessica walked out, and glancing up at Luke, Sara found his dark eyes not on Jessica but on her own face. Rattled, she looked hastily away.

By the time she finished her tour of the research facilities, Sara's brain felt overloaded. Never again, she thought, would she pick up a gadget in a store without thinking of all the people, time and risks it took to put it there.

She also felt a sense of awe at the dimensions of Luke's world, that he was responsible for something so terribly complex, for every employee and project.

As they entered the lobby she glanced up at him, remembering her earlier resolve. Drawing in a quick breath, she said, "Luke, could I talk to you? Just for a minute?" When he seemed to hesitate, she added an almost pleading, "Please!"

Looking past her, he exchanged a look with Elijah and then led her to the side of the spacious contemporary lobby and stood waiting for her to speak.

"I...I'd like to apologize," she said awkwardly. "I was angry at something that Jessica said when I described you as...as a—"

"As a man with a programmed computer for a brain and a digital heart."

"I'm sorry." She stared at his tie pin fixedly. "I truly am."

"You've hit me with worse than that before. Why the apology?"

She shrugged, unable to say that for some reason she felt her remark had been well below the belt.

"Apology accepted," he said quietly, and after a pause guided her back to Elijah, his hand feeling as if it were charged with a high-voltage current as it cupped her elbow. She left the building with an inner glow that common sense could not quell.

Once in the car and driving home, however, she found herself wondering how anyone could handle such complexity and ever expect to have time for anything else in life.

"What was your impression?" Elijah asked as she turned onto the highway leading to the foothills.

"It's somewhat daunting," she admitted. "All that to make one thing."

"In Europe, you know, they often produce a product faster, aiming for something workable. Or they concentrate on quality that only a few can buy."

"But that's what they do here."

"Not quite," he corrected her. "We tend to concentrate on what the buyer wants and needs—many buyers, usually. A bulky or ugly product that works but isn't handy, attractive and reliable won't do. So with us the buyer is king, not the product."

"Elijah?"

"Hmm?"

"Nothing."

"What kind of nothing?"

She sighed. "With all those people and projects depending on Luke, how can he ever... I mean, how could...?"

"There's a way," Elijah said, apparently understanding her disintegrating question. "But he has to choose it freely, girl."

And whatever Luke chose, Sara knew that it would not include her. She could not let the children grow in a climate where their father stiffened at the thought of her going riding alone, where contempt underlined desire, and where the best she could ever hope for would be forgiveness for a sin that she had not committed.

The lines of their lives had separated irrevocably. There was no way to correct the wrong lines, to redraw them and dip them into a chemical bath that would wash away all the lies, suspicions and distrust that had destroyed their marriage. No way at all.

CHAPTER TEN

"THE THREE OF YOU need a bath!" Sara informed Toby, Tricia and Bumper as they returned from riding several days later. "You smell of the stables! I think I must have brought horses home by mistake."

"You smell, too!" Toby rejoined.

"What? What did you say, young man?" With mock affront she treated him to a haughty glare that dissolved both children into giggles. "People mothers *never* smell like horses!" Bending, she tousled their dusty heads. "Now, off with you. Upstairs to Jeannie. Tell her to start your bath, and I'll be along in a few minutes."

As she shooed them up the stairs with Bumper at their heels, she suddenly became aware of Grey in the rear of the entrance foyer, the phone in her hand.

With a shiver that was half dislike and half the strange effect of the silent, disapproving woman in the shadows, Sara looked at her and said, "What is it, Grey?"

"It's Miss Jessica on the phone. For you."

Sara crossed the hall aware that while outwardly nothing was anything but correct, still.... She took the phone. "Yes, Jessica?"

"I just called to let you know that I'm bringing a

friend of mine along to dinner on Saturday. I wasn't sure if Luke mentioned it."

"Yes, he did. We'll expect you at about seven-thirty."

"Good." She paused. "Oh, I had better warn you that two VIPs from Texas may be invited for dinner at the last moment. You might want to warn Grey."

"I will."

"We'll see you Saturday, then."

Sara returned the receiver to its cradle slowly, wondering why Jessica was suddenly treating her as if she were truly the hostess. Luke went around her, and Grey did. But not Jessica. She frowned, then looked up at the waiting Grey. "Jessica will be bringing a friend, and there may be two more guests at the last minute."

Grey nodded, and as her footsteps faded, Sara paused in the cool shadows wondering whether Jessica was bringing someone for appearances, or whether she hoped to make Luke jealous. What did it matter? She caught herself. She was thinking that far too often.

But what did it really matter, her mind persisted as she climbed the stairs. She herself was an unwanted guest. A figurehead hostess, who might be permitted to arrange the flowers.

So, she thought tiredly as she entered her room, what did it matter? At least she would see Paul again, and learn whether her one friend from the past had also turned against her.

But when Saturday evening arrived, she found that it did matter to her not only how Paul would treat her, but also how the evening went. Edgily she watched from her window as the Girards' car entered the drive, and only then did she leave her room.

Walking down the hall toward the stairs, she told herself firmly that she would keep up appearances with a vengeance. She would be the poised hostess and wife who was considering reconciliation with her aloof and arrogant husband—no matter what.

As she descended the stairs, however, her resolution faltered, for Luke, looking disturbingly attractive in his dinner jacket, had halted abruptly at the sight of her, his dark eyes fastening on her intently.

Caught in an invisible, numbing net, she watched motionless as his eyes traveled over the smooth sweep of her sun-streaked hair into its chignon, over the golden tan of her face and throat, and then slowly down the length of her new cornflower-blue dress, pausing at the silver embroidery on its hem. Without haste his eyes made a return trip upward, lingering on the hinted curves of her slender body until she felt physically caressed.

When his eyes met hers again, she wanted to look away, but the fathomless depths of his gaze tangled with hers, and within her a swirl of feelings was suddenly clamoring to be free. Her breath catching, she ripped free and forced herself to continue down the steps with cool poise, as if her pulse were not racing, as if tremors were not suddenly weakening her, and as if she were not afraid to meet his eyes again.

At the foot of the steps she stopped uncertainly, her eyes cautiously lifting to the sensuous lines of his mouth, watching his lips part with an excruciating awareness that she was helpless to deny.

And then the doorbell chimed. With a muffled expletive Luke was turning from her to let Paul and Beth in. Feeling definitely disoriented, Sara was aware of both relief and disappointment.

"Hello," Paul greeted her, a quiet warmth clear in his voice.

"Hello, Paul," she returned, awkward with the pleasure flooding her at the realization that this man was still her friend. His hand clasping hers firmly further reassured her, as if he sensed her uncertainties as well as her need for something besides condemnation.

"I called last week," he went on, his blue eyes gentle and understanding, "but you were out." He grinned. "You're looking fine. Better than ever."

"It's so good to see you! Beth was telling me how...." Sara stopped as giggles trickled down from above. Looking up, she spotted Toby and Tricia peering through the landing rails. "Back to your room!" she ordered. "And now!"

"Oh, do let them come down!" Beth begged. "I'd like Paul to meet them."

"They are supposed to...." Sara met Luke's eyes and at his nod found herself saying weakly, "Just this once, then."

The twins, quick to spot allies and support, were already scampering down the steps, Toby lagging with his limp more pronounced at the end of a long day. But when Paul moved involuntarily to help, Sara said under her breath, "Let him do it, Paul."

She looked to Luke even as she spoke. The quick agreement she found warming his eyes added to her confusion as she introduced the children. It was only a matter of appearances, she told herself quickly as they joined Elijah in the living room, nothing else.

The twins, not long in deciding whom they did and did not like, took to Paul as strongly as they had to Beth, and clear mutual approval radiated between them and their newest "uncle." By the time Sara gathered Toby and Tricia to firmly shepherd them toward the stairs, she found herself completely relaxed and oddly happy.

She was brought back to earth with a thud when, without ringing or knocking, Jessica walked in the front door just as she and the children reached the foot of the steps.

"Ah, the children's hour!" Jessica exclaimed dryly.

Sara barely heard her, for the sight of Rufus Petrofsky following her in was like a physical blow. Sheer disbelief that even Jessica could be so callous as to bring Rufus to Spars' Nest, knowing what Luke believed, left her stunned.

Dumbly she watched Rufus crouch to greet the children, his voice seeming oddly distant as he introduced himself to them with all of his old charm. She groped desperately for her scattered wits, looking at Jessica, recoiling inwardly when for the briefest instant she saw sheer malevolence mixed with triumph in the other woman's eyes.

Then Rufus was standing with Toby held stiffly in

his arms as Tricia shrank toward Sara. "Hello, Sara," he said quietly.

"Rufus...." His named clogged in her throat. This white-haired man whose talent she had respected, whose friendship she had believed in, was a symbol of all her years alone and apart from Luke. This was the man whose lie had condemned her, and the mute appeal she read in his eyes now could not erase his past betrayal.

In the doorway Luke took in both Sara's frozen stance and the uncanny likeness of Toby in coloring to the man holding him. It was a picture that embodied fears he did not want to admit, and a savage anger rocked him.

Feeling Luke's anger instantly, Sara knew that whatever her hopes had been, the evening would now be a disaster, and that whatever fragile moments she had or had not imagined earlier, they were irretrievably shattered.

"Don't they make a lovely trio," Jessica murmured, approaching Luke.

Ignoring her, he said evenly, "Sara, the children should be in bed."

With a shudder she could not restrain, Sara took Toby from Rufus and, gripping Tricia's small hand, went up the stairs. She did not look back, but all her old fears followed her. Luke would believe the worst. She knew it as surely as if he had already launched his accusations.

When the children were settled, she closed their door and leaned her head back against the cool wood. Cravenly she wished she could manufacture a headache and simply hide in the tower until everyone was gone.

But a certainty that Luke would not hesitate to invade her sanctuary and haul her unceremoniously downstairs made her sigh and start down the hall.

The sight of Rufus waiting on the landing stopped her. "I don't want to talk to you."

"Sara, wait!" His bulk blocked the stairway. "I had to come. To see you."

"Oh?" Even as she eyed him angrily, the question she had asked herself for years burst through. "Why? Why did you do it? We were friends!"

"For your own good."

"For my own *good*!" she echoed incredulously.

"He was stifling you!" he exclaimed with all his old, slightly theatrical intensity. "He was so possessive that you couldn't expand...grow! You had to be freed. I freed you."

She regarded him with a kind of growing horror.

His hand ran through his pale hair, his intensely blue eyes no longer meeting hers. "I didn't know that you were pregnant. But even so," he repeated tonelessly, "you needed to be free of him. Sara, one way or the other Jessica would have destroyed your marriage because you interfered with Luke's work, because she wants him and his future fame. If he had really loved you, nothing could have broken you apart."

There was an element of truth in his words that hurt. Hurt so deeply that she wanted to cringe away from his naked expression of it.

But his hand was clamped on her arm as if he knew

she would withdraw. "It *was* to help you! As much as anything else. You were miserable! It was suffocating your talent!"

"Oh, dear God," she whispered.

"Admit it! Admit you've done far better away from him!"

"Better?" A revulsion of feeling for this man crowding her with his intensity swept through her, and biting back bitter laughter she said, "I haven't painted a stroke since that day."

Rufus went rigid, his eyes mirroring his shock, and after a moment they held an odd despair, as well. "That is a lie, Sara. I won't believe it!"

"No, Rufus, it's the tru—"

"Sara!"

Luke's voice, low but furious from the foot of the stairs, sent Rufus back a step and severed his hold on her arm as if his hand had been physically struck away.

Without a look or word to Rufus, Sara walked past him and down the steps toward Luke, who waited this time with only contempt in his dark eyes. Feeling battered, she tried to pass him without speaking.

His hand stopped her, and aware of how grim his face was, she kept her head bowed as he gritted, "I'll remind you, Sara, that your stay here is not a social visit!"

Her head lifted. For a brief instant her gray eyes met his with bitterness, and then, pulling free of his grip, she walked past him to join their guests as if she would not rather crawl into a cave and weep.

Her social mask was well in place a short while later when the two visiting businessmen from Texas arrived.

One, a man in his late forties, was a physicist and seemed rather preoccupied and unaware of anything outside of his own thoughts.

The other man, Will Turner, the grandson of an old friend of Elijah's, looked like a cliché of a Texan—tall, lean hipped, with sun and laugh wrinkles around shrewd yet warm eyes.

He gravitated toward her as if he were zeroing in on a homing device, and despite the tensions simmering below the surface, she found herself responding to his friendliness and humor.

"Luke told me you have a boy about to have an operation," he said after revealing that he was a widower with a grown son and two daughters in their teens. "If you have any doubts about your doctor, you call me and I'll fly the best doctor in—if I have to comb Europe, Asia or the rest of the world to find him."

Startled, she looked up, suspecting him of self-inflation but finding that he was very sincere. "I think we have the best," she said quietly. "But thank you."

"If you have any doubts, you let me know." He smiled and, taking a long swallow of his drink, added, "Did I see a tower when I drove in?"

"A small one."

"If it's possible, I'd like to see it later on—get an idea of how it's laid out. I'm designing a new home outside of Houston and I like the looks of it."

"Why not right now?" she suggested. "We have about ten minutes before dinner is served."

"I'd sure appreciate that," he accepted in his soft drawl.

She felt Luke's hard gaze on her as she led Will Turner from the room, and with a defiant tilt to her head she refused to look his way. He could think what he wanted to, she thought angrily.

When they entered the tower room a moment later, Will Turner gazed around with patent approval. "This is your room, I see."

"Is it so obvious?"

"It's warm and caring. It has heart. Yes, it's very much like you." She no sooner had wondered, appalled, if he was making an approach, when he added discerningly, "That's a fact—not a pass." Without waiting for her reaction, he crossed to the drawing table. "Are you an artist?"

"I once did portraits."

"Once?"

"The children take up a great deal of time."

His eyebrows lifted. "There's always time for the important things."

"Is there?" She thought of Luke and his responsibilities.

"Yes." There was no compromise in the single word, and as her eyes flew to his, he said, "I learned that the hard way."

"How?" she asked, knowing somehow that she could.

"Two years ago my wife became suddenly ill. It was a rare blood disease. There wasn't a thing my money or power could do. I dropped everything and spent every minute with her trying to make up for all the times I was busy wheeling and dealing. Six months wasn't long enough for me. If my daughters weren't visiting friends this weekend, I wouldn't be here."

Sara said nothing, and staring out the window at the distant lights of the city, she wondered if Luke had said something. Yet, why would he? Why, she sighed without thought.

"Funny thing," Will Turner said. "We married for all the wrong reasons. I wanted her because she was the most beautiful girl I'd met. She wanted the triumph of catching the most eligible bachelor. And... we fell in love."

"I'm glad," she said simply.

"You would think that a scientist and an artist would never team up, either. Yet, looking at what he's put together in that lab of his, I can see Luke's creative, also. I'm impressed, and I look forward to knowing both of you better."

Beginning to feel as though someone had primed Will Turner, she mumbled something, adding, "Perhaps we'd better start down."

He smiled slightly and without demur led the way.

When they joined the others again, she was laughing at a ridiculously tall Texas tale that Will had trotted out for her. Her laughter died, however, when her eyes met the smoldering anger in Luke's dark regard.

Feeling suddenly flat, she murmured to Will, "I'd best check on dinner. If you'll excuse me?"

"Of course!" was all that he replied, yet something in his expression told her that he had noted Luke's anger, and she flushed slightly as she left him.

As the evening progressed, Sara found herself feeling as if she were trapped in some dreadful play that had to be acted out. Beth clung to Paul's side as if afraid of the scarlet woman, and Jessica proceeded to spread her charms between the wealthy Will Turner and Luke like so much whipped cream.

Except for Elijah and the visiting Texans, Sara decided detachedly, all the men were angry for some reason or other. Rufus with Jessica. Paul with Beth. Luke with herself.

Realizing this, she also discovered that she did not care. She only wanted the evening to end before the toothpicks of propriety collapsed and all the simmering emotions erupted rawly.

Dinner passed under Luke's cold warning eyes as he held command over everyone, though the majority of his time was spent in whispered conversations with Jessica or discussions with the vague physicist who seemed to waken only when talking with him.

Elijah also said little, but Sara barely spoke at all, avoiding everyone's eyes. When she did reply to a remark, she had no idea seconds later what she had said and only reached for her wine to sip it continually.

Grey moved between and around them, casting satisfied looks at Luke and Jessica's dark heads, which were so often tipped toward each other. Jessica was the anointed one, and Sara was the intruder—forever under suspicion.

Her eyes lifted from her wine to encounter Beth's, only to have Beth look hastily away, her fair skin reddening slightly. Hurt by Beth's joining the pack against her, Sara wanted to rise and leave, to pack everything and run and run and run.

Instead she plowed through the evening until near the end when Will Turner and his associate left, followed by Elijah retiring to his rooms. No longer able to bear it all, she slipped away to the den.

There, the fire burning low, she opened the French windows to the garden and stood in the soft cool darkness breathing in the sweet night air, seeking strength and feeling oddly fuzzy. She shivered.

"Cold?" Paul's voice said behind her.

"Tired, to be honest. Tired of everything."

"Come inside. We haven't even had a chance to talk together."

She half turned, looking up at him and finding that he was, after all, the same reliable, easygoing man she recalled. "I thought you were avoiding me."

"I was."

"Why?"

He shrugged.

"Where's Beth?"

"Chatting with Luke. They won't miss us."

She said nothing, turning to look into the dark night again.

"You've changed," Paul finally remarked.

"I'm no longer the naive, optimistic fool that I once was. Surely you know about all my sins?"

"I never believed it."

"Luke did," she replied, wishing that Luke could have said Paul's words as calmly and certainly.

"You have a chance now," he said after a pause. "To heal the breach, to—"

"There's no chance, Paul," she replied unevenly. "I could never live with a man who couldn't trust me, who thinks every man I talk with is another target for me, and who hates himself for even being attracted to me."

Paul's fingers slipped under her chin, turning her face toward him. The soft light of the low fire and the single lamp on Luke's desk inside the room showed only compassion in Paul's eyes as they searched hers.

At last he murmured, "You poor soul. You had to go and love a man who is afraid of love." When she could only stare back at him, he sighed and then smiled crookedly. "Are we still friends, Sara? You need a few, I think."

She nodded slightly, wanting to ask him more, more about what he had said of Luke, but all she said was, "Friends."

"Friends it is. You'll make it, Sara. You have to. I care for both of you." His head bent and he dropped a light kiss on her forehead.

"Paul?"

Beth's soft and uncertain whisper straightened Paul abruptly to look to where his wife stood, her face pale as parchment.

But Sara's eyes passed Beth to where Luke loomed behind her in the doorway. Facing them in the thick silence, she read their expressions, each condemning her in a different way; Beth with the naked pain in her eyes revealing her verdict, and Luke with cynical contempt in his.

"It was the gesture of a friend!" Sara said bitterly. "One of human comfort—not that an adulteress convicted by her husband's lack of faith would be believed."

"Sara, don't!" Paul intervened.

"Why shouldn't I say it?" she cried out. "Everyone is thinking it. Why—" She broke off as Jessica, with Rufus trailing her, strolled into the den.

"Is something wrong?" Jessica asked with ill-concealed satisfaction.

"Shut up, Jess!" Rufus snapped.

Facing all of them, Sara wanted to quit. She was alien. Even Paul's simple gesture of comfort was warped by their perceptions. Her gray eyes met Luke's dark ones. "Why," she asked hoarsely, "did you force me to come back? I was content! I wanted nothing from you. Nothing—"

"That will do!" Luke ordered as if she were an employee who had stepped out of line.

She did not move, her gaze locking angrily with Luke's unheeding all of his unspoken warnings.

"Sara," Paul said quietly, his fingers touching her arm lightly, "let it go. You're upset to the point of—"

She shook off his hand. "Don't touch me, Paul! You'll filthy yourself! I'm not allowed friends. I'm a pariah."

"I think," Luke said with threatening evenness, "that you've forgotten how potent a few drinks can be at this altitude."

Sara faced him at bay, and then suddenly she was drained. Wondering why she was even fighting back against such hopeless odds, she said tonelessly, "If you will all excuse me..." and walked out.

By the time she reached her room, her throat ached with tears. Sinking onto her bed, she stared at the floor numbly, aware of only a deep humiliation, and of a terrible ache she did not want to identify. When a knock on the door sounded, she did not move.

The knock was repeated, and her head lifted warily.

"It's Beth, Sara. Please...."

Even as Sara said, "Go away," the door handle turned and Beth walked in. She shut the door quietly behind her.

"Don't bother, Beth," Sara said without spirit. "I'm not a threat to you or anyone. I just want peace."

"I know that—now." Beth flushed, and moved to sit on the edge of the bed beside Sara. "But I thought you were. I like you, and yet...." She shrugged with clear embarrassment.

"I knew."

"But I knew only that Paul was close to you once. There were...hints that you and he—"

"We were friends. He was the older brother I never had, and Luke's best friend. My one friend in a place of strangers."

"Oh, damn!" Beth groaned. "I've been an ass! We've never seriously quarreled until I heard you were coming back and told Paul that if he.... I'm sorry, Sara. Honestly sorry."

"It's all right," Sara said dully, and started to rise.

But Beth's hand forced her back. "Sara, you need friends! And you have at least two now—Paul and me. Without reservations."

"I don't need anyone! Oh, God, why did he force me to come back?"

"Because he can't forget you," Beth said softly.

Sara shook her head, rejecting it. "No!"

"Only a year ago Luke stopped by our place looking haggard. I thought it was the conference in Boston he had just returned from, but when I walked in with coffee, he was sitting with his hands cupping his face and saying with a real despair that he could not find you. He didn't know where else to look, but he had to keep looking."

"He wants revenge—only revenge." Sara rose abruptly.

There was a silence, and then Beth asked, "Sara, you implied downstairs that you weren't guilty."

The question hung in the air as Sara fought the impulse to admit guilt simply to end everything, but with a sigh she nodded. "I wasn't guilty. But I can't prove it, and never will be able to." She met Beth's sober gaze. "Were you offering friendship because you believed I wasn't guilty?"

"Either way, Sara. What you might have done five years ago, I don't think you could do now. I've come to truly like you, and liking you has given me a lot of trouble with my jealousy. But...." Beth frowned. "Haven't you ever wondered why Luke won't believe you?"

"Facts," Sara answered harshly. "Jealousy and a

single condemning situation. Circumstantial evidence. Luke's religion is science and facts. Now all he wants is revenge."

Beth went to Sara and hugged her with all of her normal spontaneity. "You're wrong, you know. But you are in no state to listen. For now, come downstairs with me. Rufus has hauled Jessica away, just after you took off. And I want Paul to know not only that I'm sorry, but also that I know I was wrong and we're friends."

She wanted to refuse, but she could not turn from the appeal in Beth's eyes; nor from the knowledge that sooner or later she had to face Luke, and it might as well be sooner.

They entered the living room together, and Sara saw Paul, who was standing alone by the fireplace, look up at Beth. Slowly the smile in his eyes reappeared, and she knew that at least their world was in balance again.

Her world, however, not only was out of balance but also was about to be violently tipped further, from the tight expression in Luke's face as he stood watching. It was with an effort that she managed to smile and say the proper words as Paul and Beth took their leave.

By the time the front door closed behind them, she was hovering between dread and anger, uncertain which would win.

Luke, though, did not hover or delay. His hand immediately fastened on her arm, and she was propelled toward the den with, "We are going to talk. *Now!*".

Once inside the den with the door closed, he spun her around sharply with easy power and demanded, "Why did you ask Jess to bring Rufus?"

She stared up at him, words clogging angrily in her throat.

"Don't both thinking up lies, Sara," he warned.

"I did *not* ask him, or tell her to bring him!"

"She called you, and you told her—"

"No! She called to say that she was bringing a friend, not who it was!"

"You're lying!"

She stilled, her arm aching in his grip and tremors racing through her. "I am *not* lying, Luke."

With a muffled expletive he pushed her away, so roughly that she staggered backward and, losing her balance as her legs hit the edge of the chair, fell awkwardly onto its upholstered cushions.

As she stared up at him towering over her, her heart thudding, she cried in desperation, "*Why?* Why do you always believe everyone—anyone—else?"

"Sara, Grey was *there*. And you told her that he would be coming!"

"That someone would be coming, but not that it was Rufus!" At his expression she added, "But of course you'll believe a servant before me! Oh, God, Luke, since the day we met you have just *waited* to be betrayed. How pleased you must have been when it seemed that you were right."

Paling visibly, Luke leaned over, his hands taking her shoulders in a powerful grip and shaking them. "And I *was* right!" he ground out, the lamp's light sculpting his face into a harsh blend of dark shadows and tanned skin. "You never gave a damn about me!"

"I did. I loved you with desperation. You were my world." Her voice dropped as she added tiredly, "But you couldn't trust me."

In reply his hands tightened on her shoulders, and she moaned involuntarily. Instantly he released her and stepped back. "You expect me to believe that? That it was all my fault? After tonight's performance with every male in sight?"

"I was polite, and with Rufus, I had as much chance of avoiding him tonight as you gave me when you hauled me in here."

"Of course."

For a long second she stared up at him, and then matching rage rolled through her. As it crested she pushed out of the chair, rising to face him taut with her own fury. "You hypocrite! You talk of appearances and then sidle around Jessica, chat up Beth and glare if I talk to any male. What did you expect me to do? Stand in the center of the damn room and stare at the ceiling?"

"Don't get flip with me, Sara! I'm not in the mood."

"That's just too damned bad! I'm not in the mood, either, for a father figure with a heavy hand!"

Her words were left to hang in an electric silence, and her eyes were suddenly locked with his in battle. She refused to yield, holding his gaze defiantly, and yet as time stretched she found herself uncomfortably aware of the pulse throbbing in his jaw, of the thin angry line scoring his tanned cheek, and of, despite herself, the vibrant male power of him.

She found herself remembering how once they had fought as angrily, only to end their battles in each other's arms. How their tensions had found a different outlet, and it was these memories that made her eyes waver in the end. Even as they did, the sudden darkening of his eyes into fathomless black pools warned her that his emotions, too, were shifting.

Her breath fluttered, and her gaze slipped to the sensuous lines of his mouth. She wanted to look away. Knew that she should look away. Instead she felt herself being slowly anchored by a languor that stole the strength from her legs, rooting her to the carpet. With an effort she looked down at the Persian pattern with fixed intensity.

"It's still there, isn't it, Sara?" she heard Luke say with an odd softness. "Despite anything we do or say to each other, it's still there for us."

"No!" It was a breathless protest as the beat of her heart drowned all warnings. She wanted to run, yet could not. She wanted to speak, yet the dangerous heated faintness held her unmoving.

"Ah...Sara..." she heard him sigh. "Don't deny it."

His hands were gentle as they cupped her face, tilting it up, and she did not protest. She felt his lean fingers thread through her hair, pulling it loose of its prim knot at the nape of her neck, and although some distant part of her told her to break free, she stood as if bewitched by the touch of him, the dark magic of him.

When he brought her against the hard length of him with barely restrained violence her lips were parted, ready to join his, and a wild thick warmth rushed through her—through her breasts, through her lips, through every cell of her body.

She let him draw her even closer, and as she molded herself to him a sweet pain, like sun-warmed honey filling a comb, flowed within her until from the depths of her a dagger-sharp spike of desire knifed through her defenses and her body arched into his, reveling in his responses.

Luke's grip tightened, and the near savagery of his passion suddenly eased. His lips were no longer uncaring, but wooing, gentle, tasting, warming—teasing and arousing her until there was nothing left but the aching joy of releasing pent-up emotions as they embraced in the shadows of the dimly lighted room, the air laced with the scent of late roses from the terrace.

Involuntarily her hands moved to caress the rough silk of his skin, the dark tangle of his hair, and her body wakened once more to the deep pleasure she had always felt with him.

There was nothing in her world then but Luke and her need of him, and as her mouth and body demanded more, as an urgency to join with him dominated her, she felt his hand unfastening the front of her dress, moving within to loosen and push aside the flimsy barriers, until she felt the cool air on her skin, and trembled helplessly as his caresses moved to match her needs.

"Mr. Luke?" Grey's voice, sharp and high,

intruded rawly through the door without warning.

Sara started violently as if Grey had entered, and Luke's hands froze.

A second knock cracked on the door, and swearing under his breath Luke left Sara to move with long hard strides to answer.

Dazed, she watched him open the door slightly to tell Grey nothing was needed and to bid her goodnight.

But the few seconds allowed a cold sliver of sanity to pierce the hypnotic spell that was gripping her, threatening to blind her to everything but her emotions. Shuddering as if suddenly chilled, Sara backed away.

By the time Luke turned back, she stood behind the heavy upholstered chair, her fingers gripping its back with white-knuckled intensity. "No more!" she whispered. "We have to stop...."

He stilled, his whole body stiffening, his eyes black flames. "I'm not buying that, Sara," he returned softly, his fingers ripping his tie loose, his wide shoulders shrugging off his jacket.

"Luke, please!" she cried out. "I beg you."

Not even pausing for the slightest instant, he kept moving slowly toward her, his shirt opening to reveal the furry mat of his chest, and the embers of the fire giving his scarred face a satanic look as he reached out in passing and flicked off the desk lamp. "No more games," he said huskily.

"I'm not playing any...game." Her voice trailed into silence, and her fumbling fingers, which had only fastened a single button, turned numb.

"Good," he breathed, and as he paused to kick off his shoes, she backed away and tried to dart around him. With effortless ease he shifted his weight and, reaching out, captured her.

The instant his hands touched her, she fought. It was as if the contact triggered an explosion. For weeks and weeks she had been boxed in, her emotions confined as well as her freedom of choice, and suddenly all the anger, hurt and rebellion erupted as once again Luke caught and cornered her to where she was losing control of her own desires.

She flailed out wildly, and as his steel grip clamped her body to his, she pummeled his chest, gasping for breath, wanting to hurt and hurt and hurt.

Grunting as she succeeded in landing a punishing blow, he loosed his strength on her without restraint, and within seconds she was immobolized against the ungiving hardness of his body, while his one hand held her wrists behind her.

"Stop it, Sara!" he growled, and his free hand cupped the back of her neck, holding her head still as his mouth lowered with a mixture of fury and passion. The taste of her, the softness of her against him, banished logic, and his intoxicated senses demanded more.

Unable to move, Sara held herself rigid. The warmth of his mouth, the strength of him, left her shattered defenses straining to keep from collapsing completely, and her reasons for not giving in to herself or to Luke slowly scattered.

"Don't fight," he said hoarsely, his head lifting as he fought for breath.

Totally confused, her emotions in chaos, she ignored his words and made a last weary effort to break free.

The brief struggle ended with her on her knees, pressed backward against the seat cushions of the chair, her hands still pinned behind her by his unrelenting grip, and her slender body caught between his muscular weight and the chair.

As she gasped for breath her head fell back, and in that instant the strain of her position tore off the single button holding her dress together. Unable to move, she felt her dress burst open, spreading into a wide vee that bared her to the waist.

Luke's breath drew in sharply. She might have been lying wantonly before him, her hair a dark golden spill of silk over the seat cushion, and her breasts forced high as he held her arched backward until it seemed as though she were eagerly offering their fullness to him.

In the tense silence, broken only by harsh breathing, he seemed to her unable to move, and only his eyes plundered her. Then, with an odd hesitancy, his hand slowly moved to touch her with the lightness of a moth's wings.

Without haste the slight roughness of his fingertips traced an ever narrowing spiral on the soft skin of her breasts until they touched the sensitive tips.

Not all her anger or her willpower could prevent the shudder of sheer pleasure that rocketed through her, could quiet nerves suddenly screaming for his fingertips to return to the pulsing nerve tips, and a breathless, agonized cry escaped from her lips.

With a groan his head bent, taking what was quivering, pleading for his touch, his lips nipping, tugging, trailing until she was moving in ecstatic anguish, her principles lost and desire streaking through her in ever increasing pulsations.

"No...no...no!" she gasped, as much to herself as to him.

He drew back, his face flushed, his breathing harsh and his body trembling as he fought for control.

"It's wrong," she whispered hoarsely, and before she could muster a coherent thought to back her words, he was contradicting her.

"It's right!"

"Please...."

With a deep tortured sound he released her wrists and his hands cupped her head, holding it fast as his mouth claimed hers.

She clutched at him, her hands gripping his back, digging into the hard sinews, to prevent herself from falling, and as her breasts were crushed against the heated tangled mat of his chest, he buried his face in her hair.

"Oh, Sara..." he rasped with raw vulnerability. "I've been so lonely...so empty!"

In that instant she stopped fighting. She was utterly vanquished by the knowledge that she held Her Luke, her lost lover, in her arms again, and even though some part of her knew that he would regret it as a weakness later, she did not care.

She cared only, she thought cloudily as he lowered

her to the fur rug before the fire, about the joy of being with him again, of inhaling the arousing and musky male scent of him, and knowing once more the touch of him in all the warm and secret places of her quivering body.

She responded to him with a measure of passion that startled him. In his blurred mind he had expected reluctance or simply acquiescence. But it was as if she, too, had hungered for years; as if she....

He could no longer think, could only feel the softness of her, the ripples of response against him, and hear her small cries of pleasure. He found himself holding back, pleasuring her, slipping backward in time, and knowing without thinking where to caress, to kiss, to knead.

No longer holding a half stranger, but the man who knew her every sensitivity, Sara cried out helplessly as wave upon wave of sensation created endless explosions of piercing desire in every cell of her body, and when she was aching with exquisite excitement, he gathered her powerfully to him, and at last she was whole again.

With his heart beating beneath her ear, and an afghan throw covering them, she fell asleep in his arms.

She wakened with a drowsy erotic pleasure coursing through her body and the slow awareness that Luke's long lean hands were gently and sensuously petting her. Lazily she drifted in a warm sea of delicious pleasure, in an intimacy from their past, until the excitement within her could no longer be contained and with an urgent hunger she reached for him again.

The chill, the absence of Luke's warmth, wakened her the second time, and slowly she sat, pulling up the afghan to cover herself and blinking at the empty space beside her.

As her brain cleared, a flat despair took possession of her. She felt tawdry in the dull gray light of predawn. There was none of the laughter they had once shared upon wakening here or elsewhere in the house or grounds, or when they had tiptoed to their bedroom before Grey appeared for her day's work.

All there was now was a feeling of stale weariness. Had she seen any vulnerability in Luke, a glimpse of Her Luke? Or had she, she asked herself drearily, seen only what she had wanted to see, needed to see, to justify her own desires?

She raised her eyes to find Luke watching her, dressed but for his tie, which hung from one hand. He seemed an alien, withdrawn male, his face darkened by his morning beard, and his eyes cool and guarded. He was the Other Luke again.

It was a need to defend herself against the objective scientific appraisal to which he was subjecting her that made her say tonelessly, "Well... you've had your one-night stand with an adultress now."

He paled, a deep weariness seeping into his bones at her words. Not certain what he had hoped for, or perhaps feared, he said, "Sara, don't."

"That's what you feel, isn't it?" Her voice was hard.

"No. I...." He stopped.

"Then you believe I was innocent!" she pressed.

There was a grayness in his face, strain etching it. "I *want* to believe! Oh, God, I want to, Sara!"

"But... you can't," she finished heavily, her slim hope a corpse. Wrapping the afghan around her in a crude sarong, she said flatly, "Then, there's nothing. Sex alone isn't enough, and it won't happen again."

"We have more than sex," he said harshly. "There are feelings between us, too, despite everything."

"That's my part, Luke," she replied with a dry humorless laugh, his last two words telling her that he would never forget. "*I* was the one who believed in loving and caring. You are the logical one! You are the scientist," she cried angrily, "who scientifically condemned our marriage."

"Sara, stop it!" It was a command.

Ignoring it, she swept on heedlessly, "You just condemned me again with your 'despite everything'! But for all your contempt, you still didn't walk away last night!"

He did not answer, and that in itself told her that he had probably already dissected their hours together and now despised himself for losing his control.

Climbing slowly to her feet, wrapped in the afghan, she faced him. "You'll never understand, will you? I have principles, too! But you never saw that, did you? You saw only an artist among bohemians. You doubted from the first with your prim prejudices. You doubted my love! You doubted my fidelity. And you never, never really knew me!"

"Listen to me," he said with difficulty.

Her head shook vehemently. "No! Never again. I

listened once. I don't want a lover! If anything, I need a friend, and you don't know the meaning of the word."

"Do *you*?" he countered, stung.

"Yes...I think I do." As she drew in her breath for her next words, her hands clenched. "I can't go on like this, Luke. We'll find a place nearby, visit but live separately."

"We?"

He said it too softly, and her heart gave an unpleasant lurch. Her eyes were instantly wary, sensing the tension in him akin to that of a panther about to spring. Desperately she choked out, "The children and I."

His head shook slowly, his eyes harbors for cold fury, but again he spoke quietly, grimly. "We made a bargain, Sara. It holds."

"Luke—" She stopped, then cried, "Why? To punish me over and over for what I've never done? Luke...please! We can't go on like this!"

"We can and we will."

"No!" Her breath caught.

"Then leave, Sara. Our bargain provided that you could leave at any time. Alone."

There was no quarter granted. She faced him in a deadly cold silence. She had lost. She wanted to strike out, to fight, to run, and knew she could do nothing, for she was trapped by his blackmail. With a cry she turned her back on him and on the ungiving hardness of him.

For several seconds Luke fought to keep his own control as he faced the slim, half-bare line of her back, his eyes captured by the golden tangle of her hair.

He was aware of anger within him because he had used his power when she could not retaliate, as well as of an intense frustration as the desire to believe warred with the facts upon which his life was structured.

With a muffled expletive he pivoted and left the room without another word.

The door slammed behind him, and although Sara flinched, she did not turn, but stood listening to his footsteps fading away into a silence that still echoed with his ultimatum.

Only then did she turn, her defenses down, her eyes stricken. She felt unable to move, but finally, catching her breath on a sob, she propped her defenses back into place and with stiff movements retrieved her scattered clothing.

Twenty minutes later she stepped from her scalding shower and slipped on her staid nightshirt. Staring at her reflection in the mirror, at a face that looked tired but otherwise normal, she wondered why the past hours had not visibly marked her.

How strange passion was, she reflected numbly. It could be so intense, yet once spent, it seemed unreal. Almost as if someone else had participated in that wild and sensual dream. Not herself, not the proper young woman regarding herself soberly in the mirror.

An aberration. Her thoughts caught at the word. Yes, that was what it had been for both of them. Not loving.

Turning away from herself in the mirror, she was unwilling to admit any other feelings, needing desperately to denigrate what had happened or else the pain would be unbearable.

She crawled into bed to huddle under the covers, and as she lay there a slow-burning anger rose within her at her own stupidity and at Luke's cruel power over her life. Somehow, some way, she resolved, she would find a way to escape, and in the futile process of seeking that way, she fell asleep.

CHAPTER ELEVEN

"Oh, it's raining!"

"It's not! It's clouds!"

"It's rain!"

"Stop it!" Sara groaned as her mind crawled out of sleep to the daily weather report of the twins. In the silence that followed she was aware of an inexpressible anger stiffening her body, and then, remembering, she buried her face in her pillow wishing she did not have to rise, face Luke and attend church as if they were a normal happy family.

By the time they left for church, however, with a remote Luke by her side and the twins chattering away to Elijah about the fog, she had managed to don a calm exterior that belied the simmering interior.

She maintained that decorum throughout the service, but at its end had no memory of the sermon. Instead her mind had relived the events of the night before, an exercise that fueled a growing rage and sense of injustice as well as helpless frustration that not even the beauty of the music or mountainside church could smother.

Nor did it help when upon their return to Spars' Nest Luke's manner chilled and with a curt nod in her general direction he disappeared into the den.

Her back stiffened, and Elijah's eyebrows rose as, without commenting, he took the children off to his rooms and left her in the entrance hall alone.

Standing motionless with one hand on the newel post, she realized that her insides were trembling violently. Raggedly she sought to pull herself together before she lost all control and stormed into Luke's den in a display that would only inform him that her vulnerability had increased. Feeling much like a pressure cooker without a release, she lifted her hands shakily to press her fingertips fiercely to her temples while she drew in deep calming breaths.

One part of her wanted to confront him and not count the cost, and the other part of her was ready to put into effect one of the mad schemes for escape that she had planned as she fell asleep. Yet overshadowing any choices was the knowledge that for Toby's sake there was no alternative but to stay and bear it.

In that instant the den door opened, and Luke's dark and powerful frame filled the doorway.

His eyes swept her briefly, taking in the tense slender form in the trim green dress, her strained expression and the dark shadows beneath her gray eyes before he announced abruptly, "I'll be going to the office shortly for the day. I should be back by six."

She nodded warily, her hands dropping to clench at her sides as she sensed more to come. It came.

"And, Sara, should you be considering running off while I'm out, remember that only a few hospitals can help Toby. He'll need that help soon, and I would have no trouble finding you."

Or in taking the children, she finished silently. With a bitter frustration, knowing there was nothing she could say, she stared back at him, finding it difficult to believe that only hours before she had held him in her arms, had wanted nothing more for many heated moments than to be part of him, and that now he had reverted so completely into a cold stranger again.

One of Luke's dark eyebrows arched in mocking inquiry, as if he suspected her thoughts, and when her silence held, he shrugged and turned away. An instant later she once again faced a closed door.

For a long moment she stared at the door, nearly overpowered by the impossible urge to walk up to it and knock it down with sheer physical power. Then with a taut and angry movement she turned away and headed toward Elijah's rooms, where the children waited to go for their promised walk.

As she entered the room, Elijah darted one sharp look at her set expression and murmured, "Easy, girl!"

"I am not a horse!" Sara ground out between clenched teeth.

"Never thought you were," he returned mildly.

"Mummy?" Tricia pulled at Sara's hand. "Toby's blood is thin, isn't it?"

"It is not!" Toby said indignantly.

"It is!"

"Not!"

"Will you stop it!" Sara ordered. "Both of you!"

"But his blood *is* bad," Tricia muttered, letting go of Sara's hand.

Sara glared down at her female offspring, her temper fraying. "Don't you ever—*ever*—say that again!" Ignoring Tricia's suddenly wobbling lower lip, she added shortly, "Now both of you get upstairs and put on sweaters. We are going for a walk."

"But—"

"Now!" Sara said implacably.

"Mummy's angry," Toby whispered audibly as he followed Tricia from the room, and with a muffled exclamation Sara let them go and started stacking their toys with sharp movements. When she straightened, it was to find Elijah regarding her with evident compassion.

"I don't need pity," she whipped out. "Or advice."

"Just someone to shout at?"

Sara stilled, and then drawing in a shuddering breath mumbled, "I'm sorry."

"Ah, girl," he sighed. "I wish I were Merlin and could cast a special spell to help both of you. But if I've learned anything in life, it's that sometimes we have to work things out for ourselves. No one else can help."

"No," she agreed tiredly. "No one else can help."

Leaving the room, she walked slowly down the hall aware of rebellion still simmering within her. It was as if the emotions released in Luke's arms had also released years of repressed anger, and Luke's quiet and ungiving squashing of her was too much to bear.

She stopped in the shadows and was trying to quell her anger when the sound of Grey's scolding penetrated her thoughts.

Her head lifted, and hearing a protest in Toby's young voice, she was drawn to the kitchen to find that he was the object of Grey's wrath.

"What's wrong?" she asked from the kitchen doorway, her eyes moving from Grey's angry expression to Toby's flushed and guilty face.

"I have told him time and time again that the puppy is not allowed in the kitchen with muddy paws! I just mopped up ten minutes ago!"

Laying her hand on Toby's shoulder, feeling him trembling as he looked up near tears, Sara again had to brush back her anger before she prompted quietly, "Toby?"

"He ran in so—so fast. I couldn't—stop him."

Sara sighed. "You could have taken him around the house instead of through the house. Now Grey has extra work—and on a Sunday when she should be off. That isn't very thoughtful, you know."

His towhead nodded fiercely. "I'm sorry, Grey," he mumbled.

Grey nodded, not looking particularly mollified, and with a small push Sara sent him to get Tricia for their walk. "I'll meet you by the stairs."

She waited until he was gone, then met Grey's peculiarly colorless eyes coldly. "I don't care how much you dislike me, but take it out on me. Not on the children!"

"I'd not harm the children," Grey returned indignantly, and with more emotion than Sara had yet witnessed in the woman.

"Then where," Sara pursued, "did Tricia suddenly learn words such as 'bad blood' and 'cripple'?

Words that she has never used in her life toward anyone, much less her brother."

Grey paled. "I never—"

"Don't lie! It's enough that Luke believes your lies."

"I have never lied!" Grey choked out angrily, her face flushing darkly.

"Didn't you?" Sara challenged with matching anger. "What about the lies you and Jessica concocted? Lies that led him to driving us off the mountainside in a rage! Lies that destroyed our lives! You hated me the day I came, and you connived with Jessica to drive me away!"

"But I—"

"I hope you're happy with the results!" Sara continued, overriding Grey. "Luke has lost his children's first five years, he's—" Sara stopped abruptly, aghast as Grey's face twisted grotesquely. With a choking sound she staggered against the heavy wooden table, her hands clawing for support.

"Grey?" Her anger forgotten, Sara stepped forward to help the housekeeper sit, aware that she was suffering some sort of attack. "Keep still!" she admonished, and went for water.

"I'm all...right," Grey breathed a moment later, pulling away from Sara's supporting arm stiffly.

Straightening as if knifed, Sara stepped back. "Don't worry," she said tautly, "I won't contaminate you."

"Mrs. Driscoll...."

But Sara didn't wait to hear. She left the kitchen, and mocking herself for feeling hurt by a woman who had never liked her, she went to meet the children.

Toby's expression was uncertain as she approached, and eyeing him with exasperation she said, "Your sweater is inside out!"

"I was hurrying," he offered.

Shaking her head, her mouth grim, she bent over him and had just pulled his sweater back on when the front door opened.

Again without a knock or ring, Jessica entered. Closing the door behind her, she paused, and her eyes darted about like those of a reptile looking for prey until they settled on Sara's less than welcoming expression.

"Something upsetting you?" she asked, her dark eyebrows lifting while her eyes mocked.

Rising from where she had been crouching by Toby, Sara countered in a low even voice, "Why did you tell Luke that I asked you to bring Rufus?"

"Where is Luke?"

"I asked you a question, Jessica."

The icy blue eyes flicked past Sara, then returned as a cold smile touched the perfectly outlined lips. "Because you did ask. Did you expect me to lie for you?"

Meeting the other woman's eyes, her own frozen pools of wintry gray, Sara quivered as she suppressed the uncivilized urge to literally assault Jessica. She knew without turning that Luke stood in the doorway of the den behind her, watching and listening.

The knowledge made her quell her anger again, and reaching out to take the children's hands, she said only, "Tell Luke Grey's not feeling well."

As they left, the twins called back, "Bye, Uncle Luke!" confirming her impression of his presence. But she did not look back, and closed the front door behind her with controlled firmness.

Outside the leaves blew across the dry lawns riding a wind chilled by the overcast skies that turned the landscape into charcoal grays and dried ochers. With resolution she shook aside everything and set off at a brisk pace.

When they reached the fork in the road half an hour later, well above Spars' Nest, the children's protests as well as Toby's more pronounced limp slowed her pace until finally she stopped to let them rest.

As they sprawled on the grassy verge at the fork, she stared up at the right fork that led to where Rufus lived and painted in his studio home. The left fork dropped to the plains of Denver, and between a deep gully gouged into the mountainside.

Moving to the guardrail, she looked down to where five years before their car had plummeted into darkness. For a moment she half heard the tires screaming again, felt the jolting shocks to her body and remembered the horrible silence that followed. A silence broken when she had cried out for Luke.

But only silence had replied, and the crackling of the engine. Gathering strength that she had not known she possessed, she had crawled to him and dragged him from the wreckage as blood streamed down his face.

Not until he had groaned as his twisted leg slid free of the car had she been certain that he was alive. And despite the terrible accusations hurled at her even as the car had screamed off the road, she had held him, calling for help and praying desperately until at last, through the early-morning fog, help had come.

"Sara?"

Jarred from her memories, she turned to find Rufus standing beneath the ancient oak tree at the end of a path that she knew led, after a stiff climb, to the back of his property.

"You were remembering," he said quietly.

"Leave me alone," she returned. "Haven't you done enough?"

His eyes moved to the children, who were kicking up the dry leaves with Bumper, and when he spoke it was to say, "I have some things of yours that you might want to stop by and pick up."

"You have nothing that I could ever want."

She expected him to take offense, but instead there was only a cryptic smile, and he said half to himself, "I wonder if we ever really know what we want—or if we're all just blind fools groping our way through life."

"Rufus... please! Just leave me alone!"

"Perhaps I should—or perhaps I could mend it all somehow."

"I...." Her lips trembled, and she shook her head—not only because she knew it was hopeless, but also because she could not trust him ever again.

Before he could say anything else, she heard a car approaching at high speed from the road below, and turning from him she called out, "Toby! Tricia! Over here!"

In the few seconds that it took to pull the children

against the shrubs on the verge and hook her fingers into Bumper's collar, she found Rufus had gone and the car whipping into view. Brakes screeched and tires squealed as it shot toward the right fork, and even as she recognized the car, there was a confirming glimpse of Jessica's taut and angry face before the car surged past them.

"There's that lady we don't like," Tricia announced.

Only half listening, Sara watched the car disappear from view with a frown. Why would Jessica, obviously angry, go tearing up the road to Rufus, she wondered, and then was forced to look down as Toby pulled on her jacket. "What is it?" she asked.

"I don't like that lady. I don't like anybody," he replied fretfully.

She paused as another car came by at a slower speed, then asked him, "Not even me?" Her throat tightened when he nodded, a small hand creeping into hers. "Come on!" she said with forced cheerfulness. "Let's go home and have a hot chocolate before your nap."

"Will I get a hot choc'late at the hospital?" Toby asked.

"I think so."

"I don't think I want to go there. Even with hot choc'late."

"Why not?" She asked it casually, holding back anxiety.

"I don't know...." He shrugged.

"'Cause sometimes," Tricia contributed offhandedly, "you never come back."

"Uh-huh," Toby agreed. "On television...that boy didn't ever come back. His mummy cried a lot."

"You'll come back. I promise," Sara said, trying to follow the advice of the books she had been reading. "That was on television. A story like dragons, but not real."

"I don't want to go there," Toby repeated, his chin jutting.

"Very well, we'll tell Dr. Nan and Katy when we visit them."

Silence replied, and judging it best to leave it there, she said nothing.

They walked slowly, and eyeing the dull sky, Sara thought it was a gray day in every way. She had a feeling that it would never end, a feeling of being hopelessly trapped, and knew a desire to launch herself at someone or something and attack until she was exhausted enough to weep.

Instead she settled the children down for their nap and then restlessly paced her room, her thoughts pounding inside her head. Why, why had Luke insisted that she stay? How could they go on like this?

Her thoughts stumbled over the intense passion of the evening before, even as his cold flat refusal to release her incited the need to escape, to run, run, far away from the treacherous attraction of him.

Abruptly she stopped pacing, and reaching for her jeans and a pullover, she changed quickly.

Moments later, Elijah having agreed to watch the children if she did not return from riding by the time they wakened, she was on her way.

She would ride and ride, she determined as she

drove toward Paul's ranch, ride until the anger gnawing at her was exhausted, and then, perhaps, then she would find some way to live with the tomorrows ahead.

IN HIS OFFICE Luke rose from his desk, and glaring across it at his lab assistant, Mike Maguire, he growled, "We are in the business of precision! Facts—not guess-and-by-gosh or fingers in the winds—are how we find answers!"

"It's still a draft," Mike said stiffly. "If you hadn't come by today and asked what it was, I wouldn't have shown it to you yet."

Reining in his temper, Luke regarded the youngest and most promising member of his research team with something close to disgust before relaxing and smiling slightly. "It's rough, all right...but it's also brilliant, Mike."

"Then you think I might be onto something?" His rather serious face lighted up.

"If I don't watch it, you'll be sailing past me."

"Oh, no! It's just a refinement of your idea. It came to me while I was working out the efficiency equation on the project. Dr. Pettiway told me that you thought I was right on the target there, so I thought I'd go ahead and try developing this. On my own time, of course."

For a moment Luke was startled, for Jess had said nothing about Mike's contribution and he had assumed that it was her own idea. Frowning, he pushed the thought aside for a moment and said, "If you have some time now, let's go over this together.

You need to establish your controls and parameters. Without precision and pinning down facts, not generalities, you'll have only an idea with no place to go."

It was an hour before Luke surfaced, finding that the ease with which his mind synchronized with his team member's had resulted in an intense exchange of concepts.

An hour during which uncertainties had become certainties through the application of trained minds, through seeking and using verifiable facts and measurable forces and materials; and during which objective reality had reigned.

A finely designed electronic system did not function on feelings. It did not care if its operator was good or bad as a person, of high or low status. Its successful operation depended on efficient design, with components accurate to the thousandth degree, and on its being put through its paces with regulated order. It had no feelings.

Emotions, whether in a lab, a shop or on the production line, led to accidents—even disasters.

His was an orderly world, he told himself, and one that had satisfied him until Sara had entered his life.

"Sir?"

Blinking, he returned his attention to Mike. "I think you have enough to go on now. If you need anything, you're welcome to the use of my library here at any time. Keep me posted, too, Mike."

As soon as Mike had departed, Luke rose restlessly and stood at the window. He felt bone-tired and knew that carrying his normally intense workload in addition to making time for Sara and the children was beginning to wear him down. A choice was approaching, he reminded himself grimly.

Will Turner might well be the solution, too, he thought, if not without a degree of resistance still ingrained in him.

With a brooding gaze he eyed the factory complex and research labs that lay before him, solid buildings housing workers who put out quality work, a place into which he had put years of his life.

For what, his mind suddenly taunted. He had almost lived here for the past years, and if his project succeeded, millions of people might have cheap energy.

A noble accomplishment, he sneered mentally. He was a successful man. And a man whose son and daughter called him "uncle." A man who was not even certain his children were his. A man who could not break free of the woman who had betrayed him.

His hand cupped the back of his neck, rubbing stiff muscles as he stared toward the spot where Spars' Nest was rooted in the mountainside. She might already be gone, he told himself bleakly. She might have realized that he had been bluffing.

Sara. He drew in a sharp breath, closing his eyes briefly, then opening them to stare blindly out the window. There was a need for her in his life that he knew was rapidly growing beyond his control—a control that he had lost with her in his arms.

Other men, and women, had come to grips with infidelity, he reflected wearily. If only he could.... A violent surge of revulsion, passionately emotional, rejected even the thought. He was helpless against it, and he tried desperately to reason his reaction away, knowing there was no future worth a penny unless he could defeat his past.

His face drawn, he lifted his eyes to the bruised clouds drawing nearer; snow clouds, yet reminding him of the day that he had found Sara again in Key West, of the booming thunder and driving rain as he had faced her fury. She had fought him then, and now—

"Have a minute to spare?"

Luke turned, arranging his face appropriately, and nodded to his security officer. "Come on in, John. What are you doing in on a weekend—looking for spies under the rug?"

"That's it!" John agreed with a grin. "Or close enough."

Luke's eyebrows rose a fraction. "Any luck?"

"Just finished a sweep on electronic surveillance, and we're looking clean."

"At least there are fewer chances today that someone will ask, 'What *are* you doing?' " Luke said with amusement, aware that it had happened despite each area's being informed shortly before a sweep, in writing, to treat the sweep team as if it were invisible, so that should there be any electronic eavesdropping, the listeners would not be warned of a security check.

"Once in a while," John sighed, "someone doesn't get the word. With the higher threat level, however, we'll do everything possible to make sure there are no slipups."

"Anything else going on?" Luke probed.

"A few reports of overfriendly, overinquisitive strangers at a couple of the local hangouts. We checked them all out, despite knowing a security alert tends to stimulate imaginations. In this business it's ten years of dullness and two hours of panic." He paused. "Are you considering teaming up with Turner?"

"I don't know," Luke admitted. "We're talking." His eyebrow asked a silent question.

"Yes, I checked him out, though I'm already familiar with the Turner conglomerate's security operation. It rivals the KGB in efficiency, and it's backed with a budget that makes me drool with envy."

"What about the Turners?"

"Hard, shrewd and about as honest as you'll find. They're not above a Machiavellian scheme to redress any wrongs they incur. A swindler who took them for a cool million found himself swindled in turn, losing his million from them plus another million. They gave the extra million to a children's home."

"The grandfather is an old friend of Elijah's who—" He broke off as the phone rang, and with a muttered, "Excuse me," he answered it.

"Luke?" Beth's voice asked, and immediately rushed on, "Sara's gone mad! She's...." Beth gulped for air, and Luke went gray beneath his tan.

"Is she all right, dammit?"

"I don't know! She arrived in a tearing rage. The next time I looked up from my baking, she had Black Storm! He's thrown her twice, and she just mounts again and heads him for another jump. Luke, it's *horrible*! Paul's gone and—"

"I'm on my way!" Pausing only to assure John that it was a personal family problem, he ran from his office, his breath knotted in his throat and a cold fear his shadow.

The object of his fears, ignoring Beth's pleas from the rail, tightened her knees as Black Storm rounded again on the bars with ground-eating strides that sent up geysers of dust as his hooves bit into the turf. Checking him, Sara then urged him into lift-off.

A split second later she knew that he would refuse again, and with a sense of futility that matched so much of her feelings since Luke had reentered her life, she knew that she was going to lose her seat.

She hit the soft dirt curled and relaxed, and rolled until she lay on her back staring into the cold sky and wondering what she was trying to prove. That she could control something, her mind replied.

"Sara! Are you all right?"

"Yes." Gritting her teeth, she rose stiffly and limped toward the huge gelding, who arched his neck as if excessively pleased with himself. She would not, she told herself savagely, quit. She would not—

"Sara, please don't!" Beth begged. "I don't care if Paul said you could ride him. You'll hurt yourself!"

"I won't get hurt. I told you, I know how to take a fall, and Paul would—"

The blare of a car horn snapped her head around. At the sight of Luke's low-slung car bearing down on her, a wild anger overtook her, and throwing caution to the winds, she ran for the horse.

His sudden fractiousness as Luke's car skidded to

a halt outside the ring delayed her, but she was in the saddle, trying to wheel the giant gelding around toward the ring rail, when Luke reached her.

His hand grasped the reins. "Get off! And now!"

"Get out of my way, Luke!"

"I said, get *off*!"

She glared down at him, trembling, covered with dust and grime, yet holding her aching body as straight as a cavalry officer's. "I'll do as I please! Take your damned hand off the re—"

He moved so quickly, she had no defense. His free hand hooked into the back of her jeans and pulled at the waistband hard and sharply, lifting her from the saddle. As her left foot hit the ground, he let her go, leaving her to fall awkwardly on her knees before him.

It was more than she could bear, and stumbling erect, she rounded on him. "I have ridden most of my life! I know what I'm doing!"

"Sara, he's only trying to stop you from hurting yourself."

"You're wrong, Beth," Sara replied bitterly. "He just wants me cornered so that he can stick pins in me and make me pay and pay and—"

With a choked cry Sara wheeled and ran from the ring to her car. She drove off with the gravel spitting from the back wheels, determined to outrace any pursuit.

But Luke did not pursue her or appear for dinner, and as the hours passed, Sara felt caught between renewed anger and relief. Unable to face Elijah's perceptive regard, she finally retreated to her tower room.

There she sat at her drawing table, unable to write to Madge as she had intended. Instead she pressed her forehead wearily into her palms, wondering what had made her ride that afternoon as if possessed. All her reasons seemed as blurred as the general ache of her body.

Restlessly she rose and moved to the window seat to sit staring blindly into the darkness. The memories were too strong. The feeling of his hard lips, the heated sweetness of his mouth, of her own loss of control, and of....

Drawing in a shuddering breath, she returned to the table and reached for her pen. She would write to Madge, and grope for the sanity and acceptable peace of Key West.

She was on the third page of her letter when she heard Bumper bark on the landing below, followed by a murmuring, and then slow footsteps on the stairs. They stopped near the top, and without turning, her pen stilled, she managed evenly, "What do you want?"

"To talk to you." He moved up the last steps, his eyes on the rigid line of her spine, the fair hair shining in the lamplight as it fell loosely down her back, and despite himself he found he was so conscious of her that his body went taut. "Are you all right?"

"Yes."

She still did not turn, and a pulse started throbbing along his jaw. "You could have crippled or killed yourself, Sara."

"Then you would have had the children, and I would have been free."

"We can't go on like this."

"Oh?"

"It's no good for the children or for us."

"So?"

His jaw tightened. "Sara, I do care."

"Bully!"

He stiffened. "What did you say?"

"I said—" she turned her head to regard him levelly "—bully."

There was a genuinely startled look on her face as he closed the gap between them in two long strides, hauling her out of the chair with effortless strength. His one big hand pinioned her jaw, the other drew her against him with a force that knocked the air out of her, and his head bent.

"Lu...." Her breath clogged in her throat as his mouth took and invaded hers violently. Desire seared her insides and her body arched involuntarily in response.

A fury rooted as much in fear of his anger as in the surge of fire in her own veins made her hand rise, and she struck out as hard as she could. The crack of her palm against the side of his head startled him enough that he jerked back, and taking advantage of it, she tore free to face him at bay.

"Don't ever talk to me like that again!" he snarled, his eyes pinpoints of black flame and the muscles of his neck standing out with strain.

In that moment it struck her forcibly that he was no longer the boy-man of their early days of marriage, but a full-grown male creature in a rage. Yet still her chin angled defiantly. "I have nothing—nothing—to say to you!"

His face still stinging, Luke regarded her with such frustration that he no longer knew if he wanted to strangle or love her. "We," he ground out, "are going to have a talk. Now!"

"Go to hell!" she tossed back, casting reason and caution to the winds.

To her surprise, he regarded her with a glittering intensity, then walked to the window and stood with his back to her. Perplexed, she let her eyes follow him warily.

After an endless time his hand moved to rub the back of his neck, and without looking at her he said quietly, "We at least agree on one point. We cannot go on like this."

"Nor any other way," Sara agreed tiredly. "Luke, it really would be best if we left."

He turned impatiently. "There are other alternatives. The children are ours, not just yours! Surely you don't still believe that I would warp them?"

"I don't know." The trembling within her was threatening to become visible. "All I know is that just before the crash...you said our marriage was a farce, and thank God that there would be no children tainted by my—" She stopped, biting her lower lip, angry at the tears threatening her.

Luke felt his face stiffen. The rage and violence of that dawn when the snapped steering linkage had sent them over the mountainside was still a nightmare to him, and her words hit him hard.

Involuntarily he stepped toward her, his hand going out, and she cringed away. His hand fell heavily to his side. "Sara, I was nearly crazed. It was the sort of thing you say. In heaven's name, I never meant it!"

"Didn't you?" she retorted with disbelief. Her eyes met his, catching the specks of gold swimming in their depths, and looking away she said flatly, "What does it matter now? It's all over, and digging up the body won't change anything."

Staring down at her, Luke felt the intense pull of her, and he wanted to say, "Sara, I still love you. The past doesn't matter." But it did. And risking betrayal again was more than he could do, for the doubts would gnaw at him and eventually eat away their marriage.

Sara bent and picked up her fallen pen. Straightening, she held it, staring at it, wanting to scream, "Let me go!" and instead waiting without knowing for what.

"Toby's surgery is only a few weeks away now," Luke finally said without expression. "With both of the children settled in, we can at least shelve our personal feelings until later. We'll talk about renting or buying nearby afterward."

"I won't need support from you. Madge will hire me back and—"

"I told you in Key West that you're still a Driscoll, and I meant it. I can't say the past doesn't matter, but we have the children to consider. They need us...a father as well as a mother."

"I've raised them well enough without you!"

"I'm not implying otherwise," he said, feeling suddenly drained. "You've been a fine mother, and no one could fault you."

He saw the quicksilver flash of surprise in her gray eyes before she looked down again at the pen she gripped tightly in her hand, and he added, "Do you think we could try with Toby's operation so close? What happened last night won't happen again."

After a long moment she nodded, all her anger gone and only a peculiar emptiness left.

CHAPTER TWELVE

Two weeks later, on a warm and quiet afternoon whose clear skies and gentle breezes denied that only a week earlier snow had cloaked the land for the day, Sara sat on a hillside above Spars' Nest feeling decidedly unsettled by recent changes.

Luke had become a stranger. He no longer mocked or challenged her. He was so distant and polite, in fact, that she felt as if she were a guest in a hotel. She told herself that the odd truce should have brought her peace of mind, yet it was inexplicably frustrating instead.

With a sigh she turned her head to check on the children playing in the tangled garden of the old ruined mansion behind her, and then almost unwillingly her eyes strayed to where Luke lay dozing on the grass nearby.

In the drowsy silence, broken only by the lazy chatter of the children and the occasional call of a bird, she studied him unguardedly.

He looked tired, she realized, almost haggard, so different from the Luke in whose arms she had lain almost in this very spot years ago. Her eyes shied away at the sensuous memories to return to the distant plains below.

However distant he was with her in the past weeks, she could not fault him on the warmth he showed to the children; in fact to anyone it seemed, but her.

After the stormy weeks preceding this sudden calm, she felt as if she had been battling her way through a hurricane and suddenly, without warning, the wind had ceased, leaving her floundering about awkwardly, trying not to fall on her face in confusion.

"Penny for your thoughts," Luke said idly.

Starting, she looked down to find his eyes still closed with their long lashes gold tipped by the sun. Her gaze shifted to the strong line of his jaw, to the thin scar marking his cheek, and somehow, inexorably, to his lips.

Flushing, she shifted her attention quickly to the golden leaves trembling on the branches of a nearby tree.

"Ten pennies," Luke persisted.

"I was thinking of Toby," she said hurriedly.

"Mmm," he sighed. "Only three weeks now."

"Two until the clinic program." She hesitated. "Luke, Toby's been fretting lately. Something about, if he has an operation, he won't come back. He got the idea from some television program."

Luke frowned, and pushing himself up to sit beside her, he joined her in staring at the plains below. "What have you said to him?"

"I haven't made fun of it, as Katy advised, and I've promised him that he will come back. As I never make a promise to them that I don't keep, and he knows it, that helped a bit. I've also told him television is just a story and we'll talk to Katy and Dr. Nan about it. I don't know what else to do."

"It sound as if you've done what can be done. Why don't you call the clinic tomorrow to warn Katy and see if she has any advice? Meanwhile I'll back what you've said if he brings it up with me. Okay?"

"Okay." Oddly enough, she felt better for the sharing, and then tensed slightly as she added, "You will be there? For the clinic program, as well?"

"I'll be there... come hell or high water."

His head turned, and as their eyes met there was a moment of silence between them that gradually became impregnated with a magnetic awareness. Without releasing his hold on her eyes, Luke shifted to rest on one hand, and his other hand moved to brush back a strand of fair hair from her smoothly tanned cheek.

She knew without words that he was remembering the times they had made love on this hillside, and she knew she should move, turn away, rise, do something—anything—but she did not.

Instead her breathing quickened, and when his mouth moved toward hers, so slowly that she could have run a mile away if she wished, she simply waited, her lips parting to receive him.

A thick flow of golden heat poured through her as his mouth plundered hers, and somehow she was lying down on the grass, the weight of him on her, his muscular thighs pinning her down, and resistance and resolve melting away.

When he raised his head his breathing was as unsteady as hers, and his pupils were dilated into pools of black velvet. With a sigh he shifted so that his lean hard length was stretched alongside her, and as he leaned on one elbow, his other hand traced a light line along her jaw.

"Luke...." She started as his hand brushed the tip of her breast and a sensuous shiver went through her. "The children...."

"And if they weren't here," he asked huskily, his eyes holding an unreadable message that went beyond his words, "what then?"

"I—"

The sudden howl piercing the quiet afternoon made them both start visibly. As quick as Luke was, Sara's instincts were faster, and she was already on her way toward the weed-covered and charred remains of the abandoned house from which the howl had originated, leaving him to catch up.

She found Tricia and Toby facing each other angrily in the middle of an arena of collapsed timbers.

"Tricia!" Sara's gaze swept the two small and flushed faces, and reluctantly Tricia lowered her fist.

"He hit me first!" she mumbled truculently.

"What happened?" Sara demanded.

"She said I'm stupid!" Toby choked out. "And I'm not!"

"Tricia?" Sara prompted in an awful tone.

"Well, he is! And it's not his cave just 'cause he found it first."

Sara's eyes went to the old rotting door frame leading to a cellar and returned to Tricia. "You were both told not to go poking in the ruins, and since when do you call your brother *stupid*?"

Tricia's lower lip jutted out. "Everyone says so... he's a stupid cripple!"

"No one says that," Luke interceded coldly as Sara sucked in a shocked breath. "Anyone who would has a crippled mind."

"That lady says so!" Tricia insisted, her lower lip trembling now. "That lady always says to Grey how awful he—"

"Stop it!" Sara said sharply. "I don't care what that lady said, she is wrong!"

"She's stupid!" Toby said with satisfaction. "Stupid."

"Yes, she is," Luke agreed quietly. "Now both of you go clean up the picnic papers. It's time to go home."

"But we found a cave, Uncle Luke!" Toby protested, backed by Tricia now.

"Now!" Luke repeated, without quarter, and after a quick look at each other, Toby and Tricia reluctantly trudged out of the ruins.

Sara did not move, but stood frozen by the realization that it had been Jessica's—not Grey's—words that Tricia had so often quoted. Jessica, who Grey had said often stopped by for a cup of coffee. With a tight fury she rounded on Luke. "'That lady' happens to be Jessica. That's what they call her!"

"I'll take care of it, Sara."

"*You'll* take care of it!" She shook with anger. "When I tried to tell you—"

"I know," he cut in coldly. "And now we both know. I'll see that it doesn't happen again, I assure you. Now let's go!"

He strode off, leaving her the option of either standing there fuming or following.

Their descent to Spars' Nest was silent. Halfway down, Sara took Toby on her back and Luke hoisted an equally tired Tricia onto his broad shoulders.

By the time they reached the rear garden, after climbing over rock beds and clutching at roots and branches to steady herself rather than ask for help, Sara had expended her anger, and she was unable to suppress a groan of relief as Toby slid off her back.

Her head lifted to find Luke glaring down at her, his dark eyes snapping. "Why didn't you tell me you needed a rest?" he demanded.

"I'm perfectly fine!" she insisted stiffly, and panting still, added, "It's only the altitude."

"You're exhausted...and I'm yelling," he returned with a sudden gentleness that nearly undid her.

"I'm all right...really," she muttered, her eyes dropping.

He took her hand and helped her to her feet, but instead of releasing her he pulled her to him. There was the briefest touching of their bodies and the lightest brush of his lips against hers before she could summon her senses to order.

A giggling about knee level made Luke peer down. "Yes, I kissed mummy, and now it is your turn!"

"Not me!" Toby objected as Luke bent and kissed Tricia lightly.

"Why not?"

"Boys don't kiss!"

"Men do," Luke returned with clear amusement.

Bending again, he kissed Toby's cheek, and grinning at his small son's confusion, he started off toward the house with two rather enchanted children trailing behind.

Standing quite still watching them, Sara knew that part of her no longer wanted to leave. Which was ridiculous, she informed herself instantly. What did it matter if he could be gentle with the children, and even with her at times, when there were other times when he was cold and unfeeling?

With something close to despair over her own muddled emotions, Sara slowly followed them in.

As it was Grey's day off, she paused in the kitchen to extract from the refrigerator a pot holding the finely chopped bits of a pound of mushrooms and a medium onion that she had sautéed earlier over high heat before adding a quart of chicken broth and letting it all simmer half an hour.

All that remained was to heat it, thicken it, add salt and pepper and then put in half a quart of milk, rather than the cream she used on holidays. With only the tossed green salad and oven-warmed French bread to prepare, she had little left to do for supper.

"Know what?" Tricia asked, wandering into the kitchen as Sara sliced half a green pepper into the salad.

"What?" Sara replied, taking the bait.

"Uncle Luke's awful mad at Grey."

Her hands stilled. "How do you know?"

"He looked mad. He went to her room and he's hollering."

"Oh, blast!" Sara muttered, and dropping everything, she headed Tricia sternly back to Elijah's rooms and hurried toward Grey's apartment above the garage, her thoughts flying back to the attack Grey had had only two weeks before.

Since then, another change in her life had been the lull in hostilities between Grey and herself, and the awareness on Sara's part that the housekeeper was not a well woman.

When she reached the open door of Grey's apartment, it was in time to catch the last few words of Luke's tirade.

"...and I won't have it! However long you've been with us, you—"

"Leave her alone!" Sara said sharply, entering the room to find Grey standing before a towering Luke looking pale and stricken. "It was Jessica, not Grey!"

"I'll thank you to keep—"

"Don't bother!" Sara cut in, ignoring the warning glints in his eyes. "Rip into your Madam Curie—not Grey!"

"I don't need help from you," Grey said stiffly.

"Well, you're getting it, like it or not!" Sara informed her shortly. "Now sit down before you fall down." The instant Grey was seated, Sara rounded on Luke. "Can't you see she's not well?"

His expression was a peculiar mixture of anger, surprise and chagrin, and had Sara not been so furious, she would have laughed. Instead she sent him for water and sat down across from Grey, who was trembling visibly.

"Never mind him," she told Grey, still cross.

"He's not used to being a father and he's only trying to defend Toby."

"I should...have stopped her," Grey whispered. "I tried...after you were so angry that day. I wouldn't hurt them—no matter what."

Sara said nothing as Luke returned with a glass of water, and as Grey drank she signaled him with her eyes to leave. Alone with the housekeeper, Sara recalled Beth's words. Once she had feared and resented Grey, but now she felt only compassion for an elderly, frightened woman.

"I'm no threat to you," Sara said tiredly. "We won't be here much longer. We can't possibly stay, for I can't let my children grow up here where I'm condemned for something I didn't do. It has already hurt them."

"I never said those—"

"I know," Sara sighed. "I admit that I thought it was you. But I should have known that however you...disliked me, you would never hurt Luke's children. But the past is like a poison in the air. Tricia never called her brother a cripple or talked of bad blood before, and some damage has been done. Toby was hurt. He hasn't any real defenses yet against cruel words."

Grey raised her eyes from the glass she clutched tightly, and with clear difficulty she said, "I should...have stopped her. I'm...sorry."

"I'm sorry, too," Sara replied gently, and couldn't help wondering if her own life might have been different had Grey, with her iron loyalties, befriended her. Rising, she pushed back a stray wing of hair and asked, "Do you need anything? We're having soup and salad. I could bring you a tray."

When her offer was refused, Sara nodded and left.

Luke was waiting in the kitchen, lounging against the counter, the set of his broad shoulders warning her he was still annoyed.

Ignoring him, she checked on the soup and then started melting the butter and measuring the flour for the thickening.

"No comment?" Luke murmured from directly behind her, making her start slightly.

"As far as I'm concerned," she said stiffly, "you can push Jessica into a pit of vipers to join the rest of her relatives, but hitting out at an old woman who would give her life for you is just plain rotten!"

"Really?" It was silky.

She drew in a sharp breath, and stirring the thickening into the soup jerkily, she snapped, "Really! And you should know better at your age!"

There was a fertile silence behind her, and then a ludicrously meek, "Yes, mummy."

She stilled, then turned to glare up at him. But the sight of his twitching lips and shaking shoulders undid her.

Suddenly they were both laughing helplessly, and before they could sober, the children were there, grinning and not understanding why their adults were convulsed with laughter, but enjoying it anyway.

Laughter that seemed to lead naturally into a warm happy evening during which time was suspended as Luke teased the children, and everyone, including

Elijah, helped wash up after supper, making chaotic fun out of a simple chore.

Lying in bed that night and looking back on the day, Sara almost wished Luke had gone to work instead of spending the afternoon and evening with them. It had been like tasting, ever so briefly, a dream wherein they were truly a family, and the knowledge that there could never be a reality made the sweetness sour.

IN THE DAYS THAT FOLLOWED she saw little of Luke, and although she knew from Elijah that he was crowding his days in order to be free the week of Toby's operation, she half sensed that Luke was also avoiding her.

Their truce held tenuously, unstrained by his slightly distant manner during the two hours he was home almost every evening for dinner. A time he spent with the children, and with Elijah always present, before departing again for his office and lab.

He said nothing about Jessica. It was only days before they were to attend the hospital orientation program that Sara learned through a remark from a less hostile, though not precisely friendly, Grey that Jessica no longer dropped by for a chat over coffee.

There was something in the housekeeper's expression as she had made her remark that left Sara wondering if Grey and Jessica were on less than amicable terms, but she could not bring herself to probe, and without comment she left to seek out Jeannie and the children.

At that moment Luke stood in Jessica's office

waiting for her secretary to locate her. His expression grim, he assessed the framed magazine interview hanging on the wall of her office.

In an odd way, he reflected, the day the article had been published had marked the beginning of all the recent changes in his life. It had been the day that he learned of the security leak, and the day that he returned to find Sara's portrait in his grandfather's sitting room.

His attention shifted to the slim folder he held, and his face hardened. His normally relaxed working relationship with Jessica had been strained since he had asked her to stay away from the house until after Toby's operation, despite her denial of guilt. Now this had come up, and he found his image of Jess was shifting significantly.

"What is it, Luke?" Jessica asked, entering her office with her white lab coat flaring as she crossed to her desk. "Is anything wrong?"

"I've just finished reading this." He tossed the file onto her desk, watching her narrowly as she slipped on her reading glasses, and catching her sudden tension as she recognized the file. "I strongly disagree with your evaluation of young Maguire."

Her finely arched eyebrows lifted as she slowly sat down. "But, Luke, he is quite competent. Why should you disagree?"

"I'm disagreeing with your quite damning faint praise. He is not 'quite competent,' Jess, he is brilliant."

"Brilliant!" she repeated. "Oh, really, Luke! Whatever makes you think that?"

"The fact that he devised the improved efficiency ratio for the system, he straightened out the feedback tangle, put me onto solving that skew we had, and is now working on an idea that may completely solve the stability problems." He paused, his eyes hard. "If that is merely 'quite competent,' may I ask what you have done to surpass it?"

She paled visibly, her eyes dropping to the file before her as her fingers nervously aligned it on the desk.

After regarding her bent head a long moment, he continued harshly, "I suggest that you think it over and forward a revised evaluation to me within the next two days. To keep young Maguire's respect, you might also recommend that his salary be upped."

"Very well." It was toneless.

"And, Jess, if Maguire should find working conditions suddenly unpleasant enough to consider leaving, I just might have to offer him your job."

Her eyes flew to his with clear shock. "Luke...you can't!"

With a disgusted shake of his head he replied, "You're not the first supervisor to stifle a promising subordinate, Jess, but let me warn you, in the long run you'll destroy your own career. It's time to stop petty tactics or I'll stop them for you."

"If you want me to re—"

"At this point," he cut her off, "take it as a lesson learned. I can tolerate almost any mistake—once. The second time the same mistake is made proves either rank stupidity or inborn dishonesty."

"It won't happen again."

"Be sure that it doesn't," he warned her. "Because I will find out, and you would be wasting your own talents on petty politics."

"Luke, I—"

"Just ask yourself where you would be now, Jess, if I had treated you that way." He pointed to the magazine article framed on the wall. "You wouldn't even have that, much less your position now. Think it over carefully."

Not waiting for her reply, he strode out, reaching his office as a call came in from Will Turner. As a result he spent the remainder of the afternoon closeted with Ralph Beaumont discussing the call, and then skipped dinner to make up the lost time.

It was nearly midnight when he arrived at Spars' Nest. Elijah's lights were on; Sara's room and the tower were dark. On reaching Elijah's rooms, he put his head in the doorway to find his grandfather watching a late film on television.

"I'm going to wash up, grab those sandwiches Sara said would be waiting for me, and a beer. I'd like to talk something over with you if you're not too tired."

"Bring me a beer, too," Elijah retorted, "and don't give me any of your looks. The doctor said a drink a day will keep him away."

Twenty minutes later Luke relaxed into the deep chair opposite Elijah, and feeding Bumper a tidbit, he said, "Will Turner called back today. They are officially interested."

Elijah grunted. "What terms?"

"Ralph's drafting them already. Driscoll Electronics will become a corporation. You and I remain majority stockholders. I'll retain control, but be free to concentrate primarily on developing the system. Royalties will be split, the percentage to be agreed upon. That's it roughly."

"Is it what you want?"

Luke stared at the tips of his shoes and then said slowly. "Yes. If we can agree on terms."

"And if Sara leaves?"

A pulse throbbed at Luke's temple before he said shortly, "I still want time for the children."

Elijah only grunted in reply.

"Buck Turner will contact me when he gets back from Europe, and Will wants to be present with two of his team for the grand finale—the final tests and operational demonstrations. We'll have to cover ourselves with them present. Legal agreements go only so far. How far can we trust them?"

"If Buck Turner tells you he'll respect confidentiality, regardless of how the trials work out, it is worth more than the finest legal document on earth."

"That's definite enough," Luke conceded. "John Gordon says he is honest, too."

"Buck has his reasons. When I first knew him, fifty or so years ago, he walked very close to the edge of the illegal in his hunger to build an empire. He wanted desperately to be someone."

"He certainly succeeded."

"He was doing well when he fell in love with Hannah's cousin. Martha was a gentle young girl who loved him unconditionally, and he became more ambitious than ever. When she was expecting their first child, Buck pulled off a quasi-legal deal that in effect stole a huge block of oil rights from hundreds of people."

"And Martha found out," Luke said dryly, not without a touch of cynicism that brought a scowl from Elijah.

"The day he closed the deal, his wife met him at the door in tears. People had been banging on her door all day, begging her to help them, to speak to Buck. She was in shock, and before she could even finish pleading, she collapsed."

"Did he lose her?"

"He lost his firstborn son. Her life was uncertain for a long while. He swore to her then that he would never cheat anyone again. She recovered, and he kept that promise. And as life will have it, a mind good enough to be that clever in crooked deals was good enough to make it honestly."

Luke was silent, then asked, "Is Martha still alive?"

"She died about eight years ago. Buck left retirement then and went back to building the Turner conglomerate with his son, grandson and now great-grandson. They're all raised to be honest, and any deal will be fair."

"Is he dealing because of old ties?"

"No, he listened because of old ties. In fact, you and Will Turner share a common ancestor, a great-great-grandmother. But any further decision is strictly business. Martha and Hannah used to visit, but I lost contact with them when Hannah died."

"Any advice?"

"I'll jot down a few ideas for you. One thing. Be sure to arrange it so that stock can transfer only to blood or adopted descendants, and that family members have first option on any of our original stock offered for sale by one of the family."

Luke's eyebrows rose.

"That way the worst a future fortune hunter can do," Elijah said, "is to share the income. The lawyers will know how to set it up right."

Nodding, Luke rose and stretched, too tired to worry about a future generation. "I think I'll take the pup for a walk and then turn in." He was at the door when Elijah spoke.

"Don't let her go, boy! We're a one-woman family—and Sara is and always has been your woman."

"Stay out of it, Elijah!" Luke said curtly. "You don't know it all."

"Then tell me!"

"No."

"You might have it wrong."

Luke shook his head wearily and without another word left. He walked in silence, ignoring the pup and trying not to think of Sara, of the times when she would suddenly hug the children and whisper, "I love you," to them, and he would feel a streak of jealousy that left him angry and disgusted with himself.

Cupping the back of his neck, he rubbed stiff muscles, and reminding himself that he had to be at work early, he turned back to the house. The next two days would be busy if he was going to be free to go to the clinic without anything waiting on him.

SARA WATCHED TOBY CAREFULLY as the day for the visit to the clinic approached, half expecting that he would balk at the last moment, even as she half expected Luke to be absent because of some crisis.

To her relief, neither eventuality occurred, and as they approached the clinic Toby was quite relaxed and had even acquired a slight air of self-importance that he seemed to think befitted the center of attention.

Katy met them at the door, and dropping to eye level, she said cheerfully, "Hello, there, Toby! I see you've brought everyone with you."

"We've come to see everything!" he informed her, making Sara's lips twitch.

"How nice! Then we had better begin right away." With that Katy greeted all of them and led the way through a corridor connecting to the hospital.

Along the way she paused often to introduce Toby and Tricia to various members of the staff. All of whom, Sara noted, not only placed themselves on eye level, but also touched the children as they told them what they did in the hospital.

"We'll stop by Dr. Nan's office first," Katy announced. "Is that okay with you, Toby?"

"I like her."

"And I like you, Toby, and you, too, Tricia," Dr. Nan said, coming up behind them.

Within minutes she had Toby on the table in her

examining room, asking him if he would pull off his T-shirt so that she could listen to his heart.

The request was another technique that Sara recalled from her readings. Having children help themselves as best they could, and also offering them choices as Dr. Nan's next question did, gave them a feeling of some control.

"Which ear," Dr. Nan asked, "should I look in first?"

Toby eyed the instrument she held with interest. "How does that work?"

"It has a light—" she blinked it on and off "—so that I can see inside your ear. It's a bit dark down there. When I finish, you can look in my ear, but not anyone else's! You could hurt them, and you can only do this in a doctor's office."

The examination took time, between Toby's and Tricia's questions and turns; and listening closely, Sara found herself completely engrossed. A glance at Luke told her that he was also impressed by the procedure that took away the strangeness of hospital equipment.

"Can I listen to mummy's heart?" Toby asked, having tried with Tricia, who giggled so much that he gave up in disgust.

"Go right ahead!" Dr. Nan told him with a smile in Sara's direction, and she proceeded to place the stethoscope for Toby against Sara's chest.

Toby listened, his head cocked, his tongue peeping out of the corner of his mouth as he concentrated. Then his eyes grew large with delight. "I hear it, mummy! Thum...thum...thum...." He looked up. "Could you make it go faster?"

Before she could find the words to reply, Luke's arm moved along the back of her chair and his fingertips nuzzled beneath her hair to tease the soft skin at the nape of her neck.

"You did! You went faster!" Toby cried, spinning to tell Tricia, while Sara flushed despite herself, aware of the doctor's amusement and even more of Luke's wicked grin.

"That was unfair!" she hissed at Luke a short while later as they followed Katy to the playroom.

"It was...interesting," he corrected unrepentantly.

Feeling peculiarly flustered, Sara had to make herself concentrate as Katy informed the children that they were all going to play doctor and patient.

When she opened a cupboard holding small green gowns, face masks and other paraphernalia, both children were instantly fascinated.

Sara knew they would be allowed to handle the blood-pressure arm band, another stethoscope and a thermometer, and to ask questions before Katy demonstrated how each item was used and explained its function.

When the structure play began, Sara saw Katy listening and watching carefully for any anxiety or misconceptions that might appear as Toby played doctor and then patient.

Half expecting his qualms about anesthesia to surface, she was startled to find that something quite different reared its head.

Toby was mimicking a doctor, and Tricia was his

patient, and he announced importantly that she was going to have an "op'ration."

"But my leg is good," Tricia protested, not quite caught up in the game yet.

"You were bad. After the op'ration you'll be good," Toby answered, and Sara stiffened. Instantly Luke's hand was on her arm in silent warning.

As if Toby had said nothing untoward, Katy asked, "But, doctor, why is an operation for bad people?"

"'Cause it hurts. And bad people always get hurt. On TV they shoot them."

"Don't good people ever get hurt on TV?"

"Yes," he agreed, "but bad people hurt them. Dr. Nan is good."

There was a logic to it, Sara had to agree, even as she wondered how Katy was going to work with his logic.

"Do you know any *real* people who had operations?" Katy asked. "Not on TV, which is makebelieve."

He thought, then looked at Luke. "Uncle Luke did. On his leg."

"Is he bad?" Katy prodded.

"I like him."

"Is he bad?"

"No..." Toby said, and was silent. Then, "Maybe he did something bad. Then after the op'ration he was good."

"Why not ask him?"

Toby hesitated. "Did you do something bad, Uncle Luke?"

"No," Luke answered casually, trying not to think of his rage that morning. "My car broke. It went off the road, and I hurt my leg."

"Oh."

"See?" Sara ventured. "And you're good, too."

"I like you lots," Tricia agreed, coming up to touch Toby's hand. "Operations are for good people."

Katy took over again and gently underlined that good people had operations, that operations were not punishments. And as the play continued, she occasionally slipped in another supporting comment, naturally reinforcing the idea.

There were other conversations, too, in which the children's perceptions were slightly twisted, and each time Katy quietly worked through the problem.

As they returned to Dr. Nan's office, Katy murmured to Sara and Luke while the children raced ahead, "If the question comes up again, be patient. Try to work through it by their logic, and don't—above all—tell them it's silly. Toby will lock it inside of himself, then. And it is not uncommon for children to think they're somehow being punished when they have surgery."

"He's said something about going to sleep and not coming back. But he didn't bring it up today."

"I noticed, and I was waiting for it after your call," Katy said. "He did get rather quiet when we talked about the special sleep, but rather than push it, we'll wait until he talks to the anesthesiologist after admission."

There were cookies and milk for the children, and coffee for the adults, when they joined Dr. Nan.

Listening to her skillfully drawing out the children about their play, Sara found herself glad that Dr. Nan had chosen years ago to take fewer patients and give more time.

"What is bad blood?" Tricia asked suddenly.

Although Sara went rigid again, and saw Luke's mouth tighten, there was only a flicker in the doctor's eyes before she said casually, "I don't know. I've never, ever seen any bad blood. Not ever."

"A lady said we have bad blood," Tricia insisted, and Toby looked up to watch Dr. Nan closely.

"She wasn't a doctor, then."

"No."

"And she does not know very much."

"I...I don't know," Tricia confessed.

"A doctor *knows*. I can tell your blood is good."

"You can?" Tricia asked while Toby still listened carefully.

"Oh, yes! I looked when I first met both of you, and I said to myself, 'What nice blood these two have! So very nice!'" She looked to Luke and Sara. "Don't they?"

"Very, very nice!" Sara responded, and as Luke echoed her, she absently noted that he moved uneasily, and dismissed it as encroaching weariness with the simple conversations.

By the time the visit was over, Sara found that she also felt reassured. Her hopes that she would be able to talk it over with Luke, however, foundered when he drove up to the front steps and directed the children to pile out.

As they scampered out, eager to join Bumper and

tell Elijah about their adventure, Luke made no move to leave the car and she turned to face him.

"Aren't you...?" She stopped, her eyes suddenly wary, as she recalled his cold and painful rejection the last time.

Luke's hand reached out toward her, to caress the softness of her cheek, and his mouth tightened when she flinched. "I'm sorry," he said, and saw she understood, even as he added, "I have to get back to the lab."

"Of course."

"Sara, I'd like to stay. But with a week left, there's a great deal to do. I'll try to get home early. It's the best I can do."

Her eyes searched his, and gradually the wariness within her was replaced by an awareness of him, of the thick silk of his dark hair, the scar slashing his cheek to the corner of his mouth, and the musky male scent of him.

Looking quickly away, she fumbled for her purse, and with a mumbled, "Perhaps I'll still be up," she bolted from the car.

The last sliver of a waning moon had already dropped behind the high mountains to the west when Luke returned. Looking up at the house as he drove in, he saw the windows of the tower and her room were dark, and was aware of an irrational disappointment despite the lateness of the hour.

Bumper greeted him, his short tail wagging hopefully. Eyeing his only greeter, Luke sighed, "Why not?" and left the house again to walk with the pup in the darkness.

As he walked, he found his thoughts returning to the day of the picnic, to the spontaneous laughter he and Sara had shared.

He had not laughed like that, he realized, since the early days of their marriage, and the realization was accompanied by an almost violent desire to somehow hold her, to keep her warmth and laughter in his life at any price—even as he knew that he could not meet her price, whatever Elijah hoped for.

He could not meet her eyes and say that he believed her innocent. Not with the evidence. Not with what lay hidden in the depths of his mind.

And yet he knew, his eyes bleak, that more and more he felt like an orphan on a winter's night, staring through a window at a family that represented all his soul yearned for—regardless of the strictures of reason.

Above him, from her darkened bedroom, Sara's gray eyes followed him as he walked slowly along the drive looking oddly lonely and vulnerable. She shied away from the impression and wished suddenly that he had not changed in the past weeks, that he had remained cold and unfeeling.

She could fight the Other Luke—his cruel blackmail, his ungiving reliance on facts—tooth and nail. But how could she fight Her Luke, the man who had called out to her as she had lain in his arms, the man who had laughed with her and who now walked so alone?

Drawing in a shuddering breath, she turned away from the window, wondering where it would all end for them, and what new scars she might carry by then.

CHAPTER THIRTEEN

FOR THE NEXT FEW DAYS Sara wakened each morning to the sound of Luke's car driving away at dawn, and lay in bed each night listening to him return in the early hours of morning.

The children missed his presence, Toby being particularly persistent in asking when Luke would be home, but Sara felt only a sense of relief, as if she were being granted a breathing space.

On Sunday afternoon, faced with two somewhat bored children, she conducted a training lesson for Bumper, much to the amusement of Elijah and the twins.

She was in the midst of the lesson when Luke appeared in the doorway, looking tired but interested in the proceedings as Tricia tried to mimic Sara's instructions to the puppy.

"Sit, Bumper!" Tricia cried excitedly. "Sit! Sit! Sit!" Nearby, Toby obligingly sat on the floor to demonstrate precisely how it was done.

Her lips twitching, Sara broke in to instruct, "Say it only once! I don't say, 'Tricia, drink—drink—drink your milk!' I say it once."

"And when she says it like that," Luke drawled, "you had better drink."

Indignantly Sara looked up to meet Luke's amused gaze, and dissolved into laughter. For a few seconds they shared, and then a sharp awareness of him faded her laughter.

Staring quickly down at the pup to cover her reactions, she heard Luke say softly as the children still giggled, "How about going out for dinner with me tonight. Just you and I."

His words brought her head up again, and she found herself feeling as awkward as if they were courting. Confused, she shook her head. "I... can't."

"Why not? No, don't bother quibbling. Forget it!"

Something in his tone made her look closely at him, intuitively certain that he was somehow hurt or angry, but there was nothing in his expression to support her impression and she looked away to Elijah, catching him staring at Hannah's picture.

Without quite knowing why, she tried to dissemble. "It's just that I'm...I'm starting on a portrait of Hannah tonight. For Elijah."

There was a silence. Even the twins felt the rippling undercurrents, and without looking his way she knew that Luke had tensed. But there was also the surprise and pleasure in Elijah's face holding her to her words, however impulsively spoken.

"You mean that, girl?"

"Sara," she corrected blandly.

"Sara."

"Yes, I mean it," she confirmed, and there was a glint in Elijah's dark eyes as if he quite understood just how impulsive her words had been, but didn't mind a bit taking advantage of them.

Nor did she mind, she realized. There was a relief in the decision to end her self-imposed embargo on painting; and to underline her decision, she said firmly, "I want to do it. I'll start tonight after the children are in bed."

Toby had risen and was standing by Luke, and as she finished speaking he tugged on Luke's hand.

"Could I talk to you, Uncle Luke?"

"Right now?" Luke asked. "I'm on my way to take a shower and...." He stopped, catching the look in Sara's eye, and without words, as surely as if she had printed the message in large letters and hung it on the tip of his nose, he knew she was thinking of her remark that fatherhood was not always convenient.

"Now!" Toby insisted, tugging again.

"Then, now it is," Luke replied, the back of his neck reddening.

"Alone!" Toby whispered.

"Oh...I see. Well, suppose you and I take Bumper for a walk. His lessons are over, and I think he'd like that."

"Okay."

"Me, too!" Tricia said instantly.

"Not now," Sara told her firmly. "Toby asked to talk to Uncle Luke alone. You can be alone with me. We'll look at pictures."

Moments later Luke found himself strolling along with Toby, his own long strides fitting themselves to his small son's. Halfway across the lawn he chose a shady oak tree and settled down beneath it.

Toby joined him silently, and after a while he cocked his head and asked, "Uncle Luke, did you have a special sleep? When they fixed your leg?"

"Yes, I did," Luke answered, doing a quick mental review of the booklet of advice from the hospital. "Why?"

"D—did it... scare you?"

Slowly Luke nodded. "A little bit."

"Me, too," Toby confided, and Luke found himself wanting to reach out and hug him.

"I know," was all he could manage.

"What did they do?"

"Oh, they wheeled me into a room on a stretcher. I was lying on my back. It felt funny."

"Oh."

"But nice, in a way. And there was a big light in the... operation room, like a sun. The people were wearing green robes and masks, and caps." He paused, groping for simple terms.

"And?" Toby prompted.

"The doctors and nurses said hello, and that they were ready to give me my special sleep so I wouldn't hurt while they fixed my leg."

"That's what Katy said, and Dr. Nan, too!"

"They are right," he assured Toby.

"Then what did they do?"

"They gave me an injection. With a needle."

"Ugh!" His small face screwed up.

"It only hurt a bit. It was so fast that before I could feel anything it was over."

"Did you cry?"

"Er, almost. It's okay if you do, you know."

"And then?" Toby pushed urgently, his blue eyes fastened on Luke's face.

"They asked me to count. So I counted: one... two...three...fouuur...fi.... And guess what happened?"

"What?" Toby's eyes were huge, his breath held.

"I closed my eyes, and opened them—right away! And guess where I was!"

"Where?"

"In the recovery room!"

"So fast!" Toby exclaimed with near disbelief.

"So fast. And the lady said, 'What is your name?' When I told her, I closed my eyes, and opened them, and like magic, I was in my room."

"And mummy was there?"

"Yes," Luke lied, realizing the reason for Toby's question. "She was right there—smiling."

Toby sighed with clear satisfaction. "You didn't go away, then."

"Of course not! It's a magic sleep, so nice and fast. So very special, too."

"Did you hurt?"

"My leg hurt, yes. But they gave me medicine to make it go away. And in a few days it did."

"I'm not afraid."

"Even if you were—a bit—like I was, it's okay."

"Honestly?"

"Honestly."

Looking down into Toby's trusting blue eyes, Luke suddenly knew that whether or not Toby was his blood son, or Tricia his daughter, in the past few minutes a final link had been forged within him, and the two children were part of him.

Rising after a quiet few moments in which it became apparent that Toby had no further questions, Luke started slowly back toward the house, a small hand creeping into his as they walked.

Sara watched them from Elijah's sitting room, thinking of how she had been certain their son would have the dark hair and eyes of Luke, and instead Tricia had inherited them.

"That's a nice-looking picture," Elijah said, following her gaze. "He's a fine boy."

"He's going to be as tall as Luke," she replied. "And Tricia will probably be a bit taller than I am."

"It's a mite early to say," Elijah commented dryly.

"Their doctor told me that if you multiply their height at eighteen months of age by two and a half, you'll be close to their adult height."

"Now you sound like Luke!"

Sara gave him a sharp look, and then returned to the photo album with its treasury of faded photographs.

That evening she started a few preliminary sketches, and within hours knew that she had hungered to paint. It was as if the gates to a dam within her had been breached by her decision, releasing a flood of creativity.

It was also an escape from emotions she was not yet ready to confront, and from anxieties she could not suppress over the nearing operation. She immersed herself in sketching the children, the pup, Elijah, and most of all Hannah from the old photographs, and the days passed.

The afternoon before Toby was admitted, she was

leafing through the old family albums and came across photographs of Spars' Nest being built.

"Why," she asked, looking up at Elijah, "did you call it Spars' Nest? I haven't seen a sea captain in the family tree, yet it sounds nautical."

"Luke never told you?"

She shook her head.

"When I started reading poetry I came across a poem written by Wordsworth, and for me the words meant Hannah. Have you ever read 'The Sparrows' Nest'?"

"If I did, I can't remember it."

"It goes, 'She gave me eyes, he gave me ears; and humble cares and delicate fears; a heart...and love, and thought, and joy.' That was Hannah. Spars' Nest is an abbreviation of Sparrows' Nest."

Before she could stop herself, she blurted, "How I envy you!"

"It's there for you, too," he said gently.

"No," she sighed. "How can it be when he distrusts me so? How can I live with him when he thinks I betrayed him?" She bit on her lower lip, then asked angrily, "Why? I keep asking why. Was there a girl he once loved?"

"Not that I know of," Elijah answered.

That night lying in bed, Sara found her thoughts returning to the question that nagged at her increasingly. She had made mistakes in that first year. She could admit it now. But she had never done anything that she knew of to warrant his suspicions, his distrust and, in the end, his relentless accusations.

Nor, as she had told Elijah, could there be a future

unless Luke could somehow believe her. How could there be, she tortured herself. Sooner or later the accusations and suspicions would surface, and sooner or later the children would become aware of it.

If they believed in her, it would alienate them from Luke, and if they came to believe him, she would lose them. Even if she could bear it herself, a lifetime of living with a man who "forgave" her, she could not do it to the children.

Wearily she forced her thoughts away from the insoluble problems to find them revolving around the operation. It would be all right, she told herself, tossing restlessly and trying not to think of how small Toby was and how frightening it might be for him despite all the preparations.

As they walked toward the hospital the next afternoon, it looked oddly sinister to her. Knowing that impression was the result of a sleepless night filled with shadowy fears that were not logical, she fought it back.

Now was the time that Toby needed her to be relaxed and confident, otherwise he would sense her fears and become afraid himself.

As they reached the steps, Toby ran ahead to step on the automatic door opener; and looking up at Luke, her gray eyes filled with the shadows of apprehension, Sara whispered desperately, "Help me!"

His arm curved around her instantly and his dark head bent, his lips brushing hers. "I'm scared, too," he admitted. "But we are both going to be as placid as two frogs sunning on a lily pad."

A gurgle of laughter rose in her. "Wherever did you come up with that?"

"I don't know." He grinned, and aware of his strength, feeling it flow through her, she was suddenly over her shakes and walked calmly through the doors that Toby kept open for them.

Katy was waiting for them, and Toby sailed through the simplified admission procedures, fascinated because everyone greeted him by name and answered all his questions.

He was also taken on a tour of his room, shown the call button, the bathroom, allowed to poke around, and then shown where the nurses' station, pantry, playroom and sitting room were, with explanations of who did what and what sort of noises he might hear from his room.

He had brought his teddy bear and his own pajamas, though he remained dressed until bedtime. When his lab tests were over, with small games and more explanations, he was visited in his room by the anesthesiologist and the nurse who would greet him in the recovery room in the morning.

"That's just what Uncle Luke said," he informed the anesthesiologist, David, when the procedures were reviewed. "He had an op'ration on his leg, too."

"Good," David replied. "Now let's look at the mask we'll put on you. It's like the ones jet pilots and astronauts use."

Toby's blue eyes lighted up as he was given a black molded mask. "Where's the long thing?"

"In the operating room. We didn't bring the hose out. Try it on, Toby."

Obediently Toby did so, making what Sara presumed to be jet noises.

"Did you know," David asked him, "that Colorado has produced quite a few men for the astronaut program?"

"Oh!"

As they continued talking, Luke murmured to Sara, "Did you ever hear what they did to Scott Carpenter when the mayor of Denver asked him to dedicate a new pool for a community center?"

She shook her head.

"The mayor gave a brief speech along the lines of, 'When you open a highway, you cut a ribbon. When you dedicate a building, you lay a cornerstone. And when you open a pool....' With that the mayor paused, and they all rushed their guest astronaut and tossed him into the pool."

Sara laughed aloud, and soon Toby was clamoring to hear the story. The moments seemed to speed by, and when Dr. Nan had been to visit in her surgical gown, letting Toby see her with her mask on and promising to wink at him, Luke took his leave.

"Tricia will be waiting," he reminded her.

Sara nodded, trying not to reveal the hollow feeling his departure was creating. "I'll call her at eight tonight."

"I'll be here in the morning as soon as I'm certain that she's settled with Beth and Jeannie in riding class."

She looked up at him wordlessly, and with an effort managed a smile of sorts. "I'll be fine."

"Get some sleep," he murmured, and bending to touch her lips gently with his, he strode off.

To her surprise, she slept, waking only moments before the nurse entered to explain and give Toby his preoperative shots.

"Which side first, Toby?" she asked as he gripped Sara's hand tightly.

"Doesn't m-matter," he said tremulously.

"What is your teddy bear's name?"

"Teddy." He jumped slightly as the first shot went in.

"Doesn't he have another name?"

"No."

"Say ouch, ouch, ouch!"

His eyes widened slightly. "Ouch—ouch—*ouch*!"

"All done!" the nurse said even as he flinched, a hint of tears in his blue eyes. "Thank you," she added. "You really helped me by not wiggling. That wasn't too awful, was it?"

He shook his head, slightly surprised, and then his eyes began drooping and his grip loosened. "Mummy?" he said drowsily.

"I'm right here," Sara assured him, brushing his fair hair back gently. "I love you, darling."

"I...love...you...too," he sighed.

Too soon she was walking by the stretcher, the nurses explaining everything to Toby despite his sleepiness, and then he was wheeled out of sight.

There was nothing left to do but wait, and feeling lost and shaken, she entered the surgery waiting room.

"Have you had any breakfast?" Katy asked, joining her.

"N-no. I don't think I could."

"It will help. Honestly."

"I'm being silly, I know. There must be children far more ill than Toby in here, but I'm still petrified." She looked at Katy, and her voice wobbled as she added, "He's so very small!"

Katy's hand covered Sara's. "I know...I know.... I feel the same with every child I see here. But Dr. Nan's the best, bless her." She smiled. "And I know she would never let a fellow Canadian down."

Something between a laugh and a sob escaped Sara's lips, and she drew in a steadying breath.

"How about tackling breakfast now?" Katy prodded as an orderly entered with a tray.

"I'll try," was the best Sara could manage, though common sense told her that Katy was right.

"Good." Katy rose. "I'll be down in the playroom if you need me or would like to come and watch. I keep an eye on the children's play after surgery to spot any lingering shock. It often comes out in the playroom as the children chat with each other."

It was an effort to eat, but Sara doggedly made herself finish everything, and found she did feel better, after all. A glance at the clock told her that less than a half hour had passed in what she had been told would be at least a three-hour operation.

Rising, she went to the window to stare out blindly, willing the time to pass and saying little silent prayers for Toby before once again looking at the clock. The minutes ticked by with excruciating slowness, and she tried desperately not to think of what might go wrong, of Toby's trusting blue eyes and how much the little boy he had looked as he was wheeled away.

When Luke walked in, she did not pause to think, she simply walked into his arms and buried her face in his shoulder.

As if knowing, even sharing, her need to be close and united at this moment in time, he said nothing, and gradually she calmed, only then aware that she had been shaking inside for hours.

His arms loosened slightly as she drew back and said huskily, "I'm so glad you're here."

"So am I." Gently he pushed back a strand of hair from her face, and then, glancing at the breakfast tray, he added firmly, "Come. We'll get us a cup of coffee."

"I don't...."

"I need a cup after coping with Tricia, and they'll know where we are."

"What happened with Tricia?" she exclaimed in alarm.

"Calm down! It's actually hilarious. Those two imps are no more predictable than you are."

She let the highly unjust remark from Mr. Unpredictable himself slide by, and allowed herself to be guided down the hall after being informed sternly that he would divulge nothing until he had his coffee.

In the cafeteria he selected not only coffee but a huge slice of chocolate pie with whipped cream.

"Luke, it's only eight-thirty in the morning!"

"That's what's great about being grown up," he countered with a grin. "Mummy can't stop you."

Despite her anxieties, she could not help smiling back, and by the time they were settled in a small booth, she was a great deal more relaxed.

"What happened with Tricia?"

"First I must have one mouthful of pie," he decreed.

"Luke!" she warned, tempted to give him the whole slice in his face, even as she knew that he was deliberately distracting her.

"Mmm, that is good!" he sighed, and lifting an eyebrow at her as she shuddered, he added, "Tricia is peeved, piqued and in a pucker."

"Why?" she prodded, ignoring his alliteration.

"Because she can't have an operation, too."

"Because she...." Sara's eyes widened. "Oh, for heaven's sake!"

"She doesn't think it's fair."

"Life isn't fair."

"Yes...but she insists that she should have an operation, too. It seems the program here has completely sold her on the desirability of a stay." His dark eyes held amusement as he shook his head sadly. "I'll have to have a talk with Dr. Nan about this. Shouldn't oversell like that."

"You and Tricia are absolutely ridiculous!" she pronounced with mock disgust.

"Think how green with envy she'll be when she sees Toby's cast with all the drawings on it."

Shaking her head, Sara reached for her coffee, resigned to Luke's nonsense even as she was grateful for it.

But when they returned to the surgery waiting

room, a silence fell, and glancing at the clock, she returned to the window, aware of Luke standing beside her quietly.

"Let's sit down," he finally suggested.

"No, I...." She saw the lines of strain marking the tanned features, and letting her protest trail off, she nodded.

Leaning back on the sofa, Luke raised his feet to rest on the low table before it, loosened his tie and stretched an arm out to pull her next to him, tucked against his chest and shoulder.

"It shouldn't be too long," Sara said, letting herself relax against his strength without question.

"He's going to be fine."

"I know. It's just—"

"He's going to be fine!" he repeated harshly.

Slowly she raised her head, her eyes searching the darkness of his. "You care!" she whispered. "You really care!"

"What kind of remark is that?" he said curtly, appalled at the thought that she might have sensed his earlier innermost reservations.

A confusion of feelings surged through her at his response, denying her the power to reply, and when Luke jerked her around, roughly pulling her against his chest with something close to a violent need, she lay passively against him, drawing on his closeness for strength.

He hugged her tightly, and after a long silence he ground out, "Yes, dammit, I care!" In a complete non sequitur he added with a groan that was more nearly a tortured cry, "Oh, Sara, why? Why you, too?"

She tried to lift her head, feeling his pain, unable to make sense of it, yet wanting to comfort him. But his hand pinned her head against his chest, and she could only lie listening to his heart beating beneath her ear, to the rasp of his breathing and to the echo of his cry in her mind.

A desperate hopelessness suddenly swept over her. It seemed as if they stood at a fence, each in a different land, yearning to cross over. A fence with open spaces through which they could reach, and also with vicious clusters of barbed wire waiting to tear the flesh and soul of the foolish. If only, her heart cried, there were a way to reach each other, to truly reach each other.

How could there be, though, when she knew that she was afraid even to question what, "Why you, too?" meant, for fear he would withdraw at this time when she most needed him.

When after an endless time he released her without a word, she looked up, and finding his face closed and withdrawn, she leaned back against the sofa beside him and let the silence be.

Within moments, however, the separation became unbearable, and after a brief struggle with the fear of being hurt, of being rejected, she moved her hand through the space, braving the invisible barbed-wire clusters, and covered the clenched fist that lay on his muscled thigh.

It was a gesture that sought both to give and to receive comfort, and she felt him start at her touch. Then slowly his clenched hand relaxed and turned to grip hers.

There were no more words. They waited. The

clock ticked away time inexorably. Another couple entered, their faces also drawn, to sit across the room whispering. The sounds of the hospital wove their muted theme around them, and Sara silently prayed.

When Dr. Nan finally appeared in the doorway, still in her green gown, they both started and then rose hurriedly to their feet.

"It went perfectly," she said with a broad tired smile. "If I do say so myself. He's in recovery now. They'll call you as soon as he wakes up and can return to his room."

Hardly knowing what she babbled in reply or what Luke said, Sara was swept with relief and joy simultaneously, and blindly she turned to Luke, seeking him, clinging to him as tears of happiness streamed down her cheeks while she sobbed over and over again, "He's all right, Luke! He's all *right*!"

CHAPTER FOURTEEN

THREE WEEKS LATER Sara paused as she worked on Hannah's portrait to look out the tower window at a landscape of vivid autumn colors, her thoughts drifting over the past weeks with a tenuous hope she dared not examine too closely.

The days had passed peacefully and with a contentment of sorts. Toby was up and about, swinging along on crutches with the agility of a gymnast and trailed by an envious Tricia, for whom a chance to use her brother's crutches was a treat indeed.

Luke's project was a success, also. On his insistence Sara had been present on the big day, and there had been no pretense for public appearances in her pride at the completely successful demonstration. Nor had her uninhibited response to his exuberant hug and kiss in front of everyone been pretended.

She sighed, and then felt her body warm with awareness as she saw Luke's car sweep along the drive. It was a reaction to his presence she was finding increasingly difficult to control, and moving nervously from the window, she busied herself packing up for the day.

"Mummy!" Tricia called impatiently from the bottom of the steps. "Uncle Luke is here! Hurry!"

"Coming!" Sara replied, aware that the twins were eager to start on the promised trip to the zoo. Since the successful demonstration of his energy system, Luke had started taking off afternoons every few days to spend with the children, and they were looking forward to this trip with great excitement.

Elitch Gardens, thirty-six acres of delight, contained a zoo that was the first zoological garden west of the Mississippi River. There were also paths and walks through bountiful gardens below ancient trees, sections for children, a dancing pavilion and theater, and an amusement park that included among its fascinating rides a miniature train.

With Toby's leg still in a cast, they chose the zoo for the afternoon treat, with Luke promising a visit to the amusement park at a later date. As the twins had never been to a zoo before, there were no protests.

"Can we have a skunk?" was Toby's first excited exclamation at the children's section.

"Absolutely not!" Sara replied with amusement. "When they squirt, the smell is dreadful."

"You'll see skunks at the ranch next spring," Luke added, as if there were no doubt they would go. "Just remember to stay upwind."

"What's that?" Tricia asked.

"Always have the wind blowing on your back when you face a skunk. They don't spray you then."

"And if there's no wind?" Sara asked blandly.

He grinned. "Then stay away and don't scare it."

With that he led them all on, taking command without thought and keeping up a running commentary on everything. When two lions suddenly started a spat, Luke's comment to the children was, "Watch their ears! Every animal that fights with its teeth lays back its ears when it fights."

"Like horses," Tricia said, nodding knowledgeably.

"I'll have to start watching your ears," Sara murmured to Luke, then blushed at the look he gave her, adding hastily, "What other tidbits have you stored away?"

"You can tell," he obliged mockingly, "whether a zoo is well run by how many offspring are produced. Unhappy animals don't breed."

"Marvelous," Sara returned dryly.

"Monkeys are usually nearsighted," he continued, straight-faced, "and you can tell one lion from another by the pattern of the whisker holes on its nose."

"How do you get close enough to look?"

"That is a personal problem," he replied with a laugh, and even as she laughed back at him, there was a sudden acute awareness of him, a sharp desire to.... She looked away quickly and bent confusedly to murmur something to Toby.

She was tugging Toby's sweater into order when a smothered expletive made her look up at Luke. With a sense of shock she saw that his face had hardened, and a look of black fury was focused on her as he demanded with ill-concealed contempt, "Did you plan this?"

"What?" she gasped with genuine bewilderment, her heart sinking.

His eyes snapped past her, and she turned to see Rufus strolling toward them, a sketch pad in hand and a smile of greeting on his bony face.

"No!" Her eyes flew to Luke's pleading silently. "Luke, I swear it...on the children's heads...I did not plan for or encourage him to be here. I didn't know he would be here!"

He was silent, his dark eyes seeming to hunt out the corners of her soul, and then, with an almost imperceptible nod, he relaxed the tenseness of his stance and the corded muscles of his tall frame slightly, if not totally.

There was no time to say anything, for Rufus was upon them, greeting them all casually and then squatting down to show the children his sketches of the animals and spectators alike.

They were talented and clever sketches, but Sara barely saw them, for she was so tense, so frightened that Rufus might take it upon himself, for whatever twisted reasons, to imply that she had agreed to meet him.

But his conversation remained bland, and after a few minutes he wandered on. If he had briefly marred the afternoon, there was the compensation that Luke had believed her. It was a beginning.

IN THE WEEKS THAT FOLLOWED there were other expeditions, unmarred by Rufus's unexpected presence. Trips to a wax musuem; to Larimer Square in downtown Denver, with its turn-of-the-century atmosphere; and to the Garden of the Gods, south of Denver, where stark monoliths of red sandstone, carved by the winds sweeping down the mountain slopes, stood awesomely high against the sky-scraping peaks.

In the evenings they drifted into the habit of sharing a snack and chatting about their day and the children, and she knew she was allowing her life to move in a direction carrying new implications, but could not bring herself to question it.

Hannah's portrait was beginning to come together for her. Working from dozens of old photographs, Sara strove to capture the essence of her personality while Elijah told her of their life together, of the happy times, sad times, of quarrels and triumphs, until she felt that she had once actually known Hannah.

The painting appeased the formerly stifled hunger to create, but another hunger grew within her as she listened to the lifetime of sharing that had existed between Hannah and Elijah.

Thanksgiving Day came and went too quickly, for it was a day Sara knew she would remember whatever the future held. Toby's cast was off. He was walking, slowly but evenly.

At the church service her prayer of thanks was more meaningful than ever before, and afterward, with Beth and Paul, there was feasting as a family. She feasted not only on the traditional roast turkey and pumpkin pie, but also on the sight of her small son restored to normal.

It *had* been especially wonderful, she reflected some nights later as she sat in the window seat of the tower, tired after a long session with the portrait. Sighing, she closed her eyes, leaned back on the soft pillows and wished that Luke were not in the lab with the attentive Jessica by his side, but by her side, in her arms.

It was long past midnight when Luke returned home to find Sara asleep on the window seat.

For a long moment he simply stood quietly staring down at her, knowing he had sought her deliberately, missing her companionship for the late snack they had come to share, and yet fighting the knowledge at the same time.

His eyes left the delicate contours of her face, relaxed and vulnerable in sleep, and shifted to the canvas on the easel by her drawing table.

It held his attention instantly. Though only roughed in, the portrait already showed Sara's unique magic. The pose with Hannah's face glowing with light, her hair loose, was timeless. It was, he sensed instinctively, Elijah's Hannah—the lover, mate and lost half of his life—not the public Hannah.

Moving closer, he stared down at the scattered sketches of Hannah on the desk, and among them he found others of Toby frowning, Tricia in giggles, Elijah dreaming and even Grey scowling. Not one of them was of himself. He frowned, and then a stirring behind him made him turn.

Sara wakened, aware only of stiffness at first, and not opening her eyes, she sighed foggily and rubbed her prickling legs. When she suddenly realized that Luke was there, however, she stilled, the very cells of her body quickening with awareness.

"That's an awkward place to sleep, at best," he murmured as her eyes flew to his, wide and still not finely focused.

His mundane words flowed through the velvet night, and striving to clear her sleep-befuddled mind, which was already too unguarded to stop a purely emotional response to his towering presence in her sanctuary, she managed a bland, "What time is it?"

"Two o'clock." There was a pause, and then he asked, "Did you really stop painting for all these past years?"

"Yes...." Her breath caught as he moved closer. "I was too busy."

"You once said it was like breathing for you."

"D-did I? How awfully young of me." She spoke with false lightness, trying to draw in scattered feelings as her heart beat in slow heavy strokes.

"Sara...?"

Hesitantly, her whole body feeling weighted, she raised her eyes and was trapped by the darkness of his, by the nearness of him and the irresistible male scents of him.

Very slowly his hands moved to cup her face, his fingers sliding through her tousled hair, and she shivered as his lips touched hers lightly, feathering, and then with sure possession.

The silky fabric of her caftan teased her skin as she moved against him, drawing him to her until his weight slowly lowered her back on the pillows and she was lost in a beautiful sensuous dream.

When at last his head lifted, she looked up at him, her eyes dark with her need for him, her lips swollen and parted as her breath fluttered excitedly through her. "Luke...."

His name was only a breath, a soft cry, and Luke's mouth lowered once more, his lips teasing the corner of her mouth, moving along her jawline to nuzzle below her ear and trail deliciously along her neck as his hand moved up from her waist to cup and hold her breast, his thumb teasing and arousing.

With a cry in the back of her throat, her mouth sought his, invading and being invaded, captured and plundered with sensuous delight. As her hands dug into the steel muscles of his back, she delighted in the weight of him, the masculine hardness of him, and the roughness of his beard against the softness of her skin, and with a deep unsatiated hunger she reached for the feeling of wholeness again, just one more time.

When his hand moved around her to slide the zipper down, she shifted to ease his way, her own fingers fumbling at his shirt, her breathing quick, her skin flushed and hot.

"What the—" Luke exclaimed as his hand struck something, sending it flying.

"Never mind..." she said huskily, and then stiffened as he sat up abruptly, his eyes on the floor.

"Luke...?" Bewildered, she turned her head to follow his gaze, and saw nothing but the slim volume of his mother's poetry lying on the floor. Questioningly she looked up.

"Is that the sort of trash you read?" he said with cold accusation.

"Luke!" she cried with shock. "It's beautiful!"

"It's *garbage*!"

"It's not! How can you—"

Her words were stopped forcefully by the roughness of his hands imprisoning her face, and this time his fingers ripped through her hair with uncaring power.

Even as she cried out with pain, he was kissing her savagely, bruisingly, as if he wanted to hurt her. It was an assault with the bitter taste of hatred and a ravaging desire to inflict pain.

Then without warning he pushed her harshly away from him and rose to stand over her, his big body shaking with rage, his face a mask of stone. "What's wrong? You were eager enough moments ago! Or did your reading excite you so that any man would do?"

"Luke, don't! Please, *don't*!" she whispered raggedly through lips that bled, her eyes stunned and horrified.

His gaze swept her body, her disheveled state, with clear disgust. When he reached her lips, however, he seemed to wince, and with a muffled oath he wheeled and was gone.

Numb and badly shaken, Sara turned onto her side, curling up defensively as she wondered, with the despair of shattered hopes, what else would become grounds for accusations and punishments.

She could not speak to another man without Luke's vile suspicions. Now she could not even read poetry that sang softly of love. And next?

With raw pain she lay alone, her blood curdling with unsatisfied passion, her emotions blanched by his inexplicable cruelty.

SHE WAS LATE FOR BREAKFAST the next morning, and the children were already outside with Jeannie as she entered the room. The sight of Luke waiting for her alone made her flinch visibly despite herself. Only pride kept her from walking back out.

He waited until Grey had poured her coffee and served her toast, and when they were alone he said roughly, "Sara...I'm sorry."

She could almost hear his pride creaking, and refused to look at him or acknowledge his stiff apology.

"I was exhausted last night...edgy. The sight of.... I'm sorry I hurt you."

"Why?" she said at last through bruised lips. "That book was your own mother's poetry!"

"I...mistook it for something else."

Her eyes dropped to her coffee. She knew him too well and, knowing him, knew that he was lying. But she also recognized the inflexible look on his face, and baffled by his lie, she tiredly accepted his apology.

That afternoon, however, she showed the volume of poetry to Beth, and giving her time to read selections, she asked earnestly, "Do you think it's trash?"

"Decidedly not." Beth closed the book, her hazel eyes as puzzled as Sara's. "I think it's sensitive... touching."

"Listen to this," Sara said, opening Elizabeth's diary. "'We had a row today. There's no one I'd rather fight with than my Simon-Robert. It is utterly exhilarating, and afterward absolutely lovely to end up laughing and loving.'" Sara looked up. "They must have had a very special kind of loving."

"Do you suppose that deep inside of him he can't forgive his parents for dying and leaving him? Children do that...and it can linger subconsciously."

"I don't know." Sara absently refilled her coffee cup and glanced out Beth's kitchen window, checking on Toby and Tricia. "Luke must be something like his father," she said thoughtfully.

"In what way?"

"From what I've read of Elizabeth's diary, she started teasing Simon during their courtship about being a dry businessman, but gentle and sensitive when he was her lover. Her special name for him became 'my Robert.' All her private letters to him started with, 'My darling Robert.'"

"Why not dub Luke 'my darling Michelangelo'?" Beth offered, and promptly dissolved into laughter, which Sara could only pretend to share as she thought of Her Luke and the Other Luke. "It would be romantic," Beth sighed.

"What would be?" Paul asked, entering the room and slipping his arms around Beth's waist from behind to trap her in her chair. "The view, the subject or me?"

Listening to their relaxed banter, Sara found she had to shake herself mentally to keep from wallowing in an irrational trough of self-pity.

As if sensing her reaction, Paul released Beth and circled the table to give Sara a quick hug. "I had lunch with Luke today, and together we have cooked up a special evening. How is that?"

Sara regarded him blankly, wondering if Luke had agreed to something because of appearances or as a further apology.

"It will relax you," Paul assured her. "You've had a rough time and Toby's doing great, so we are going to drive down to Colorado Springs to have dinner at the elite and hallowed Broadmoor and then watch an ice-skating competition. You two can enjoy the ice dancing and ogle the young men, while we will ogle the spinning ladies."

"That's great!" Beth said with enthusiasm.

It was perfect, Sara discovered a week later as she sat in the darkened arena watching a young couple skim the ice in weaving spotlights to the romantic strains of Tchaikovsky. She ached to paint the fantasy of it, and glanced up at Luke next to her to see if he, too, was captured by the spell.

His face was relaxed, his eyes following the skaters, until without warning they were looking into hers. For a brief instant there was only his nearness, the spell of his dark eyes and the beauty of the music permeating everything.

Then applause welled around them like a wave crashing upon a quiet beach, and she was fumbling awkwardly for her program and desperately trying to push that brief moment of intangible touching away.

Driving back to Denver there was little conversation, and after they had switched to Luke's car at Paul's home, there was complete silence back to Spars' Nest.

The first words Luke spoke were at the foot of the stairs, when she was about to ascend to her room. It was then that he reached out to her, and drawing her slowly to him, he said hoarsely, "Sara, what are we going to do?"

She did not try to reply or resist, but let her lips

join with his, felt the gentle searching of his mouth and a warm sweet pleasure that in its way was more penetrating and intense than passion.

For long sweet moments she let herself float in soft sensations of delight, and when his lips left hers she stared up at him wordlessly, wanting only to stay with him, never to leave. But he moved away from her, his eyes seeming to ask something, and then without a word strode away.

The following afternoon, as Sara frowned over her asparagus plant—which was showing decided signs of displeasure by dropping fine yellow leaves everywhere—the sound of Luke's car made her turn nervously and look down from the tower room. Setting aside her plant's woes until later, she descended to meet him, somewhat doubtful about how to greet him.

He solved her minor dilemma by entering scowling and obviously out of sorts with the world. "Where are the children?" he greeted her.

"With Jeannie."

He grunted, left his briefcase on the foyer table and disappeared down the hall to his room. Feeling oddly hurt, Sara mocked herself for being foolish and went to tell Grey to prepare a tray for him. When he entered the den twenty minutes later, she had his coffee and sandwiches waiting.

"I'm not hungry," he muttered ungratefully, and proceeded to scatter notes and drawings across his desk.

"What's wrong?"

"Nothing!"

"Oh. And how are you when something *is* wrong?" she asked sweetly.

His eyes narrowed, and then he said in a rather disgruntled tone, "Part of the system isn't holding up properly. It has to be changed somehow." Absently he picked up his mug of hot coffee and swallowed, only to swear virulently as he burned his mouth.

Suppressing a bubble of amusement, she asked, "Why isn't it going properly?"

"If I knew why," he said silkily, "I wouldn't be here trying to solve the mess."

"Should you be? What about security?"

He scowled at her in reply.

"Why not tell me about it?"

"You!"

"How unflattering," she rallied.

"It's not that," he muttered, his one hand raking through his dark hair. "It's complex...technical."

"Simplify it."

He eyed her grimly and then, shrugging, began to explain. Slowly at first, then more quickly, and nearly an hour later, with Sara still following his lucid explanations, he reached the point of his impasse. "It should be working smoothly, but it isn't."

"Does it have to operate precisely that way?"

"Of course!"

"Why 'of course'?"

"Because it must!"

"Why?" Sara persisted intently.

"Because...." He hesitated, frowning. "Because...." He drew in a sudden breath, and slowly his eyes went out of focus.

Recognizing the signs, Sara sat quietly, and when he leaned forward to reach for pencil and paper, she rose silently and went to the door. There she paused to look back.

This they shared, the compelling grip of creativity. It was as Elijah had said. Luke was also a creator, one who used the universe for his paints and canvas.

With a soft sigh she left and returned to tend her ailing plant absently, knowing she wanted to share a great deal more.

That evening as they had coffee after dinner in Elijah's sitting room, Luke was called to the phone. He returned to say tersely, "Jess is coming over shortly."

Sara tensed visibly. "Here?"

"Yes, here." His gaze shifted to Elijah. "She's picked up something on the Turner proposal and is in a panic."

"Isn't she aware of the terms?" Elijah asked.

Luke's dark eyebrows lifted. "As R. and D. director?"

"What did he mean, 'as R. and D. director'?" Sara asked when Luke had left, trying not to think of Jessica in the house and grateful that the children were in bed.

"'R. and D.' stands for 'research and development.' It is not a line position—not a power position—just as personnel and functions like public relations are not usually power positions in a company, but support positions. As such, Jessica would not be included in the negotiations, especially as Luke is directly involved in the research."

"What negotiations?"

"I'll leave that to Luke to tell you."

"As I'm not in a power position," she returned dryly, "it's not likely he will."

Elijah ignored her remark. "I'll wager that Jessica's panicked all right, and that she will blame you for the changes."

"What she's probably worried about," Sara said with rare sarcasm, "is whether anyone's going to steal her Nobel Prize!" She grimaced and then looked at Elijah. "He couldn't really win it, could he?"

"It's not impossible, from some reading I've done since you last mentioned what Jessica told you."

"When Einstein, Edison and the Wright brothers didn't?"

"Why they didn't is a mystery of the times and perhaps the internal politics of the Academy of Science. But the prize in physics has been awarded for inventions as well as for discoveries. Marconi, for instance, won the Nobel Prize for his development of wireless telegraphy."

"But Luke's work is a company project. Wouldn't that disqualify him?"

"Not at all. Three Americans who worked for a corporation shared the physics prize in 1956 for their discovery of transistor effects. Replacing vacuum tubes with transistors was an invention. However, it changed electronics all over the world. And the development of the electrocardiograph was a matter of discovering a mechanism for doing a specific task. No, the project might qualify when it's done."

"Then Luke...could be eligible?" she asked, stunned.

"By the time he refines his system, yes. But it's early days yet."

"And Jessica?"

"She'll have the prestige of working on the project from the beginning and recognition as one of the experts on the system."

"But you said that three men shared a prize."

"Yes, but she did not contribute to the theory or design of any major component of it. If you design the first airplane, the engineer who follows your instructions, however brilliantly, cannot claim credit for conceiving the idea or implementing it."

"She was so certain that day she lit into me, and so...." She paused as something struck her. "And so afraid! How odd! I just realized it, Elijah. She *was* afraid."

"Knowing her background, wouldn't that be logical?" he asked.

"Her background? I would guess it's elite from the way she dresses and carries herself. A spoiled only child."

Elijah shook his head. "She's the youngest of four girls from a dirt-poor family."

"Jessica is?"

"Her eldest sister married an alcoholic and died in a car wreck with him. Her second sister married a man who deserted her and her children. The third one became involved in drugs."

Sara regarded him with disbelief. "Jessica came from a background like that? It seems impossible!"

"She told me once that she was only nine years old when she decided that she was going to be different. It meant working, saving, studying—not just schoolwork, but how to dress, walk and act. She won scholarships and worked harder, determined to be someone and never to go back."

"She certainly succeeded," Sara conceded reluctantly.

"She's part of a social phenomenon. Given five children from a miserable background, one copes while the others are crushed."

"*Has* Jessica coped?" Sara asked, thinking of her cruelty.

"In her way. I suspect she's sacrificed a good part of herself in the process. Buck Turner had his love for Martha, and it saved him. Jess has nothing but her work."

"She has... Luke," Sara said with difficulty.

"I don't believe it," Elijah rejected flatly. "They have only the closeness of two people working together intensely on a common task."

Sara was silent. If Elijah chose to ignore that two people, both of whom seemed to fear emotions, might marry because neither would make demands, she could not. Nor could she ignore the fact that if Jessica succeeded in marrying Luke, she would not only have reached her career goals, but would also have done what her sisters had failed to do: married exceedingly well.

"I cannot pity her," Sara admitted to Elijah. "Perhaps when I'm in my eighties I shall have more compassion, but all I can see is how she hurts people.

She's like a nasty child who can see the world only in relation to herself and will attack anyone in her way."

"The fear of failure can warp people," Elijah replied mildly. "And that is the other side of the coin when you find someone desperate to succeed."

Rising, Sara crossed to the window, knowing she could not find it in herself to forgive Jessica for what she had said about the children, whatever her past, whatever her accomplishments.

She was in time to see Jessica's car arrive at the front entrance, and her lips compressed as the other woman left the car and, clearly in a distraught state, hurried into the house.

"You're a fool to think she's ever been more than a colleague to Luke," Elijah said from behind her.

"Yes...I'm a fool," she agreed tiredly. "I'm a fool to stay, and a fool to let his accusations and suspicions hurt me."

"When two people love each other, they can sometimes be very cruel to each other in their pain. For loving means also learning your loved one's most vulnerable places. That can become a terrible weapon."

"Then I shall stay invulnerable," she said harshly, and knew as she said it that it was already too late for her. Moving away, she added, "I'd better get back to work on Hannah's portrait."

She stopped by the children's room and then entered her room, intending to change into a loose robe before going to the tower. Instead she found herself restless, and knowing she would not be able to work, she shrugged on a warm jacket and moments later slipped quietly from the house with Bumper at her heels.

She was unaware of Luke's dark brooding gaze following her from the window of the den, or of his tall frame tensing as she disappeared down the drive.

She knew only that as she walked down the road, with her walked the knowledge that she could no longer deny that what Luke did, or did not do, mattered. The admission frightened her, for it implied accepting a future with a man whose tenderness and sensitivity could change without warning to a cruel callousness, a future that could be unutterably bleak.

By the wayside she paused to stare pensively down through the cold fine rain at the blurred lights of Denver that glowed through the low-lying clouds like candles in a phantom city.

With a sudden intensity she missed the sound and scents of the Keys, of the night winds ladened with salt, and the soothing infinite rhythm of the ocean.

What she needed, she told herself wryly, was a stringent dose of Madge Wintertree's common sense, telling her not to be a fool because of a physical attraction and a precarious truce.

Sighing aloud, she called Bumper to her and set off at brisk pace as if she could outrun her thoughts, oblivious to the time and the chilled damp air.

At Spars' Nest Luke found himself at the window for the third or fourth time, grimly straining to pierce the mistlike rain that shrouded the night.

"Luke!" Jessica said sharply. "Are you even paying attention?"

Turning reluctantly, he regarded her with weary irritation. "Suppose we just call it a night."

"Forget her!" she replied angrily. "What good will it do to run after her? You know as well as I do that she can reach Rufus in fifteen minutes if she took the shortcut, and where else could she be after nearly two hours on a night like this?"

"I'll forget you said that, Jess," he warned in a dangerously soft tone.

"And will you also forget all the time we've lost because of her and her children? Divorce her, Luke—before it's too late!"

"Get out, Jess. And stay out of my private life."

"Luke...."

"Just get *out*!"

She faced him stiffly and then started to gather up the notes and drawings on the desk.

"Leave them," he ordered curtly.

Her head lifted, her eyes startled. "I can at least start on them in the morning."

"Jess...."

With uncharacteristic nervousness she crossed the room, only to stop at the door and say, "I apologize, Luke. After nine years together, I can't help caring."

She left without waiting for his reaction, and alone he stood battling the very suspicions that Jessica had verbalized. With a muffled oath he strode from the room in long angry strides, moving swiftly toward the stairs. Her room was empty. Tricia stirred slightly as he checked the twins' room, and whispering a soft assurance he sought out the tower.

Moments later he returned to the entrance hall, uncertain about whether or not to call the sheriff, search for her himself or believe what Jessica had said. In that instant the front door rattled, and his whole body went taut.

Sara pushed open the door with Bumper in her arms, unaware of Luke's presence. Blinking in the light, she was bending to free the pup when a looming angry shape confronted her and a big hand reached out to jerk her upright.

Luke's eyes traveled her sodden state with a mixture of emotions before he asked harshly, "Do you realize you're asking to come down with pneumonia?"

"I've been wet and cold before—" she shivered "— without coming down with the slightest of colds."

"And where the hell have you been?"

"Out."

"Out *where*, Sara!" His voice was hard, and she stilled, small tremors running through her as her eyes met his and read his meaning.

"As I've managed well enough most of my life," she made herself say evenly, "if I want to walk alone and think, whatever the hour, I do not need anyone's permission."

"Ah, yes!" he sneered furiously. "The martyr speaks again! The poor wronged woman who raised her children alone!"

Sara stared at him numbed by pain. His cynical mocking of the years of sheer grueling effort, after their times of closeness in the past weeks, left her feeling as if he had physically struck her. Her face went pale, and she turned to flee up the stairs before he could wound her further, before he could see her vulnerability.

"No running this time!" he ground out, his hand clamping on her shoulder, his thumbs digging into her soft flesh as she tried to pull free.

"You're hurting me, Luke!"

The sight of her gray eyes swimming with tears sobered him, and his grip loosened abruptly. "Sara—"

"Don't! Just don't hurt me anymore!"

With the words she darted away and ran blindly into the cold wet night, seeking only to escape.

"Sara!"

Ignoring his pursuing cry, she kept on running until the sheets of thin rain shielded her.

He was halfway through the door after her when angry words were thrown at him from above. "You're bad!"

Wheeling, he stared up at Tricia, who stood on the landing with her teddy bear dangling from her hand.

"Tricia, what—"

"I don't like you anymore!" she sobbed, tears starting to stream down her face. "Not anymore... ever!"

With a muffled expletive he went up the stairs, three in a stride, even as Tricia lifted her teddy bear and threw it at him with, "I don't want your old teddy! I don't want Bumper! I don't want you!"

He ducked, caught the teddy bear, tripped and slammed onto his left knee on the stair edge with his full weight, and with a heartfelt oath he still managed to grab at Tricia as he sprawled on the stairway.

With a wail she crumpled against his chest, crying without restraint, and Luke found himself smoothing back her hair and murmuring to her until she was reduced to dry hiccups.

"Tricia?" he whispered tentatively, forcing himself to ignore his own pain. "Don't you ever get angry at Toby?"

There was a stillness in the small form curled against his chest, and he could almost hear her thinking his question over before giving a reluctant nod.

"But you don't stay angry, do you?"

"You hurt mummy!" Tears flowed again.

"My hand was accidentally too tight. I didn't mean to hurt her." He paused. "She was out walking so long I was worried. I really didn't mean to hurt her, honestly. And I'm very sorry."

Slowly Tricia's head lifted, and she regarded him with a long sober look that he found somewhat unnerving. "Are you going to say you're sorry to mummy?"

"As soon as I have you back in bed, I will."

"Promise?"

"I promise. Cross my heart."

There was another thinking pause that he did not dare to interrupt, and finally her hand crept into his. "Uncle Luke?"

"Hmm?" He smiled somewhat crookedly.

In a breath her arms were around his neck and her face was buried against him. "I do love you! And teddy. And Bumper."

"And I love you," he assured her roughly.

Ten minutes later he limped out into the drizzling rain, a spare jacket over his arm. His knee, vulnerable since the car accident, was becoming increasingly painful, yet all he could think of was the pain in Sara's eyes, and his own stupidity.

He found her not far from the gate, walking disconsolately toward him, a lone road light casting a pale glow on her through the rain.

With a surge of relief he closed the distance between them and wrapped the dry jacket around her.

"I'm sorry," he said quietly, drawing her shivering body against him and folding her inside his own jacket, as well. "I was so damned worried that I lost my temper...said things I didn't mean. Sara, please!"

For an endless time, it seemed, Sara simply leaned against him tiredly, soaking up his strength and warmth, feeling and not yet able to think.

Somewhere in the long silence, held by Luke on a cold night not unlike one long ago in Toronto, Sara accepted quietly that she still loved him. As illogical and hopeless as it was, she still loved this strange man who lacked faith in her.

On the heels of her realization, she heard Luke whisper her name, and almost hesitantly she looked up.

His lips were a breath away, then joining with hers. It was a long, gentle searching kiss. Never wanting its peculiar sweetness to end, she moved her arms to circle his waist as she answered his silent questions.

When his mouth finally left hers, he held her

against him, and feeling his powerful body trembling, she found herself hoping against hope.

It was not until they started walking back to the house that she noticed he was limping badly. Her exclamation brought an account of what had happened, finished with, "She settled down after assuring herself that I was on my way to 'make up.'" He paused as they reached the steps, and looked down at her. "Sara...could we try?"

"Luke—"

"No, listen! Remember the day Dr. Nan said that sometime in life we have to choose? I've chosen. I agreed to sign with Turner the day we went to the Broadmoor."

"Why?" she asked, needing to know.

"Not to pressure you," he said firmly. "I had been toying with the idea ever since we returned. But the day when Toby tugged on my hand and said he wanted to talk to me alone—that day...I knew. I chose. Come what may, I was going to have time for him, for Tricia."

"How can we...?" Her voice broke.

"We can. I want to try. I want you to become my closest friend, to share with you, to be needed by you in all ways." He paused, then added hoarsely, "I'll soon be free to spend evenings at home, to have our weekends together. We'll have time to try. To really try."

She stood within the circle of his arm, her throat aching, her slender body quivering with uncertainties. "I...I don't know. There's so much we haven't—"

"But we could *try!*" His hands gripped her shoulders. "Sara...meet me halfway. That's all I ask."

Her head bowed, and after a long moment during which Luke tensed with conflicting emotions, she nodded.

CHAPTER FIFTEEN

"I CAN'T STAND IT another minute!" Sara exclaimed with a grin several days later as she lunched with a radiant Beth. "You are sitting there positively glowing!"

With a laugh Beth admitted, "I'm not hiding it very well, am I?"

"Hiding what? Has Paul landed some stupendous contract in town?" she asked, aware that it was Beth's dream.

"One could say that...in a way," Beth replied mischievously.

"What way?" Sara demanded.

"I think I'm pregnant."

"Oh, Beth!"

"I'm not absolutely certain," Beth cautioned, then added, "Well, I am. But I've an appointment with the doctor in an hour, and I want to be absolutely certain before I tell Paul. We've waited so long." Her voice shook.

"I'm so happy for you!" Sara said sincerely. "You both are terrific with children."

"You have no idea how long the past years have been!" Beth returned. "I'd begun to think it would never happen. Every time I looked at the twins, I felt almost miserable because it seemed we would never have a child of our own. Now...." Her voice trailed off.

"I suspected as much," Sara admitted. "Sometimes you looked at the children so wistfully."

"Enviously," Beth corrected. "It seemed so terribly unjust that there were other people who didn't want children, who screeched at their children as if they hated them, and Paul and I were just *aching* for a child."

"What are you hoping for—a boy or a girl?"

"It doesn't matter! After years of trying, of doctors shaking their heads and telling us the chances were very small of having a child at all, I'll take a healthy child—period."

"Perhaps nature will endow you with twins as compensation," Sara teased.

"Good grief!" Beth exclaimed dramatically. "Paul would go into shock."

"Let me know what the doctor says."

"After I tell Paul," Beth promised. "I may have to revive him." She laughed with uncontainable happiness. "And what are your two imps up to?"

"They're with Elijah, helping him finish two walking canes—one for each of them."

"Two what?"

"Luke fell on the stairs the other night and injured his knee, the one hurt in the accident five years ago. He's using a walking cane, and Toby took one look and wanted one."

"Which meant Tricia had to have one, too!"

"Right," Sara confirmed with amusement. "After

being done out of an operation and a lovely cast with pictures on it, you bet she wanted one, too. So Elijah's making them each a walking stick. He's waxing the canes down today, after making the twins sandpaper them until their arms ached."

"Which they enjoyed."

"True. Elijah firmly believes they'll value them more after working on them, and I have to agree."

There was a comfortable silence as the waitress filled their teacups again, and when she had gone, Sara looked up to find Beth studying her. Her eyebrows lifted in silent question.

"I was thinking," Beth said frankly, "how much more relaxed you're looking."

With a faint flush Sara murmured, "Probably because Toby's through the operation now."

"Oh...of course!" Beth agreed, her eyes laughing silently as she added, "And how is Luke doing these days? Aside from a bunged-up knee?"

"Just fine."

"Mmm," Beth murmured. "Well, don't tell him my news until tomorrow. Paul has to know first."

"One look at your face and he'll know," Sara predicted. "But I won't say a word. And as Luke's working late tonight, I probably won't even see him."

But despite her words to Beth, that evening Sara found herself listening for Luke's car as she worked on the portrait in the tower, hoping he would return early.

She had barely seen him in the past days, yet there had already been a subtle shift in their relationship during the late hours of each evening as they shared coffee and sandwiches as well as the events of the day.

It was a fragile time, she knew, and any future meant accepting that Luke would always doubt her in some secret corner of himself, however much he tried to hide it.

It was a bitter pill to swallow, but she knew she had to if there was to be a future.

If she did not try, if she did not even *try*.... She drew in a shaking breath and forced her attention back to Hannah's portrait. It was nearly finished, and she had banned Elijah from the tower more than two weeks before, certain she could finish it without his help, and wanting the pleasure of seeing his expression when it was complete to the last detail.

The hum of an approaching car on the road, however, intruded, and she stilled, listening. When it passed the gate her shoulders slumped slightly, and giving an impatient exclamation she conceded defeat and packed up for the night.

Luke, driving home through the quiet streets, found himself hoping that Sara would still be up. There was a new and growing need within him to end his day sharing it with her, instead of shielding her as he had done before. A need that drove him to leave early, telling himself that he could study the proposed agreement with the Turners at home just as well as at the office.

Suddenly his hands gripped the wheel, and he swore with sheer exasperation as he realized that he had left the proposal lying on his worktable in the lab. The temptation simply to call back to the security guard was rejected by the knowledge that to do so could create unpleasant repercussions.

If the man read it, even unintentionally, there would be a strong temptation for him to discuss it with others, and rumors along with unnecessary panic would sweep the company.

His mouth compressing, he turned the car and headed back to the lab. Fifteen minutes later he walked through the production area, which was closing down as the night shift ended, and entered the deserted hallway leading to the research wing.

The rubber tip of his cane made a soft padding noise in the eerie silence, and he was scowling at the twinges in his knee when he rounded the corner.

His first warning that something was awry was the absence of the guard at the security desk in front of the steel door to the research laboratories.

He paused and his eyes swept the area, assessing, seeking, yet finding everything normal but for the guard's absence. He moved forward again, aware that the guard might have stepped into the men's room despite security procedures.

It was a possibility that died at the sight of the uniform hat lying upside down next to the empty chair, specks of blood spattering its lining.

With reflexive speed he pressed the silent alarm, and only then noting that the entrance door was not completely shut, he slipped through it and moved with careful speed down the hall lit only by nightlights. As he neared the door to where the solar model was housed, he heard a scuffling sound, and bending low, he entered at high speed.

He expected to be confronted by the guard struggling with the intruders, or by the sight of the files ransacked. He did not expect someone to be waiting.

The blow missed his head due to his low profile, but still caught him full force on his left shoulder, instantly deadening his arm.

With a grunt he pivoted and in a football block drove his right shoulder into his assailant's midriff. He heard the forceful expulsion of air and the solid thud of the man's body hitting the floor, even as he went to his knees.

Gasping for breath himself, Luke knelt, his head hanging, aware of the molten streaks of pain shooting up his leg and the contrasting numbness of his shoulder and arm as lights flashed on and the footfalls of the approaching security team sounded in the hall.

Raising his head slowly, he sought out the figure sprawled on the floor, and as his gaze reached the man's face, his eyes widened with shock.

An hour later, flexing a sore but otherwise sound shoulder while his left leg was propped up on an opened bottom drawer of his desk, Luke sat in his office regarding Ben Hadley with a cold contemptuous anger.

Outside the office door two policemen waited along with the company's guards. Within the office Ralph Beaumont and John Gordon also waited, their expressions grim.

"Alone!" Ben Hadley repeated sharply. "I don't want them here."

"*If* there is any deal at all," Luke said flatly, "we negotiate here and now. But don't count on it, Hadley."

Pale and disheveled in the rumpled guard uniform he had used along with forged passes, and his knowledge of internal security Ben Hadley looked at the three men and then shrugged.

"I'm offering a trade," he said. "I'll get out of town and stay out. You drop the charges."

"In return for what?" Luke asked coldly.

"The name of the person on your staff who leaked the project."

There was a brief silence in the room, then Luke spoke again. "If our guard weren't in the hospital with a concussion and broken nose, I might have considered trading. But I draw a damned hard line between violent and nonviolent crimes."

"I wouldn't have hit him with the gun if he hadn't tried to disarm me."

Luke did not reply, not trusting his self-discipline in the face of such a shallow and egocentric defense.

"If you don't deal," Hadley said with sudden nervousness, "I'll tell the newspapers who did it. When I'm through you'll look like a fool to the whole industry and town."

"No deal," Luke said quietly.

"Even if it blows your marriage sky-high?" Hadley asked with a sneer.

Luke's jaw clenched, his insides convulsing into a steel knot, but his face remained expressionless. "Regardless of who leaked the—"

"Even your mistress?" Hadley cut in, his eyes calculating.

"My mistress?" Luke repeated mildly, despite instantly comprehending. "I don't happen to have one, Hadley."

"Everyone in the company knows Jess is into you!" Hadley snapped. "They don't dare say a word against her, no matter how the bitch treats anyone who's even a shade lower on the scale than she is. She's the boss's piece of—"

"That's enough!" Luke cut him off harshly. "No deal."

"Then we'll see how the press likes the story. Your mistress who couldn't keep her mouth shut! She had to brag to Drew Barrister that she was on the road to Oslo, and solar energy was her ticket. She started it all. She told Barrister and he sold the tip. She put me here, and now she can pay the piper!"

"You put yourself here," Luke countered coldly. "And it's still no deal." He nodded to John Gordon, who rose and went to the door.

"I'll smear you, Driscoll!" Hadley threatened furiously.

"Remember the laws of slander when you do," Luke returned with apparent indifference.

"You think you're her only lover? Well, ask her—"

"It's of no interest to me," Luke replied, his expression hard.

Ben Hadley stared at Luke, meeting the cold contempt in the other man's eyes. "You really don't give a damn, do you, you cold bastard."

"You finally have the message."

"If you press charges," Ben Hadley said hoarsely, "my family—"

"You should have thought of that before you tried armed assault."

"Dammit, man! Can't you feel anything?"

Luke did not reply and silently watched him ushered out by John Gordon, the door closing behind them.

"You'll press charges?" Ralph asked.

"Yes." Luke rose tiredly, wincing as his shoulder and knee protested. "I meant it. I draw the line at violence, especially premeditated—which it had to be. We'll prosecute."

"And Jess?"

Luke crossed the room and pressed a recessed button. A panel slid open noiselessly, revealing a well-stocked bar. "I'm not yet sure. Drink?" He caught Ralph's expression and ignoring it poured the drinks. As he handed one to his general manager, he said flatly, "Jess is not, and never has been, my mistress."

Ralph's shrewd eyes probed as he accepted the drink, and then he nodded. "Hadley was saying what just about everyone believes. She's been considered untouchable... except by you," he ended dryly.

"So I've recently come to realize." Luke took a long swallow of his drink. "It was convenient, I suppose, not to comment. She acted as a buffer while Sara was missing."

"Let's hope it doesn't boomerang on you now."

Sinking into his chair, Luke forced himself to maintain an expressionless facade. "Suppose you tell me about Jess. All of it."

Listening wearily to Ralph Beaumont's succinct recital, it seemed to Luke that he could hear Sara warning him, as she had almost from the first day they met, that people were not machines.

He had treated Jess, he reflected as Ralph confirmed many of his recent suspicions concerning her, as if she were a convenient mechanical assistant. Ignoring her invitations for more, ignoring her except where she directly touched upon his research interests. Even in the beginning, he was forced to acknowledge, he had hired her because her mind moved with his, her efforts to be someone, her accomplishments, only incidental to him. In a sense, he thought, he carried some guilt.

"In all," Ralph summed up, not without a touch of cynicism, "she hasn't done much more than other fair-haired bastards. The slip—or leak—was probably inadvertent, and she's sharp in her field, if poor on teamwork."

"We can tolerate a player whom we may not personally admire," Luke said, picking up Ralph's vernacular, "but...." He was silent. "If John can confirm tomorrow morning what Hadley said, notify Jess that I want to see her after lunch. Make it at one."

Ralph nodded and, rising, paused. "By the way, I think we can keep Hadley quiet."

Luke's eyebrows rose. "How? I won't deal."

"We can link him to ETI. I'll pass the word to Joe Webster in their head office that if Hadley talks, we talk. ETI won't want that."

"Thanks, Ralph," Luke said quietly. "I'd appreciate it."

The following afternoon Luke received confirmation through John Gordon that the free-lance writer had indeed named Jess as the source of the tip he had sold. Her boast during lunch after her interview for the magazine article had meant a lucrative addition to his fee.

His face drawn, he stared out his office window waiting for Jessica to arrive. He felt battered. There had only been time earlier in the morning to sketch out the night's events to Sara, and not enough time to remove the questions in her eyes.

Swiveling his chair around to face his general manager and security officer, he regarded them both for a long moment before saying, "We'll play it your way, Ralph."

"There won't be any doubts that way."

Even as he nodded, Jessica appeared in the doorway, and looking up, he slipped into his role with a casual, "Come on in, Jess. This might interest you. John has just confirmed who was responsible for that leak."

"Ben Hadley, I assume," she said with distaste as she settled into a chair.

"No, it wasn't Hadley. It was one of our top people. We've been weighing years of excellent work against an accidental indiscretion."

"You'll fire him, of course," she said coldly. "I certainly would."

"For an unintentional remark against a nearly unblemished record?"

"For endangering all the years of work and money we've put into our project."

"And the contributions toward—"

"I don't care what he's done!" she said heatedly.

"He could have destroyed everything! And through sheer carelessness."

He studied her for a long moment and found his predominant reaction was pity. It was the years of fine work, along with his knowledge of her background, that made him persist. "Calm down a moment, Jess. My feeling is that years of damn fine work should count."

"I disagree. We all know the importance of security. We all know what is at stake."

"Everything indicates it was an off-the-cuff remark," Ralph interjected mildly. "We're not considering firing. The choice is between a letter of reprimand and a fine, or—"

"What good would that do?" she attacked.

"It will delay any promotions, especially as the company enlarges, for several years. It will mean a transfer to different, probably less vital, responsibilities. And it will give the individual time to learn to work with the team."

"The other choice," Luke picked up before Jessica could reply, "is to ask for a resignation, which would bar the person, according to our contracts, from working in the solar-energy field for a year. In view of past work, we would provide a year's salary as separation, and unblemished recommendations at the end of the year. A year that could be spent at a university."

"You'll all do as you wish, but I'd still vote to fire him."

"No matter who it is, and how much that person has contributed?"

"Yes." It was said uncompromisingly.

Tiredly Luke nodded to Ralph Beaumont and John Gordon. When they were gone he noted the complacently triumphant look in Jessica's eyes and knew that she assumed he was accepting her recommendation.

His mouth tightening, he pressed the intercom lever to say quietly, "No calls or interruptions, Ellen." Releasing the lever, he saw the first flicker of uncertainty in Jessica's eyes, and despite regrets, he proceeded to wipe away all the complacency by requesting her resignation.

"He's still in conference," Ellen Ross informed Sara nearly an hour later. "If it's urgent...."

"No! No, it isn't. Actually," Sara said jerkily under Elijah's amused regard, "I'd rather he didn't know I called, Mrs. Ross."

"Make that Ellen, please."

"Ellen." Encouraged by the secretary's calm friendliness, Sara continued, "Luke told me what happened last night. He insisted he wasn't hurt, but he looked terrible this morning, and he's favoring not only his leg but also his shoulder and arm. I thought you might know whether or not he's seen a doctor."

"Dr. Howton has seen him," Ellen assured her, adding the doctor's recommendations. "He's bruised and under orders to head for home as soon as this conference is over."

"You're certain?"

"I wouldn't slap him on the shoulder, or cling to it, for a few days," Ellen advised with a low laugh.

"Male pride or not, he'd probably crumple at your feet."

Sara couldn't help smiling, and thanking Ellen, she hung up.

"That wasn't so difficult, now, was it?" Elijah said blandly, as if he hadn't called Ellen himself after watching Sara fretting and then handed her the phone without warning.

She gave him a speaking look. "The company doctor has ordered him home, though Ellen doubts that he'll be here before five. I think he's with Jessica now."

"Feeling a pang of sympathy for her? It's the end of her dream. Once Luke decides, that's it."

"All I'm sure of," she said, "is that I hope she never comes near here again."

"Or near Luke?" he asked, and when she did not reply, he added, "Better check with Grey. She'll know what his leg needs."

"Moist heat," Grey told her when she sought her out in the kitchen. "There's a heating pad in the pantry. You might put that in his room. He also needs to stay off that leg for a few days and take aspirin for the inflammation."

"Which he will never do," Sara said dryly.

"Short of tying him down," Grey agreed with a dry humor that had only recently surfaced. "And I'm not about to try it."

"Don't look at me!"

"Take that box of Epsom salts on the lower shelf, too. A warm bath might help."

Moments later, her arms ladened, Sara entered

Luke's room and stopped dead, nearly dropping everything, as her eyes fastened on her own portrait hanging over the mantel.

Why, she wondered, and managed to walk to the chair by his bed and sit down. Only then did she realize the portrait was positioned so that he would easily be able to lie in bed staring at it.

The thought unsettled her; it seemed somewhat akin to discovering that she was being watched while she slept. How often had he lain in bed staring at it, hating her, filled with contempt, wanting revenge?

She shook herself mentally. Perhaps he had—once—but not now. Surely now there was caring, even possibly the beginning of belief. For a long moment she looked up at the portrait and gradually started to see it in perspective, almost as if it were of someone else.

It was, in a way, she thought suddenly. The Sara in the painting was much younger, so untried and full of dreams. The years had changed her irrevocably, and Sara knew she could never paint herself in just that way again.

Rising, she prepared the room and Luke's bathroom, and then with a last look at the self she had once been, she left the room and bumped into Elijah.

His eyes went past her, then returned to her face. "It's been there since the day it came back to Spars' Nest." He paused. "You know that he loves you, don't you? And you love him."

Her eyes met his, and then she said quietly, with a sense of relief, "Yes, I love him. I can't help it."

"I never doubted it," he said gently. "Never once."

"It doesn't solve everything."

"It's a foundation for solutions," he countered.

"If only...." She sighed and looked up at him. "Am I asking too much, Elijah? Can I live all the rest of our days together knowing he believes what he does, knowing the suspicions that lurk in the shadows of his mind?"

"In time they may fade away," he replied, and unwittingly echoing Luke's words, he added, "All you can do is try."

Nodding, she murmured unevenly, "I'd better check on the children. They'll be waking up from their nap any moment."

They were not awake, however, and glancing out at the gray day, she suspected the weather as much as anything was extending their nap. Restlessly she left the room, and once downstairs, she decided to take a walk.

Asking Grey to look after the twins if they wakened before she returned, she promised to be back within a half hour.

"Be sure to wear a warm coat," Grey advised. "It's near snowing."

Startled, Sara paused, and Grey flushed slightly. "Thank you," Sara said. "I will."

Wearing comfortable walking shoes, dark green plaid slacks and a navy sweater, Sara added a fingertip fleece-lined coat and left the house.

The sky was a dove gray with dark charcoal clouds decapitating the mountain peaks, and the air held a crisp chill that confirmed Grey's prediction of imminent snow despite the warm sun of the previous day.

The changeable weather, so typical of Denver, reminded her of the Denverite Elijah had mentioned once, who claimed the weather was so confusing that her cat was storing acorns.

Snow or sun, she reflected as she walked, she felt a quiet exuberance and growing sense of optimism that was somehow connected to finding her portrait in Luke's room. A room she knew she wanted to share.

She found herself looking back over the past months at the Luke she had met again, in a sense, and found she could no longer believe the threats he had hurled at her. Somehow Her Luke and the Other Luke had become fused, and neither part of him was invulnerable.

Fighting him had been her defense, her battle for emotional survival, and she had been so involved in defending herself that she had failed to see that for all his threats and anger, even contempt, his actions were contradictory.

He had claimed to have no feelings for her, yet he had stayed by her bed when she was ill, he had insisted on protecting her, he had been there when her own courage had wavered, and his caring had been in every kiss and touch and caress.

As if she were creating a three-dimensional portrait, she searched out other pieces of his personality, and it was during this process that she suddenly stopped with a look of horror on her face.

Beth! She had completely forgotten that Beth was stopping by at four. A look at her watch told her it was just past four, and half running, she turned and hurried back to the house even as the overburdened clouds released a steady flow of heavy snowflakes.

She was within sight of the gate, and had paused to catch her breath and ease the stitch in her side, when the sound of a car coming down the road behind her at a reckless speed made her step hastily onto the snow-covered verge.

There was only time for a glimpse of the driver, of Rufus, with his face set in grim lines, before the car skidded as he applied the brakes and swung wildly through the gate.

With sudden alarm and dread, Sara began to run, her heart thudding with fear. She was gasping for breath as she rounded the curve in the drive just as Rufus, his car parked alongside of Jessica's, dashed into the house.

The driveway, which had been empty when she left, was now crowded with cars, and somehow she knew that Jessica had come for revenge.

Rushing up the steps into the house, she was greeted by a scene that froze her in her tracks.

Jessica, ranting hysterically, was confronting a rigidly controlled Luke, whose knuckles were white as he gripped his cane. Rufus had just caught Jessica's swinging hand, and Beth looked on with clear fright.

"I'll tell everyone!" Jessica was screaming. "I'll sue you! I'll tell them what kind of rotten lover you are, what kind of a thief you are, and—"

"Either you tell me exactly what happened just now with Grey," Luke cut in, his voice as frozen as the mountains outside, "or I'll have the sheriff here so fast your head will spin!"

"To hell with Grey!" Jessica shouted. "She's turned against me like all of you!"

"Answer him, Jess!" Rufus snapped.

"The truth," Luke demanded coldly, ignoring Rufus. "You were in the kitchen with her; what did you *do* to her?"

"Nothing! She's a stupid old woman."

"Grey," Luke said with a deadly softness that Sara knew only too well, "is lying on her bed now with a handprint across her face and a nasty cut on her head."

"She fell and then became hysterical!" Jessica threw back almost insolently. "What else do you do with someone who's hysterical but slap them!"

"So hard that she was unconscious for several minutes and bleeding from a head wound?"

"She fell," Jessica reiterated, "and those damned brats started screaming."

Involuntarily Sara moved forward, and looking up, Luke said curtly, "Leave this to me, Sara!"

Jessica's head whipped around. "Yes, leave it to him, Sara! The man who doesn't believe your children are his! Who's willing suddenly to play the noble, forgiving— Ah!" She reeled as Rufus's hand struck her cheek with a force that shocked not only her but also everyone else in the room.

Before anyone could react, Rufus gripped Jessica's upper arm in a punishing grip and looked at Luke. "There will be no further trouble from Jess," he said quietly. "She won't be suing, and she won't be babbling about stolen credit or Nobel Prizes. She's retiring. If your offer allowing a resignation is still open,

Jessica's will be in the mail tonight along with a statement that will protect you against any further charges."

There was a barely perceptible nod from a grim-faced Luke, and then they were gone, leaving a vacuum behind.

Sara, whose eyes had instantly gone to Luke's face as Jessica screamed her accusations, hardly heard what Rufus said, for one look had told her that whatever else Jessica had lied about in the past, this time she spoke the truth.

Luke had doubted that he was the father of the twins. The color seeped from her face, and even as Luke met her eyes in the silence left behind by the departure of Rufus and Jessica, Elijah spoke from the stairway.

"The children are missing!"

"Oh, God, no!" Sara cried, wheeling toward Elijah, her heart seeming to stop.

"Easy, girl," Elijah said, his eyes moving past her. "All this can wait. Right now there's a mean storm howling outside, and the children may have run off into the middle of it."

"No!" Sara whispered. "How long? How long have they been missing?"

"Could be anything from twenty minutes to a good half hour."

"Why would they run away?" Sara cried. "They must be in the house!"

"From what Grey told me," Beth said quickly, "Jessica struck her so violently that she fell against the kitchen worktable and collapsed. She thinks she heard Jessica say something to the effect that the children had killed Grey."

"But—"

"Details can wait!" Elijah said sharply. "What we need to do right now is find them."

"Let's be certain that they're not hiding somewhere in the house," Luke said, taking command. "Elijah will check the basement, Sara upstairs. Beth and I, this floor and garages."

Numbly, not looking at Luke for fear her control would crack completely, Sara fled up the stairs. As she searched rapidly through the rooms and the attic, her lips shook so badly that when she tried to whistle for Bumper, barely a sound emerged.

When they met in the entrance hall again, Luke read the naked fear in Sara's eyes as she said hoarsely, "They aren't here! Bumper would answer a call. They have to be out there!"

Leaning heavily on his cane, his left leg refusing to take his full weight any longer, Luke moved his free hand to comfort her. She stiffened and then flinched away from him. "Sara, I can explain. Give—"

"If anything happens to them," she cried, "I'll never—"

"That's enough!" Elijah interceded angrily. "Luke, call the sheriff!"

As Luke obeyed, Sara held her silence, knowing Elijah was right. But unable to stand there doing nothing, she left them and cut through to the kitchen. There she leaned against the counter as a wave of weakness washed over her, staring blindly into the snowstorm outside, and praying desperately.

As the first shock wave passed, her eyes suddenly focused on the ground outside. With a muffled exclamation she was out the back door, crouching and studying the suggestion of footprints next to the steps that were nearly covered by the new-fallen snow. Bumper's paw pads were still visible in mud already frozen by the rapidly dropping temperature.

Slowly her eyes lifted to the forbidding mountains.

"Where?" she whispered as if they could answer. "Where!"

And then she knew. She stilled, wondering how Toby could possibly make it with his leg still weak. The thought seemed to paralyze her until suddenly she knew what she had to do.

Wheeling, she raced inside and up the stairs, ignoring Beth's startled look from the phone, where she was speaking to Paul.

It took only moments before she was down again, dressed in three sweaters, her woolen slacks and her riding boots.

The pantry held a flashlight, first-aid kit and food. She piled them helter-skelter into a rucksack and tossed Elijah's mac on top. She had just filled a thermos flask with hot coffee and was adding sugar when Luke found her.

"Where— You are not going out in that storm alone, Sara!"

"I am."

"There will be plenty of others here shortly!"

"I'm not waiting."

"Dammit, you don't even know where they are!"

"They're heading for the ruins. To their cave. I'm sure of it."

"You could be wrong."

"I know them, and I'm going."

"Then I'm going with you, and to hell with my leg!"

"For two children you don't believe are your own?" she cried bitterly.

"Sara, it isn't that way!"

"I saw your face, Luke!"

"Then you saw wrong, Sara."

His hands gripped her shoulders as he tried to force her to listen, and not caring, she struck out at his injured shoulder.

The blow sent him staggering back, his face gray with pain, and in the few seconds he needed to recover, she had scooped up the rucksack and was gone into the storm.

"Sara! *Sara!*" His injured leg dragging now, he stumbled after her. "Sara! Come back!"

But she was gone. Sucked into the dark vortex of the storm, into the eerie silence of snow that was rapidly turning his hair white even as he stood helplessly chained by his injuries.

And as the coldness crystallized in his bones, he knew that above all else in his life he wanted her back safely—on any terms, just safely.

"Luke?"

He did not move, his eyes searching upward through the darkness, fury raging within him because he could not follow, and despair searing him because of what he had read in her eyes.

"Luke, the sheriff's deputy is here."

He turned heavily to face Beth. "She's gone up there alone."

Beth studied his face an instant before saying gently, "She's strong, Luke. She'll make it."

"She has to," he said huskily. "She has to, Beth. All of them."

"They will. Paul is on his way, and the sheriff's deputy needs to talk to you. Please come."

Nodding heavily, he followed Beth into the house, and ignoring the snow melting on his head and shoulders, he ordered, "Check the bathrooms, Beth, and bring me any elastic bandages you can find."

"Luke, you can't!"

"If there are none, bring a sheet and we'll cut it in strips."

"No, Luke! You'll cripple yourself."

"Then I'll find something myself, dammit!" Gritting his teeth against the pain, he limped into the den to find the deputy studying a map laid out on his desk.

As soon as Elijah had completed introductions, the deputy asked, "Where do you think they might be?"

Tersely Luke brought them up to date, tracing the path on the map. "That was the route we took up there. The children were with us. If she's right, and they are heading for the ruins, they'll follow that path as best they can. But in this storm...."

"If they left nearly an hour ago, they may have reached the ruins before the storm really broke," the deputy said. "We'll send teams in from both directions as well as search the surrounding areas in case the children did not head up there."

As the deputy left the room, Luke swore angrily and looked up to find Paul and Beth entering. "Where are the bandages?"

"You'll do permanent damage," Paul said crisply, "and in the end you'll collapse and waste the search party's time."

"Either I find something and do it myself, or you help me."

Paul and Beth exchanged a brief glance, and then Beth sighed, "I'll see what I can find."

"She should have waited!" Luke ground out.

"Would you have waited?" Elijah asked gruffly.

"Hell, no," Paul answered for Luke.

"I've called in the volunteer search teams," the deputy announced from the door. "One of our men knows of an overgrown road near the ruins. Unless the storm covered it completely, we should get through with a four-wheel drive."

"I'll start from down here," Paul said. "If you'll brief me on the signaling system should they be found by one of us, I'll get ready."

Beth entered at that moment, several elastic bandages in her hand. "While you're gone, I'll start sandwiches and hot coffee." She knelt by Luke. "Roll up your pant leg!"

"I can do it."

"I'm awed," she said caustically. "Now, do as I say."

To his own surprise, Luke found himself obeying. He was standing up, testing his leg with in inward wince, when a voice said from the door, "I've brought Dante. He has a good nose."

Luke went rigid as he looked up to find Rufus in the doorway, a retriever by his side. "We'll manage without your kind of help!"

"You need all the help you can get," Rufus replied levelly, his blue eyes steady. "Jessica caused this mess as well as you."

"What the hell does that mean?" Luke demanded tightly.

"When you're ready to listen," Rufus said quietly, "come see me. Meanwhile—"

"Meanwhile," Paul stepped in quietly, "we can use you and the dog."

Even as Luke started to speak, Elijah's hand came down on his shoulder. With grim resignation Luke nodded and forced himself to wait as the search was organized.

Where was Sara, his mind asked over and over. He tried to concentrate, but a part of him continued to ask desperately, where was she? Had she fallen? Was she lying half-covered with snow? And the children?

"We'll find them," the deputy said, glancing at Luke's drawn face. "It's a matter of time."

How much time was there, Sara wondered with fear as she climbed the hostile slopes. If Toby fell, if either of the children faltered, they could freeze to death before they were found.

Desperately she searched the spinning darkness with her flashlight for any sign of tracks, the cold thin air searing her lungs.

They would both get the length of her tongue when she found them, she promised herself, sick with worry as she doggedly pushed herself on.

When she was forced to pause again, she stood panting, her hands already stiffening within her gloves. The snow fell in silence around her. No lights were visible anywhere. It was as if she had stumbled out of the world into some primeval past.

Impatiently she pushed away the fantasy and went on, her pace slowing despite herself. Time and time again she paused to call, "Toby! Tricia!" Time and time again there was only the eerie sighing of the wind in reply.

Her legs felt heavier, and her strength was gradually being sapped by the exertion, the cold and the high thin air.

What if she passed them in the dark, she fretted, and tried to tell herself that surely Bumper would bark. Surely.

The pauses gradually became more frequent, and vaguely she was aware of frozen tears on her cheeks. She kept calling, but each time it seemed the wind was stronger, the night colder, the snow more smothering.

Exhaustion started to make her clumsier, and inevitably she missed her footing and went sprawling and sliding down the rocky slope until she collided violently with the trunk of a tree.

The light flew from her hand, spinning wildly beyond her reach, to stop with its pale beam filled with falling snow. Stunned and winded she lay there unable to move.

It was in that moment of feeling an utter failure that she heard the barking.

"Bumper!" she cried hoarsely, her voice cracking. "Here!"

The pup was upon her so suddenly that she fell back beneath his welcoming assault. It was several minutes before she could stagger to her feet and, ignoring her bruises, whisper to him, "Find Tricia! Find Toby!"

As if he understood, the fawn puppy bounded ahead, circled back, then rushed on as she retrieved the light and followed.

"Mummy?"

The small cry sent Sara stumbling the last steps to find the children curled together under the snow-ladened branches of a thick shrub. In seconds they were in her arms and she was whispering, "I'm here, darlings. I'm here. Mummy's here!"

"We didn't hurt her!" Tricia wept.

"You didn't," she agreed. "Grey is all right. It wasn't your fault at all." She reassured them over and over, and as they calmed, she eased the thermos from the rucksack and fed them the thickly sweet coffee.

"We're not far from the ruins—the cave," she told them. "We'll go there. They'll be looking for us there."

They protested, but she firmly insisted, shrugging out of the extra sweaters she had worn and bundling each child into a thick cocoon of wool.

Once again she started climbing, but the children were soon unable to make it through the drifts and whimpered with cold and weariness. Finally, knowing they were all too wet to stay still, she carried Toby on her back and Tricia in her arms, and staggered on in a daze until out of the darkness came a huge black dog barking wildly, and behind him Rufus and... Luke.

An hour later she was back in Spars' Nest, surrounded by warmth and light and protesting, "I'm fine, Beth! Please!"

"You're bruised and scraped and still half-frozen. Here! Get into this robe!"

Wrapped warmly, Sara turned. "Are you sure Toby and Tricia are all right?"

"They're fine, and ready for bed. Just as you are."

"I'm not going to bed," Sara refused, and started toward the connecting door. Beth firmly turned her back and pushed her onto the bed's edge. "Beth, I want to see them!"

"Slippers on first."

Muffling an exclamation, Sara shuffled them on impatiently even as a shiver rippled through her slender body and her eyes blanked for an instant.

"Sara?" Beth asked softly. "Are you truly all right?"

"I'll never be all right," Sara whispered, half to herself.

"Don't let Jessica Pettiway's lies destroy your life!" Beth retorted sharply.

"I'm leaving. She and Luke can do what they want—together or apart, I don't care."

"She was out for revenge, and hysterical on top of it."

"She told the truth, Beth. I saw it in his face. What hope is there now? I thought...I thought that even if he did believe Rufus had been my lover, we had a chance. We haven't. There's nothing but an endless series of suspicions because he has never trusted me, and never will."

"Perhaps Jessica told him something in the begin—"

"Don't! Dear God, Beth, *leave me alone!*"

There was a long stiff silence that Beth finally fractured somewhat hesitantly. "Sara, if you should leave.... Come stay with us until you can work things out somehow."

"I—"

"Promise me that much, Sara. Toby still needs therapy, and tonight may have set him back. No, he's fine! But come to us, please."

Sara nodded tiredly, knowing she was grateful and feeling unable to cope. "I...I'd like to see the children now."

The sight of Luke with Toby and Tricia sitting cross-legged on each side of him on one bed, both faces directed confidently up at him, stopped her in her tracks.

He looked utterly drained, yet somehow still masculine and powerful with his arms around them protectively. With an effort she dragged her eyes from the lean drawn lines of his face to concentrate on what he was saying.

"...and she is gone!" Luke finished firmly.

"Forever and ever?" Toby asked.

"Forever and ever. And you know why?"

Both children waited, regarding him with clear trust. Misplaced trust, Sara thought savagely, her hands clenching.

"She's gone because she hurts people, and because she lies. Do you know what a lie is?"

They nodded simultaneously.

"She lied when she said Toby and Tricia have bad blood. She lied when she said I didn't like you or want you. I love you, both of you."

His dark head bent, and without self-consciousness, he brushed his lips against each soft cheek. Her throat tightening unbearably, Sara turned and fled back into her room, only to collide with Elijah.

"Whoa, girl!" he murmured, and wrapped his arms around her, holding her. "You're safe now. They're safe. It's all over, girl."

She leaned in the circle of his arms, wishing that it were truly all over—and finding that something inside of her had frozen in the dark cold storm raging over the mountains. She could not cry, could only shake.

Elijah did not speak, waiting until her trembling subsided before finally releasing her. "Luke's gone, child. Go in to the children."

For an instant her eyes met his, saw his awareness of the grief within her, and then, turning, she left.

By the time she entered Elijah's sitting room half an hour later, she found Paul and Beth with him, but not Luke.

"Has Rufus left?" she asked, just recalling that he had been there, and not willing to ask where Luke was.

"A short while ago," Paul answered her. "Sara, Luke's beside himself and in rotten physical shape. He may have—"

"I am tired of hearing what a terrible time Luke is always having," Sara cut in coldly.

There was a stunned and awkward silence, and Sara let it sit, finding she was too frozen inside to care.

"We'd better be going," Paul said at last.

"I meant my offer," Beth murmured as she hugged Sara goodbye. "Come to us if you leave."

When she was alone with Elijah, she avoided his brooding regard, and crossing to the hearth, she stood staring into the fire—waiting.

It was not long before she heard the uneven steps that warned of Luke's arrival, and turning, she faced him, her whole body rigid.

"Sara...." His hand moved toward her.

"Don't touch me!" she warned through her teeth.

Though his eyes narrowed, he still closed the gap with a swiftness that made him grimace with pain, but which also ended with her wrist captured by him. "It's over!" he said sharply. "Get hold of yourself!"

"They could have *died*!" she cried with clear anguish. "I told you years ago she hated me! You knew what she had said to the children, how she hurt them!"

"I didn't know that she was in the house until it was too late!"

"I'll never trust you again, Luke. I'll never believe you again."

The blood drained from his already pale face, his scar a white line against his now sallow tan.

"All these months," she went on brokenly, "you pretended to offer friendship—to care. And all the while you were wondering if I was palming off another man's children on you. How could you?"

"Because I couldn't stop loving you, no matter what I thought or feared."

"Loving! You don't know what it means. But I'm through! Even a dog knows better than to come back after three kicks."

"Do you think it was easy for me?" Luke demanded angrily. "It was possible, knowing the past. Rufus could have fathered them. Yet I loved you enough, came to love them enough, to fight my suspicions and to accept them as my own children, without reservation."

"It's going to be much easier in the future, Luke. We're leaving. This time I won't be blackmailed by your threats to take them away from me. I have Jessica's testimony that you have been lovers for years, and I can match any accusations you care to throw back."

"Sara, she is lying! We have never been lovers!"

"Of course not! I wouldn't expect you to admit it," Sara mocked bitterly, and with her words she echoed his own of years before when Rufus claimed to have been her lover.

"I tell you—" He stopped, and she saw the shocked awareness in his eyes.

"No more, Luke," she said tautly. "This time I'll fight you in court. I'll even deny you are their father, if I must."

"Sara...!"

But she tore free of him with a violence that rocked him, and was gone, leaving him staring after her in shock.

CHAPTER SIXTEEN

A WEEK AFTER THE STORM Sara entered Luke's den to find him at his desk, staring bleakly out the window. His face, etched in lines of fatigue, seemed almost gaunt in the gray morning light, and he did not turn to look at her until she halted on the far side of his desk.

Fighting an irrational desire to comfort him, she steeled herself and said flatly, "We're ready to leave. Grey is well enough now to handle things. We'll be with Beth and Paul while I look for a place to live until Toby's therapy is finished."

He rose as if he were aged, and when he walked around the desk, she eyed him warily, even as she noticed that he was limping a great deal less.

He stopped a stride away, his eyes guarded and his face expressionless. "Sara, if we could talk it over—just once."

"No." Her head shook tiredly, and her gray eyes were shuttered. "It's done and past."

"Not like this," he refuted. "If you need more time—"

"It is over! It never really was."

"Dammit, Sara, *no!*" His hands gripped her shoulders, and she was hauled against him and imprisoned before she could react.

"Don't!" she choked, her body rigid, yet aware of the lean hardness of him. She tried to avoid his mouth, but his large hand fastened in her hair, forcing back her head, and then his mouth was plundering hers with a deep, demanding passion.

Even as she resisted responding, his lips became gentle, wooing, and what violence had failed to do, the soft caressing of his mouth succeeded in doing.

The yearning to hold him one last time conquered her, and her hands stopped pushing him away and instead curled around his head as she kissed him with equal desperation.

"You're staying!" Luke groaned. "We'll work it out somehow."

Her denial was lost as his mouth rejoined hers and his hands touched and brushed and held her body until she felt the familiar weakness, the familiar prelude to passion, spreading within her.

When she was trembling and breathless, he loosened his hold to cradle her lightly in his arms, and her head dropped weakly onto his shoulder.

"You're staying," he said hoarsely.

"No," she whispered, and drawing on the last remnants of her willpower, she pulled free of him as if he were a whirlpool trying to claim her.

"You don't mean that."

"I do." Her voice wobbled. "We were always... strongly attracted to each other, but it can't replace trust and friendship."

"We have much more than sex between us," he denied angrily. "You're wrong!"

"Goodbye, Luke."

Moments later she shepherded the children and the pup into the small station wagon. She would send it back when they left Denver. Once Toby's therapy was over, she would accept nothing ever again from Luke, however difficult the future was.

"Are you angry at Uncle Luke?" Tricia asked.

"Yes," Sara replied briefly, opting for honesty.

"Are you going to make up?" Toby queried worriedly.

"I don't know."

In the instant before she stepped into the car, she paused to look up at Spars' Nest, her eyes resting on the tower. A house built with love, she thought with pain, and for two generations there had been love, but not for her.

Lifting her eyes to the sky, she stared up blankly. It looked and felt like snow again, she thought numbly. It was another cold and gray and miserable day.

IT WAS STILL COLD a week later, and also wet.

Icy rain pelted past the windows of Elijah's sitting room as Luke sprawled in one of the deep upholstered chairs by the fire. Abruptly he raised his hand and drained his glass in one long swallow.

"Is that what you're planning to do the rest of your life?" Elijah asked roughly. "Drink yourself blind every night?"

"Any better suggestions?" Luke asked without interest.

There was a pause. "No, you seem to enjoy being right where you've put yourself."

"I did, didn't I," Luke agreed obscurely, quelling

the need to talk to Elijah, to exorcise the past in the hope of a future, for he knew he could not. Never to Elijah.

"Have you tried to see her?"

"No."

"Did you doubt that Toby and Tricia were yours?"

"Yes," Luke admitted heavily without looking up. "Jess...." He stopped.

"They each have a very faint indentation on the right side of their forehead, about a finger's width above the eyebrow," Elijah said quietly. "I have it, too."

"Everywhere I look," Luke whispered hoarsely, "I'm damned."

"Call her!"

Luke rose with sudden anger to face his grandfather. "Keep your advice and platitudes to yourself, old man! I don't need them! I don't want them!" With the words he threw his glass into the fire and strode out of the room, thrusting back the urge to return and apologize.

In the silence of his room he stopped, breathing heavily, and then almost reluctantly his hand moved to the light switch.

Only the light above the painting on the wall facing him came on, and he stared at it hungrily. As always, her portrait drew him, making him ache to appease that silent yearning in her eyes.

He felt gutted without her. He felt as if he were skin and bones that were hollowed out and still moving. Inside he was screaming day and night, and nothing smothered the pain...not drinking himself blind, not working in his lab, nothing.

Turning, he walked from the room and out of the house into the cold rain and darkness of night.

He had no idea of how much time passed before he found himself outside Rufus's studio. He knew only that he was there, wet and frozen and recalling the enigmatic words of Rufus, "When you're ready to listen, come see me."

Haggardly he stared up at the modern cedar house, at the lights illuminating the studio with its vast windows, and then slowly he moved toward the door.

Beyond the barest flicker of his eyes, Rufus betrayed no surprise on finding Luke at his door. He took in Luke's state with one look and said brusquely, "Come in, man, before you drown or freeze to death."

Luke entered stiffly, mechanically dried his head with the towel Rufus silently handed to him and then replaced his sodden sweater with a dry one.

It was only after Luke had swallowed half a mug of laced hot coffee that Rufus stopped pacing to stand in the center of his huge studio room with his legs braced apart and his hands in his hip pockets.

"I'm listening," Luke said tersely.

"Well," Rufus drawled in a hard tone, "I'm damned if I know where to begin." For spaced seconds he said nothing.

Then with an angry movement he wheeled and strode to the canvases stacked against one wall. After searching for several moments, apparently oblivious to Luke, he extracted two canvases from behind a corner stack. Without a word he turned one toward Luke.

It was a portrait of Luke, and he knew instantly that it was the one Elijah had referred to once, but which he had never seen himself.

It was also a portrayal of himself that made his throat go taut, for the man looking back at him was painted in sunlight, and smiling with a tender amusement in his eyes. It left him feeling an infinite sense of loss.

"This," Rufus said quietly, "is what she was painting when your marriage started. Several months before she left, she turned from it in despair. She told me it was a lie...to throw it out. I did. Simply to see what her reaction would be as I tossed it into the trash pile outside. Do you know what she did?"

Luke shook his head with an effort.

"She cried. Her face dropped into her hands, and she wept, asking me over and over why she loved you."

With an angry shrug Rufus turned to the second canvas. "She decided to paint something historical, to escape into the past, perhaps. Instead she painted the end of your marriage, her innermost feelings about your endless suspicions. It was her last painting here. She dubbed it *The Faithless*."

He turned the canvas slowly toward Luke and watched as the man's face went rigid with horror. Inwardly Luke recoiled from the terrible cruelty of the inquisitor's face, a face not unlike his own, but reflecting the worst of himself. When his eyes shifted to the victim's face, to the pleading eyes... his own face grayed.

"Long before she ever painted this," Rufus told him evenly, "we discussed that time in history. She told me she had always thought that it was not the victims who had lacked faith, but the inquisitors. I doubt if she realized consciously that you and she are the main characters in this."

The indictment was clear, and Luke had to force himself to stand. "I'd better go."

"Not yet," Rufus disagreed. "This painting is the truth, Luke."

"I know...I know." The painting left no doubt of her innocence, and he felt ill.

"Surely you want to know how and why I repaid her naive trust with a lie that destroyed her marriage to you!"

"Go on."

"Your jealousy showed from the beginning. Jessica wanted Sara gone, and she promptly took advantage by planting doubts in a mind ready to doubt. On her visits to Grey she used to 'borrow' some item of Sara's. Remember the times when you saw a scarf or purse of Sara's lying in view here when Jessica just happened to drop in with you? Remember how it reappeared in view at home...as if Sara had been tucked away in my bedroom during your visit?"

Luke's face tightened with the memories of his accusations, of Sara denying tearfully that she had been at Rufus's studio that day.

"You snapped up those clues like an inquisitor panting to prosecute," Rufus continued coldly.

"Just as on that last day, when Sara arrived in the afternoon for tutoring. Realizing I was quite ill, she stayed, and when Jessica called and found out, she saw her chance. You came running."

"What kind of people are you?"

"Self-centered ones," Rufus said bluntly. "What kind of man are you? We set it up, but *you* bought it. You never once, that I know of, defended Sara."

"Why?"

"Don't you know yet?"

"Jessica...for you. For her?"

"For Jess? Don't you know that she's a scrawny little alley cat inside? That's she's clawing her way to respectability, to success, and most of all to fame? Sara got in the way. The pinnacle was the Drs. Driscoll together accepting the Nobel Prize. It was her obsession."

"That's not normal...or even realistic," Luke rejected.

"Obsessions never are. My obsession with her isn't, either. Yet I can't help seeing and wanting that little alley cat who is a passionate child, afraid of emotions—something I suspect you share, and which first drew you two together."

"Rufus—"

"Jess came to me the night after I told you Sara and I were lovers."

Luke's eyes closed as he absorbed it. "Whatever you thought of me, how could you do it to Sara?"

Rufus sighed tiredly. "You think there are some things you would never do. You think you're a decent person. Then you meet someone you need so deeply and so terribly that you find you'll do anything. That's when you discover you're not so decent after all."

"And you sell out a friend?" Luke said harshly.

"You tell yourself it really isn't that way. You're helping. I was helping to free Sara to paint. It's easier than facing yourself."

Luke knew in that moment that he could not indict Rufus without condemning himself. He had needed Sara terribly, and because of that very need, he had also destroyed her. He and Rufus were both guilty.

"There's no logic, Luke. I suspect you know that already. Was it logical to believe a friend instead of the woman you loved? Would you have listened to me before tonight?"

There was no need to reply, and Luke could only stand there gripped by a growing horror as the truth penetrated fully and finally. Almost blindly he turned away and crossed to the door. As his hand touched it, Rufus spoke again.

"It's not too late, Luke. Not with a woman like Sara."

Luke looked back at him, white lipped, and gave a harsh raw laugh. "Not too late! After putting her through hell because of what you did?"

"Because of what *you* did. If you know why, there's still a chance."

Wrenching open the door, Luke strode back into the darkness. The rain had stopped, but he was barely aware of it as he walked unseeingly into the night.

Dawn found him entering Spars' Nest with no real memory of the hours since he had left Rufus. Half stumbling on a weakened leg, he entered his den to sit there with his head in his hands, wondering how he could go on.

A weak sun was sending its light into the room when he finally reached out for a pen, and drawing a sheet of paper toward him, he slowly began to write.

CHAPTER SEVENTEEN

SARA CIRCLED A RENTAL LISTING in the morning paper and reached for her coffee absently.

"When are you going to make up with Uncle Luke?" Tricia asked across the breakfast table.

"Someday," Sara replied evenly, having become accustomed to the question during the past week.

"You know something, mummy?" Toby asked.

"Hmm?" Sara circled another listing.

"Uncle Luke would make an awfully good daddy."

"Yup," Tricia agreed succinctly.

Sara stilled and then looked up, her throat tight. She should let the remark pass without comment, she told herself, yet found she had to pursue it. "That would mean we won't go back to Florida, we would always live at Spars' Nest."

"Uncle Luke said he'd like to be my daddy. And Tricia's, too," Toby revealed casually.

"He could kiss us good-night all the time!" Tricia offered with clear enchantment, adding generously, "and he could kiss you, too."

"But...." Sara stopped, and aware that they were truly in favor of the idea, she said feebly, "But we wouldn't see Aunt Madge again."

"If you *marry* Uncle Luke first," Tricia explained patiently, "then we can go on a honeymoon to Aunt Madge. All of us."

"What an intriguing idea," Beth remarked lightly as she entered the kitchen.

Flushing slightly, Sara frowned repressively at the children. "That's enough now! You'd best go help brush the ponies and finish your morning chores."

"But, mummy—" Toby started.

"Now!"

"Okay." Both sighing, they left with abused expressions on their small faces.

"It seems they're all for the idea of Luke as a daddy," Beth said casually as she helped herself to a glass of orange juice, having been told that coffee was not good for the baby.

"Let's not discuss it," Sara replied, pointedly returning to the listings.

"Luke's commissioned Paul to design a research center."

"I'm so glad for you," Sara managed, Luke's name plucking a nerve.

Beth grimaced and eyed Sara with despair. "Sara, you look awful! You can't go on like this. You're losing more weight every day."

Sara shrugged slightly. "It will come back. It did last time."

"It's not *right*!"

Startled by Beth's vehemence, Sara looked up.

"You're both desperately in love with each other, and yet— All right, I'll be quiet! You don't have to leave. I...." The doorbell stopped her, and as Sara looked toward the hall warily, Beth waved her hand. "Relax! It's probably someone inquiring about the horses."

Still, Sara listened tensely to Beth's murmuring and the deeper male voice that responded. She was out of the chair, hovering by the back door, when Beth returned.

"It's Elijah." She cast an exasperated yet compassionate glance at Sara. "He wants to talk to you."

Uncertainly Sara's hand clutched the door latch, and then, as she hesitated, Elijah was there with his familiar, "Easy, girl. It's only an old man who's still your friend." He waved her to the table and followed, grumbling, "Though I don't know why I should be, considering you haven't called me once in the past ten days."

Facing him across the table, Sara found herself not knowing what she hoped or feared as she watched him help himself to coffee.

"Good coffee," he said after a swallow. Replacing his cup, he eyed her somberly. "You're looking in the peak of health. Obviously you are quite happy now."

Her lips trembling perilously, Sara whispered, "Please don't joke. I don't think I can bear it."

"Then let me say my piece right out." He cleared his throat, and withdrawing a packet of envelopes from inside his coat pocket, he laid them before her. "These are the legal documents that settle trusts on Toby and Tricia."

"I don't want anything from Luke!" She pushed them away.

"They are from me, girl!" he reproached her.

"For your supposed grandchildren?" she asked bitterly.

He shook his head, and his gray eyebrows lowered in a frown. "As I told Luke, they carry the Driscoll mark—if I needed proof."

"What mark?" Her tone was derisive.

"That slight crease in the forehead above the right brow. I have it." He pointed. "It skipped Luke." He sighed. "Whatever doubts Luke may have had, did you know that he changed his will shortly before Toby's operation and made you and the children his major beneficiaries?"

"How noble!"

"Don't, child," he chided gently.

Sara rose and went to the counter to stare out the window, her throat taut.

"I've also," Elijah continued behind her, "settled a sum on you. There is a bank passbook in one envelope. You are reasonably well-off now and able to meet any expenses. And with your pride, you'll need it."

Sara stiffened. "You think I'm wrong, then."

"I don't know. I do know there's loving, but I don't think you ever accepted Luke as a man with human faults. And to me it looks mightily like you're running again."

Her fingers gripped the edge of the counter until her knuckles were white, and her slim back was straight, her face haunted. "Leave me alone, Elijah," she whispered.

"Oddly enough," she heard him say mildly,

"Luke said the very same thing to me, but far less politely."

Her head bowed. "I'm sorry. It's just...." Her throat clogged with unshed tears, and she heard him rise and come up behind her.

"That portrait of Hannah," he said roughly. "It's so beautiful that I ache when I look at it. Sara, you must—"

"Please...Elijah."

His hand rested on her shoulder, and she felt his lips brush her hair. "Will you promise an old man two things, Sara?"

She hesitated.

"I'll play fair." When she nodded, he said, "First, whatever happens, don't cut me out of your lives. And second, read this letter."

He placed an envelope on the counter near her hand. "It's from Luke. He gave it to me before he left."

"Left?" whispered Sara.

"He left two days ago. Said he'd be back when he came back."

She did not want to ask, yet she had to. "Where? Where did he go?"

"He wouldn't say. But when I said that I was coming to see you, Grey asked me to tell you Luke's gone to the cabin. I called the ranch manager, and he confirmed it."

"Grey?"

"She went completely over to your side the day you defended her against Luke's anger. She had been slipping your way since you came back. That's really why Jessica struck her. For daring to defend you."

Before she could reply, Elijah left and she was alone. Alone with a bulky white envelope.

Outdoors she could hear the children laughing, the pup barking, the horses nickering. Inside the house was quiet, as if it were holding its breath.

Uncertainly her hand moved to the letter, touching it, then picking it up. Returning to the table, she sat down, and after a long moment she opened it.

"My darling Sara," she read. "You have always been that to me. Did you know that? Did you ever know that I have loved you from the first day I met you, and I never stopped loving you despite what I believed? Did you know that the more I loved you, the more I was afraid to trust you? What a hell of an inverse ratio that is between a man and the woman he loves."

She drew in a trembling breath, and in spite of everything, joy flooded through her and a broken laugh escaped her lips at his phrasing.

"Forgive me," she read on, "if I'm a bit incoherent. Last night I slammed into the truth at the speed of light. Oh, God, I'm getting scientific again, when my heart is being torn out by its roots."

Blinking rapidly, she turned the page.

"I went to see Rufus last night. What I saw was myself, and you're better off without me. Perhaps I've always known that. Perhaps...."

Sara's eyes blurred, and angrily wiping away the tears, she managed to steady herself enough to read on. To read every detail of months of evidence against her, of incidents that she had known nothing of, and finally she stopped reading for the sheer horror of it.

"Oh, Luke!" she cried. "Why did you let them? Why didn't you believe in me?" Her eyes returned compulsively to his letter, and as if Luke had heard her cry, his answer was there.

"Sara, I've loved, really loved, only two women in my life. You and my mother. Because of what I've done to you, you should know about her."

The shade of ink changed, and she sensed there had been a long time lapse before he continued writing.

"Everyone talks of how ideal my parents' marriage was. The perfect couple. The perfect marriage! How my mother called my father her Robert. What they don't know is that there *was* a Robert. My mother had a lover, and no one knew, least of all my father."

Sara gave a stifled protest, and her eyes moved more swiftly.

"I found a letter of hers on my twelfth birthday. I had gone up to the hills above the ranch with a volume of her poems. Tucked inside its pages was a letter. A letter begging Robert to go away with her for a weekend, leaving Simon behind."

"No!" she said involuntarily. "You're wrong!"

"I still remember tearing up the letter and pounding it into the ground with my fist, crying and swearing, and then hitting the shreds with a stone until they were gone and my hands were bloody."

"No...no...no," she whispered.

"From that day on I was afraid of loving, of trusting. When I fell in love with you, you became my victim. From the moment we married, some part of me was preparing for the day you would betray me. So how can I blame Jessica or Rufus when I alone am fully to blame?"

"Oh, Luke!" Sara cried aloud. "You're so terribly wrong."

"Sara? What's happening?" An alarmed Beth appeared in the doorway.

"He's a fool! A damned fool!" Sara sobbed, tears streaming down her face. "Why did he never tell me? Why couldn't he tell me? That's why he called her book trash. That's why!"

"What *are* you babbling about? Calm down!"

"No...no. I must finish." Her eyes moved through the last page, and then despair clouded their grayness. At last her head lifted. She stared at Beth bleakly. "He's divorcing me...for my own... good."

"Nonsense!" And then Beth was kneeling beside her, saying intently, "You know that's nonsense. It's what he thinks he has to do!"

"He's always believed that Robert was his mother's lover," she choked out. "And all these years he's been protecting her in spite of what he believed!"

Beth froze. "Oh, Sara! He can't—not if he's ever read Elizabeth's diary or Simon's letters to her!"

"But he does believe it...he always has!" Sara sobbed, and suddenly she was crying helplessly, unable to stop as years of tears flowed, slowly thawing the coldness inside her since that night of the storm.

She wept for the lost years, for her failure to realize that there had to be some deep reason for his fears, for her failure to fight to find it, and because she had always run away. There were tears for Luke, and for the boy-man who had guarded his mother's secret for so many years at such a terrible cost.

When the deluge finally receded into damp hiccups, Beth leaned back, her own eyes wet as she asked softly, "What are you going to do?"

For a long moment Sara stared back at her dazedly, and then the answer was so clear, tears flooded her eyes again. "I'm going to him."

"What else?" Beth replied shakily.

Sara rose. She was no longer going to run, she knew, except toward Luke. "Watch the chidlren for me, Beth. I don't know how long I'll be."

"But—"

"Tell them...tell them I'm going to make up. They'll understand. No! No, of course I have to tell them. And then I need to go to Spars' Nest for Elizabeth's diary and Simon's letters. The ones where he asked her to go away with him, and signed them as Robert. Luke will have to believe the truth then."

IT WAS NOT AS SIMPLE as she hoped, for there were explanations at Spars' Nest that delayed her until she thought she would never get away.

But at last, six hours later, the proof resting beside her, Sara drove cautiously up a steep snow-rutted track. Despite her care, the car skidded just when she was in sight of the cabin, and in an instant it had buried its nose deep in a snowbank.

Not caring, she turned off the engine and leaned

back wearily. All that mattered, she thought tensely, was that she was there.

After a moment she climbed stiffly out of the car, and once she had verified that there was no damage, she stared up at the cabin.

It nestled beneath a stand of dark pines, spruce and the winter skeletons of aspens. Built of logs that had been laid under the supervision of Hannah's grandmother, it was modernized inside. Its basic frame, however, still stood sturdily after more than a century of winters and storms.

Standing there with flurries of snow whirling around her, she suddenly felt exhausted. All the energy and emotions that had propelled her seemed to seep out of her, and the loss of sleep during the past nights abruptly became a physical weight.

She shivered as a gust of wind swept the harsh slopes of the high mountain, and feeling depressed, she told herself that she was a fool to expect miracles.

"Don't be a coward!" she said aloud, needing to hear it. "You're *not* going to run away this time. You are *through* with running!"

With the words she drew in a deep breath, and telling herself that she was shivering because of the cold, and not because of cold feet, she marched herself up the snowy slope to the cabin.

He was not there. With a dreadfully hollow feeling she entered the cabin, closing the door behind her and then leaning back against it with weak relief as she saw the fire burning in the stone fireplace. He was there, if absent.

Slowly her eyes scanned the room. The polished

hardwood floors covered by scattered rugs, the long sofa flanked by easy chairs around the hearth, and the round oak dining table and chairs were all much as she remembered.

Once she had been deliriously happy here. Once this cabin had been a magic place for her. This time.... She straightened and walked over to the sofa, discarding her jacket on it. She was pushing a wing of fair hair back from her still cold cheeks, uncertain what to do, when a noise made her turn.

He was there, standing in the back doorway, unmoving as a rush of cold air swept past him. His expression was closed, his dark eyes forbidding, as he shut the door slowly behind him and crossed the room to stand with every male line of his powerful body as taut as a coiled spring long strides away from her. A cold distance away.

She knew then that she would have to fight for their marriage. Fight his pride as much as anything. There was no welcome in his eyes, and although his look would ordinarily have made her quake, she could not help seeing the small boy in him who was desperately loyal and who had denied himself any help or compassion.

"Sackcloth and ashes," she said rather inanely, "are not your style at all, Luke."

"What's this?" he asked coldly. "A rescue mission? Your good deed for the year? I thought you told me that even a dog doesn't come back after three kicks."

"But then, I'm not a dog," she rejoined, adding quickly, "I've brought you something to read."

"Read?"

"These." She held out the diary and packet of letters. "Read them through. Then we can talk."

He scowled down at them, off balance. Then his head reared back suspiciously. "What are you trying to prove?"

"Nothing...everything. Read them! Please, darling."

Still he hesitated, and she thrust them impatiently at him. "I'll make some coffee while you read."

His eyes met hers, and slowly his hand went out.

When he had shrugged off his heavy sweater and was settled in the easy chair by the lamp, she went quietly into the small kitchen and prepared a platter of sandwiches and a pot of hot fresh coffee.

He drank his coffee and ate his way through the sandwiches hungrily, if absently, his eyes absorbing what he read word by word, line by line, letter by letter. At last he put them aside and sat unmoving, staring into space.

Sara leaned forward. "Luke...you must *believe!*"

"I want to," he said, half to himself. "I want to."

"It was an easy mistake for a small boy to make. I could well have written you a note saying, 'Let's leave the other Luke behind and run away together.' A stranger might think there were two men involved. It was a natural mistake, darling."

His face unrevealing, he rose and crossed to the hearth to stand staring into the fire, his hands gripping the mantel until his knuckles were white. She knew that he was fighting to believe, and she yearned to go to him, to hold him against her breast, the hurt child who was inside the grown man now fighting to destroy his own particular devil.

But she held back, knowing that he had to find his own way through, and watching him, she saw his shoulders gradually relax until his head dropped forward between his braced arms, and his tall frame sagged wearily.

"Thank you," he said hoarsely. "Thank you for freeing me, when I would not have blamed you for keeping silent in revenge."

"Oh, Luke," she sighed. "Do you know me so little?"

He turned violently. "Dear God, Sara! Do you realize that now I don't even have a reason for what I've done to you?"

"You had all the reason in the world, believing what you did."

"The wrong reason."

"Is that what bothers you? Being wrong?" she challenged.

"Of course not! Look what I've done to you. Don't tell me that doesn't matter!"

"It doesn't," she replied simply. "What chance did you have when you were so resolutely loyal to her, when there was no one to ask why you were so quiet suddenly, to hold you and love you so that you could confide, and not spend all these years with your secret locked away... even from Elijah."

"Pity!" he rejected harshly, the muscles of his throat corded steel.

"Who's offering you pity?" she shouted with sudden anger. "If we have to start throwing spears, my score is pretty miserable, too."

"Against my throwing you out? My treating you with contempt? My blackmail?"

"Blackmail without heart," she said gently. "You looked after me when I fell, you bullied me into accepting the help I needed, you supported me when my courage failed, you were so caring with the children... who adore you and should know that you are their father."

"Sara...." He was shaking his head, his pride sticking in his throat.

"No, you listen to me, Luke. If you don't, I'll stay here and cling like a leech until you do listen. You were the one who wanted to talk. Now I'm ready."

His mouth set into a stubborn line, and her chin rose defiantly, her hands clenching. "I'm not going to run this time, Luke. I ran five years ago. I didn't wait until you were out of the hospital, over the shock, and try to face you and fight for our marriage. I ran."

"Do you think I could blame you?" he said with clear pain.

"You should. I tried to run when you found me again. I tried to run after I came back. And I'm so very tired, Luke, so very tired of running. I simply can't spend the next fifty years of my life alone just because it took us five years to find each other and to understand each other."

"Nothing you say can excuse what I've done," he reiterated with a pigheadedness that made her want to shake him violently.

"I don't give a damn who did the most wrong!" she returned furiously. "Or who did the least. All I care about is you and me. And I want you *in* my life for at least the next fifty or sixty years. And I can be stubborn, too. As stubborn as you, any day of the week. *Very* stubborn," she finished emphatically.

He wanted to give in, wanted to take her in his arms and accept all that she offered, and yet he could not.

"Oh, I could shake you!" she cried, realizing it. "Forget logic! Let the scientists and lawyers argue technicalities. This is a matter of loving! It's all of us! Not just the rational part. I *love* you. You love me. Isn't that what matters in life? So we both failed! Failed because we were afraid to share our weaknesses as well as our strengths. Afraid to love."

"There's no way to make it up, Sara. How do I live with that?"

She regarded him with frustrated exasperation. "Luke, there's only one, *one* way to make up for the past, to expiate the sins you are obstinately clinging to. If you must carry the whole burden yourself, then to make up for the past—forget the past. Don't make me and your son and your daughter pay."

"It's not that easy."

"Exactly! But I'm asking you anyway. It *will* make up for everything, if you will start over with me, darling, and love me and love me and love me all the rest of our lives. Can you bear that penance, my dearest love?"

She waited then, exhausted, not knowing what else she could say, how else she could plead her cause and his, and her eyes were fastened intently on his face, hoping...praying.

It was like watching the sun come through the darkness of storm clouds, the slow light growing in his eyes and spreading to warm her, as well. The smile appeared in his dark eyes first. Long before it reached his mouth, she knew there would be a future for them.

"Well, my dear blockhead," she asked with joy, "do you accept the penance?"

"I've never been logical around you yet, and I accept," he said huskily.

He had not finished speaking before she was in his arms, and holding her against his heart, he knew that he loved her so much that not all the days of his life would appease his hunger, his need for her. "There's a condition," he said, his voice cracking.

"Condition?" Her heart fluttered, and calmed when his lips brushed hers gently.

"Promise me that even when I falter, when I'm unbearably obnoxious, when I am incredibly pigheaded, you will never, *never* say goodbye to me again."

Her head lifted and her eyes met his steadily. Eyes that held no more pain, no haunting pleading, but only loving. "Never," she promised. "Not ever."

Held close to his heart, she knew that she meant it with all her soul, and after a quiet time there were soft confidences to exchange, so much to tell and be told that time flowed by swiftly and gradually talk faded into touching and exploring with a sense of newness.

"We'll have another church wedding for us and for the children," she whispered to him, her fingertips tracing the scar on his cheek, her lips following.

"They'll like that," he said absently, kissing her earlobe.

Shivering, she added, "We'll sacrifice ourselves for the children, force ourselves to love each other to eternity."

"Hmm...." He nibbled at the silkiness of her neck and lowered her to the pillows scattered before the fire.

"And we'll have forty dogs."

"Um-hm...." His lips trailed across her cheek to claim her mouth.

"And twenty-four more children," she managed breathlessly, her eyes dancing as his head lifted.

"Great..." he murmured, his big hands sliding beneath her back.

"And open a zoo," she added softly.

He stilled, and looked down at her with abrupt awareness. *"A zoo!"*

Suddenly they were laughing in each other's arms, laughing and then they were loving.

What readers say about SUPERROMANCE

"Bravo! Your SUPERROMANCE was super!"
R.V.,* Montgomery, Illinois

"I am impatiently awaiting the next SUPERROMANCE."
J.D., Sandusky, Ohio

"*Love's Emerald Flame* is one of the best novels you have published."
A.B., Oregon City, Oregon

"Delightful...great."
C.B., Fort Wayne, Indiana

*Names available on request.

SUPERROMANCE

Longer, exciting, sensual and dramatic!

Here is a golden opportunity to order any or all of the first four great SUPERROMANCES

SUPERROMANCE #1
END OF INNOCENCE
Abra Taylor

They called him El Sol, golden-haired star of the bullring. Liona was proud and happy to be his fiancée...until a tragic accident threw her to the mercies of El Sol's forbidding brother, a man who despised Liona almost as much as he wanted her....

SUPERROMANCE #2
LOVE'S EMERALD FLAME
Willa Lambert

The steaming jungle of Peru was the stage for their love. Diana Green, a spirited and beautiful young journalist, who became a willing pawn in a dangerous game...and Sloane Hendriks, a lonely desperate man driven by a secret he would reveal to no one.

SUPERROMANCE #3
THE MUSIC OF PASSION
Lynda Ward

The handsome Kurt von Kleist's startling physical resemblance to her late husband both attracted and repelled Megan—because her cruel and selfish husband had left in her a legacy of fear and distrust of men. How was she now to bear staying in Kurt's Austrian home? Wouldn't Kurt inflict even more damage on Megan's heart?

SUPERROMANCE #4
LOVE BEYOND DESIRE
Rachel Palmer

Robin Hamilton, a lovely New Yorker working in Mexico, suddenly found herself enmeshed in a bitter quarrel between two brothers—one a headstrong novelist and the other a brooding archaeologist. The tension reached breaking point when Robin recognized her passionate, impossible love for one of them....

COMPLETE AND MAIL THE COUPON ON THE FOLLOWING PAGE TODAY!

SUPERROMANCE

Harlequin Reader Service

In the U.S.A.
1440 South Priest Drive
Tempe, AZ 85281

In Canada
649 Ontario Street
Stratford, Ontario N5A 6W2

Please send me the following SUPERROMANCES. I am enclosing my check or money order for $2.50 for each copy ordered, plus 75¢ to cover postage and handling.

- ☐ #1   END OF INNOCENCE
- ☐ #2   LOVE'S EMERALD FLAME
- ☐ #3   THE MUSIC OF PASSION
- ☐ #4   LOVE BEYOND DESIRE

Number of copies checked @ $2.50 each = _____
N.Y. and Ariz. residents add appropriate sales tax $_____
Postage and handling $_____
TOTAL $_____

I enclose_____.
(Please send check or money order. We cannot be responsible for ca sent through the mail.)
Prices subject to change without notice.

NAME_____
(Please Print)
ADDRESS_____
CITY_____
STATE/PROV._____
ZIP/POSTAL CODE_____

Offer expires November 30, 1981   105567: